Inside the Jaws of Agnes

Edgar L. Biamonte

First Edition

Biographical Publishing Company
Prospect, Connecticut

Inside the Jaws of Agnes
First Edition

Published by:
Biographical Publishing Company
95 Sycamore Drive
Prospect, CT 06712-1493
Phone: 203-758-3661
Fax: 253-793-2618
e-mail: biopub@aol.com

Copyright © 2014 by Edgar L. Biamonte
Editing: Jack Solomons, Tom Willkens, and Edgar L. Biamonte
First Printing 2014

PRINTED IN THE UNITED STATES OF AMERICA

Publisher's Cataloging-in-Publication Data

Biamonte, Edgar L.
Inside the Jaws of Agnes/ by Edgar L. Biamonte– 1st ed.
p. cm.
ISBN 1929882114
13 Digit ISBN 9780991352111
1. Title. 2. Disasters and disaster relief. 3. Historical novel.
4. Documentary. 5. Satire 6. Hurricane. 7. U. S. Government.
8. HUD.
BISAC CODES:
    SOC040000 SOCIAL SCIENCE / Disasters & Disaster Relief
    FIC014000 FICTION / Historical
    POL028000 POLITICAL SCIENCE / Public Policy
Dewey Decimal Classification: 809.7 Historical satire
Library of Congress Control Number: 2014943434

Foreword

Inside the Jaws of Agnes is a historical documentary and satire about hurricane Agnes which struck upper New York State in mid-June, 1972, particularly Elmira and surrounding towns. Two weeks after the Chemung River flooded Elmira, newspaper reports praised The United States Department of Housing and Development (HUD) for supplying trailers successfully and quickly for the victims, but this was a lie. The bungling, waste, and stupidity that began then and continued throughout this crisis was mindboggling, much like what was destined to happen during Katrina.

The truth is that only half a dozen trailers had arrived at the Fair Grounds staging area at that time. Crowded like animals in schools, churches, the Armory, and elsewhere, victims were suffering and depressed. One had already committed suicide. More would follow suit.

City Hall officials were still haggling about where to set up the victims' trailers, mostly because the fortunate escaped the flood, refused to have them parked near their homes.

HUD hired this writer to help in the operation. A party-like atmosphere greeted him when he entered the office trailer. Large groups of mostly young men were sipping coffee or smoking while chatting, joking, and laughing in the combined living room and dining room.

The supposed Chief of Ground Operations was dressed like a cowboy. Wearing dingo boots, he resembled a cowhand or hillbilly, and was enjoying himself similarly during this disaster.

Receiving no instructions from him about what to do during the ensuing days, these men began signing in and congregating at the coffee urns for the usual. The moment he left, they followed suit: playing poker in the trailers, getting in a round or two of golf, or pursuing whatever they wished. All of them would return at night to sign in for their weekly pay. Several even obtained other jobs on the side while still employed with HUD.

This writer started keeping a daily journal about such unbelievable behavior. Considering so much foolery and indifference that prevailed unabatedly while the victims suffered, this book is a study in pathos also.

Except for a few minor events, all of the book's incidents are true. Even much of dialogue is accurate. Only characters' names are fictitious. Any reference to any real person is accidental or coincidental.

Though the Chief of Ground Operations was practically nonverbal and lacked basic reading and writing skills, the Peter Principal had apparently prevailed. Because he was a crackerjack maintenance man at the recent Rapid City disaster, higher-ups had *promoted him* to this critical position, instead of searching carefully and responsibly for an intelligent, conscientious, resourceful leader during this tragedy.

Not only did he lack the capacity to handle such an operation, but he never stopped personnel (located in the Rand Building miles away from the office trailer for some mysterious reason) from hiring and sending to the office what resembled a conglomeration of high school dropouts, losers, and some drug enthusiasts.

Ironically, despite his inability to act quickly and decisively, he had personnel hire his eighteen-year-old girlfriend for his secretary. Spoiled, ill-mannered, and immature, she was insensitive, non-caring, and a shrew. She also kept disorganized records. Throughout this disaster she never stopped shouting disrespectfully at contractors and toters (those who trucked in the trailers), belittling them. Often they had to wait for her to finish gossiping on the phone or completing a sentence in a personal letter before she gave them vital information about setting up trailers. She frequently hung up on flood victims begging her to help them get into trailers, stunning this writer.

The first site finally opened two weeks after the flood. But instead of paying eight men (including this writer) to drive their own vehicles to this site, HUD arranged to supply them with old panel trucks that were constantly breaking down. More incredible is that they were unneeded for anything connected with the disaster.

The height of absurdity was the Chief of Operations ordering this handful of men to inspect these trailers and rectifying problems while dozens of others signed in daily for their usual, boisterous morning snack, and bee-lining out the door after the Chief left.

Though two weeks had passed, tools still hadn't arrived for some uncanny reason, though the local hardware stores sold them. Upon finally reaching this site, this small group of concerned men used their own, borrowed them from the contractors there, or even from the few flood victims whom Social Services was fortunate enough to assign into the handful of trailers.

Once tools arrived, they eventually vanishing like the vacationers, including chain saws, circular saws and many other needed tools. Weeks later, lacking supervision or quality control, many from this same group received tags enabling them to charge HUD for tools at a local hardware store (whose salesman, treated them with shocking indifference, despite the disaster.) But this also enabled many to obtain tools for themselves.

Though the crisis required quick, physically action, HUD official at the Rand continued pressing the office trailer's secretarial staff to send them ridiculous and useless paper work related to inspections, dispatch tickets, and other non-essential items while the victims continued suffering.

Finally learning about the thievery, HUD officials considered taking inventory which was the height of stupidity. Accounting for stolen goods (which included Red Cross donations) would have required an enormous amount of man-hours and time, even if they could have caught the culprits. The point is that disasters require physical action not clerical paper work.

As more sites eventually opened, the large group of vacationers simply transferred their lounging and coffee-drinking to the trailers that arrived. Awaiting instructions about activating electricity and water that higher-ups (detained for unbelievable reasons), many sunned themselves outside the trailers. Others slept inside overnight. Only the same half dozen of concerned men handled the overwhelming problems.

On one occasion at a site, this dedicated group needed help from the local Water Board. But spared from the flood, they refused to open before nine o'clock, "flood or no flood," they told them.

More incredible was that despite receiving overtime pay, the electricians refused to work at the sites on Saturday, much less Sunday.

Two hundred and fifty trailers finally arrived at the Fair Grounds in mid-August, almost two months later than necessary. Unbelievingly, because neither Fair nor HUD officials anticipated the Fair, all trailers had to be toted to the Holding Point, wasting more time and taxpayers' money.

A temporary cement block warehouse was finally set up there, and the company deliberately raised their prices because of the crisis. They also sold contractors uncured cinderblock that crumbled underneath trailers (already sinking because of excessive rain), causing monumental problems and more unnecessary expense.

On one occasion, lacking supervision, toters unhooked and parked their trailers in the dirt road *alongside* clearly-staked pads, not inside the provided space. At another site, toters parked them so closely to posts (containing electrical outlets), that entry inside the trailer was impossible without doors banging into them. Unable to find a site, some toters simply unhooked their trailers and left them in the street.

Personnel hired a supposedly experienced carpenter (or someone impersonating one) to replace cinderblock steps with wooden risers. To assist him, he selected a crew from the loungers and problems soon arose. Not only did the group fool around with circular saws, endangering themselves, but why higher-ups failed to choose buying risers locally, which would have saved time and money, was another one of countless unknowns.

The head carpenter, the Chief, or some unknown (since leadership was helter-skelter at best) mistakenly ordered ten-inch-wide wood for the steps instead of eight, according to "specs." This author and others insisted that wider steps would be safer and would save time exchanging them, but we lost.

Since no one told the head carpenter how many to produce, he and his gifted entourage never stopped hammering them out. Consequently, by mid-August, mountains of them surrounded the parked cars, the office trailer, and both sides of the macadam road leading out the gate.

Towards the end of this operation, a HUD expeditor and his assistants finally appeared, but much too late. Needing time to learn about what was *really* going on, their spokesman ordered a meeting. He told the men to continue what they were doing, which they did after they left: chatting, joking, and laughing during coffee time, slipping out the door and returning to sign in at night.

The expeditor and his assistants finally made some progress. But instead of firing the Chief of Operations, his secretary and his clique, HUD officials simply transferred this wondrous group to the Wilkes-Barrie disaster area in order to help out during their cleanup operations. At least officials were kind enough to allow him to drive his group there in his fine, 1972 government-issued car. All this is just a fraction of the unbelievable fiasco detailed in this book.

Chapter 1

Hurricane Agnes thrashed Florida in mid-June, 1972, and continued into New which was most unusual according to NOAA's record keeping. By Thursday, June 23, a day before the school year ended at Southside High School, Elmira, New York, where Sal D'Angelo taught English, several rare weather fronts had surrounded the hurricane's eye and had already held it stationary above the Southern Tier, causing rain to slash the area nonstop for two consecutive days.

Leaving for school the next day, Sal D'Angelo, age forty-two, finished breakfast, and succumbed to a raincoat. He grabbed his black briefcase, kissed his wife, and emerged from the backdoor of his old farmhouse which they had been struggling to remodel together, since they moved in with their four children ten years ago. He eyed several lengths of weathered, white siding that needed replacing, as did the house's entire north side. Lean but strong, and possessing almost inexhaustible energy, he shrugged, though not because of endless work that lay ahead, but because he was in good spirits, despite another gloomy day. A mild gust swatted his thin face with a splash of pesky, innocent drops. Grinning, he wiped his face and gold-rimmed glasses with his handkerchief and entered his "61" Chevy. He backed out of his dirt driveway, drove ahead, and churned up the poorly maintained gravel road that led to the highway and Elmira, twenty-eight miles away.

Recklessly running up an enormous bill for materials at the local hardware store, he was hopelessly in debt, yet still optimistic, somewhat irresponsible, and a trifle insane living in the woods, three miles from a microscopic town that boasted a population of under seven hundred.

Teaching mostly average and below-average classes containing apathetic, rebellious seniors, a carryover from the raging Sixties, he had already given three final tests which he marked as his students handed them in. Having entered the grades in his register, he only had two more finals to give. Finally wised up, he praised himself for having completed so much so soon before Friday, the last school day, something he had never accomplished before during his eleven, wild, teaching years.

Driving through the picturesque hills, he stopped before the sole red light before Route17, switched off his wipers rubbing monotonously against the windshield because of slackening rain, and turned left. Reaching Elmira twenty minutes later, he crossed over the Madison Avenue Bridge and arrived at the school. He headed for the dirt parking lot in back which contained potholes saturated with water.

Eyeing the teachers' cars parked haphazardly on higher ground further ahead, he slowed, found a space, and parked. He grabbed his briefcase and exited. Warm rain swatted his face, and he hurriedly strode between the potholes and entered the school. He checked his mailbox, found a few miscellaneous notices, and proceeded to his homeroom.

He gave the finals to both of his unruly senior classes and marked and entered their grades into his register during the tests like so often before. Remaining at his desk, he started transcribing their grades onto special IBM cards with his number two Faber pencil. Oh, no, he anticipated when three stragglers from his last class entered and plunked down noisily into the seats before him. *I guess that want to know if they passed. But why couldn't they sit down quietly?*

The trio looked up inquisitively with anticipation at him, as if expecting the often odd Mr. D'Angelo to unleash another dramatic, witty dissertation about their poor English skills, primary concern with sex, drugs, and money. Plus their lack of self-esteem, ambition, poor sense of values, and so much more, he reviewed mentally.

"How'd we do, Mr. 'D'?" asked Kevin on Sal's left, a lanky senior with wispy, almond hair and traces of a mustache below a fragile nose.

Possessing a refined, gentlemanly face, the bespectacled English teacher regarded the marijuana leaf neatly penned on the boy's arm. Suppressing a smirk, he continued bubbling in tiny circles underneath the appropriate grades. "Worse than usual," he teased and sighed.

Sitting in the middle, the incomparable Bruce Allmendinger, nicknamed Dinger, tilted his head upward and stared at Mr. D'Angelo through thick glasses that magnified his eyes grotesquely. "Like, did *I* pass, man?" he enunciated but haltingly, in order to attract attention or because he was slow-witted, as Sal often speculated.

About to give in and answer, Sal stalled because of cumulative stress and an urge to punish them for aggravating him all term. Rain splattered the windows, stopped, and he evaluated water streaming down the panes. He rechecked a card from the stack beside his briefcase, penciled in another bubble, and regarded the threesome wearing shabby, torn jeans. *Thought I recognized the smell*, he told himself, singling out Dinger who possessed enlarged, languid eyes. He studied the young man's stringy, dark, fanned-out hair resting on Dinger's round, beefy shoulders. Having occasionally sniffed the young man's repugnant body odor throughout the term, he almost winced. "That's what you came in for? Figured you came in for extra help," Sal teased because he was good-natured, often joked, and established a good relationship with them. He studied their clothes, long hair, and dirt. It suggested a movement among some of the new generation to retreat back to Thoreau's woods which he considered uncivilized and stupid, despite his

2

liberalism and tolerance for the underdog, independents, and those who refused to follow others blindly. "You just finished the test minutes ago," he enunciated, often directing such exasperation at such students' stupidity, pretended or real, their microscopic effort, or their general misbehavior.

Their abuse was familiar. Only the faces had changed during these eleven years, he seemed to moan inwardly. Perspiring because the old school lacked air conditioning, he ordered himself to calm down. "How could I possibly know your grades already?" he moderated in his often fatherly manner, especially since he planned to pass them all anyway, based on attendance rather than grades or how often they cut his class, which he also deemed absurd.

Suddenly catching himself stalling in order to get even with them, inconsistent with his character, he became upset. Thank God school is ending so I can take the family on a vacation. Sure, he answered sarcastically. With what money?

Aware that Sal was sincerely concerned about them, they laughed, like they did during similar incidents all term.

"Besides, final averages won't be given out till tomorrow," Sal droned, which he had repeated days before and even during the test, but they rarely paid attention to him. He adjusted his stylish glasses which fit perfectly above a slight bump on his nose. "School rules," he quipped, as if he followed them fanatically. Dinger studied Sal.

"Far out," he commented in a monotone, as if to criticize Sal for wearing a white, short-sleeved shirt and tie.

Penciling in another grade, Sal caught another whiff of foul air intermingling with dampness and body odor, and smirked.

Kevin regarded their studious-looking teacher whose shadowy face suggested that he had a dull razor blade, rapidly-growing hair, or both. "We won't snitch, if ya tell us now."

Sal darkened another bubble.

"Because like, man, you're a real fast grader, Mr. 'D,'" Dinger patronized slowly. Laughing, he turned sideways, slouched, and kicked Kevin's chair for no reason. "You should clue us in now, man, 'cause we ain't comin' in tomorrow," he seemed to threaten, and eyed the shiny Lincoln cent wedged between the leather in his loafer. Catching Sal's attention, he frowned, as if to remind Sal that he disliked school, the establishment, and teachers generally.

Though Sal appreciated that students liked him because he was warm-hearted, rarely put anyone on detention, and often identified with their concerns and problems, he was appalled how callous and indifferent they were about school. "Why? You're planning to skip, even on the last day?" he retorted incredulously. Having hardly excelled on the secondary level himself, mostly because of Attention Deficit Disorder and other reasons, Sal was almost fanatical about the importance of learning in general, especially after having struggled through college on the Korean G.I. Bill with three children, the fourth having arrived during his senior year.

"Ain't cha heard, man?" Dinger responded. "The Chemung's crestin' 'bout midnight. Elmira's gettin' flooded. So's this dump," he unfolded with slow giddiness that always annoyed Sal. "It's gonna float away, man. There ain't gonna be no school ta'marra," he sing-songed.

The threesome burst into outrageous laughter.

Don't you wish. Besides, what's so funny? "There *isn't* going to be any school," corrected the well-groomed English teacher possessing thick, wavy black hair interspersed with strains of white.

"Whatever, man," Kevin added and the others laughed again.

"There won't be school if you had anything to do with it," Sal responded dryly. "Can't believe you guys. You're hoping for a vacation from loafing? It's the last day," he emphasized.

Rain sprinkled the windows from a different direction during more of their laughter and both stopped.

Eyeing their jeans again, Sal remembered catching two teens in the lavatory laughingly ripping theirs into the desired look. "You wouldn't mind Elmira getting flooded out? Just for another day off?" He darkened another bubble. "What about all the damage? People losing their homes, suffering, and even dying? Where's your compassion for others?"

"Go for it, I always says, Mr. 'D,'" Dinger offered slowly.

"What's that supposed to mean? I'm sure the flood victims would appreciate your concern," Sal quipped.

"What?"

"Nothing. Forget it," he replied without eyeing him.

The others laughed still again.

You're even too lazy to pronounce my complete name, Sal grumbled inwardly. He sniffed sickening odor and exhaled quickly. Lack of motivation, he explained, almost shaking his head. "The Chemung hasn't flooded in twenty-six years," he scoffed. Aware that he would give in because he respected them as humans despite their faults, he entertained stalling further, though it meant absorbing more of their badgering that would invite more stress.

"Didn't ya catch how high the river was, Mr. 'D'?" Dinger droned happily. He turned to Terrance staring out one of the wide-open, casement windows.

"Didn't know anybody threw it," Sal remarked smartly, eyeing the window.

None laughed.

"Like, the river's in front, man," Dinger reminded him and the others horse-laughed as if they had heard the ultimate joke.

"Thought they moved it," Sal muttered.

Terrance watched Sal darken another bubble beneath an *eighty*.

"I ain't never seen the river so high," Dinger unloaded slowly.

"Which bridge did ya come over, Mr. 'D'?" Terrance asked.

Perspiring in the stuffy, humid room, Sal felt too stressed out to answer and he suppressed a sigh.

Dinger stretched his legs and slouched. "How're we gonna have graduation Saturday if there's a flood?" he entreated just as slowly. He peered up lazily at Sal through his thick glasses encased in thin, crooked wire, which he or someone else must have somehow fashioned but sloppily. Like they did everything, Sal reminded himself.

Sal slid the card under the stack. How are these celebrities going to make it on the outside? Covering a yawn, he inhaled his own soap and resumed blackening another bubble which the trio seemed to study intently. "They'll just cancel graduation. None of you will graduate. School rules," he teased, as he often did in order to offset his own seriousness, which often bordered on the profound.

"What?" Dinger demanded, but comprehending the tease, finally grinned. "Far out, man."

Straightening, Terrance lifted up his buttock's left side.

Oh, no, Sal braced himself, expecting him to pass gas which he sometimes did in class, but Terrance simply loosened his jeans stuck to the seat because of the humidity, relieving Sal.

"Tell you what, Mr. 'D'," Terrance resumed with familiar playfulness. Lifting his desk an inch, he dropped it for emphasis, annoying Sal who had tried to tolerate such absurdities instead of constantly scolding them. "You seem cool," he flung flippantly, as if Sal were a teenager. "Don't tell me if I passed."

"I won't," Sal inserted. Catching his own pretended indifference, he glanced at them and almost grinned. Why do those kids who hate school the most, always hang around the longest? He regarded each of their young, flippant faces briefly and lowered a folded sheet of paper under the next line of grades in his register.

"Here's the deal," Terrance continued unperturbedly. "You give me your car keys, and I'll drive your clunk right up to the back steps, if ya pass me, man. Then ya won't have ta slosh through the water ta get it."

Sal waited for the others to stop laughing. "That's all I need. Pass you and get fired for accepting what's really a bribe."

"We won't tell," Terrance promised during the other's laughter.

"Appreciate it," Sal chirped. "I'm sure I could depend on you birds

5

not to turn me in."

They laughed louder.

"Besides, you'd probably hit a parked car on the way. What water?"

"You ain't checked the flood in back recently?" Terrance inquired in a tone suggesting that Sal were stupid.

"It wasn't that bad when I arrived this morning," Sal seemed to dismiss, since such teens were constantly lying, teasing, or trying to fool him. Shading the last bubble, he slid the IBM card under the stack and positioned the sheet under the next name. About to bubble in another class average and final test grade, he surveyed the trio again. "Flood or no flood, I'll never get done if you guys keep chewing up my time with your baloney."

"It ain't baloney," Kevin contributed.

"Gimmy yer keys and *I'll* drive it over," Dinger announced slowly, despite having failed Driver Education twice, although mostly because he hardly attended class. "Don't worry. I gots a license," he lied.

"Yeah but can ya drive?" Kevin asked and the others broke up.

"Can you speak English? That's the thing," Sal mumbled.

"Did ya bring yer hip boots?" Terrance resumed pointedly. "You're gonna need 'em gettin' ta yer car."

Sal eyed him with renewed suspicion.

"We've been chauffeurin' teachers' cars to the back door all morning," Terrance explained with a grin.

"Unless ya wants ta get your feets wet," Dinger offered belatedly.

"*Feets?*" Sal repeated and rechecked the dismal morning through one of the recently installed windows. Four years of English has elevated them to this level of proficiency, he sighed. Rising curiously, he headed for the far end of the windows, hoping to see the parking lot, and the threesome scrutinized their imperial-looking English teacher who caught sight of the now-flooded area. "Huh. Now there's a few drops," he admitted facetiously, as if to appease them, and they exploded into laughter, as if delighted to know more than a teacher.

"It's not *that* funny," Sal dispensed again. "It wasn't that bad when I arrived this morning." Sitting, he felt the seat's clammy-dampness through his trousers, pictured sloshing through the water to get his car, and smirked. Have they really been chauffeuring teachers' cars, or are they lying? Deciding to suppress such concern to such an unsympathetic group, he hurriedly finished filling in another bubble. Maybe I can trust one of these bandits to do just that. But which scholar? He examined Kevin's slumped body, Dinger's defiant, folded arms, and Terrance's cocky aloofness, all reminiscent of another frustrating year. Shuddering inwardly, he reexamined the windows suddenly slashed with rain. All they think about is graduating, so they can start earning thirty bucks an hour. Yeah, sure, he scoffed, picturing recent graduates working at McDonald's.

Ah, what the hell, he conceded, eyeing the clock above the door. About to settle back on them, he glanced at his briefcase, as if to avoid their electrifying indifference as long as possible. "Meet me at the back door at twelve o'clock, a half an hour from now. If it's still raining, I'll have one of you bandits drive my car to the curb. Which one, I haven't decided yet, because all of you lie like rugs. I don't even know how bad it is out there. Besides, how do I know who can *really* drive?"

All insisted they could.

"Yeah, sure," Sal replied, darkening another bubble. "If whoever manages to drive it to the back steps without bashing a parked car, getting stuck, or racing the engine like a maniac, I'll tell you if you passed. "If not, well, we both lose."

Laughter followed, intermingled with offended assurance that he needn't worry.

"But can we depend on *you, man*, to be there at twelve?" Terrance teased, referring to Sal's frequent lectures about the importance of being responsible, upholding one's word, and particularly getting to class on time.

Checking the next card, Sal finally grinned. "Okay. Terrance, you're it." Because you gave me the least trouble and have more brains than the others. "And you're all excused. Goodbye. Leave quietly," he emphasized, "so I can finish what I'm doing."

Stumbling noisily to their feet, they stormed boisterously out of the room.

Thanks. He shook his head and started entering the grades into his register. Could I get my final check now, instead of tomorrow? he began reflecting. Not that it really matters, since pressing bills are going to devour it. In fact, I'll have to get another dumb summer job like every year since I started baby-sitting. Unless I can get a job teaching summer school, he tried to think positively, though aware that the district gave older English teachers priority.

Slashing rain caught his attention. Watching water streaming down the windows, he recalled last year's fiasco when Mr. O'Reilly, vice principal then, mistakenly handed out the checks before the last school day. Relieved from teaching the rebellious, many teachers left for Europe, the Caribbean, and other exotic places and never returned. Forced to locate them in order to rectify omitted grades, IBM mistakes, incorrect averages, and whatnot, Mr. O'Reilly, now principal, was furious. He also felt slighted about not receiving the usual last day's "goodbye" according to tradition.

What if the school *really* gets flooded out? Sal analyzed and started entering their test grades onto the IBM cards. Finishing at eleven forty, he tied each of his five class tests separately, dropped them and his cards into a carton, and carried it to the office, as Mr. O'Reilly, had requested.

Clicking typewriters and air-conditioned coolness greeted Sal as he entered, and he observed Mr. O'Reilly studying *The Star Gazette's* sport section while clutching the counter's edge with his large hands. Approaching the counter, Sal stared outside through the large aluminum window, as if he were trying to discern the Chemung River that bisected the center of town five blocks away. He handed the cards to Mr. O'Reilly, who checked them randomly, tossed them into box behind the counter, and initialed Sal's final sheet.

The principal eyed him curiously since teachers handed in cards last. "Done already?"

Sal glanced at the pretty Audrey McConnell. Sitting behind one of the new, maroon electric typewriters, she seemed to be clicking away happily because of the innovative daisy wheel. "Yes," he announced proudly, realizing he had finished first which he had never accomplished before either. "Exams all properly bundled and scored."

Mr. O'Reilly signed the bottom of Sal's sheet.

"Can we have our checks now?" Sal nevertheless ventured despite what happened last year and held his breath.

Reflecting, Mr. O'Reilly frowned. Seeming unsure, he paused briefly.

Sal looked away in order to avoid embarrassing him. O'Reilly opened a drawer in a cabinet behind him. Flipping through the stack, he found Sal's check, handed it to him, and resumed reading the sports section.

Beautiful, Sal commented to himself, picturing leaving the children home and visiting Pennsylvania Dutch country for a few days with his wife Trudi, as he had promised her. But suddenly studying it as if it were a death warrant, he comprehended sadly that the amount was less than he had roughly calculated repeatedly beforehand and never enough, as usual. Pressing bills and other expenses would quickly consume a thousand dollars plus. He visualize limping through July and penniless by August like every year. September bills would haunt him, give Trudi sleepless nights. His tongue would seem to hang, then drag while he awaited his first, regular check. Bills would devour it and appear to lunge for his sanity.

What a life, he moaned inwardly. Cool air poured out of the humming air conditioner. Though last year's senior class chipped in and presented it to the school as a gift during an assembly, the administration accepted it instead of passing it on to the faculty hold up in a stifling, windowless faculty room.

Despite what happened last year, Sal toyed with the idea of asking if he had to return tomorrow. But wording seemed more important than good teaching because of the strictly construed Taylor Law that pitted teachers and administrators against one another, which Sal believed was ridiculous. Both sides often misconstrued good-natured teaching as camouflaged insults, he knew, staring outside at the gloomy grayness. Teachers can't even send students for paper clips without the office asking who wanted them, why, and for how long. At least at Southside High, he qualified regretfully, wondering how to ask him. Hell, *I* wouldn't skip.

Suddenly comprehending how much money the government had withheld, he whisked out his check from his side pocket and restudied it briefly. Shit, he selected, despite rarely metalizing or verbalizing profanity at this point in his life, and slid it back. Fingering his wavy hair, he reevaluated Mr. O'Reilly reading about the Yankees. "Are we still supposed to come in tomorrow anyway?" he finally pursued in a tone suggesting ludicrousness. Refusing to patronize the principal with a grin, he glanced at Audrey still clicking away with stiff resolve at the keys.

Rain splattered the windows and then stopped, as if it were undecided about continuing.

Looking up, O'Reilly frowned again. "You mean because of the rain?"

Studying the man's mostly barren skull, save for strands of wavy hair, Sal mentally constructed O'Reilly's full head of hair as a young man. What else, Chief? "Yes," he told the large, overbearing man, the kind that unrealistic Boards hired in order to scare unruly males who were rarely frightened.

"Avoca got hit pretty bad," he admitted, but as if attempting to protect the District in case they closed the schools unnecessarily.

Badly, Sal's English mind corrected. You're the principal, remember?

Slapping sounded again, as if someone had just dumped a pail of water on the windows, and once again the groomed English teacher with a full head of hair studied water streaming down the large pane.

"Couple of bridges washed out west of us. The Chemung's rising an inch an hour," O'Reilly commented.

Scanning the newspaper upside down, Sal shook his head. A fanatical Met fan, he was tempted to search for their write-up but heard that they lost, and changed his mind in order to avoid irritating himself further. Penny wise, Sal criticized, having learned that the town had rejected dredging the river since extended rains and major spring thaws had never flooded it. "You mean they might close school on the last day?" he inquired as if surprised that troublemakers could be right about anything. Concerned about conveying total dedication in a world of educational appearances, he didn't want to sound like he wanted the day off and berated himself for asking.

"I didn't say that," Mr. O'Reilly hedged as if he were on trial. Seemingly bursting with stress, he managed to smile away a suggestion of annoyance. "But if this keeps up, well, who knows?"

Both spent several minutes discussing what was a "pesky storm containing heavy gusts," according to the weather bureau, plus the peculiarity of a dying hurricane having ventured so unusually far upstate and inland.

Hang around any longer and he might lunge for your check, Sal warned with a laugh. Stranger things 've happened. Suppressing an urge to dash for the door, he walked out casually. Approaching his desk with a "last-day" mentality, he sat. Pulling out his first drawer, he discarded the year's mimeographed bulletins, old tests, and whatnot into the waste can. Students' absentee notes followed, including the usual forgeries that many teachers ignored like him because of overwhelming school work and unnecessary bureaucratic paper work. Besides, aware that the reward for Gestapo-like interrogation was more forgery, he emptied all the drawers, relieved that the school year had ended.

Realizing it was 11:55, he rose. Could Terrance and the others *really* be awaiting him at the back door? He grabbed his briefcase, slid it off the moist desktop, and the resulting path surprised him.

Arriving in back, he peered outside through the upper glass door. He shook his head, although not because the outside steps appeared to lead weirdly into what resembled a small, rippling, muddy pond that had reached several cars' wheels including his, but because Kevin and the incomparable Dinger were standing fully-clothed and ankle-deep in muddy water, playing touch football with several other boisterous males. About thirty feet to his right stood Terrance. Also immersed in water, he was leaning against the cyclone fence like a casual spectator at Wimbledon on a sunny day.

Unbelievable, Sal withheld, but recalling his similar odd behavior during high school, he almost grinned.

Kevin crouched, and the group, mostly seniors, hurriedly lined up on opposing sides of an imaginary scrimmage. Steadying the football about to float away, he flipped it between his legs to a heavyset teen called Joe standing with outstretched hands like a quarterback.

"Shit," Joe cursed, missing it, and the ball splashed into the water.

Shouting, laughing, and cursing, the bodies pushed one another aside and sloshed after it.

Sal eyed eyeing their mud-soaked pants and t-shirts. All worthy of mom's tears, he sighed.

Hands grabbed mostly water at first. Finally caught, the ball squirted out. More hands slapped away until they retrieved it.

"Shit, my glasses," bellowed Dinger.

Ignoring him, bodies dashed after the carrier who almost fell. Kevin tagged him, and all trudged back to where they had scrimmaged in order to search for them.

Sal pushed the bar. The door cranked open. Using his briefcase for a hat, he stepped outside, descended several steps and paused. Catching Terrance's eye, he reached into his pocket and underhanded the keys to him.

Terrance lunged for them, missed, and the keys disappeared in the water.

"You might know how to drive, but you can't catch," Sal scolded playfully.

"No problem," Terrance responded with a laugh and splashed ahead. Bending, he submerged his hands into the water. Finding the keys, he paused without surfacing them, and looked up at Sal. "Did I pass?" he threatened as all watched.

Sal grinned. "Did you find them?" he shouted back.

"Maybe," Terrance hedged. "Did I pass?"

"No. None of you did," Sal announced, and Dinger and Kevin frowned along with several others. "I passed all of you anyway," he emphasized. "On the curve."

"All right," Terrance responded.

"Cool, man," Kevin added amid some applause.

"Far out," Dinger contributed lazily.

"Decent," someone else contributed.

All resumed searching for the glasses which Joe found, and the future scholars of America lined up for another play.

Rising with the keys, Terrance stamped towards Sal's car, splashing water obliviously along the way, and Sal shook his head. Entering the Chevy, Terrance started the engine and the wipers. He backed up wildly, swung around a station wagon, and almost clipped a new truck.

"Easy," Sal shouted belatedly, eyeing muddy water furrowing out from his front wheels as Terrance dipped in and out of craters filled with muddy water.

Bounding over the submerged curb, Terrance continued along the hidden sidewalk.

Holding his breath, Sal observed Terrance driving up several steps, almost to where Sal was standing, and the car stalled. Terrance rolled down the window and looked up. "How's that grab ya, man?"

Windy showers caused Sal to reposition his briefcase protectively. "Very nice. You're ready for Daytona."

"Thanks." He rolled up the window and exited. "See ya around."

I hope not, Sal suppressed.

Terrance splashed toward the others lining up for another play.

Imagining an administrator or reporter observing Sal from a school window, he hurried inside his car and backed down the steps carefully. Swinging around, he waited until the play ended and crossed the hidden sidewalk.

Watching, the group paused to direct him over the curb and onto the muddy road near where they had been playing. Sal thanked them and waved. Reaching the water-soaked, deserted street, he drove away quickly, lest he read about the incident in the morning paper. He approached the Madison Avenue Bridge, turned on the radio and slowed in order to view the Chemung River which had risen to almost three feet below the bridge according to a report. Muddy water was churning massively with odd debris breaking in and out of the surface. The river had engulfed the weeds, saplings, and trees along the banks and was spreading toward the poorer homes lining the opposite banks. If there's a flood back home, it's the end of the world, he reminded himself, thankful that he lived on a high hill. Staring at the river, he observed a leafy limb repeatedly turning as if it were a huge celery stalk in a boiling pot of soup. Shaking his head, he proceeded toward Route17.

Chapter 2

Because local networks reported "sporadic flooding from occasionally heavy rain," Elmira's inhabitants were unprepared for what followed. Nor could anyone blame meteorologists for underestimating a supposedly lifeless hurricane. Only the police seemed to understand the significance of the Chemung "backing up through the city's sewer system," according to the news. Responding quickly and independently from city officials still quibbling about how to act, if at all, they kept warning motorists to avoid Elmira unless an absolute emergency. They had also been detouring vehicles from flooding streets all day, and had enough sense to close the streets *after* rush hour.

Soaking rain persisted intermittently into the evening, causing school closings, Sal heard over the late news, and he pictured the three teenagers and others celebrating with joy.

Thickening streams continued pouring muddy water into the Chemung after Sal and his family retired. The bulging river, reached Corning, a sister-city to the northwest. Trucking sandbags in order to steady an old, wobbly bridge from collapsing, drenched men gave up. Hoping to save the bridge, Amtrak supplied an engine that pulled away the heave load of freight cars parked on an unused track.

The next morning, Elmira's officials ordered all of their bridges closed until further notice, as did Corning, as if they didn't wish to be outdone. As more rain continued to swell the Chemung, a news bulletin urged Elmira's inhabitants to evacuate their homes along the river. But few took the warning seriously or even heard it. Many home owners were too preoccupied carrying belongings upstairs from flooding basements. Others were curiously watching the dark, ominous river from upstairs windows, as if it were entertainment

Scattered power failure also prevented most from hearing further television bulletins. Many residents had already retired or weren't home. Fear motivated others to evacuate their homes and visit relatives or friends living on higher, safer ground. Others abandoned their homes and drove their families to Southside High and other schools, churches, and the Armory. The police and volunteers in pick-ups rescued many fleeing the scene on foot, as the unsuspecting D'Angelos slept peacefully.

A patrol car's light pulsed red and white as the vehicle motored slowly and eerily from house to house along River Road, south of the Chemung. Inside the car, officers Corey Smith and Dave May took turns warning residents over the loudspeaker to abandon their homes.

Noting what appeared to resemble a flickering figure festooned to a window, Corey braked. Both men exited into the splattering night. They knocked politely on the front door, but the figure stayed put. When pounding had no effect, they raced to the back door, found it unlocked, and entered. They eventually reemerged out the front, escorting the hysterical Mr. Fowler, a senior citizen raging about his rights, even threatening to call the police for being "dragged out" of his "birth-house" in the middle of the night.

"Metal was crackin'," he kept repeating almost incoherently, while the officers led him along a muddy path, and he paused some distance from the idling patrol car. "I heard it. Just before," he whined as the car's windshield wipers swished back and forth monotonously. "Somethin' funny goin' on out there, I tells ya."

"Sure, sure," Dave conceded, coaxing the skinny, trembling senior further ahead.

"Where's my umbrella?" Fowler demanded.

"Don't worry about that now," Dave answered.

Fowler halted again, as did the officers, and he began describing "pinching steel" emanating from the Walnut Street Bridge's vicinity and something "twisting," and disappearing in the "dark, ugly night. There's something live out there, I tells ya. Go take a look," he cried, clutching a World War I toilet kit and tattered trousers.

May opened the vehicle's back door and politely nudged him inside.

Already behind the wheel, Smitty inched ahead slowly. A twenty-year veteran, he held a tiny microphone before his mouth as the wipers swept aside tiny circles of slackening rain. "Attention all inhabitants," he resonated through the loudspeaker and repeated the warning about abandoning homes.

Fowler rested his arms on the upper part of the front seat. The vehicle hummed past houses that appeared to glow weirdly from candlelight power. Peering into the semidarkness, he claimed to have heard a horrible snapping of something huge that broke, slid into the water, and vanished "like a spaceship."

Anticipating Walnut Street leading to the bridge, Smitty kept glancing to his left. "Should be coming up. Right about . . . now," he emphasized, stopping alongside the street sign.

All stared ahead into the shadowy darkness between the trees and brush.

About to repeat the warning, Smitty switched off the mike. "Where the hell's the bridge?" he directed at the foreboding nothingness, which distant city lights had glowed ominously.

"I'll be damned," Dave declared. "It's gone."

"That's what I been tellin' ya, fer Krist sake," blurted Fowler while they evaluated the emptiness beyond the water-soaked trees and dripping vegetation.

Smitty backed up, turned onto Walnut Street for a better look, and his brights illuminated the wet street that seemed to lead toward a vaguely discernible drop-off, some distance ahead.

"It *is* gone," Dave emphasized.

"I tol' ya," stammered Fowler. "I tol' ya."

"Okay, slow down, Mr. Fowler," Smitty urged, pulled back onto River Road, and resumed cruising ahead slowly.

Light from a break in the clouds brightened the distant skyline. Becoming distinguishable, houses appeared to kaleidoscope past, as if the trio's eyes were separate cameras photographing them.

Smitty hurriedly reactivated the mike. "Attention. This is an emergency!" he boomed, his voice almost cracking, despite a reputation for coolness. "Leave your homes immediately," he directed at a flickering light inside one house. "The Chemung's overflowing. The crest is heading this way. I repeat–"

Ten miles north of Corning, where the Chemung River became the Cohocton, a savage wall of black water bulged along. Overflowing the banks, it uplifted and collected homes, barns, and docks. It swirled around an innocent oil-storage tank, wobbled it fifty feet beyond the bank, and deposited it on a flooded field. Lunging ahead like a runaway roller coaster, the surge swung around a bend, met the Cohocton, and ballooned, consuming a cluster of empty stores, restaurants, and businesses. Fanning out with squirming cattle, partitions, rafters, trees, furniture, rugs, and debris, it devoured more homes, a filling station, a drive-in, and McDonald's. It even roared into St. John's Church and floated out many of the pews.

Finishing her shift at Pazahanick's all-night diner, waitress Cindy Robinson stepped outside. She heard a massive crack, looked west, and observed the freight cars sliding off the bridge. Rolling and twisting grotesquely along with the bridge's girders in the dim light, they splashed into the raging water and disappeared, only to resurface sporadically, as if they refused to sink.

Reaching the Chemung in Elmira, the river popped up manhole covers, sending one so high that it bounced off a half-submerged car. Geysers soared from underneath the sewers for a spell, until gushing street water swallowed them into redundancy. The river inundated a cemetery, scooping up everything in its path including coffins that it floated eerily by.

Massive water submerged Elm Chevrolet's car lot, tossing cars about as if they were toy boats in a tub. A wave scooped up a car, leaned it against an oak, and parked another upside down behind a grocery store.

Muddy water uprooted sidewalks that scattered and broke like saltine crackers. Similar slop spread north and south along South Main

Street. Pressing against stores, it bowed plate-glass that burst, skimming splinters of glass inside. Tons of water veered into Miller's Pharmacy, filled the basement, splattering cases of drugs, creams, and merchandise and belched everything out the windows and doors.

Clad in pajamas and skimpy clothing along South Main, confused folks sloshed through water shouting hysterically for help.

Water filled Harper's Sub Shop, then Nate's Insurance Office. Knee-deep in cellar muck at home, Nate was hurriedly handing up boxes to shaky hands belonging to his screaming wife. About to wade back for more, he discerned a loud thump and stumbled frighteningly upstairs, barely avoiding a mass of water that flopped inside through the windows.

Herman's Hardware's basement filled in seconds. Rising water pressured storage bins until nails squirted out like frightened minnows. Reaching the main floor, water floated boxes and buoyed counters that drifted, thumping and bumping against one another.

The raging river splashed into Sam's Bar next door, dislodging the bar. It buckled the walls, buoyed his wooded booths, gum-side up, and burst the contents onto South Main–all this as Sal and his family slept comfortably.

Peering out her second floor window, Pat Kinney was aghast. A seemingly unseen force appeared to be moving a fleet of floating furniture west on Partridge Street. Ugly water tore inside the bank along South Main, the Steele Memorial Library across the street, and up the steps of Southside where many residents had been fleeing after having abandoned their homes. Swelling from merging streams, tons of water slopped inside the cafeteria, immersing stoves, crates of food, dishes, tables, and chairs. Filling the band room, it flipped the Steinway, legs side up and poured into cabinets, floating out cases of trumpets, clarinets, and violins.

Stunned with surprise, the residents scattered up Southside High's second floor stairs. Others left out the back door that Sal had exited the day before. Splashing in wild disorder through the engulfed parking lot in the semi-darkness, others headed south toward the Remington Rand Building and higher ground.

The D'Angelos woke about nine o'clock the next morning. No big deal, Sal dispensed, observing their drenched lawn with a yawn. The sky brightened during breakfast, and he drove to town. Anxious to pay an overdue insurance bill before banking his check, he entered Carl Frisbie's Insurance.

Friendly, middle-aged, and possessing a weathered face with puffy cheeks, Carl had known Sal for years. Accepting his check after they exchanged greetings, Carl handed Sal a receipt, and leaned back, squeaking his swivel chair. "So? *Now* are ya glad ya don't live in Elmira?" he emphasized. "The trip's not gonna bother you none right?" he insinuated, referring to Sal's complaints about the long drive, and his flushed face lacked his usual joviality, Sal noticed.

Sal slid the receipt into his jacket pocket and frowned perplexedly. "Why? What do you mean?"

"You haven't heard? Southside got flooded out. Ain't that where you teach?"

Sal smiled curiously. "Yes."

"Southside High got eight feet of water in the basement."

Sal pictured the normally immaculate cafeteria filled with gooey, muddy water. "What?"

Carl picked up *The Star Gazette* from the floor. "See for yourself." Opening it to the front page, he handed it up to him.

Sal glanced at the headlines, looked below, and settled on an aerial photograph of neatly-spaced stores and homes standing in a seemingly enormous lake. "My God I don't believe it."

"Believe it, believe it," he insisted. "Keep the newspaper."

"Thanks," Sal responded and left.

Chapter 3

Sal deposited his check and paused to read the news in his car before driving home. Thousands had lost their homes. Basic cleanup operations had already begun. Advising inhabitants to avoid entering Elmira unless it was an emergency, city officials announced that HUD would soon be setting up trailers for the victims.

Several days later, the District wrote Sal that they had hired others with more experience to teach summer school at a neighboring high school that had escaped the flood *Couldn't they think of a better excuse? I probably have more experience teaching the kind of losers that will probably sign up, than anybody,* he sensed, sitting at his desk inside the large pantry that he had converted into his studio.

Picturing seeking part-time work, Sal remembered how badly landscape employers treated him working as a helper during two different summers and as a security guard on another occasion. *Maybe I could work for HUD,* he considered, but felt guilty about doing so at the expense of others' misfortunes. *What's the difference? If you don't, someone else will. But if you're lucky enough to get the job, who would work hard trying to help them other than you?* his other self reminded him.

Elmira became partly accessible by July 5, and he headed for the Elmira employment office, as he had every summer for the last eleven years.

Passing through his microscopic town three miles away, he chose the long way to Elmira because the weather was warm, sunny, and pleasant. Twenty minutes later, he stopped for a familiar red light at the Route 17 intersection. Listening to chirping sparrows intermingling with leaves tinkling from a soft breeze, he couldn't imagine a flood disaster in Elmira, ten miles away. Arriving, he took the Church Street exit which was still muddy. Store merchants had piled damaged cabinets, furniture, rugs, and other paraphernalia on both sides of the muddy, cluttered street. He slowed behind a line of cars, passed blocked-off streets filled with similar refuse, and stopped before a National Guardsman rerouting traffic toward one of two operable bridges out of four. Poking his head out of the window, he inhaled polluted mud reminiscent of the Chemung where he often fished with his three sons. "How do I get to the Employment Office?"

Frantically signaling another car approaching a long line, the soldier looked over annoyingly. "Been washed out. It's over in the Rand Building now, next to HUD's office," he barked and motioned him on.

You're kidding, Sal contained, complying. Catching up to the line moving slowly ahead, he sniffed carbon dioxide and braked behind an old

Ford. He followed it motoring over the Madison Avenue bridge. Reaching Southside High, he eyed the basement windows clogged with weeds and other debris. The water line, he realized, noting what resembled a crooked rope connecting them. Passing a muddy side street, he headed toward what was once a familiar row of houses that were absent. a sign leaning against cement steps covered with similar river debris. A sign leaning against cement steps covered with similar river debris was all that remained of the first house on his left.

WE NEED HELP, NOT GAWKERS AND CAMERA FIENDS, it read.

Momentarily embarrassed, as if it particularly meant him, he faced forward. But the temptation to survey the damage was too great for someone so curious as he, especially because other drivers in the line ahead were just as curious.

Iron poles that supported the main beam was all that represented the next home. Haphazard furrows scarred what he remembered had once been its manicured lawn.

The roof and outside walls were gone in a house that exposed only muddy inner walls.

A disorderly pile of siding, floorboards, doors, and pieces of soaked sheetrock represented the house on his right.

Struggling not to stare, Sal observed just a cellar foundation on the opposite side of the muddy street.

The next property was bare, save for an elderly man carrying old bricks toward a crooked pile tilting beside a stack of salvaged wood and miscellaneous debris. Looming surreal minus the house, was a flimsy jamb barely holding the front door in place. A crooked sign hung from the doorknob.

RING BELL AND WALK IN, it read.

About to grin, Sal shook his head sympathetically. He cruised past similar devastations, veered around a pile of bunched cars in the middle of the street and reached the Rand, a four-story building that had escaped the flood. Viewing the long row of cars parked some distance behind the building, he parked and exited. Huge elm trees shaded the muddy street. A sharp blast of dank air stung his nose. Where's some loose bass and pickerel? he questioned with a laugh, inhaling a strong, fishy odor while zigzagging between leaves, muck, branches, and haphazard lines of furrowed gravel. Entering the back door, he noticed long lines of distraught flood victims filing for unemployment.

Jobs were plentiful, he soon learned from the receptionist who handed him an employment card. Because of their experience with hurricane disasters, the government had flown many Southerners to Elmira in order to help with cleanup operations, she explained.

I see, the facetious Sal suppressed.

"Hilda will call you. Just take a seat."

Sal thanked her and obeyed. Called up, he described his experience remodeling his house. A pleasant woman, Hilda listened to him selling himself well. She offered him a job helping a glazier or setting up trailers for HUD. Since both, $3.18 per hour, Sal pictured helping the flood victims and chose the latter.

"Take this introductory card to Mrs. Harrison at the Fairgrounds. Her office is inside a short, one-bedroom trailer. You'll find it, because there's only about a half-a-dozen trailers that have arrived there so far. Her trailer is near the main headquarters office. It's a four-bedroom trailer. Do you know where the Fairgrounds is?"

Sal did, thanked her, and left. Hearing more chattering sparrows on such a beautiful, sunny day added to the disaster's surrealism. Backtracking along the same debris-filled street, he entered his car. He followed another long line of slow-moving vehicles heading back to the Madison Avenue bridge, but because of so much rerouting, the ten mile trip took him almost an hour. He located the trailer, filled out another card, and Mrs. Harrison, a local woman in her mid-thirties, called him to her desk. Sitting alongside, he described his basic experience again.

"Take this to the employment office in Rand Building," she announced innocently, handing him a different card. "HUD is operating from there. Do you know where it is?"

What is this, a broken record? I was just there, he withheld, studying the card. This is the government, he reminded himself. "I teach at Southside."

"Oh, I graduated there years ago," she revealed enthusiastically.

Sal looked up.

"Well, not that long," she modified, misinterpreting his expression. She touched the end of her red lips affectedly and mentioned several teachers, most of whom Sal knew. "Oh, I'd love to see him again," she specified at one point.

Basically tolerant and polite, despite detecting her indifference about the crisis, Sal was anxious to start helping the victims and squirmed impatiently.

"He taught math, my best subject."

"Oh."

"Who was the principal then?" she asked and frowned thoughtfully. "Trying to think. Oh, a fine gentleman. Oh, what's his name?"

"Mr. Brown?"

"Oh, that's him. Whatever happened to him?"

If there ever was a time to be abrupt because of the flood victims, this was it, he reasoned. "He got fired for stealing students' locker money," he deposited dramatically.

"What? Really? And Miss Voorhees?"

She married him, he teased inwardly. "She's still there. I just came from the Rand," he finally divulged impatiently.

"See Millie Jackson," she told him, wrote her name on a half sheet of paper and handed it to him. "Sell yourself like you did me, and you should get hired."

Sal thanked her, left, and agonized through more bumper-to-bumper traffic on Church Street. Hard-working, responsible, and constantly demanding the best from himself, he skipped lunch, hoping he would be hired quickly for the flood victims' sake. Standing on line again, he waited another fifty minutes before filling out a special application. God, they're in no hurry.

Millie called him. Sal sat alongside her desk and she nibbled a cold McDonald's hamburger while reviewing his application. Middle-aged, bespectacled and thin, she appeared dedicated, efficient, and conscientious. "Ah see you've done electrical and plumbing work."

"Yes, on my house," he explained and elaborated for the third time.

"Know anything about trailers?"

"No, but they're really like houses," he tried to assure her confidently without sounding like a braggart, and he studied her slender, freckled fingers holding his application.

"Are you applying for an inspector or maintenance job?"

Simple question. But Sal had worked many part-time jobs during college and afterwards. Frequently disqualified because of age, face, mannerism, education, and being overqualified, that is, "unfit for manual labor" as one employer put it, and other discriminations, he hesitated. Because so much is involved when one human evaluates another, he started battling against paranoia and even fear. "Inspector," he finally chose, accurately concluding that it was more responsible and probably paid more. Sensing that she was examining his face, he struggled to appear nonchalant. Why can't the intelligent make good laborers? he always wondered. He was about to modify his expression–somehow throw in a dash of stupidity–when she spoke.

"You might have to do some maintenance work," she cautioned, as if worried that he didn't look the part, Sal sensed.

"That's okay," he tried to say casually, hoping a Southern employer–particularly a female–might somehow consider him differently than the many cold, mercenary Northerners he had encountered.

"You'll need to check in with Roy Nichols. He's running field operations from the headquarters trailer at the Fairgrounds. Do you know where it is?"

Not again, Sal concealed. "Yes." You mean I'm hired? Or is it up to Roy? Why can't they just say, "You're hired" and shake on it? he always questioned despite sensing the low caliber of part-time jobs he was forced to take. God, what a problem we have giving others work so they can pay for food and a roof, he grumbled. "I was just there," he nevertheless uttered but pleasantly.

"Oh, good. So you know where it is."

"Yes." God, what red tape. You'd think this *wasn't* a disaster, he enunciated and departed. Locating the office trailer, he parked and ascended cinderblock steps. Knocking brought no one to the door. Opening it, he stepped into a combined dining and living room. Smoke and the smell of coffee greeted him intermingling with familiar body odor. Sal observed a packed crowd of mostly young men, some with long hair, beards, or both. Shutting the door, he noticed most holding cups of coffee and cigarettes while talking and laughing, surprising him. Others were lounging informally on inexpensive chairs or a single couch. What is this, a hippie reunion?

Dingo boots caught his attention on his left, plus a thick belt around a narrow waist belonging to a man perched on a disheveled desk strewn with papers. Seated behind the desk was a young, pretty woman with slightly bucked teeth. About eighteen years old, she seemed to be struggling to read or comprehend something written on a paper she held before her eyes.

His arms folded and a cigarette dangling from his lips, Roy Nichols looked up without abandoning the desk. "You ain't Mr. King from Metropolitan Propane, are ya?" he asked with a Southern drawl.

Hell of a greeting, Sal criticized, comprehending Roy's cowboy shirt tucked into denims without really regarding either. Didn't know the rodeo was in town, flashed a thought. "Not really," he confessed. I'm not even Richard Nixon in disguise, he rejected joking because of the occasion's gravity. Is he Roy Nichols? he considered asking the young women who possessed wavy brown hair. Or is he for real? Maybe he is *really* Roy Nichols, and *isn't* for real. Because how could anybody be wearing that shirt and those boots during a disaster?

Roy's eyes narrowed because of his own smoke. "How about Rod Thomas from the Elmira Water Board?"

Would believe Sal D'Angelo from the woods? he almost verbalized. "Would you believe Sal D'Angelo from the Employment Office?" Hell of a way to introduce myself.

Listening, several men laughed, momentarily distracting Sal from asking if he were Roy Nichols.

Roy unfolded his arms and pushed off the desk. "Damn."

Sor-ry, Sal suppressed. Peering between the crowd, he regarded the couch full of men and turned to the woman in order to ask her about the nature of the job. But noticing that she and others were studying Roy, he did also, and regarded the man's fair complexion below sandy, almost delicate hair. "Are you Roy Nichols?"

Roy removed his cigarette. "Call 'em again, Doris," he ordered gruffly.

Yes, I am. How do you do? Sal mentally provided for him.

"Ah done called all a them, Roy," Doris wailed angrily with an equally heavy Southern drawl.

Thanks for introducing him to me, Doris, Sal also scolded.

"They ain't in. None a them," she responded, silencing several nearby talkers who looked over.

Sal studied Roy's droopy, almost listless eyes.

"Some people work regalar hours, nine to five, ya know," she barked and exchanged menacing eyeballs with Roy, surprising Sal.

"I said call 'em all again," Roy growled and more men stopped talking to listen.

"You heard the boss. Call 'em," Skip Reynolds delivered from the couch and jerked a wad of unruly hair in place.

Sal observed Skip's saucy, elongated head containing a non-focusing eye that he suffered in an amateur race-car accident.

"Shut up," Doris told Skip, further surprising Sal.

What the hell's going on here? he reproached.

"Are you done ready to call now?" Roy demanded.

Doris folded her arms and snapped her head. She sunk back into her seat and sulked.

"Doris, you ain't worth a damn. Gimmy that phone," he demanded sharply and reached across the desk and grabbed it before she could react.

Sal watched Roy dial. Are these two serious?

Roy held the receiver to his ear for some time and hung up in disgust.

"See?" Doris needled nervously. "Nobody's home. Whad ah done tell ya?"

Roy dialed another number, waited, and slammed the receiver back down. "You'd think they wasn't no flood, no nothin'. Damn."

How's that for proper English, professor? Sal needled himself.

"Damn," Doris mimicked sarcastically.

Roy reinserted his cigarette and finally checked Sal. "Who sent you?"

Sal regarded the sagging ends of Roy's eyes. "Millie Jackson."

"Can you work twelve hours a day?"

For $3.18 an hour I'd work twenty-eight, he suppressed. "Yes."

"Seven days a week?"

Sal visualized paying off bills with savage giddiness while helping the victims. Is he kidding? "Absolutely," he declared convincingly.

"You're hired," Roy declared.

Sporadic laughter resounded along with a few cheers and a whistle, catching Sal off-balance and he smiled uncomfortably.

You've got a weird style, Roy, but I'll tolerate it, Sal cried inwardly. But wasn't I just hired?

"Whad ah done hire you as?" Roy asked with a straight face.

More laughter rose and fell.

Sal had trouble with Roy's heavy drawl. "An inspector," he answered belatedly.

"Ever inspect a trailer?"

"No."

"Good," Roy cried. "We need guys with no exper-iance."

Laughter rattled again.

"Welcome to the club," someone chirped.

What's going on? Sal wondered. Wasn't there a disaster?

Roy grabbed a small, white pad on Doris' desk. He wrote something down, tore off the page and handed it to Sal. "Take this to Millie. You needs ta fill out a application."

You've *got* to be kidding, Sal responded, accepting it. "I already did before."

"How long was it?"

Eight and a half by eleven, Sal squelched, a carry-over from forever reacting similarly to his raging financial problems.

"'Bout a page."

"You ain't seed nothin' yet."

Seed? And I thought my rowdies couldn't speak English.

"Them government applications is half a mile long."

The onlookers laughed still again.

"Ah'll see ya tomorrow morning at 7:30 if you done finish by then," Roy added, grinned, and absorbed another blast of laughter.

"Hire him," Sal read. This is worthy of framing.

Roy timed Sal's head about to look up in order to evaluate him. "What's your regalar line of work?"

Surrounded by such a sordid group, Sal felt self-conscious. "I try to teach young people who don't want to learn," he unfolded, catching attention.

"A schoolteacher?" Roy remarked loudly. "Hear that, Doris?" Absorbing her smirk, he reconsidered Sal. "What do ya teach, schoolteacher?"

"English."

"English? My worst subject."

I believe it, Sal kept it to himself and left. Hilda sends me to Mrs. Harrison, Sal started reflecting while driving back. She sends me back to Millie. Millie sends me to Roy who sends me back to her. Talk about disorganization and wasting time. And why are so many guys just standing around? Why aren't they helping the victims? he demanded and reached the Rand several hours later. This is dumb, he complained, filling out the long application that not only requested information about his past employment but his private life also.

Chapter 4

Sal reentered the office trailer shortly after seven the next morning. Wearing old, clean clothes, he inhaled smoke and coffee and was surprised to see mostly the same gathering of disheveled, unshaven young men. Didn't they go home? Wearing faded, tattered jeans, most were holding cups of coffee, smoking, talking, sipping, and laughing like the day before. Sal noticed Skip Reynolds sitting on the end of the couch reading *The Star Gazette* with his good eye, and Sal regarded Roy sitting behind Doris' desk tapping a pencil. "How're you doing?" Sal greeted him informally.

Roy mumbled incoherently and handed him a clipboard.

Sal contemplated the many signatures. What happened to verbal communication? Realizing that it was the sign-in sheet, he signed it, and handed it back.

Roy accepted it with his free hand without stopping the pencil tapping, and yawned.

"Anything you want me to do?" Sal offered above the droning voices.

The pencil stopped. "Not now. I'll let ya know. Grab yo' self a cup over there," he entreated, nodding at a large urn, "or in the kitchen," he specified almost friendlily.

"Thanks." Appreciating the offer despite rarely having more than one cup at home, Sal nodded. Breaking away, he angled between several long-haired men. Peering through a serving space, he observed the kitchen equally packed with mostly young men and decided to head there out of curiosity. They certainly hired enough muscle, he appreciated innocently, and the men parted as he proceeded along the narrow hallway. Except there's not a single black man in either group. Guess what that means? he announced to himself. Squeezing inside the kitchen, he nodded to unfamiliar faces, and veered toward those standing beside a mimeograph machine on the counter to his left.

Several men nodded back but cautiously, as if fearing that such an older, serious face belonged to an official, Sal sensed. His casualness allayed their fears, and he overheard someone describe the looting of abandoned river-front homes which he had already heard over the news.

Minutes later, Roy squeezed past the kitchen overflow in the hall and entered the last room in back. Now what? Sal entertained, hearing the door close behind him. When nothing happened for a half hour, he sauntered back into the noisy living room with a cup of coffee.

A man sitting in the middle of the couch agreed to buy doughnuts, collected money from a half dozen others, and left. Wonder what I'm supposed to do? he questioned, taking the man's seat. Tough job, he criticized. He regarded an elderly man sitting alongside and introduced himself to Norman Meriwether, a kind, unpretentious farmer with thick, steel gray hair, and they shook hands. Wearing baggy overalls, Norman resembled someone modeling for the Almanac or Bean's Mail Order House, Sal concocted mentally. When do we start working? he was itching to ask him, but Norman began describing incidents in his life, as if they were friends.

"Had my own feed company," Norm continued above the talking and occasional blasts of laughter. "Made nearly a hundred thousand one year, then lost it all. My own men was farming on the side, using my feed, even my trucks without me knowing it," he deposited and exhaled.

"Sorry to hear that," Sal responded sympathetically, despite becoming restless and impatient.

"Almost killed my wife, she took it so hard," droned Norm. "Picked up the pieces a couple of years ago. But at sixty-three, I'm broke. No retirement, nothin'. Just gots the farmhouse. Built it with my own bare hands, me and my son."

"Now you're working for HUD at $3.18 per hour," Sal contributed.

"Right. Puttin' in the hours as inspector," he revealed, sighed regretfully, and his mood changed. Laughing at himself, he flashed a row of unevenly-spaced upper teeth.

"If you call this work," Sal responded and checked his watch. "It's past ten. What're we supposed to be doing and when?"

"Beats me. Probably nothin'. Government job." Norm clasped his hands behind his head and nestled back comfortably against the cushion. "Them jobs is all like that. Hired three days ago and ain't done nothing since." He yawned, squinted, and coughed. "I just sit, talk, and drink coffee. Inspected one trailer."

Sal frowned in disbelief. "You're kidding. The flood happened over two weeks ago. How come they're not doing anything?"

Overhearing him, a tall man in his late twenties with a slightly pink, upturned nose, disconnected from a nearby group. Holding a cup, Craig Stevens checked Sal's concerned face. "Don't worry, you'll be havin' more work than shit," he divulged with a laugh. Turning, he reconnected with the same semicircle of young men, and Sal regarded his fine crop of thick, duck-tailed hair that was a shade darker and fuller than Roy's.

Whatever that means, Sal scoffed. "Is he one of the bosses?" he asked Norm who shrugged.

"Got me. Who knows? Clings to Roy like he is or hopes to be," he answered and laughed easily again. "Never know. Can't trust nobody," he warned and began discussing the merits of farming for himself rather than working for someone else.

Sal glanced across the room at hands removing doughnuts from several bags on a small table in the dining room. "What time is lunch?"

Norm laughed. "Any time you're hungry."

Noting Sal's expression of disbelief, several men laughed.

"How come they run such a tight ship?" Sal ventured, and more laughter erupted from the listeners. "This is ridiculous. Isn't anybody worried about the flood victims?"

Shrugging again, Norman began what sounded like a lecture about new farming techniques, but the sound of shuffling interrupted him. He stopped, eyed several men heading for the front door, and checked his watch. "Guess it's about that time," he conceded, rose and headed for the door, as did Sal.

"We're going to inspect some trailers?" Sal asked.

Stalled because of those ahead of him, Norm turned back and smiled. "Hell no. It's time for lunch."

Sal noted 10:46 on his watch. "Tough morning."

Norm laughed. "Ya get some like that."

"I don't get it. People 've been flooded out. We've been hired to inspect trailers or set them up, and we spent the morning doing nothing."

Norm smiled almost fatherly. "Ain't got no trailers."

Studying the pleasant, weathered face, Sal frowned. "There's about a half a dozen out there in the field right now."

"That's nothin'. We needs hundreds, maybe thousands. Who knows? Hundreds is supposed to be comin'. But it don't make no difference. Only one site's open, Edgewood. A couple trailers is already set up on pads there."

"That's it?"

"City Hall still can't agree about where to put trailers when they starts comin'."

"You're kidding." Because they don't care enough about others, he recognized. Or they would agree–come to a loving decision, and quickly. "There's tons of land surrounding Elmira. What's the problem?"

Norm smirked. "Folks don't want trailers parked in front of their houses. Bulldozers gotta clear sites when theys open. Water and electric is gotta be put in. We inspect trailers here before they get drug ta the pads."

Men cutting ahead of them and storming noisily out the door, reminded Sal about his male rowdies rushing out of class after the bell. So they can fall asleep in the next class, he criticized. Although liberal enough to accept their shoulder-length hair, he refused to tolerate their indifference and apathy throughout the school year. "These birds know how to inspect trailers?" he inquired curiously above the noise and confusion. "Even *I* don't know."

"Probably not," Norm replied with another laugh. "But it ain't hard."

Sal reached the clogged doorway with Norm. "How come somebody–this Roy guy–doesn't take this bunch outside and demonstrate how it's done?" You're rocking the boat, his other self warned. Somebody should, his conscience answered.

"Ya got me. I only work here. Maybe they's waitin' for more trailers. But the government's paying us, so who cares?"

Everybody's got to care, especially about one another, or what good are we? It's so simple, Sal philosophized internally. "What about Roy Nichols?" He flicked his head toward the far room in back. "What's he doing to speed things up?"

"Probably as little as possible. Ah, maybe he's sleeping," Norm explained and laughed.

Mellowing over Norm's easygoing manner, Sal followed the chunky man outside. Parting, Sal entered his car, turned on the news, and opened the first of several neatly-wrapped sandwiches Trudi had made. He tasted fried eggplant, one of his favorites, analyzed the distant hills surrounding Elmira, and listened to a familiar report describing thousands of homeless victims cramped in churches, schools, the Armory, and other buildings. One man had even committed suicide.

The problem is that the office trailer isn't in the center of the disaster, he speculated innocently. Ah, maybe trailers 'll be arriving soon, he tried to concede optimistically and reentered the office after he finished eating. He edged past a toter, that is, a toter standing before Doris sitting behind her cluttered desk, and angled between several milling men chatting with one another while smoking, sipping coffee, or intermittently doing both. Doesn't anybody clean up around here? he reacted, regarding papers, folders, paper cups, and whatnot strewn atop a row of cabinets against the wall to Doris' right. Now what? I'm supposed to mingle? What else can you do? he answered, pushed the clutter aside and elbowed atop the first cabinet somewhat awkwardly.

"Are you mean to kids?" a female interrupted his thoughts.

Realizing Doris was referring to him, Sal was off guard. He regarded her youthful green eyes, flowing brown hair, and full lips bulging slightly because of bucked teeth. Attracting the loungers' curious and somewhat hostile attention (because I'm a teacher, Sal surmised), he smiled self-consciously. "Not really," he responded accurately, recalling their abuse, and prided himself in being tolerant, kind and just. "It's probably vice versa."

The toter handed Doris some papers which she dropped disinterestedly on her desk. "Vi-ce what?"

Waiting impatiently, the toter glared at her and exhaled annoyingly.

"What's that mean?" she inquired loudly enough to turn heads, including Craig's, and she smiled, appreciating their attention. "Ma, what big words."

Didn't they learn ya none in school? Sal dramatized internally. Or maybe you didn't pay attention.

Sitting on the couch, Skip slanted his head, as if to contemplate her with his good eye. "That's Northern language, Goldilocks. You wouldn't understand."

Sal smiled. Thanks.

The toter examined Sal's neat clothes and studious face curiously, as if hoping Sal were a higher-up about to scold Doris into hurrying on his behalf.

"*They're* often mean," Sal emphasized.

"*They're* mean?" she disagreed incredulously, as if teenagers were beyond reproach.

Why doesn't she take care of that toter? Sal questioned.

"How come?" Doris asked Sal.

"Because that's the way many teenagers are. Not all of them, thank God," he revised quickly. And you typify the inconsiderate, because you're ignoring him. "Maybe you should take care of this man." He flicked his head at the toter glaring at her. "Didn't he just bring in a trailer for the flood victims?" he ventured because he wasn't positive.

"He can wait," she replied, stunning Sal, and she eyed the grimacing man. "Can't you?"

Unshaven, perspiring freely, and tired from hauling a trailer hundreds of miles, the man frowned. "How long?" he growled.

Ignoring him, Doris settled on Sal who sensed that she was evaluating him with familiar resentment against teachers in general. "You probably think all teenagers is brats."

She's trying to intimidate me, he recognized, studying her smooth, youthfully plain, pretty face. Bad enough putting up with such disrespect during the school year. "Not really, just the ones who are," he quipped sharply.

The toter stared at his own papers which Doris finally acknowledged with a glance. "Need 'em signed," he hinted irritatingly. "Sometime today, if it's all right with you."

A cup in one hand, a cigarette in the other, Craig broke from his circle and approached. "Yes, sir," he obliged him, grabbed the papers from underneath Doris' inattentive eyes, and started reading them.

"Need 'em signed," the toter repeated angrily now.

"Gimmy 'em back," Doris spat.

31

"Hey, what do you know? A trailer just arrived," Craig announced undauntedly.

"Stranger things 've happened," Skip flung, standing nearby, and repositioned his hair.

What the hell's going on? Sal demanded, grimfaced. Are these people for real?

Stooping, Craig signed several papers on his knee awkwardly. He was about to hand them to the toter, when Doris rose.

She snatched them out of his hand angrily, shoved them into a disorderly pile near the phone, and sat, astonishing Sal. "Hand me a folder," she ordered Craig, stunning Sal further, and flicked her head at the first cabinet.

I don't believe her, Sal protested, stepping aside. Much less all of this, he added, eyeing the usual groups smoking, drinking coffee, and laughing, and the blond-haired man with the duck-tailed hair complied reluctantly.

"Another trailer's comin'," the toter told Craig. "Two altogether. My buddy's just pullin' in."

Craig turned to peer out the window, but several men perched on a vacant desk below it, also rose to look, blocking his vision. "Beautiful," he nevertheless remarked, broke away from the group which hardly parted for him, and headed toward Roy's office.

"Know why they give you trouble?" Doris resumed incongruously at Sal re-elbowed to the next cabinet in the row of three, and the men stopped talking to listen.

"Because ya probably pile it on," she scolded, and slyly removed several sheets of personal stationery from underneath the disorderly pile.

Catching "Dear Mom," Sal was stunned. Write to Mom on your own time, woman. "The problem is with parents," he oversimplified, attracting more unwanted attention. "Most of them aren't teaching their kids values. Most kids don't want to study or learn," he moderated almost pleasantly.

"That's because your classes is probably dull," she stabbed, rattling him and he flushed during the laughter.

Go to hell. What the hell do you know? he grumbled internally. Tolerance, his other self injected, and he suppressed an urge to reciprocate scathingly. "Did you ever think that what's dull to you might be interesting to someone else?" Dummy, he concealed. Realizing that she could hardly help who she was at this moment in her life, he mellowed further. "It's all relative. What should we do, turn the schools into some kind of club to accommodate kids who don't want to learn?" he threw in and immediately regretted for inviting an obvious response.

"Hey, why not?" someone agreed.

"Sounds good ta me," cried another.

"The problem is that most kids consider school a hangout, a place to socialize. Like the local tavern." And you're probably one of them, he withheld, unsure how she fitted in with the leadership.

"You tell 'er, Teach," Norm agreed, standing beside a group of conversing young men.

Roy returned from his office and handed Norm a clipboard of inspection sheets. "Wanna get them two? Show him how to inspect them?" he asked Norm, referring to Sal.

Norm nodded. "The trailers what just come in?"

"No, this one," Skip teased.

Laughter surrounded Norm who joined in.

Sal pushed off the cabinet. 'Bout time.

"Far out, man," a familiar voice cried from deep inside the crowd.

Oh, God, no, Sal thought, glanced worriedly at the packed group, and regarded Craig. "Not sure I know how to inspect one."

"Neither does anybody else," Skip barked and snapped his hair back.

"Welcome to the club," quipped someone else and the men laughed.

"Ah needs Scotch tape," Doris clamored. "It's in the first cabinet," she shouted to no one in particular, then nodded at a man holding a cup.

Walking there obediently, he waited until Sal moved aside and opened the top drawer.

How come she doesn't get it herself? Sal reproached. And why do some men feel obligated to wait on women, especially spoiled brats like Doris?

"Not that one. The second one down," she screeched and more laughter filled the room.

What is this, a zoo? Sal protested. Where's the humor, particularly in view of the flood victims?

"Don't let that bother you, Teach. Nobody tells you nothin'," Norm expressed. "Learned myself everything."

Sal managed to nod tolerantly and they left. But finding both trailers' doors locked, they returned to ask Doris for the keys. Observing her talking on the phone, they paused before her desk.

"She day-id?" Doris drawled loudly enough into the receiver in order to attract attention and appreciated many eyes regarding her.

"You got the keys to the new trailers?" Norm interrupted her and the men quieted.

Doris covered the mouthpiece and looked up. "Shhhh," she rebuked Norm, removed her hand, and eyed Sal contemplating her disbelievingly.

Norm turned to Sal. "Whatever happened to respect fer yer elders?"

"This is all too unbelievable. During a disaster?" he whispered to

Norm who shook his head in agreement.

Doris glanced at several men studying her, and then considered papers on her desk, as if to pretend indifference about their attention. "What time did they get back to the motel?" she asked loudly into the receiver, and finally smiled coquettishly at those listening. "Is that raght?" she almost shrieked.

Craig disconnected from his group and approached Sal and Norm.

"Far out," penetrated the same voice like before.

Dinger? Is that possible? Sal considered, whirled in order to investigate again, but the dense crowd blocked his vision. He settled on Craig whose long sideburns and thick, duck-tailed hair seemed out of place amid so many men sporting long hair.

"Both trailers is locked," Norm told Craig. "Need the keys."

"Don't cha know how to get into a trailer without one?"

Oh God, Sal moaned.

Doris cackled into uproarious laughter. "Is that raght?   Who, Ginger?"

"I'll show you sometime," Craig promised and checked Doris. "*She's* got 'em. Good luck getting the right one," he said and returned to his group.

"Probably mixed in with all them papers," Norm declared, reached over, but Doris slammed her hand down, blocking them. "Hey," Norm protested, snapping his fingers in pretended pain.

Doris covered the mouthpiece again and glared at him. "Whaddaya want?" she asked sharply.

This is too unbelievable, Sal admonished.

Norm repeated his request.

The second toter entered, holding papers, and he positioned himself before Doris' desk.

"I'm on the phone," she snapped at Sal, Norm, and the toter.

Is she for real? Sal demanded.

Doris resumed speaking confidentially into the mouthpiece.

Sal exchanged a meaningful glance with Norm, and the toter leaned forward with anticipation.

Doris hung up. "What do *you* want?" she deliberately asked the young toter, rather than Sal and Norm.

"Just pulled in," the toter revealed.

Rising, Doris snatched his papers.

"This girl's a piece of work," Sal breathed to Norm who frowned in agreement.

Doris signed appropriately, tore out the man's copy and almost flung it at him.

"How could anybody hire somebody like her at a time like this?" Sal asked Norm beyond her hearing.

Norm shrugged.

Doris contemplated Norm briefly. "What do you want?"

He told her.

"Ah don't know nothin' 'bout no dumb keys," she stormed, checked the crowd and seemed pleased that many men were still focused on her.

"For any trailers out there," Sal enunciated. "Not necessarily the two that just arrived."

Once again Doris merely glanced at Sal and Norm disinterestedly, as if their faces were too old to have any value.

Sal pointed to the papers on Doris' desk. "Maybe you have the keys for the two trailers that just arrived, amongst those papers."

Doris glanced at them. "What? They didn't give me no keys."

"What's going on?" a familiar voice drawled.

Turning, Sal regarded Roy holding a cup and wearing the same cowboy boots and shirt. Nice belt, Sal uncorked sarcastically, settling on Roy's oversized silver buckle depicting a silver, embossed steer. What time's the rodeo?

"They're talkin' 'bout some dumb keys to some dumb trailers," Doris confided annoyingly.

It's for the dumb victims, Sal almost quipped angrily as Norm explained again.

"So, where's them keys?" Roy asked her.

Let's *look* for them, Sal enunciated to himself. Or get into any trailer somehow. So we can really start doing something.

"How should ah know?" she barked at Roy. "Ah gotta do everythin' round he'a. We needs more office help," she insisted angrily and slapped her messy desk emphatically. "Ah ain't even made up yesterday's report."

"Help's a-comin'," Roy assured. "Ah done tol' you. Didn't that trucker give you no keys for that trailer what just come in? What about them trailers what's already out there?"

How's that for English, big guy? Sal asked himself again. Is there an interpreter in the crowd?

Doris smirked above her bucked teeth. She pushed the pile of papers aside, opened the drawer, and grabbed a handful of keys. "Maybe they's somewhere in here," she declared, dropped them on the desk, and the onlookers laughed.

Roy squinted, smirked, and sipped. "How comes you didn't label them when trailers come in?" he scolded and turned disgustedly to the crowd. "Where's ma key man?" he shouted.

"We're all key men," Skip asserted, standing with a cup of coffee

35

near the couch, and drew some laughter.

Faces turned to the sound of footsteps in the hallway, and a curious body started working its way through the throng.

Could it be? Sal questioned, barely glimpsing large, wire-rimmed glasses and long hair parted in the middle. Familiar enlarged eyes and slightly hunched shoulders came into view. Oh, for God's sake I don't believe it.

"Hey, Mr. 'D'," Dinger greeted him sleepily. "What cha up to, dude?"

Laughter responded.

Careful, he could be your boss, Sal warned. God forbid, he replied and silence seemed to ease back. "Very little, Dinger. That's the problem," he admitted cryptically. Detecting familiar body odor, he stepped casually aside, and appreciated that Dinger didn't offer his hand for shaking which would have necessitated washing his own. Surrounded with such a motley group, Sal had difficulty maintaining his dignity and felt self-conscious. But they're all humans, his other self interceded. Much like the bandits you've learned to tolerate and help. Sure, he responded sarcastically, but nevertheless resolved to maintain the same positive, caring attitude he had as a teacher and human being.

"What cha need, boss?" Dinger asked Roy.

"How 're them master keys comin'?" Roy inquired.

"Fine."

"How many sets you done finish?"

"None."

Laughter rose and fell.

Roy sipped his coffee. "How come?"

"Like, the goddamn key machine don't work, man," he droned lethargically as if were on drugs.

Skip slanted his head and approached. "Yeah, like its key operator."

Sal frowned during more laughter. I don't believe all this.

Looming formidably despite a small but well-built frame, Roy stared blankly at Dinger. "Why'n hell didn't you tell me?"

Skip also regarded Dinger who was his cousin, Sal was destined to learn. "Probably 'fraid you'd fix it, boss. Then he'd have to work."

More laughter reverberated.

Dinger parted his hair, though it didn't need parting. "You never asked, boss."

Roy slid his hand into his tight-fitting jeans' pocket. "Figured you was a mechanic," he quipped good-naturedly.

"Not really," Dinger answered.

"Lemmy check it out," Roy offered, turned toward the hallway, and the men parted, as if Roy were Moses about to wade into the Red Sea.

"Far out," Dinger answered, following him angling between the men. Though the first toter had returned and was standing almost obediently before Doris' desk, she dialed her phone and paused. "Tammy? So then wot?"

You've *got* to be kidding, Sal remarked to himslf. Noticing the toter's annoyance, Sal shrugged. "She hasn't heard about the flood yet," he told him.

The toter shook his head. "She signed in the wrong place."

Sal shook his head, stepped closer to Doris' desk, and pointed to the pile of keys. "One of them has got to work." He forced a smile but Doris disregarded him.

Lunging, Sal grabbed most of the pile before she could react.

"Hold it, Tammy," Doris shouted into the receiver, then palmed it. "Make sure ya bring 'em back," she shrieked, watching Sal stuff them into his pocket.

The telephone rang on another line.

Sal grabbed the rest and handed them to Norm. Both paused to listen curiously, as did most of the men.

Doris put Tammy on hold, answered the caller, and hung up. She reached under her desk, pressed a button, and staccato buzzing sounded in Roy's office. "Telephone, Roy," she screeched down the hallway. "Ain't cha got no ears?"

Skip jerked his hair in place. "Not anymore."

"A real winner," Norm whispered to Sal and both stepped outside. "Would you believe her and Roy is a pair?"

Sal inhaled the fresh morning air. "A pair of what?"

Norman laughed while they headed toward the trailers. "Had my share of 'em in business," he reproached as the sun struggled to penetrate the dense fog.

"That woman's a shrew. She should be fired. The place is completely disorganized. Dozens of men hanging around doing nothing. Where are all the trailers? What's the delay? People are living like animals in the Armory, in schools–all over."

Norm shrugged. "What can I tell ya?"

"Roy's running operations?" Sal objected incredulously. "I've got nothing against hillbillies, but that's what he is. Who could have hired him, much less put him in charge?"

"Heard he was a crackerjack installer at the Rapid City disaster."

"Installers don't necessarily make good leaders," Sal declared but Norm didn't reply. Realizing he was overwhelming him, Sal ordered himself still.

Reaching a trailer, they spent a twenty minutes trying one key after another before Sal fitted one and they entered. Poignant formaldehyde mixed with stifling heat greeted them, and they opened windows hurriedly.

Both surveyed the packed furniture throughout the living room connected to the dining room. "We're supposed to unpack all this and set it up?" If so, how come that bunch inside didn't take care of it already? he left unsaid.

Untying furniture, Norm wasn't sure if that was their job, and they reentered the office in order to ask Roy. Squeezing between the living room loungers, they passed the usual kitchen overflow, and knocked on Roy's door. He invited them inside almost incoherently, and they eyed him sitting behind his desk frowning at what appeared to be the first page of a report in his hand.

Either he needs reading glasses or he can't read, Sal realized while contemplating his cowboy shirt.

Norm asked Roy who was supposed to unpack and assemble the furniture.

Roy looked up, caught Sal's eyes, and turned away almost self-consciously without answering Norm.

"We needs tools to set up the kitchen table. And one of the couch's legs needs screwing," Norm revealed and "screwing" loosened Roy's smile, further annoying Sal.

"Telephone," Doris shouted from the front and pummeled Roy's office with buzzing.

Why scream down the hall? Isn't buzzing him good enough? Sal wondered disbelievingly. What about answering Norm's question, Chief?

Roy gazed down the hallway. "I knows it," he bellowed back to Doris and picked up his receiver. "Yeah," he answered into the mouthpiece, eyeing several pencils on his desk. "What? Where?" he questioned and frowned. "Be right over," he announced, hung up, and rose.

"We needs tools if ya want *us* to put the furniture together," Norm reminded him still again.

Bypassing them, Roy started swaggering up the hall. "Water's a spoutin' all over Edgewood," he justified to Sal and Norm. "Craig," he shouted. "Get me Craig," he shouted to Doris and the kitchen overflow pushed one another inside, so he could pass. "Check with Lenny for tools," he shouted back to Sal and Norm, and the front door slammed behind him apparently without him finding Craig.

"I take that for a *yes*," Sal told Norm who laughed.

They started heading back up the hall when clusters of disheveled men suddenly poured out the kitchen, blocking their way.

Where are *they* going? Sal inquired, watching them stumble

laughingly out the side door and front door. They're all driving to Edgewood? he analyzed, waited with Norm for rest to leave, and they entered the kitchen.

Realizing that Roy had just left, Lenny jumped awkwardly onto the counter. Sprawling alongside the AB Dick duplicator, he clasped his hands under his neck as if preparing to sleep, despite the unlit cigarette dangling unlit from his lips.

How's that for a friendly greeting, Sal asked himself with a laugh, sniffing mimeograph fluid. Oh, God, can't get rid of them, he remarked, realizing Lenny was a former student.

Lenny Norquist opened his eyes, glanced at Sal, and looked away indifferently, forgetting that Sal had passed him for simply attending class regularly.

So he could sleep in back, Sal recalled.

"Fucken machine," Lenny appeared obligated to breathe to Norm and he slid off the counter just as awkwardly.

No need to say hello, Lenny, Sal concealed, eyeing Lenny's bulging blue veins on his unusually thick, dirty forearms.

Norm asked about the tools.

Mostly non-verbal, like many of Sal's worst students, Lenny flapped a stack of paper recklessly between the machine's metal guards, disturbing Sal. He started the machine but it jammed.

Why is he bothering with that toy? Sal questioned. Just get us some tools, son.

"Shit," Lenny spat and Norm inquired about the tools again. "Phillips screwdrivers is all checked out," Lenny barked and repositioned the stack, smudging the top sheet.

"What other tools ya got?" Norm asked.

Lenny restarted the machine. "Nothin'." The drum rotated without printing paper, and he turned off the machine in disgust.

A major disaster and we're running off paper or trying to? Sal criticized. Lenny was like Kevin, Dinger, Terrance, and the others. Refusing to do anything connected with English, they often resorted to pencil tapping, desk lifting, and kicking anything (or anyone) whenever they weren't yawning in boredom, talking, or hiding one another's books, Sal reviewed with irritation.

"We needs some, anything," Norm insisted.

The dirty hands seemed to pause. Both men studied Lenny's smooth, almost playful face beneath his curly-brown, zigzagging hair.

"Everybody needs some, man," Lenny breathed.

Because of his supposed knowledge about how to run a mimeograph machine, HUD hired him as a G-7, Sal was also destined to learn with disbelief.

Lenny adjusted a knob and restarted the machine. "Ain't cha getting none back on the farm?" he asked Norm. Laughing breathily, he regarded Sal briefly, and then stared back at the machine spewing defective sheets and torn paper out the opposite side. "Shit," he barked. He grabbed the paper angrily, tore good and defective sheets alike and threw the stack into an overflowing waste can, bothering Sal who could barely afford to buy typing paper.

Nice hands. "What are you trying to mimeograph, son?" Sal couldn't resist inquiring.

Ignoring Sal's facetiousness and the malfunctioning machine, Lenny crumpled more sheets and calculated the distance to an overflowing waste can nearby. Poised like a basketball player, he shot, missed, and cursed.

Sal eyed other apparently missed shots with annoyance and turned off the machine. This place is a mess, he suppressed.

"The place is crawlin' with cooperation and skilled help," Norm told Sal who shook his head.

Lenny removed the torn pieces that fluttered to the cluttered floor. Ignoring them, bothering the meticulous Sal further, he glanced at both men again. "Tools is on order." Checking the drum's stencil, he reinserted new paper that included his thumbprint on the top sheet. "You guys got inspection sheets?" he breathed.

Norm placed his hands against his thick waist and smiled. "We needs tools, not inspection sheets."

"How're you gonna inspect trailers without inspection sheets?" Lenny demanded in a whisper and restarted the machine. "That's what I'm runnin' off."

Sal folded his arms. Same way you got a diploma–without knowing anything, he answered. God, if it wasn't for the flood victims and $3.18 an hour, I'd be gone.

"Don't rightly know," Norm retorted, as all watched copies floating into the tray. "But so far I worked a week without 'em."

Lenny flashed a sullen face. "Worked? Where?" He laughed breathily. "Worked a hole in your pants from sittin' maybe."

Two young men drifted inside and headed for the coffee urn. Lenny glanced mockingly at them and repositioned the tray about a half an inch. "They're gonna be needin' a new couch from all the sittin'."

The two men started conversing loudly with each other. "Hey, hold it down. I can't hear the fucken machine," Lenny cried, frowned during their heckling, and he shook his head.

Sal stared at copies slapping the tray which was out of line. "Where can we get inspection sheets?"

Lenny appeared to freeze, as if he were surprised about the question. "Whadaya think I'm runnin' off, Mr. 'D'," he revealed mockingly, as if Sal were stupid for not knowing.

"How are we supposed to know, if you don't tell us?" Sal responded. "I left my crystal ball at home."

Norm and the two men laughed.

"Had Mr. 'D' years ago," Lenny told Norm.

Take it easy, Sal warned himself. He's just a child. "You can call me Sal," he suggested friendlily, but the inattentive Lenny missed it, like so much during English.

"Ask Doris to staple these inspection sheets when I give 'em to ya," Lenny breathed again.

Norm raised his hands in protest. "And get chewed? No thanks. I'd rather grab a buzzin' chain saw."

"Whadaya think, she's a, a secretary or somethin'?" Lenny asked. He smirked into laughter and removed the stack clumsily from the tray with his dirty hands.

"Was he like this in English?" Norm asked Sal.

"Hard to tell. He only showed up so he could sleep."

"And you passed him?" Norm pursued.

"How else can you get rid of them?" he answered and was anxious to leave. Arriving up front with Norm and a clipboard containing several inspection sheets, Sal removed Doris' stapler and stapled the sheets together, while she flirted with several nearby standees.

The telephone rang several times before she answered it, and Sal returned the stapler unnoticed.

"We ain't got no trailers yet," she snapped at a flood victim, stunning Sal. "Ah got no idea. Ah don't know," she answered angrily and slammed down the receiver. "Damn pests."

Too incredible, Sal varied, shook his head, and followed Norm outside. Hearing a familiar thumping sound, he was more astounded than ever. Most of the HUD workers were sitting inside their parked cars, talking, laughing, and listening to rock. Maybe we'll all start working tomorrow, he nevertheless encouraged. He grabbed his Phillip's screwdriver from his glove compartment, caught up with Norm, and reentered the same trailer.

Norm tightened the couch legs with Sal's screwdriver and hung storm windows while Sal unpacked and installed globes, tightening nuts by hand. They assembled the kitchen table, coffee tables, and bed frames. Removing mattresses' plastic coverings, both lifted and positioned the mattresses on beds in the two bedrooms. Norm inspected the bathroom sink and toilet, announced that both unscratched or blemished, and Sal checked them off on his inspection sheet.

"Them inspection sheets are important," Norm explained. "Doris sends the blue copy to the Rand. That's how contractors get paid after they sets up trailers and we inspect them again."

Sal nodded. Watching Norm open the mirrored medicine cabinet, he experienced a familiar, uncomfortable feeling–that he was sinking deeper inside the jaws of someone else's stupidity. "Whose brainstorm is this?"

Examining the glass shelves, Norm looked over, eyed him curiously, and squinted. "Come again?"

"Hundreds, maybe thousands of victims are cooped up all over town," he began as if lecturing in class. "And we're fussing around checking for a scratched sink, missing screen, or we're making sure the front door ·closes properly. Do you really think the victims give a damn? Many can fix all that themselves," he assumed. "They're suffering living in cramped quarters. All they want is to get out of wherever the hell they are. Besides, only two guys–you and I–are doing this while seventy-eight free-loaders are getting paid for vacationing in and out of the office. It's too unbelievable." We're two specks of hope surrounded by rampant disorganization and incompetence, his poetic mind embellished. "I've been forced to do dumb things in my life, but this beats it all."

Norm grinned, exposing spaced teeth in a pumpkin-like face. "What can I say? Government job," he tried to justify, as if Sal were a pesky young son inquiring about sex. Fingering the cabinet door from underneath, he closed it carefully and looked back. "Maybe we're making sure companies don't screw the government. They could send broke stuff, or forget ta include a bed or couch."

Sal burst out laughing. "Pennies compared to so much money HUD is wasting paying the freeloaders. What about quality control? How come trailers aren't inspected carefully before they're sent out? Put the damn trailers on the sites anyway right now," he insisted angrily again. "Even if water and electricity haven't been activated. Take care of all that later. How come officials haven't figured that out?"

"Couldn't do that. They need water ta wash and use the toilet."

"HUD could set up portable toilets and send in truckloads of water bottled water for drinking. It's all simple, if the leaders had any brains, ingenuity, and love for others," he repeated.

"Sites ain't ready yet," Norm reminded him again with contrasting calm. "Trailers haven't arrived yet."

"Why not? What's the delay? What's going on?"

"You can't change the world," his mother once told him when he was young.

"Why not?" he had answered and frowned in the present.

"Wasting time and energy to save the government a few cents is too stupid," Sal remarked. "No wonder this country is almost a half a trillion in debt. These two trailers should have been dropped off at Edgewood, not here for this stupid inspection, damn it. And what about the other trailers out there? Why are they still here? Are we supposed to inspect them?" Chill out, he ordered. You're losing control.

Smiling, Norm shook his head. "We's just the little guys. Medicine cabinet okay."

Calming down, Sal checked the sheet appropriately.

Norm turned to the toilet. "Can't fight City Hall," he muttered and jingled the handle. "Toilet okay."

Talk about dumb. What could be wrong with a tub? he suppressed, watching him run his hand along its side. Reading further down the itemized list, Sal sniffed derisively. "Ceiling and walls? Are they kidding?"

"In case they comes up missin'," Norm finally teased back.

Sal laughed sarcastically and Norm rose. "We're supposed to check that everything's here in good working order. That trailers weren't slapped together. Ain't a piece of junk."

Sal followed Norm into the hall. Glad somebody finally explained my job, he grumbled internally, regarding Norm's navy-blue overalls. "So, what if we find something missing or broken?"

Entering a bedroom, Norm glanced back. "The company's gotta make it up."

Sal eyed the ceiling Norm was surveying. "Roy told you all this?"

Norm laughed easily again. "Not really. You picks up bits of info everywhere: Dunkin' Donuts mostly, the john. The best place is the couch, dependin' on who's sittin' there. By the coffee pot in the kitchen's a close second," he specified whimsically.

Appreciating the man's innocence and positive attitude, despite the situation's absurdity, Sal almost smiled.

"Keep your eyes and ears open I always says. Be alert. Never know who you're gonna learn off. Yesterday a toter showed me how to inspect the roof."

Sal visualized the toter boosting Norm up. "How?"

"Ya borrow somebody's truck unless ya gots yer own. Pull it up alongside, stand on the cab, and look," he told the pensive teacher who finally broke up. "Think I'm kiddin'? Beats climbin' up."

"Why doesn't HUD just buy a ladder or have somebody bring one in, if the government can't afford it? They can even borrow mine. 'Course I'm too poor to own a truck. Maybe the government would be dumb enough to buy one for me so I could use it to stand in the bay and look up."

Norm laughed.

Finishing the rooms, they stepped outside and inspected the doors and windows. Checking the yoke, Norm copied down the trailer company's serial number.

"Another detail," Sal persisted. "If there's a broken window or whatever, how do we know who's responsible, the factory, the toter, or vandals?"

Norm paused to analyze the bespectacled teacher seemingly glowing under the morning sun. "Beats me. I'll say one thing fer ya. Ya got a active mind. I never think a them things."

Exhaling, Sal fell silent while they headed for the second trailer. You've got two choices, he finally announced. Tolerate this stupidity and incompetence, do whatever you can to rectify it, or quit without trying to help the victims. Then waste a few days' pay or longer looking for another job, if you can find one. No way, he answered. A bird in the hand is better than . . . You also can give the stupidity and incompetence a chance to work itself out, his other self interrupted. Be patient. Maybe it will, he struggled to reconsider optimistically.

Finishing the trailer, they returned to the office and Sal handed Doris the keys and sheets. "You ought to tag the keys with the trailers' serial numbers and–"

"Oh, God. Can you file this for me?" she interrupted. Eyeing Norm, and she handed him a folder.

Accepting it good-naturedly, Norm analyzed her perplexedly. "Ain't sure I figured out your filing system. You don't always file by the number, do you?"

Assuming he was joking, Sal almost grinned.

"Tsk," Doris replied with annoyance. "Just set 'em on one a them cabinets," she ordered abruptly. "Ah'll get ta them later."

The door banged open, and in rushed dozens of men. Practically stumbling into one another, some headed for the couch and chairs, while others continued down the hall to the kitchen.

"I guess Roy's on his way back," Norm told Sal who smirked.

During the next two hours, Sal moved from crouching beside a chair in the living room, to leaning against the cluttered kitchen counter. He poured another cup of coffee out of boredom. Relieving himself in the bathroom, he looked up at a small sign pinned on the wall above the toilet.

HAPPINESS IS A NORTHERNER REPLACED BY A SOUTHERNER.

Oh, God, can you take it? he inquired, accurately blaming Doris, and he zippered up. You already chose to do that, he reminded himself and flushed the urinal. Ugh, he thought, noticing the dirty sink. Even the soap's dirty. Should I use it? You've got no other choice or forget about washing your hands. Just wash the damn soap first, man. It'll save time for more loafing, he scolded sarcastically, almost laughed, and left.

The sound of droning voices and the smell of coffee intermingling with smoke intensified as Sal headed for the kitchen. Entering, he angled between the usual crowd of talkers, spied Norm near the cream-colored refrigerator, and approached. Leaning against the wall, he felt the paneling give.

"Careful, ya might fall through," Norm warned and Sal shook his smirking head.

A thin, disheveled young man with long hair opened the refrigerator, withdrew a soda, and slammed the door shut. He pulled off the tab and discarded it on the floor near a paper wad.

Mom 'll get that, Sal suppressed.

Reopening the refrigerator, Norm removed a can also.

"Who's supplying the soda?" Sal asked him.

"The Red Cross."

"And *we're* drinking it?" Sal had trouble believing, especially since soda was a luxury that he couldn't afford. "Anybody can just take some?"

Norm tossed the tab into the waste can and smiled. "On this job, you does anythin' till stopped by a wall or Doris' mouth."

Laughter blossomed and died.

"Whatever comes first," another man agreed.

Sal removed a can. He walked between two shaggy men, who stepped begrudgingly aside, and fit himself between several others leaning against the counter.

Dinger entered. He surveyed the group as if he were a pick-up cook at a local tavern, and his large, magnified eyes seemingly bounced weirdly from one small knot of talkers to another. "Ain't nobody gonna eat? It's time for lunch."

"You buyin'?" Skip inquired, attracting attention.

Dinger laughed. He removed a filthy piece of paper from his shirt pocket, unfolded it, and out tumbled flecks of dirt, disturbing Sal. "Yeah, with your money," he uttered sleepily. He grabbed a ballpoint from the table and commenced taking orders from several men with even greater deliberation.

A man wearing a soiled bandana and an earring handed him a twenty.

Sal took a sip. Wonder where *that* came from?

"Far out," Dinger cried and folded the bill around change that he withdrew from the same dirty pocket.

"Hey, how many hours a day are we supposed ta work?" a man wearing a black leather jacket piped up incongruously.

"'Bout twelve. But only when we're this busy," Norm said and the crowd broke up. "And if ya start on the half hour in the morning, ya get credit for the whole hour," he obliged personably, attracting more attention. "My brother told me," he informed the inquisitive faces. "Works for the government in Chicago. Didn't like callin' him long distance, but how else 'er ya gonna learn anything?"

"Should'a called Nixon," someone ventured.

"Call him what?" inquired another.

"It's Mister President ta you," someone else corrected.

"Why call 'im? The White House ain't flooded," returned another vaguely familiar, flippant voice.

Scanning the many faces worriedly, Sal recognized the delicate nose above a wispy mustache and spied the marijuana leaf on the young man's arm. Kevin, he announced and surveyed the rest of the crowd. And Terrance, he spied standing with folded arms near the sink. He must've just been hired, he assumed accurately and sipped again. Imagining either of them becoming his superior somehow, he almost sighed. In fact, remembering administrators pressuring him to lower his standards in order to pass some of his worst rowdies, he almost choked. Mellow out, he urged, catching himself about to sink into self-pity. You'll live longer.

"Another thing," Norm resumed, silencing Sal's rampaging thoughts.

"You gets paid for lunch and supper time."

Accepting a belated order, Dinger looked over. "You mean we get paid for lunch and supper, man?" he inquired lethargically.

"No, he means we get paid for lunch and supper," Skip mocked, stimulating more laughter.

Dinger paraded his enlarged eyes about the room and smiled. "Far out."

"But ya gotta sign out on the hour or close to it, not the half hour," Norm emphasized. "Or ya lose money. Don't ask me why," he told the inquisitive faces including Dinger who seemed to be regarding him with protruding eyes. "Just make sure to sign out on the hour."

"What do you mean?" Dinger mistakenly asked and several men jeered him into silence.

But puzzlement remained widespread, and Norm suddenly became payroll advisor extraordinaire.

"When's pay day?" the man wearing the bandana asked.

"Every two weeks on Friday," Norm provided with a smile.

"Is Sunday double time?" Kevin inquired.

"Not unless it's a holiday," Norm obliged.

Dinger disconnected from several men and tilted his head back at Norm. "Thought Sunday *was* a holiday."

Craig stepped forward, holding a paper coffee cup, and all turned to the tall, heavyset man with thick, duck-tailed hair and the upturned, pink nose. "We don't have holidays. "Every day's the same. This is a disaster. You work every day."

"Then how come we're standin' around?" Dinger asked.

"Because there ain't enough chairs, dummy," Skip scolded, snapped his loose hair back in place and the usual laugher responded.

Chapter 5

Someone had trouble opening the office's front door Friday morning. A young man assisted, and in clunked Mrs. Rota Peters wearing spiked high heels. Surprised, the men moved aside, and the petite woman appeared to usher in an odor of cheap perfume. Her full, auburn coiffure was well-groomed, attracting momentary interest from the sitters, standees, and those wedged in their favorite slots. The chattering dipped slightly. But when a closer examination revealed a thin, middle-aged face that moderate makeup failed to soften, the talking resumed almost to full intensity and pitch.

"Good morning," she chirped, eyeing Doris tapping a pencil during a lengthy yawn. Smiling enthusiastically, Rota flashed oversized and slightly-crooked front teeth above a pointed chin that Sal regarded briefly, sitting in the middle of the couch, and he was annoyed that Doris was ignoring several contractors apparently mentally undressing Rota.

"You the new secretary?" Doris drawled, attracting Craig's attention.

Sipping coffee beside his clique of coffee cohorts, he ogled the woman also.

"Yes," Rota introduced herself to Doris who merely frowned, and Rota unbuttoned her light blue summer coat.

"Good. You can help me– Oh, my lord," Doris shrieked, almost dropping the pencil. "Hot pants!"

Voices halted. Quiet spread like floodwater. Heads jerked back to Rota. Noting surprisingly large breasts for a small woman, many sets of eyes simply rested there. Others dropped in order to study her bare, rather shapely, tan legs.

"Get a blanket," Skip urged, standing with folded arms beside the couch.

"Got my girlfriend's picture in my wallet," protested Kevin sitting beside Terrance on the floor alongside a second desk that had been placed beside Doris'.

Sal had trouble stopping his head from shaking incredulously.

Smiling mischievously rather than coquettishly or self-consciously because of so much attention from the many gapers, Rota searched for a place to hang her coat.

"What's my mother gonna say?" Skip asked.

Sitting beside Sal, Norm folded his arms behind his neck and smiled.

"What's goin' on?" inquired a slow, hidden voice. A body-like figure, seemingly belonging to some kind of mutation emerging from a cave, stumbled through the crowd. Dinger swept aside his long, straight hair and scrutinized Rota's legs and breasts boldly. "Decent."

Though the legs might have attracted more attention had they been shapelier, several pounds heavier, and the owner twenty years younger, the men studying her curiously.

Rota clunked toward hangers hooked to a wall lamp behind the second desk.

Sitting directly underneath the lamps, Kevin stared at her legs.

"Roy said you could wear 'em?" Doris practically screeched, jolting her momentarily.

About to respond, Rota tried to reach the hangers, but Kevin was in the way. Realizing that he was too engrossed ogling her legs or perhaps appreciating it, she frowned.

"Roy said I could wear these," Skip insisted, slapped his jeans, and laughter resounded.

"Guess that's my desk," Rota told the men sitting on it, but too engrossed studying her, none moved, hardly fazing her. More interested in hanging up her coat, she reconsidered the hangers and leaned toward them which were directly above Kevin who gave her panties a serious workout.

Well, what do you know, he's finally motivated himself about something, Sal scoffed with a laugh.

"Look out," Norm warned, nor could anyone determine whether he was warning Rota to steady her balance or Kevin's seemingly bulging eyeballs.

Whatever the case, Rota froze, possibly in order to satisfy Kevin, the onlookers, and Terrance who slid over as if to keep Kevin well focused, although no one could be sure about that either.

"Far out."

Rota stretched further, pulling Kevin's eyes up even higher into the forbidden area.

"Need any help?" Skip asked Rota.

"No, I'm fine," Kevin supplied.

"Same here," Terrance contributed and savage guffawing tore loose.

Rota smiled indifferently. "Got it," she announced, grabbing the hanger.

"So did I," Kevin admitted, as if he were a photographer, and was slain with savage laughter.

Rota inserted the hanger inside the arms of her coat. Timing her leaning back to hang it up, Kevin and Terrance looked back up.

"Lend 'em your glasses," Skip advised Dinger who ignored him.

Rising slightly, Kevin managed to bring his face to within six inches of her panties. "No need," he assured, and guffawing ricocheted off the thin walls.

"Guess you finally found something worth studying," Sal told Kevin and smirked at the absurdity of it all.

"There," Rota uttered obliviously, hung up her coat, and straightened.

Kevin hurriedly settled back down and Terrance slid back to his spot.

"Where?" Skip asked.

Rota flashed a reserved smile, eyed the desk, and the men finally slid off reluctantly.

Stepping on a small, brown scatter rug, bunched under her chair, Rota stumbled momentarily.

"Take it easy, Rota," Norm cautioned. "You don't wanna be too anxious to work."

"Yeah, 'cause there ain't none," Skip announced, snapped his head, and his hair fell back in place.

Rota smiled graciously and sat. Not until the legs folded and disappeared safely under the desk did the gawking start to diminish.

Lenny broke through the thick crowd, noticed Rota, and approached her desk. "Somebody said something about work?" he asked and all watched him settle his eyeballs on Rota's breasts. "Where?"

"Not there," Skip explained and laughter broke lose again.

"Maybe she's got the wrong trailer," Lenny breathed.

"Could be. Nobody works here," a man declared.

Rota frowned in puzzlement.

"Ah'll wear mine tomorrow," Doris vowed, ignoring Bob Updike, a heavy-set contractor standing before her desk with a paper in his hand.

"Thanks for the warnin'," Skip cried.

"Go to hell," Doris snapped, surprising Rota who began opening drawers and checking inside.

Finally catching Doris' glance, Bob asked her when more trailers were arriving for him to set up at Edgewood, but Doris ignored him.

"What time does Mr. Nichols arrive?" Rota asked no one in particular and quiet seemingly whip-lashed back as Sal watched and listened incredulously.

"Mr. Nichols?" Skip cried in disbelief. "Who he?"

Laughter rumbled back.

Craig disconnected from a group containing practically the same faces belonging to the same bodies standing almost in the same places as yesterday. Holding a cigarette, he approached Rota's desk. "'Bout seven forty-five."

Rota checked the watch on her slender, tan arm. She glanced up at

Craig's handsome baby face, flashed another smile, and looked away self-consciously. "He's late."

Raucous laughter surprised her.

"Late for what?" someone inquired. "He don't even work here."

Rota frowned again. "I'm confused. What? Isn't this the office trailer? Isn't this headquarters?"

Craig grinned. "Don't listen to them. "He's in back, the far room."

"Why didn't somebody tell me?"

"We just did," someone answered.

"You never asked," Craig agreed.

Rota rose. She paused to pull up her hot pants, emerged from around her desk, and pretended not to notice the men staring at her legs and breasts.

"Far out," Dinger commented and laughter slithered loose.

The men parted as she approached, and their eyes remained glued to her shapely legs unfolding one after the other as she clunked past. Some men refused to give her breasts a rest, while others appeared to enjoy alternating between the two body parts.

Walking past the dining room, Rota smiled pleasantly rather than haughtily or conceitedly, disappeared down the hall, and returned shortly afterwards. Gathering more stares, she hopped back around her desk, and sat. "He's on the phone," she told her audience, and regarded a stack of inspection sheets Doris had placed on her desk.

"For the files," Doris shouted, though Rota was no more than four feet away.

Rota stared at the top sheet.

"The 050's are filed under *three* and the 900's under *six*," Doris explained and once again groups of men stopped talking in order to watch and listen.

"Sounds logical," Skip chirped, finally loosening an incredulous smile from Sal's expression of disbelief.

Thumbing through several sheets, Rota regarded Doris with puzzlement. "What? What do you mean?"

Doris smirked. "Inspection sheets is filed by the number." Rising impatiently, she ignored the smirking contractors waiting for her to attend to them, and placed a stack of contracts beside the inspection sheets. "These go in the bottom drawer. By contract number," she shouted and slapped them.

"What? My desk drawer?" Rota inquired.

"Not your drawer," Doris practically shrieked. "In the cabinet behind me."

Rota eyed the row. "Which one?"

"Take your pick. It don't matter," explained an unshaven, young man wearing a baseball cap, and Rota frowned.

Annoyed, Bob Updike asked Doris what trailer he and his crew could haul to Edgewood.

Doris finally regarded him. "How should ah know?" she fumed.

"She only works here," someone inserted.

"I'll show you," Craig obliged and took a giant step backwards from his group. Walking to the window, he looked out, pointed, and turned to Bob who had approached. "That one. Closest to us," he advised and returned to his group.

"Don't mix the inspection sheets with conditionals or the delivery tickets," Doris blurted to Rota, returned to her desk, and accidentally brushed her stapler on the floor.

"God," Rota complained about Doris' loud voice.

"Gimmy that," Doris ordered the contractors and one of them obliged.

"Conditionals?" Rota inquired, frowning at both piles. "Delivery tickets? What're you talking about? Nobody told me anything."

"Far out."

"Welcome to the club," Lenny announced.

Craig stepped back again and frowned at Doris.

"You were supposed ta block a two-bedroom trailer, not a *three*," she boomed at Bob.

"You told me ta pull any trailer off a the field," he whined and Rota studied his muscular torso above his white, t-shirted beer-belly. "How was I suppose to know? I figured they was all *twos*," he growled, placed a hand on his waist, and lowered his head to peer out of Rota's window again. "You never told me."

"You never asked. Ah got more things ta worry about than what ya'all pulls outta here," Doris barked sternly and Bob fell obediently silent.

"It was on your copy of the inspection sheet," Doris added.

"Far out."

"See, right there. Two bedrooms. Can't you read?" Doris asked and Rota stared incredulously at her.

"No, our schools don't learn us nothing," Bob sneered.

Doris glared at him. "Ah believe it."

"How am I supposed to know the difference between a *two* bedroom trailer and a *three*?" Bob demanded.

"*Three's* one more than *two*," Lenny threw into the fray and laughter filled the room.

Grinning, Bob became serious. "All them trailers look alike. I'd have to check inside. I don't even have a key."

"Key man," Skip called.

Faces turned to Dinger who tilted his head upward defensively, and his eyes, magnified by his thick lenses, suggested something alien.

"They're on Doris' desk," Sal told the others.

"Can't make no more keys," Dinger unfolded slowly. "Roy fixed the machine, but we ran out of blanks," he unfolded sleepily.

"Use yourself," Skip recommended.

Doris looked up at the smooth-mannered Bob. "Boy, you Yankees is dumb. If ya reads 2-A-72 printed on a trailer, *two* means two bedrooms, get it? 'A' is for Agnes, the hurricane, remember?"

Bob glared. "Oh, there was a hurricane here?"

"You're lookin' at her. They changed Doris' name ta Agnes," Skip supplied, stimulating the usual.

Craig walked over to help the distraught Rota.

"How come you never told me that?" Bob stormed.

"Can you guess what seventy-two means?" Doris continued.

Bob appeared to be studying Doris' slightly bucked teeth. "Your age?"

"She ain't that young," Skip slipped in.

"Oh, you Yankees is real funny," Doris scolded following another avalanche of laughter.

Bob shook his head. "Gee, I don't get it," he sneered sarcastically in a juvenile voice.

Norm turned to Sal. "See what I mean? You picks up bits of info everywhere, even from Doris."

"This is ridiculous. Everyone should have been briefed about all this in some way before."

Norm nodded.

"What trailers have you been pullin' outta here all along?" Doris barked at Bob.

"The first trailer I come to."

Doris' mouth opened in dismay. "How 'm ah gonna know how many *two* and *three* bedroom trailers is at Edgewood?"

"Same as we do everything here–guess," Skip suggested.

Bob shrugged. "That's your problem," he snapped.

"It's printed on the trailer. She just told you," Sal told Bob exchanging glares with Doris.

Waiting impatiently for her to attend to their similar needs, the other contractors shook their heads in disgust.

"You only asked me to check serial numbers. I always wrote them down and handed you the sheet before pulling out, remember?" Bob insisted. "So, now what? I don't get paid?"

"Rota," Doris shrieked.

Chatting with Craig, Rota palmed her ears. "My ears."

"Don't file none a Updike's contracts. They gotta be pulled and checked," Doris stormed.

Rota removed her hands. "What?"

Doris repeated herself a shade quieter.

"What contracts?" Rota inquired. "Where are they? You mean from this pile?" she inquired, touching the stack. "What?"

"Tsk. Ah'll take care of it later," Doris sneered.

"I'll check the trailers we just hooked up and let you know," Bob told Doris. "Only thing is, I don't know what ones is mine. Other guys 've been haulin' 'em to Edgewood too. They're all mixed up."

Sal was aghast. "There's no record of what trailers have been moved where?"

"*You're* keepin' track of 'em, ain't you?" Bob asked Doris.

Checking papers on her desk, Doris looked up. "Me? Don't you got no park map?"

"I borrowed it from a contractor who ain't around," Bob explained.

More laughter erupted except from the somber Sal.

"How's a map gonna tell me where all *my* trailers are?"

"Nothin' like a smooth operation," Skip said.

Bob grinned briefly. "Roy's supposed to be getting new maps. But it don't matter. Lot numbers ain't even been assigned yet," he whined annoyingly.

Doris stared in disbelief. "Are you sure? They're supposed to be."

"What the hell's the difference?" Bob demanded. "Long as we get people inta somethin'."

Doris registered alarm. "Yes, it does," she shrieked. "Some families gets a *two* bedroom trailers or a *three*, dependin' on how many's in the family. How's HUD gonna sign up families to a *two* or a *three* if'n they don't know how many bedrooms is in a par-tic-aler trailer?"

"It's printed on the trailer," Sal reminded Doris who ignored him.

"So, if they get assigned to the wrong one, can't they get reassigned to the right one?" Bob insisted. "No big deal."

"Doris glared again. "Papers is all written up on each one," she shouted. "They gotta sign a lease," she added just as loudly. "God, 're you dumb."

"Thanks," Bob replied.

'You're welcome," she answered.

Flirting with Rota, Craig finally broke away. "Can I help?" he asked Doris who hurriedly briefed him about the problem.

Doris whirled back to Bob. "You ain't getting' paid if you're blockin' wrong trailers," she stormed.

Bob turned grim.

"Anybody got an Alka-Seltzer?" a standee asked.

Dinger peered up from a niche between the couch and a chair. "Who's got a headache?"

"Your mother, ever since she brung you inta the world," Skip remarked.

Doris stared at the far room during the laughter. "Roy," she shrieked. "Come 'ere. We gots problems."

"Come back here," Roy shouted back, and heads turned toward the hallway.

"No, damn it. Come 'ere," she screamed and heads jerked back to Doris.

"You're serve," Skip injected.

"No sense nobody movin'. You're both doing fine from where you are," Lenny breathed during more laughter.

"Thank God they ain't further apart," Norm told Sal. "They'd be even louder."

"That ain't possible" Skip disagreed.

"Two to one Roy moves first," someone predicted.

"Moves what?" Dinger asked.

A distant chair pushed out along the linoleum in the far room, causing heads to look back as if all were awaiting the returned shot.

Arriving holding half a doughnut, Roy stumbled through an opening in the living room crowd.

"Told ya," the same voice said.

Dinger stepped forward to stare longingly at the doughnut, but Roy threw it inside his mouth before reaching Doris' desk.

"What's all the frettin' about, woman? Roy leveled at her while chewing away. Suddenly observing Dinger's strange, angled head eyeing him, he frowned. "Who you?"

Laughter erupted anew.

Doris began cackling out the problem and all stopped laughing in order to listen.

Doesn't Roy remember hiring him? Sal wondered.

"Dinger," he introduced. "Bruce Allmendinger," he delivered slowly.

Roy studied Dinger's long, swept-back hair and strange face with curiosity. "You puttin' me on?"

"No, he's for real. That's the way they grow 'em in the Bronx. From the eyeballs down," Skip uncorked and laughter bounced back.

"Roy, are you listenin'?" Doris shouted.

Rota palmed her ears again. "I can't think."

Roy shook Dinger's hand. "Glad to know you. Whad ah done hire you as?"

Is he serious? Sal protested.

"A garbage can," Skip provided dryly. "Eats everything that don't move and sometimes stuff that does."

Roy contemplated Dinger's enlarged eyes. Frowning again, he grinned during more laughter and awaited Dinger's answer.

"A maint–a," Dinger attempted.

"He can't even pronounce it, let alone do it," Skip told his audience and snapped back some disorderly hair.

"He's another key operator," Norm explained.

Roy started nodding as if he finally remembered.

"Mr. G-7 himself," Skip reminded the listeners.

Several applauded and Dinger grinned proudly.

Lenny appeared through the crowd. "We ain't got no blanks ta make extra keys," he reminded Roy who ignored him.

Sal eyed Lenny's dirty hands. Doesn't he ever wash? came more wonderment.

Roy rechecked Dinger still examining him. "Hope ya remember what ya are when yer out at the site. Wouldn't want ya inspectin' when ya should be maintainin'."

"What?" Dinger asked. "Mr. Nichols, I ain't done nothin' since, since they sent me over from, from–"

"Bellevue," Skip inserted.

Roy looked back. "Just hang in there, son. Hang in there."

"Yes sir, but–"

"Roy, did you hear me?" Doris stormed.

"Yeah."

"What should ah do?" Doris asked.

Roy eyed her meaningfully. "Just hang in there, woman."

"Lotta hangin' goin' on," someone injected.

"But drop yo' voice a shade, first," Roy recommended and he grinned during the cheering.

"I smell dead fish," Skip offered. "Hey, Dingle. Move yo' buns outta the way. Can't see Doris through the smoke."

"Consider that a blessing," someone told him.

"What smoke?" Dinger asked, nevertheless complying.

"Thanks," Sal told Skip.

"No problem," Skip answered.

Several men stepped aside and moved further away as Dinger approached.

This is a farce. Where's Shakespeare. Sal thought and considered complaining to the higher-ups about the chaos. I should be a hero? he suddenly refused. I don't even like informing, unless it's something serious. This *is* serious, he answered. But where do I go? Who do I see? Giving up, he folded his hands behind his neck and leaned back. But realizing how easy it was to do nothing, instead of rising above a difficult situation and doing the right thing, he unclasped his hands, leaned forward, and draped one leg over the other while evaluating Roy. What could you possibly accomplish by complaining? Except give yourself more grief? Besides, who's to say Roy isn't doing everything possible under the circumstances?

"Roy, what about them wrong trailers Bob blocked?"

"What about 'em?"

"Roy, for God's sake–"

"You're the secretary, ain't cha? Start secretaryin'.

"Bob should unblock them, so's my paperwork comes out right."

"Unblock 'em?" Roy cried incredulously. "Hell no. Our job's settin' 'em up," he clamored.

"Good," Bob agreed.

Doris folded her arms, slouched, and smirked. "Well, if he don't give a damn about the screwed up paperwork neither do ah," she told the contractors who were grumbling about being ignored.

About to leave, Roy noticed Rota and paused. "How're you doing?"

Rota looked up and smiled, exposing uneven teeth. "Fine."

"Who're you?"

Rota introduced herself as the new secretary and asked him if he wanted her to file the conditionals.

Pain transformed Roy's placid face.

"Ah done told you, didn't ah?" Doris shrieked at Rota, staggering her.

Roy maneuvered his tongue inside his closed mouth. "Yeah. File 'em," he seemed to fling recklessly, causing laughter.

When in doubt, file, Sal left unsaid.

"What else should I do?" Rota persisted, holding Roy's fragile attention.

Silence spread with anticipation, especially when Rota smiled suggestively.

Hardly creative even with sexual vulgarity, Roy also lacked wit. "How're you at making coffee?"

Missing the absurdity, the loungers resumed talking, particularly when Rota began unfolding a long dissertation about her cooking to several of them. It was so good that her husband had left her, she revealed accidentally. "He's back now but we haven't talked for weeks."

Removing a cigarette from his pack, Roy regarded her breasts. "Is that raght?" he drawled. "We could use a bigger coffee pot," he pursued incongruously. "You got one?"

"She's got two," someone injected, stimulating the usual.

Staring at Roy in puzzlement, Rota appeared to be fighting off a smile.

Roy turned to Sal. "English teacher, whadaya call them big pots?"

"Percolators?" Sal asked.

"That's it. We could use a larger one for the kitchen," Roy persisted, turned back to her, and the two eyed each other curiously.

"Oh, I've got a nice large one, Mr. Nichols," Rota obliged. "We used to have a small restaurant and–"

"Ya got two, I'm tellin' ya," interrupted a hidden voice.

Rota smiled. "I'll bring it tomorrow."

"Good," Roy replied.

The government could only afford that small coffee pot in the kitchen? Sal wondered. They have to borrow necessities from employees?

"Roy?" Doris demanded.

"We're leavin'," he barked as if hoping to silence her.

"What? Now? Where?"

"Ah'm takin' you to lunch."

Doris checked her wristwatch. "It's only nine."

Roy eyed his. "Is that raght? Well, ah'll be damned. Let's go for breakfast then."

"We done had breakfast," Doris insisted.

Still waiting to receive information about trailers to block or tote to sites, the contractors frowned and sighed.

"We de-ad? Did we eat supper last night?"

"No."

"Let's go for supper then," he suggested, caught a few laughs, and turned to Rota. "Can ya hold down the fort, till we get back?"

"What? Oh, yes. Certainly, Mr. Nichols," she declared as if he were the company executive.

"Five minutes is plenty of experience on this job," Skip commented.

Roy turned to the circles of standees throughout the room. "These guys can help."

Fearful about changing the status quo, the men moaned.

Roy turned to Lenny. "How're them inspection sheets comin'? Done run off any more?"

Silence descended.

"No," he breathed, ushering in more laughter.

Roy regarded the medium-built Lenny whose rolled-up sleeves exposed his thick, veined arms. "What's wrong with it?"

"Duplicator's broke."

"It's got a faulty operator," Skip provided without snapping his head.

Dinger approached, as if it were his cue to recite his part in a bad play.

Turning to the strangely tilted face containing thick glasses, Roy seemed to catch Dinger's body odor and retreated several steps.

"It ain't copying," Dinger explained.

"No kiddin', Dingle," Skip cried. "Broke machines usually don't copy, copy?"

"What?" Dinger asked.

"Let's check it out," Roy offered.

The crowd started parting like before. Dinger followed Lenny and Roy into the kitchen and Roy removed a jam, solving the problem. He left with Doris. The men continued sipping, joking, and laughing, until Dinger reappeared from the kitchen.

"I just seen a horse go by," he announced slowly, catching their attention.

"What did he buy?" Skip inserted.

"Like, nobody was even riding it," Dinger spoke even slower.

"Shit, give up the weed, man," Skip suggested. "Of course nobody was riding it. Everybody knows horses ride people. Why the other day–" he attempted but laughter smothered him.

Norm, Lenny, and several others looked out the window above the couch, blamed Dinger for "seeing things," and returned to their slots.

"Take your thumb off a your glasses," Skip advised.

Dinger looked out the same window. "I ain't kiddin'. I seen a big, black horse."

"Couldn't be mine," Norm offered. "I got a horse of a different color."

"Maybe ya seen yourself, Ding. You're a dark horse."

"There he goes," Dinger shouted.

The men looked back out the window behind Rota's desk.

"You guys are a scream," she cried and resumed flipping through inspection sheets.

"What's a horse doing here?" Lenny asked as the animal trotted along the rough toward the back gate.

"Probably looking for a job," Skip entreated. "We're runnin' outta men ta hire," he told a laughing face.

"Maybe it's a sign," Rota commented without turning back.

"Yeah, a sign of tryin' ta get the hell outta here," Skip offered.

"Probably just finished totin' a trailer," Lenny breathed. "Drivers is scarce."

"Far out."

Norm unclasped his hands and yawned. "A sign of six more weeks of loafin'."

"They show horses here," Rota explained.

"Show 'em what?" Dinger asked.

"Manure," Skip answered. "People come from all over to check ours out."

A car appeared, then slowed before the horse reached the opened gate.

Dinger surveyed the others. "People come to see horses here?"

"No, horses come to see people, Dingdong," Skip revised. "That's why the horse is tryin' ta leave. Couldn't find no people."

The car caught up with the horse which suddenly reared. "See that?" Dinger cried.

"No," someone answered.

"Dinger, run out there and get that horse," Norm suggested.

"One look at Dinger and it'll get a horse attack," Skip quipped.

"Someone ought to do something," Rota suggested.

"We are–watching," Kevin commented.

The horse galloped ahead of the car, shot out the gate and disappeared from view.

"Hey," Dinger exclaimed. "It's gone. Probably looking for a female horse."

"They call 'em mares, cuz," Skip corrected. "That horse ain't never gonna find a mate."

Dinger rested his magnified eyes on his cousin. "Why not?"

Skip snapped his hair in place. "'Cause this is only a one-horse town, dummy."

"Oh, man," Norm responded.

Chapter 6

Too much nonsense, Sal ridiculed inwardly, driving home that night. I'll give it one more day. Entering the office the following morning, he inhaled coffee mixed with the usual strange odors. He walked between the chatterers, exchanged nods with several familiar faces, and entered the kitchen. He observed the red light on the percolator near the sink and Rota's milky-smooth tan legs.

Wearing pink shorts that matched her blouse, she was stooped over washing dishes.

"Grab a cup," Norm invited.

"Doesn't look too safe," Sal remarked, eyeing dirty dishes, a column of paper cups, and an opened box of stale Dunkin' Donuts soaking in spilled soda. Flies were buzzing around curdled milk.

"The donuts ain't too bad once you get past the flies," Norm encouraged with a laugh, studying Rota's legs along with several other men.

"I'll pass," Sal replied, leaning against the counter.

"Looks like Rota finally learned what they's hired her for," Norm commented.

Rota wiped a rinse cup on a towel, turned, and glared at him. "That's what you think. We're going to start taking turns," she threatened unconvincingly.

Sal evaluated the men's waning interest. "Good luck."

"I believe in women's lib," she asserted meekly.

Skip grinned. "Yeah, but nobody else does, and you're outnumbered," he delivered and rearranged his hair.

"Never touched a dish in my life," Norm remarked, leaning against the counter awkwardly. "Dishes is women's work."

Rota glanced at Skip folding his arms. Turning back to the sink, she washed a saucer. "You guy's 're all the same. You believe women were born for certain jobs."

"Weren't they?" Skip inquired.

"I know one job you'll never get out of," Norm offered obligingly. Rota added the rinsed saucer to the pile and looked back.

"Giving birth."

"I'll say," she agreed and submerged a cup into one of the twin sinks filled with water.

Lenny scrutinized Dinger striding toward the doughnuts. "What a nose."

"He smells the flies," Skip explained.

"They's rancid," Norm warned.

"What, the flies?" Lenny asked.

"No, Dinger," Skip remarked.

"Mixed with slop, flies, everything," Norm completed.

Dinger grabbed a doughnut, took a bite and Sal winced. Dinger turned to Norm while chewing. "Flies gives 'em flavor."

"Hate to see food wasted but this is too much," Norm declared, straightened as if about to leave, and slumped back against the counter. "I believe he'd eat manure."

"Only if it's seasoned," Skip provided with a laugh.

"Think I'm gonna puke," Rota objected without turning back.

"Don't hit the dishes," Lenny warned.

"Most of these cups and dishes are mine. I'm taking them home tonight," Rota vowed. "Then I wanna see how you're gonna get along."

"Ah smells beautiful fresh coffee," someone drawled, and the usual parting occurred for a familiar figure wearing a different cowboy shirt sporting the picture of a bear and the same dingo boots and denims with the outrageous steel buckle.

Finishing the last cup, Rota glanced at Roy working his way further inside. "Brought the percolator," she announced, wiping the counter.

"Right on, Rota," Roy responded, poured a cup, and left.

Entering the office, Doris promenaded through the living room, and practically stumbled into the kitchen. "Told you ah'd wear 'em," she shouted.

All turned to inspect her legs which resembled two bulky, straight columns protruding down from a pair of oversized, blue hot pants.

"Yuk," Lenny uncorked breathily. "I think *I'm* gonna puke."

"Go to hell," Doris spat. Folding her arms awkwardly across her breasts, she moved aside as if waiting to hook an arm at a square dance, and pretended not to notice the men inspecting her legs.

Minutes later, a young, pretty, dignified woman entered the side door and paused before the kitchen doorway.

Voices diminished and heads turned to regard her leather riding boots matching her pants and jacket.

"Excuse me, but did any of you happen to see a black horse?" Struggling to avoid the gawkers, she settled on the sober, matured-looking Sal leaning boredly against the refrigerator.

"He's in back talking to the boss," someone uttered before Sal could answer, and the laughter disturbed her.

"I beg your pardon?" she responded, surveyed several long-haired heads, and turned back to Sal who hadn't laughed.

"Ask the boss," Lenny suggested, sitting before the duplicator, and he pointed to an up-tilted head devouring a fourth doughnut.

The woman studied Dinger's long, parted hair and strange glasses and frowned. *"He's the boss?"*

"You should see him when he ain't eatin'," Lenny offered, angled his thick, veined arms up awkwardly for her analysis, which she missed, and the men laughed.

"It's the job," Skip explained as the laughter subsided. "They got him workin' so hard, he hardly eats," he explained and sighed.

The woman reevaluated Dinger amid renewed laughter.

Skip yawned. "Yeah, he's the boss," he reaffirmed in his usual deadpan manner. "We're so short of help, he put himself to work."

"You're joking, of course," she responded in annoyance.

"Of course," Lenny quipped. "He really ate at home. This is his second breakfast."

"Tsk, no I mean–" she attempted but laughter rattled her again.

"Sorry about that," Sal apologized and explained about seeing the horse yesterday.

"Thank you," she replied, glared at the others, and left.

Coffee sipping and idle chatter persisted until Craig stepped inside. "How many of you guys drive?"

The men paused to exchange glances.

Never volunteer for anything, Sal remembered from the service. This is different, his other self disagreed, and he raised his hand. So did Norm, Skip, and several others, including Dinger.

"Good. Follow me," Craig ordered.

Finally, Sal announced, complying with the others.

Pausing before the front door, Craig turned to watch the group maneuver between and around the usual standees. "We're pickin' up HUD's panel trucks at the Rand at ten thirty. So pile in a couple of cars, yours and yours," he said, singling out Norm and Sal. "You guys 'll chauffeur us there, drive back with a truck like the rest of us, then get somebody to drive you back later for your cars."

Arriving at the Rand Building shortly afterr ten, they parked near a line of tan panel trucks but Tony never showed. Irritated and impatient, Sal offered to look for him inside with Craig who agreed, and both entered the building.

An employee directed them to a large room filled with secretaries typing at their desks. Tony's desk was off to the side, but his chair was empty, and none of the secretaries knew his whereabouts.

Talk about indifference during a crisis, Sal criticized, and Craig started flirting with a pretty secretary, annoying him further. Am I the only one who's concerned? Smirking, he picked up a stray *Star Gazette* from a nearby chair. Sitting, he read that conditions had become so unbearable at the Armory and churches that two more flood victims had committed suicide.

A half hour later a slim, cocky man in his fifties headed for Tony's desk and sat, squeaking the swivel chair.

Sal gave Craig the eye, and they approached him like two FBI agents about to make an arrest.

"Are you Tony Grannis?" Craig asked.

"What if I am? Who's askin'?"

Sal expected Craig to scold for not meeting them in back, but the tall, blond-haired man introduced himself and Sal cheerfully, surprising Sal.

What's *his* problem? Sal berated, referring to Tony who disregarded his extended hand. You're bored? With so many people out of work, you're lucky to have a job.

Tony opened a bottom drawer, withdrew a stack of 5 x 8 index cards, and slammed the door shut, as if he disliked being bothered.

"We came to pick up the trucks," Craig divulges almost boyishly.

"I know what yuz come for," Tony snarled defiantly in a deep, crisp voice and regarded the desk's glass top with savage contempt.

This is an emergency. Where the hell 've *you* been, jerk-face? Sal almost exploded. Picturing getting fired, he reduced his irritation to glaring at Tony staring arrogantly at the cards.

Tony tossed them on the desk and reached for a black, government pen shaped like a zeppelin. "How many guys ya brung?"

"About a dozen," Craig replied.

Tony looked up, revealing a dark, withdrawn face beneath receding, black hair. The ends of his mouth curved downward slightly, suggesting sarcasm. "Don't cha know?"

Craig's grin disappeared. Placing hands on his waist, he shifted his feet uncomfortably. "We got enough men for all of your trucks," he assured pleasantly. "Don't worry," he added with almost the same high school tone.

"Oh, I ain't worryin'. And you ain't gettin' all of 'em," he warned and looked away angrily.

"I thought you said over the phone–" Craig attempted.

Wrinkles invaded Tony's wide forehead. "I never told ya how many. Don't be puttin' words in my mouth. You guys are all the same."

What guys? Sal pondered.

"Hey, you said–"

"I tol' you we had some panel trucks," Tony barked crossly. He rechecked the secretaries for their reaction, but none looked his way, pleasing Sal.

"We counted eight trucks out there, and–" Craig resumed.

"You're tellin' me how trucks I got?" he interrupted sharply. "I know how many's out there. Two guys to a truck in case ya need help or whatever. And nobody drives, 'less he's got a license."

"Oh, I'll make sure," Craig agreed and grinned sheepishly.

"Oh, you'll make sure," Tony mocked. "That's what they all say."

What HUD imbecile put this asshole in charge of transportation? Sal demanded. These beauts should take a course on how to love their neighbors like themselves, then get thrashed for having the audacity to be alive.

Craig looked away self-consciously.

Tony squeaked his chair into a new position. "I'm puttin' you responsible," he scolded Craig. "And if a truck breaks down, nobody does nothin' 'cept call me, got it?"

"Got it."

Stop kissing the jerk, Sal scolded.

"I don't give a shit where the hell ya are. Push the damn thing off the road. Keep your goddamn hands off the motor. Don't touch nothin'. Just call me."

"Oh, my guys wouldn't–"

"Oh, your guys wouldn't. How the hell do you know what your guys would do?" he fumed, paused, and typing seemed to penetrate the silence. "There's more bum mechanics than, than, experts," he sneered, checked Sal for the first time and looked away. "One asshole tears the motor apart, *then* calls me. Wanted ta know where the plugs go," he berated, then eyed Craig squarely. "Don't give me none er ya shit," he growled, then, as if remembering, swung around to scrutinize the secretaries recklessly, but none reciprocated, pleasing Sal again.

"So, how many trucks can we take, Tony?" Craig pursued.

Tony swung back sharply. "Keep yer shirt on. I'm comin' ta that," he barked belligerently. "And nobody changes trucks. Everybody keeps the same truck ya sign them up for. And you're responsible, got it?" He waited until Craig nodded and continued. "I don't give a rat's ass if ya gotta walk ten miles to the nearest phone or if somebody else's truck's handy. No swappin' trucks," he emphasized. He continued lecturing similarly for a full minute, realized Craig was staring at the cards and stopped. "Ya can take seven trucks," he appeared to concede so quietly and begrudgingly that Sal wasn't sure he had heard him, until Tony started raging that the eighth truck parked near a telephone pole was "broke down" and needed repairs. "Don't touch it, got it?"

"*I* got it," Sal responded facetiously. "What about you?" he asked Craig. "Did you get it?"

"I got it," Craig answered.

"He got it," Sal informed Tony who eyed him suspiciously.

"I'm givin' ya seven keys," he announced, opened his top drawer, grabbed the pile, and dropped them on his desk. "See these tags? The plate number's written on each one," he shouted and turned to catch whatever secretary might have caught such savage manhood.

None did again and Sal smiled this time.

"And don't try startin' a truck with somebody else's key. The hell's the matter with you guys?" he demanded as if Craig's crew had been responsible. Noting Craig threatening to disagree, he unfolded a long, profane dissertation about someone who had. "Cost the government thirty-eight bucks."

Picturing how much the government was wasting paying the loungers, Sal almost burst out laughing.

"See them cards?"

Sal suppressed a yawn, hoped for a *no* from the handsome face with the pointed nose and duck-tailed hair, but Tony resumed before Craig could respond.

"Each man signs the card with the right truck license number, follow? And no trucks roll 'less I get a signed card, got it?"

"No problem," Craig varied but too pleasantly, annoying Sal.

"Then how come everybody drives wrong trucks?" Tony accused, surprising Craig.

"Yeah, you laugh. And how come I don't get cards back?"

Don't answer the asshole, Sal suggested.

"I'll return 'em," Craig assured.

"Make sure ya do," he grumbled and the duo finally left.

Sal complained about Tony's attitude, and Craig revealed that he had been a Rand foreman. "Some kind of ball-buster, I hear. Now he's one of HUD's big boys. Scares ya how some guys make it to the top, don't it?"

"I'll say." The Peter Principle is still alive and well, Sal mused.

Craig distributed the cards and keys but problems soon arose. Sal's and Craig's keys didn't fit into their ignitions, and they returned. Tony was on a coffee break, according to a secretary and reappeared nonchalantly with his cup, twenty minutes later.

Sitting boringly nearby, Sal joined Craig who explained the problem.

"You ain't gettin' no other keys 'less I get the cards back," Tony stormed, then, as if he was battling stress, reopened the same drawer begrudgingly, removed another handful of keys that he dropped on his desk.

"Are you always this friendly?" Sal inquired.

Craig burst out laughing and Tony regarded the secretaries who refused to look their way, satisfying Sal again.

Craig collected the keys and they left. The men wasted an hour finding the right ones to start the vehicles. Worse, Norm's truck tires were almost flat and Skip's truck kept coughing, sputtering, and stalling.

Jerk-face be damned, Sal sneered. Pulling up alongside Craig's car window, he suggested that they try finding the key for the eighth truck. "I'd give it a whirl, but my truck will die if I take my foot off the pedal."

Craig complied, was surprised to find a key already in the ignition, more so when it started, and he drove alongside Sal. "If we take it, how the hell am I gonna explain it to Tony? All his paperwork's gonna be screwed up."

"Like Tony," Sal responded. "He's probably not even there."

Skip flipped his hair back in place. "We could always bash the engine. Then his paperwork would be right," he shouted from inside his vehicle and Craig laughed.

"These old trucks probably haven't been used in months," Sal told Craig.

One of the men found some tools in his truck and Skip, a former mechanic, managed to get all the trucks running hours later.

Craig signaled the others to follow him. Sal was about to do so when his passenger door opened.

"What's up, Mr. 'D'?" inquired a familiar voice slowly.

Give me a break, Sal moaned inwardly noticing Dinger. "Figured you were driving with Skip."

"Craig tol' me to go with you," he responded, hopped inside, and Sal smirked.

Last to follow the caravan moving slowly behind a long line of vehicles, Sal slowed.

Reaching Route 17 with the others almost an hour later, Sal started losing speed. "Now what?" he muttered, when his vehicle sputtered and stalled. Quickly shifting into neutral while coasting, he couldn't restart the engine. Veering onto the wide shoulder, he halted, just in time to regard Dinger who parted his long, stringy hair which he swept back onto his hunched shoulder.

Sal stared with aggravation at the others proceeding ahead without him. "Dinger, what do you know about engines?"

"Nothing."

"Great. Neither do I." I'm sure I'm going to sit here and do nothing, he thought sarcastically, recalling Tony's warning, and exited. Hell of a mechanic, he scolded, unable to find the latch that unhooked the hood.

Dinger poked his head out of the window. "Need any help, Mr. 'D'?"

Sal glanced at the faulty wire surrounding Dinger's lenses, and struggled not to laugh, although mostly about the situation. "No, stay put," he uttered grimly. And try not to aggravate me more than I am, he concealed.

"Want me to try pushin' 'er, Mr. 'D'?" he asked languidly.

"No, that's okay." How could Craig pair me up with him? he questioned and paused to scrutinize the vegetation across the highway. Maybe he did out of some deep, psychological resentment against teachers, he answered and reentered the truck. He watched a semi lumber past on the opposite side, flipped the key, and the engine started, surprising him.

"Far out."

"Unbelievable, like everything else," Sal muttered. He drove about a quarter of a mile and the engine died again. Shifting back to neutral like before, he tried restarting it, was unsuccessful, surprising him, and he stopped, lest he weaken the battery. It's got gas, he assumed, since the needle was pointing to "F," and he coasted back onto the shoulder in disgust. Unless the gauge is broken, he considered, eyeing a low-flying Piper Aztec spraying disinfectant on the city. He tried restarting the engine shortly afterwards and was equally surprised when it did. Pulling away, he drove for a spell, stalled, and veered back onto the shoulder and halted again.

"Aren't we gonna go?" Dinger asked, reminding Sal of students who often faked stupidity just to irritate him.

"Not if I can't get it started," he explained as if addressing a child. The engine kept turning over repeatedly, refused to start like before, and he stopped.

"What's goin' on, man?"

Sal looked over. "Dinger," he announced while cars whizzed past on both sides of the highway. "Don't worry about it, okay?"

"What?" Dinger teased with a laugh and Sal ignored him.

Probably not getting enough gas, he concluded, appreciating that Dinger kept still. He fumbled through a pile of dirty papers inside the greasy glove compartment, found an odd pair of pliers, and exited. Analyzing cars humming past, he gave up on a state trooper passing by, finally located the latch, and open the hood. He removed the air filter, and considered pouring gas inside, all he knew about the possible problem. But how do I siphon gas from the tank without a siphon? He unloosed a fitting. Gas began pouring out freely, pleasing him, and he re-tightened it. Need a bottle or a can, he realized. The truck's back floor only contained old newspapers, a short chain, and cigarette wrappers. Picturing a discarded bottle in the weeds beyond the shoulder, he exited.

Descending the embankment, he paused to view the peaceful Chemung sparkling in the distance. Never forget those days, he called to mind almost sadly, remembering Trudi sunbathing on the bank with their daughter Vicki while he and his three sons backpedaled in the river, casting for smallmouth bass. Finding an empty Coke bottle, he filled it with gas, and poured some into the carburetor. Sal started the engine which petered out like before and he kept repeating the process until he finally arrived inside the Fairgrounds over an hour later.

At least the government's paying for all this nonsense, that is, my dollars as a taxpayer, he revised, exhaled in disgust, and both exited. Though a weak consolation, he might have embellished it, had he not recalled the victims again. If you don't bend a little—toward the absurdity of it all, like when kids forget their pencils, books, homework, or they skip class; if you don't start laughing at it all, you'll go off the deep end, he warned and entered the office. But life was odd, he analyzed, passing between the usual clusters of shaggy loungers laughing, sipping coffee, and smoking. You strive to learn, struggle to rise above your problems and survive life's abuses, especially as a teacher, then find yourself forced to tolerate stupidity, even your own because we're imperfect, he philosophized. Unable to find Craig, he strode down the hallway in order to reveal all to Roy, and entered his office.

Sitting incongruously behind his desk, Roy was peering down at some papers and lifted up his blond head.

Greeting him, Sal started describing the trucks' terrible condition including his.

"Oh, Teach. Didn't even know ya left," he interrupted.

At least he's honest, Sal consoled, glancing at Roy's droopy eyes. "Should we call Tony Grannis and tell him that we need better trucks?" What's this *we* stuff? he scolded and almost broke up.

"Who's he?"

Startled, Sal pulled himself together and placed his hands on his hips. "Why do we need trucks anyway? It's a waste of money," popped out unexpectedly.

Roy frowned. "What?"

Sal struggled to suppress exhaling irritatingly. Forget the trucks, he ordered, realizing that the real problem was Roy's inability to act hastily, efficiently, and utilize so much manpower loafing at government expense.

"Fuel pump, ya think, eh, Teach?"

He's either struggling to comprehend what *really* happened or can't decide what to do about my truck.

Frowning, Roy reexamined his papers, as if he were trying to impress him, Sal sensed.

How can America be truly great if we put nincompoops in charge of rectifying major disasters instead of the creatively intelligent and the educated? he demanded, almost slipping into the jaws of cynicism and despair. "Maybe you could call Tony and tell him to send over a mechanic to fix my truck. Unless you want me to. And somebody's got to drive us back, so we can pick up our cars."

71

Roy couldn't handle that many angles. "Hah? What?"

Sal repeated himself verbatim.

"Yeah, okay, good, do that."

Which one? Take your pick. "Things have been awfully slow around here," he pursued carefully. "I haven't done anything since you hired me. When are we *really* going to start helping the flood victims?"

Roy picked up an order form, began analyzing it as if it were an amendment to the Constitution, and maneuvered his mouth, as though he were trying to dislodge food from between some teeth.

Need a toothpick? Sal asked himself with a laugh.

Roy dropped the form. "More dang paperwork than ya can shake a stick at."

What's a stupid form got to do with what I just asked you? he was tempted to ask him and scolded himself for nodding patronizingly.

Roy folded his hands behind his neck, leaned back, and glanced at Sal trying to read *The Star Gazette's* headlines upside down.

"You'll be inspectin' more trailers than, than–"

Wait, I'll get a dictionary. But what about what I just asked you?

"Than you ever seed in this here yo-nited States."

Seed? You mean as in planting? How's that for English, big guy? Wait, I'll get Dinger or Kevin to teach you the language.

Roy yawned.

Sal examined gold in several molars, and the Chief of Field Operations closed his mouth in order to manipulate his tongue.

Forget your tongue. You needs a toothpick, man, Sal dramatized. Wait, I think I got some in my car. Or is the mouth getting ready to speak? Stop fooling around, he scolded himself. He can't help who he is or what he has become. Or can he? "But when are we going to *really* start helping the victims?" he repeated hurriedly, lest a guffaw break loose.

Roy rearranged his tongue and opened his mouth. "Today or ta'marra. Trailers is comin' in full blast. Don't cha worry, Teach."

About to ask Roy if he were positive, Sal found himself staring inside Roy's yawning mouth. Oh, for God's sake, I give up.

"Tired," Roy admitted.

You're working too hard–on your teeth, man.

Roy snapped his head as if to wake himself up.

Sal had enough. "Catch you later." When you're all yawned out and finish tooth-picking, he added and departed.

Chapter 7

Craig drove Sal and the others back to the Rand for their cars. Returning, both entered the kitchen and added themselves to a group listening to Skip describe what befell the other trucks. Two had run out of gas though their gauges had registered full, and Norm's radiator had boiled over. Skip almost hit a tree because of brake failure, and he left his truck to buy brake fluid with his own money. "Nothin' like decent trucks," he concluded.

More laughter responded, died, and then flourished during Dinger's halting rendition about Sal's fiasco.

"Thank god this ain't no emergency," Norm declared so pleasantly and with such a nice smile that Sal momentarily believed that he had fantasized the disaster.

"Why the hell did HUD rent us such bad trucks?" Terrance demanded.

"Like the good ones is in Vietnam gettin' bombed," Lenny breathed, devising a new form at the table.

"Government officials gets staff cars," Norm declared. "Nothing cheap for them."

"So they can ride around and dig the disaster, man," Skip contributed.

Craig sipped coffee, lowered his cup, and turned to Skip then Sal. "You guys weren't supposed to touch your trucks. You were supposed to call Grannis."

Oh, another follow-dumb-rules fanatic, Sal labeled. "Where would I find a phone on the highway? Give me a break."

Lenny ruled a line, then shook his head. "Wouldn't touch them trucks with dirty hands."

All turned expectantly for the rebuttal from Skip slanting his head because of his bad eye.

"That's all you got, man," he obliged.

"They might blow up," Lenny completed during more laughter.

Sal studied the veins bulging in Lenny's thick, dirty arms, and Skip evaluated Lenny with pretended aversion. "When 're you gonna finish that masterpiece, man?"

"After he washes his hands," Norm supplied. "Meaning never."

Lenny looked up at Skip. "What're you, the boss or somethin'?"

"Somethin'," someone supplied.

"The boss," Skip declared impudently. "No one else is."

Norm looked over Lenny's shoulder and stared at the form. "What's the difference? By the time he finishes, it'll be so black he'll have to redo it."

Lenny lifted it up and studied it. "Not really. It's got the right shade right now."

"What the hell's that?" Terrance demanded, looking over from where he was standing near the percolator.

"Who, Lenny or the form?" Skip asked.

"I'll be a work of art when I'm done," Lenny predicted breathily.

"More a work by a fart," Skip corrected.

"When it's done?" Terrance protested amid more laughter. "It's taken him a day to draw one line."

"That's because he forgot to use a pen or pencil," someone contributed.

"Far out."

"And Rota had to teach him how to use a ruler," Skip included.

"Somebody should teach him how to wash his hands," a new voice commented.

"He knows how," Skip assured. "Towels is his problem. He ain't figured out what they are. He keeps drying his hands on his sleeves. That's why he rolls 'em up. Ta hide the dirt."

"Think that's bad," Norm contributed. "You should 've seen his hands after he worked on his car yesterday. On government time," he enunciated.

"You should've seen the car," another heckler contributed.

About to rule another line, Lenny turned to his mockers. "That's what happens when you're the only guy what's on task," he retorted superiorly.

"Yeah, sure," Skip disagreed. "Next time do a motor job on your own time."

"I did," Lenny insisted. "I couldn't help it that I'm also workin' for HUD."

Skip slanted his head and stared at Lenny's dirty form.

"Duplicator ink," Lenny blamed. "Hard to remove."

"'Specially when you keep wearing the same dirty shirt," Skip retorted. "I'll have you know Mr. Norquist washed that shirt just last year, gentlemen. He's been wearin' it ever since."

"Hate to see the color of his bed," someone supplied.

Lenny ruled another line, then looked back. "Oh, it's clean," he answered indignantly.

"Why, you don't sleep in it?" Skip asked.

"You guys 're just jealous because I got an inside job."

"We got outside jobs?" Skip protested.

74

Lenny eyed him during more laughter. "Wait 'll tomorrow. You won't be stayin' in here much. Why do ya think Craig just left?"

"The coffee in the living room is more fresh," someone else offered.

"Because we're short of help," Skip explained but few laughed. "And overworked," he added, was more successful, and he surveyed the group. "You should've heard Tony when I called and told him about the seventy-five cents I paid for brake fluid. Almost blew a gut. We're only supposed to stop at HUD authorized stations."

"What's a HUD au-thor, au-thor–" Dinger attempted and gave up.

Skip turned to consider his cousin's up-tilted head, thick glasses, and long, stringy hair. "It's a new service station, cuz. They're openin' up all over since the flood."

The tall, heavyset young man with the blond, duck-tailed hair reappeared and the laughter petered out. "Gentlemen," Craig began.

Quiet descended, and more heads turned to analyze the face containing the slightly pointed, pink nose.

"Where?" Skip inserted.

"The boss wants to know," Craig resumed, capturing even Lenny's attention, plus several men who had just entered. Craig threw them a nod and cleared his throat. "The boss wants to let you know that he fixed the urn in the dining room," he completed.

Howling laughter exploded and Sal merely shook his head. "What the hell's so funny?" Craig inquired.

"We didn't know it was broke," Skip commented and Craig smirked.

Chapter 8

That's it. I can't take it, Sal admitted. Driving home that night, he decided to complain vehemently to Roy or Craig about the lounging, incompetence, the broken-down trucks, and general indifference. But arriving at the office the next morning, he discovered that Roy had left for Edgewood and Craig had gone to the Rand to pick up two-way radios.

What for? Sal objected. Contractors and the crews are doing the heavy work, not us. More fun and games, he answered, and attached himself to a small group in the living room. Listening to the usual small talk, he pictured the seven idle trucks profiting HUD at taxpayers' expense. What waste. Nobody cares. Nobody acts, and dumbbells are at the helm, he reminded himself and headed for the bathroom. Should'a put a flood victim in charge of operations. People don't have to suffer to sympathize with the suffering, but it helps. What a mess, he scolded, eyeing the overstuffed waste can and scattered paper towels throughout the floor. Roy ought to order the slobs to stop being slobs. Urinating, he looked up at the sign that someone had changed.

HAPPINESS IS A NORTHERNER REPLACING A SOUTHERNER, he read.

Bunch of kids. Smirking, he left for the living room. Outflanking a lounger heading for a space beside Skip sitting on the couch, he picked up part of *The Star Gazette's* sport section before sitting, commenced reading, and the hours dragged.

Sometime later, Dinger took orders for hamburgers and left with Norm for McDonald's. Both returned to the living room comtaining men munching away and talking near the urn.

Too nervous to eat, Rota offered her French fries and milkshake to Dinger staring at both, and he almost stumbled reaching for them.

Skip evaluated the loungers and yawned. "It's the job," he told Rota. "Look at these punks. Check how much stress they're under, talking, laughing, and downing coffee."

Preoccupied with paper-work, Rota looked up and stared bewilderedly at him.

Skip rose and Sal followed him outside to eat his bagged lunch in his car. Blessed with considerable energy, which he consumed doing school work, remodeling his house, and attending his vegetable garden during the summer, he had never been so bored. No sense rushing back inside, he realized. Listening to the news, he was stunned to hear that another flood victim had committed suicide. Grim-faced, he watched different groups reenter the office. After supposedly having had lunch, they realized that Roy and Craig were gone, and stumbled back outside. Sal reentered, spent the afternoon reading the newspaper and several sports magazines on the couch, and the men didn't start filtering back until evening.

Roy and Craig arrived at 8:15 p. m., and Craig began distributing a notice to everyone including those lining up to sign out. "Let me have your attention," Craig shouted and all quieted. "This is a short message from Hugh Brennig."

"Who's he?" a gloomy man called Miles asked Sal who shrugged. "To HUD Employees," Craig enunciated loudly and clearly.

Papers rattled as the men began reading the same directive along with him.

"I'd like to take this opportunity to congratulate you for your rallied support during the terrible disaster that struck the Twin Tier area. I know I speak for all the flood victims who thank you for the great job you are doing."

Howling laughter responded, surprising him, and he frowned.

Too unbelievable, Sal moaned, accepting a belated sheet. Amazing how some people can look at a horse and call it a tree.

"He must be at the wrong disaster," Skip quipped.

"Hope they don't find out. We might not get paid," a young man answered.

"We're not. This is volunteer work," Skip explained.

"What?" Dinger injected.

"That's us?" commented another.

"Maybe they use the same notice for all disasters," cracked a stocky-built lounger.

Hugh Brennig. That's who to see, Sal realized.

"There's more," Craig resumed. "Effective immediately. All right, hold it down," he barked and paused for silence. "The work day will increase from twelve to fourteen hours until further notice."

"We're gonna work fourteen hours a day?" Dinger asked Craig.

"No, it means you're gonna keep doin' nothing for an extra two hours," his flippant cousin provided.

"Far out."

Skip snapped his hair back in place. "I'll be damned," he cried outrageously. "We got praised so's they could suck more loafing outta us."

Murmuring peaked and subsided.

Dinger tilted up his head at his cousin. "But we don't do nothin'," he insisted as the men resumed signing out.

"What the hell do you mean, man?" Skip disagreed in mock anger. "You don't call this hard work, standin' around talkin', sittin', drinkin' coffee? Eatin'?" he enunciated. "Come on."

"No," Dinger confessed.

"You mean you don't get tired walkin' to the coffee pot, cleanin' out a cup, and holdin' it under the faucet? Then turnin' it on?" Skip protested.

Rota began giggling amid more laughter.

"Are you puttin' me on?" Dinger asked.

Roy disappeared out the door and Craig joined the others standing on line.

"Oh, Dinger, you're a scream," Rota delivered without looking up.

"Fourteen hours? When do I see my wife?" someone asked.

"You don't," Lenny breathed, signing out. "You stay her and *I'll* check 'er out."

"What job?" another asked. "Didn't know I was workin'," he commented and laughed.

Terrance eyed Craig about to sign out. "Fourteen hours a day? Are they nuts?"

"That's ninety-eight hours a week," calculated a man waiting to do likewise.

"Forty hours at $3.18 per hour. That's about a bill and a quarter a week," offered another, and he turned to the man in back of him. "Plus time and a half after forty-eight, that's, that's–"

"Yeah, yeah, go ahead," his friend encouraged with a grin.

"That's, that's a hell of a lot of bucks," he concluded. "They're going to have to raise the national debt."

"Comes to exactly $403.20 per week just for the forty-eight hours," calculated a short, young man with long, stringy hair. "Then there's fifty hours overtime."

"You figured it out?"

"Holy shit," Terrance declared.

"Four hundred more'n we're worth," Skip announced.

"We might not get paid for overtime," Craig inserted.

"I'm no glutton for work, but when 're we going to start *really* helping the flood victims?" Sal asked Craig.

"Don't worry. You're getting paid," he responded.

"That's not the point. All these guys are standing around doing nothing while families are living side-by-side in cramped quarters. What's this Hugh Brennig doing to alleviate the situation? And where is he, behind a desk?"

"I know," Craig admitted but laughed. "Don't worry about it," he sing-songed.

Sal stared at Craig's pink nose. "Don't worry about it? Are you serious?" he objected. "If *we* don't, who will?"

"We're going to *really* start doing something very soon."

"When?" Sal demanded.

"Tomorrow," he emphasized. "Trust me," he added, signed out, and stepped outside.

Chapter 9

Sal milled around in the office trailer for over an hour the next morning. Irritated, he broke away from the living room coffee-clutchers and headed down the hallway. He was about to complain to Roy when his door opened.

Craig emerged and walked past Sal without regarding him.

Good morning Sal supplied sarcastically.

"All you guys that got trucks yesterday, meet me by the front door," he bellowed, strode up the hallway, and several standees stepped out of the kitchen in order to consider him.

Reaching the crowded living room, Craig repeated himself. "We're headin' up to Edgewood. I'll supply each driver with one passenger. Like, he'll be your assistant. Like," he added and laughed.

Finally, Sal announced, heading up front.

"What's goin' on there?" Norm asked Skip pausing near the front door with Craig and others.

Skip flipped back his hair. "Nothin'. He just wants us ta head up there."

"Gas up and sign for it at the Texaco station outside the front gate," Craig shouted.

"We gotta drive there for gas?" Dinger inquired slowly.

"No, we're gonna leave the trucks here and pull the hose over," Skip obliged. "What 'er you worried about? You ain't drivin' a truck."

"When you get to Edgewood, look for a HUD guy named Lyman Bludiamond," Craig instructed.

"Why, is he lost?" Skip inserted.

"He's been working there. He'll tell you what to do," Craig specified.

One man's been working there? Just one man? Sal responded in disbelief.

"Who's he?" Dinger asked.

"Shouldn't be hard. He's black," Craig told the group. "I'll be up later. Lenny made master keys for the trailers that's there."

"Nice goin', Len," Norm said.

"Thanks," Lenny responded.

"Get a set from him before leavin'," Craig instructed.

What for? Sal inserted. One of us might steal a trailer? Why bother?

Lenny waved a sheet. "Ya gotta sign out for them," he breathed.

"Hey, Lenny, we get to use your form," Skip cried.

"Yeah," Lenny confessed with a smile.

"Far out, man."

"It's about goddamn time," complained Miles, a bony-faced man in his late forties. "Tired of sittin' around doin' nathin'."

"Now you can *drive* around and do nothin'," Skip answered.

Miles turned away in disgust.

Sal reminded Craig about his inoperable truck.

"Did you tell Roy?" Craig asked.

"Yes. He might even call Tony. Accidents do happen."

"What's-his-name didn't come in. Use his," Craig replied and turned to the others.

Who's what's-his-name? Sal wondered.

"Radios come in. They're in back," Craig resumed. "One per truck. Pick them up now. Ya gotta sign out for them too."

"Hey Lenny, we get to use even another one of your forms," Skip shouted.

"Go to hell," Lenny cried.

"What radios?" Dinger piped up.

"We're gettin' them for the trucks," Skip quipped. "How the hell can ya listen ta the Mets if ya ain't got no radio?" he asked so convincingly that Dinger nodded.

"Them radios cost $900 apiece," Craig resumed. "So, take care of them."

"I'm a Yankee fan," Dinger disagreed.

Skip frowned. "Maybe they'll give ya a Yankee radio."

"Nine hundred bucks?" Norm said.

"What the hell do you care? It's the taxpayers' money," Terrance commented.

"Like, I thought trucks *had* radios, man," Dinger enunciated slowly.

"Yeah, but I'm a taxpayer," Norm objected. "You bums scare me."

"You're responsible for the radio you sign out for," Craig enunciated and Dinger parted his hair aside as if he were about to wash his face.

"What radios?" he asked Kevin.

"Two-way radios," he obliged.

"Who don't know how to operate a two-way radio?" Craig queried.

No one answered.

"I ain't operatin' no goddamn two-way radio," Miles protested, sulked, and several men contemplated his stern, withdrawn face. "They didn't hire me for that. Them's too complicated for me."

"Give him a one-way radio then," Skip suggested. "He can talk to himself."

"I don't know how ta work them radios either," Dinger confessed during more laughter.

"You're not getting one," Craig told him. "You're riding with Skip."

"Thanks," Skip returned and Craig grinned.

"Was hired as a maintenance man, not a radio operator," Miles grumbled.

"So, where's that form?" Skip asked Lenny.

"Ain't finished makin' it yet," Lenny admitted with a yawn and had trouble shaking off scattered laughter.

"Okay, let's get them radios," Craig urged, and the group followed him inside the second bedroom. "Keep the radios with you at all times," he instructed, standing before several rows of them that were the size of a standard dictionary.

"Oh, *them* kind of radios," Dinger realized as Craig began handing them out. "Do they need batteries?"

"No," Skip replied. "We plug 'em in here before we take 'em to Edgewood. They come with an eight-thousand foot cord."

"This is crazy," Norm confided quietly to Sal who had just received his. "How the hell 're we supposed to figure out how it works?"

"I think I just turned mine on," Sal said as the men began questioning Craig and one about how to operate it. "I heard a click."

"That was Dinger," Skip explained. "He just turned on his brain. 'Bout time, cuz."

Dinger held the receiver to his ear. "I don't hear nothin'."

"Nobody's transmittin' right now," Craig explained.

"Dingle," Skip sing-songed. "You ain't getting' no radio," he reminded him.

Dinger reached back, rearranged hair resting on his thick, hunched shoulders, and tilted his head upwards defensively. "Why not?"

"Because you're over-qualified," Skip retorted and Norm laughed.

Where are the simple, step-by-step instructions for those with average intelligence? Sal kept to himself.

"What's their range?" Norm asked.

"Twelve miles I think," Craig answered. "You go through base relay for longer distances. They've got a powerful station near Elmira. Everybody's responsible for recharging their batteries every night," he bellowed and displayed a wire with plugs at both ends.

"You worry about your sex life. I'll worry about mine," Norm inserted with a smile.

Craig grinned. "This end goes in your radio, and this, into one of them sockets." He pointed to them and tossed the wire near others on a bed containing boxes, light fixtures, faucets, and similar paraphernalia. "Each man 'll have his own number that you have to memorize. Lenny, 'll give out the numbers."

Why isn't he explaining how to work the damn thing? Sal was about to ask.

"Craig, another trailer's pullin' in," Doris screeched from her desk, interrupting him.

"Glory be," Skip declared and applause sounded in the living room.

Maneuvering between the men, Craig strode into the hall. "Sign out for your radios," he shouted. "And meet me outside in ten minutes."

Who's responsible for locking this door? Sal worried, regarding the rest of the radios. Shaking his head, he signed out for his, received his number from Lenny, and departed out the front door with the others.

Since Sal was the only one who knew Edgewood Trailer Court's location, passing it on the way to school, Craig ordered everyone to follow him.

Sal entered his truck, lowered his radio to the floor, and met Elmer Christianson already sitting on the passenger's side. He shook hands with the young man, read "Capabilities" printed above his shirt pocket and realized he was retarded. Very commendable of Capabilities to find jobs for the handicapped, but pray tell, what kind of help can they offer during a disaster? Who makes these decisions? What's the difference? Nobody's doing anything anyway, he answered. Checking his mirror, he noticed the others waiting for him, and he sped ahead of them.

"This is unit five. Come in, unit thirty," boomed Sal's CB radio.

Now what? Sal asked, remembering that that was his number. Reaching down, he grabbed the receiver, pressed it to his ear, and squeezed the lever. "Sal, here," he ventured, motoring toward the front gate. "That you, Craig?" What could he possibly want? Rechecking his rearview mirror, he barely discerned the blond-haired man driving in the fourth truck behind him.

"This is unit five," Craig repeated, bristling with officiousness. "Unit thirty, what's your 10-20? Over."

Sal reexamined Craig in his mirror. Is he kidding? What's a 10-20? Glancing at Elmer peering unconcernedly out his window, Sal drove out the gate.

"Unit thirty, this is unit five," Craig radioed again, and Sal slowed for the others to catch up. "Identify yourself by number before speaking," he emphasized. "Ten-twenty means present location, over."

He knows where I am. Why is he– Breaking off, he realized that Craig was teaching him how to use the radio. So, why didn't he explain this to everyone before? How come I'm his guinea pig? This is more exciting, gets more attention. It's an ego trip, his other self answered. He also gets to humble a teacher, Sal sensed and squeezed the trigger again. "This is unit thirty. Thanks, unit five," he responded and lowered the receiver back between its black prongs.

"Unit thirty, unit thirty. This is five," Craig sing-songed. "Come in unit thirty. Over."

Sal reached for the receiver. "This is unit thirty," he complied and waited.

"This is five, thirty. The word *over* must follow every transmission," Craig explained.

Sal regarded Craig's truck in his mirror.

"Do you copy? Over."

"This is unit thirty. I copy." Remembering, he added *over*, fitted the receiver back, but forgot to squeeze the lever.

"Unit thirty, this is five. "Come in thirty, over," Craig's voice sang.

This is unit ridiculous, Sal derided. Grabbing the receiver, he pressed the lever. "This is thirty, come in, five," he radioed, released the lever, remembered to squeezed it, and transmitted "Over."

"Unit five. What's your ten-twenty? Over."

Squeezing the lever *after* I say *over*, cuts him off. Releasing it gives him a chance to radio me, he comprehended and waited. When Craig didn't respond, he squeezed the lever in order to answer him. "This is thirty. We're approximately two miles from Route 17. And a mile from a large oak tree. "Over," he added quickly.

"This is five. That's a Roger, thanks. Over and out."

No problemo. And thank God, Sal thought and clunked the receiver back between the prongs.

"This is unit five. Come in unit thirty."

Oh, for God's sake, Sal protested and reached down again, as Elmer scrutinized the scenery. "Unit thirty, he–a," he dramatized, using a Southern accent. "Come in five, over."

"Unit five here. Did you copy? Over."

I don't believe this, Sal mocked, pressing the lever. "This is unit thirty. I copied. Over and out," he emphasized and returned the receiver.

"Unit thirty, this is five. Come in, thirty, over."

Geezus, man, take a break. "This is thirty. Come in five. Over."

"Thirty, this is five."

No kidding.

"Do you happen to know Norm's number? Over."

How could I possibly know that? Even though I do, he praised and pressed the lever. "This is thirty. Six, I believe. Over and out," he barked, stopped for a light, and exhaled. Tolerating this is harder than tolerating my bandits.

"Unit six, this is unit five. Come in six," Craig's voice blurted through Sal's radio but silence followed.

Sal gunned ahead, checked his rearview mirror and watched the others following behind him. "This is thirty. Unbend, five. Over."

Craig transmitted part of his laugh. "Unit thirty, does unit six have his radio turned on? Over."

Sal stared back disbelievingly into his mirror at Craig. Is he out of his tree? How should I know? Wait a minute, I'll step out and check, he smothered with a laugh. "Hard to tell through the mirror, five," he transmitted but forgot to identify himself. Hell with it, he decided with a smirk. Oh, help the boy out, he reconsidered, and pressed the lever. "I'll check and get back to you. Thirty, clear." But not by radio. Had enough of that beast, he grumbled, slowed, and veered onto the shoulder, aware that all would follow suit.

"Five standing by. Thanks, thirty. Five, clear."

"Thirty clear," Sal announced.

Norm pulled up behind him, then the others, including Craig.

People 're homeless and destitute, and we're playing with radios. If they only knew. Hopping out quickly, Sal told Norm and the others to turn on their radios, reentered his truck before Craig could exit, and droned ahead.

"Unit six, this is unit five," Craig's voice boomed almost immediately.

"Norm Meriwether, here. What's up?" he uncorked and Craig spent several minutes describing how to operate the radio.

"Break, break," interrupted a crisp voice. "Baseman here. Operators are requested not to indulge in unnecessary chatter. This radio system is designed for emergency communications, not for conducting a seminar on how to transmit messages."

"Amen," Sal cried. Thank God for the National Guard, he praised, and so did Elmer belatedly.

Approaching Edgewood, Sal recalled that it had opened five years ago and now contained about a dozen HUD trailers. And destined to fill to capacity with more, he had learned, and he turned into the entrance. Zooming ahead with the others behind him, he observed a young, obese woman and a short man about the same age facing each other in the middle of the dirt road. He pulled over beside them and stopped, as did the others behind him. He rolled down his window, poked his head out, and discerned the sound of heavy machinery. He eyed the man's muddy boots and mud-splattered t-shirt, was about to ask him if they knew Lyman's whereabouts, but they were arguing.

"So what the hell do you want me to do?" the man asked her, and she glanced at Sal's truck.

"Ain't that the HUD guys? Ask them."

Oh, no, Sal thought, noting his stern expression as he approached.

"Good morning. I'm Sal D'Angelo and–"

"Now look," the man interrupted. "I don't wanna get in no goddamn hassle with–"

"You're gonna have to," she flung at his back and he whirled back at her.

"Will you shut up?"

"It's half my court," Jill snapped, folded her chubby arms across her breast, and fell begrudgingly silent.

"That's women's lib for ya," he told Sal and introduced himself as Shorty. "They want half of everything ya got, even your conversation." Evaluating the idling trucks, he checked Elmer and settled on the bespectacled English teacher with the wavy black hair interspersed with gray. "Contractors is gonna park trailers where *we* say, not where *they* say," he fumed.

"I take it you two own Edgewood?" Sal inquired amid the panel truck engines humming behind him.

"I don't give a damn if their trailers is already blocked," Shorty stormed. "That's *their* problem. Whose place is this, theirs or mine, goddamn it? They're gonna have to un-block them at *their* expense, not mine, goddamn it."

"Ours," Jill reminded him.

"Shut up," he barked and turned back to Sal. "This shit's gotta cease."

Nothing like a little compassion for the flood victims, Sal admonished.

"You tell 'im," Jill encouraged.

"They got maps. Why the hell can't they follow 'em?" Shorty asked Sal who turned grim.

"Why can't they leave them where they are now?" he ventured, aware that *they* would be collecting the victims' rent money. People profiting from others' losses or misfortunes, he suppressed.

"No way. They're too far from our main water and gas lines," Shorty snorted. "And them trailers look shitty parked where they are."

Amazing how emotional people get over complications that calm intelligence can rectify easily.

"I ain't bringin' in a backhoe ta move 'em at my expense because they got their heads up their ass. *They're* movin' 'em, and that's it," he told Sal. "And when the hell 're you guys bringin' steps?"

What steps? What's he talking about? "We're working on it," he improvised.

"Yeah, you're working on it," Shorty sneered. "And where's this Lyman guy?"

Sal shrugged, turned off his engine, and reevaluated the man's angry face. "I was about to ask you."

"Ain't seen hide nor hair of his ass all morning."

What about the rest of him? Sal questioned, and the panel truck engines shuttered into silence.

"And another thing," Shorty continued. "The electric company don't wanna pay their men anymore bucks ta put up the poles today. They're already paying them time and a half because it's Saturday, they says."

A warm breeze fluttered Jill's slightly-bleached blond hair. "They wanna quit at twelve."

"Did you remind them that this is an emergency?" Sal probed, following Norm's suggestion to try and learn as much as possible from anyone.

Shorty looked away sarcastically and turned back. "Shit yeah. They told me ta wait 'til Monday. What kind of shit is that?"

Sorry. I'm no authority on defecation, Sal concealed, suppressing a grin, and shook his head sympathetically.

A panel truck door opened, slammed shut, and Norm approached.

"Another thing," Shorty resumed. "Three trailers got leaks. Who's fixin' 'em, HUD or the contractors? Contractors say HUD. Lyman says the contractors. Wish somebody'd make up their minds."

"The doors," Jill reminded him.

"Some doors ain't closing properly. Didn't you guys inspect them before hauling them down here?"

"They might have gotten knocked out of whack when they got towed in," Sal inserted.

"Ain't broke windows the company's responsibility?" Shorty complained. "And some trailers got electric burners, 'stead of gas. Electric cost a ton in this area. Didn't HUD think about such shit?"

"Flood people can afford electricity?" Jill questioned Sal studying the dirt road ahead. "Have them send only trailers using gas."

Yeah, sure. You're lucky to get *any* trailers. "I'll see what I can do." With so many problems, how come a squadron of beatniks are lounging at the office? And where the hell is Roy? What's he doing?

Panel truck doors opened, slammed shut, and the others arrived.

The flood victims be damned, Sal realized, having also learned that trailer court owners would have the option of buying the trailers afterwards. It's the money factor, greed, and selfishness again. They're worried about having trouble renting trailers using electricity instead of gas afterwards.

"What's up?" Norm asked congenially.

Sal hopped out, introduced everyone to Jill and Shorty and explained everything.

"We're looking for a guy named Lyman. Know where he is?" Craig asked them.

Learning Shorty's last name, Craig wasted ten minutes asking if he was related to Jeff (who married Craig's cousin, Beatrice), then ordered everyone back into their trucks so they could search for Lyman.

"Why not try radioing him?" Sal suggested.

Craig tried but unsuccessfully.

Sal drove ahead. The caravan followed for a spell, then veered off in different directions.

"Unit twelve, here," a voice crackled officially over Sal's radio. "I'd like to report an empty panel truck on Blossom Lane, approximately two kilometers south of 4th Street," he unfolded with fierce indifference.

Skip, hamming it up, Sal recognized.

"Said vehicle probably belongs to one Lyman Bludiamond who ain't nowhere in the vicinity. Am standing bah said vehicle, awaiting orders," he dramatized. "Oh-va."

"Call in the artillery," Sal muttered.

Elmer laughed, surprising Sal and mass confusion ensued.

Norm radioed Craig that he was lost. Miles questioned if Blossom Lane was near Locust Avenue, and Dinger radioed that he had just left the Fairgrounds in a truck, surprising everyone.

Sal shook his head. Whose truck is he driving? He doesn't even have a license. How did he get a radio? Whose is it?

Miles cut in. "I ain't sure if nobody can hear me, but I ain't workin' no radio."

You're already working it, man, Sal inserted. Are these guys crazy?

"Break, break," interrupted base relay, and scolded the men for too much "unnecessary chatter."

The men began cruising throughout Edgewood in search of Blossom Lane or 4th Street. They eventually pulled up alongside Skip kneeling beside his radio. All exited their trucks like a SWAT team and Craig ordered them to spread out and search for Lyman.

Sal shook his head. God, what nonsense. Why waste time searching for one man? He should be able to find us.

"Why didn't I wear boots?" Norm asked, eyeing the surrounding muddy embankments reluctantly.

"Because you didn't expect mud at the office where we usually loaf," Skip obliged.

Norm laughed. "Thank God some of us got a sense of humor."

Noting several men blocking a trailer, Sal and Norm asked them if they knew Lyman's whereabouts.

A young man, carrying a roll of copper tubing, paused. "The nigger?"

Not again, Sal sneered. "Not really. He's black, Afro-American."

"Same difference. Ain't seen 'im."

Frowning, Norm removed a set of specifications from his work shirt pocket. He studied the second page briefly, eyed the trailer's piers, and settled back on the man. "Are you the contractor?"

"Yeah."

Crouching, Norm pointed to a column of bricks supporting the steel frame. "Ain't supposed to use brick according to the specs. What's the matter with you?" he barked angrily, surprising Sal.

"Ran out of block," the man defended.

"Get some," Norm advised icily.

Sal suddenly caught on. Nice going.

"Who're you?" the man asked Norm.

Rising, Norm pointed to *Inspector* written above the name tag on his shirt.

The contractor turned to a man soldering the fitting and shrugged."I'll take care of it, don't worry."

"Make sure you do or ya won't get paid," he dug and the man regarded him with annoyance.

"We'll get 'em in there," he promised, begrudgingly directed them to where he last saw Lyman, and the duo left.

"Can't stand prejudism," Norm remarked, plodding toward a recently-blocked trailer with Sal.

Prejudice, Sal corrected inwardly, having long since resolved not to criticized anyone beyond the classroom.

"It wasn't the Lord's intent."

Amen, Sal thought.

Both observed muddy shoes protruding from underneath the trailer.

"Lyman?" Sal called and the toes commenced digging into the soft earth.

"If they'd tighten the nuts in the first place–" grumbled the owner working his way out. Holding a small crescent wrench, the muscular Lyman, age thirty-two, eyed the two and rose. He dusted off his jeans and maroon t-shirt.

Norm introduced Sal. All shook hands and they discussed the disaster.

"So, how's the coffee at the office?" Lyman inquired.

Sal grinned with embarrassment.

"Roy finally told you guys how ta get here?" Lyman asked.

"Somethin' like that," Norm revealed. "Hate ta tell ya, but this trailer might have to be moved," he announced and elaborated.

Lyman turned to stare at the siding, and tiny hills appeared across his sweat-soaked t-shirt, suggesting impressive abdominals. "Are you kidding?" What the hell's going on?"

Norm continued explaining undauntedly.

Lyman's head started shaking negatively. "We're gettin' in our own way."

"You could use some help," Sal offered sympathetically.

Lyman turned in disgust. "What for? It's over three weeks since the flood and we still don't even have tools. Look at this," he declared, pointing his wrench at Sal. "A six-inch piece of shit to tighten king-sized nuts. Borrowed it from a contractor. And contractors are scarce for some reason, man, believe it or not." He glanced in the distance at the men removing the faulty bricks from under the trailer. "And the damn electric company wants to quit at twelve."

"So we heard. Just remembered something," Norm interrupted. "We forgot our radios."

Lyman snorted sarcastically. "Shit, left mine back in my truck. They're worthless. Craig keeps radioing to ask what I'm doing or what my 10-20 is. How the hell can I do anything if I gotta keep answering that squawk box?"

All watched the men carrying the bricks back to their pickup.

"I finally told him to stop pestering the shit out of me and baseman bit my ear off," Lyman continued. "Can't swear over the radio," he added and finally grinned.

"Guess we missed all that," Norm told Sal.

"Craig sent us," Sal told Lyman. "You're supposed to tell us what to do. When do we start inspecting?"

Lyman laughed and shook his head. He analyzed the trailers placed interestingly on the surrounding knolls and regarded Norm, then Sal. "You can't. Not till the contractors finish setting them up."

"When's that?" Sal asked.

"Whenever they get around to it," he barked in frustration and nodded at three nearby trailers. "They ain't even been blocked yet. And half the contractors don't work Saturdays. Like the electric company's primadonnas. Then contractors run outta solder, water pipe, block, you name it," he fumed. "Things 're so disorganized–" he attempted, halted, and shook his head. "*We're* the disaster. We outta get the victims to straighten *us* out."

Sal and Norm laughed sympathetically. Studying a fly rubbing its front legs together on the beige siding, Sal ruled out feeding Lyman's helplessness and irritation with his own. "We'll help. Just tell us what to do," he offered positively.

"Nothing," Lyman replied. "Not until we get tools," he emphasized.

Sal smiled sarcastically. "What's the problem? The government can't afford to buy them for us?"

Lyman glanced at a crow flying past and laughed. "HUD still ain't found a local merchant that wants to give us credit."

Sal examined the man's strong, handsome face beneath closely-cropped black hair.

"Guess they think the government's a bad risk."

"You're kidding," Sal returned. "That's the problem?"

"Part of it," Lyman replied.

"Who wouldn't want to give HUD credit? HUD's part of the government."

Scrutinizing three empty, forlorn trailers, Lyman smiled sarcastically.

"Roy's the other part, man. Somehow Roy, Brennig, or the government brass are out ta lunch, man. Or they're just slow. Who knows?"

"It's not the government," Sal disagreed. "It's the people working for the government. People always make that mistake."

Lyman looked away. "Whatever, man."

"But the flood victims," Sal began, realized that his voice was rising and paused momentarily. "Hell, I've got tools at home. Everybody's got some kind of tools, even in their cars." You just need somebody with enough intelligence to evaluate the situation, improvise if necessary, then act, organize, and lead, he fumed inwardly. "We could've saved days."

Lyman looked back and shrugged helplessly.

"Why didn't you complain to Roy?" Sal asked him.

"Me?" Lyman protested. "A black man with Southerners running everything? You're kidding." He laughed and Sal looked away with embarrassment again.

"Hell, I did anyway," Lyman insisted. "But it was like talking to a wall. Still is. Who cares what Roy did at Rapid City or wherever they drug him from? He don't know a disaster from a sunny day. So I've been workin' out here. On my own." He turned his neatly-chiseled face toward a parked dozer some distance away and looked back. "Besides, I couldn't handle hangin' around in the trailer doin' nothin', man."

He's a better man than you, Sal scolded. "Guess I'll bring some tools tomorrow," he muttered.

Noticing Sal's guilty expression, Norm laughed.

"Forget it," Lyman said. "Roy's supposed ta check out this one hardware store in town. Maybe we'll finally get tools. Three weeks after the flood. Can ya believe that?"

"Looks like she's leakin'," Norm declared.

Eyeing several drops clinging to a recently-soldered copper fitting, all crouched for a closer look.

"Ain't contractors responsible for everything below the trailer?" Norm asked.

Lyman regarded Norm with suppressed aggravation. "The hell's the difference who fixes what? The pay's the same. The sooner trailers is ready, the sooner people can move in, man. It don't matter who gets 'em ready. People 'er livin' like pigs in schools and tents, you name it. Me and my family got flooded out. We're livin' in a Catholic church. And we don't even follow Catholicism," he cried and burst out laughing.

"But just for the record, ain't HUD responsible for only what's inside the trailer?" Norm pressed.

"Technically," Lyman responded. "But who knows? Roy says one thing, lover-boy with the hair and comb says somethin' else, and so does Shorty and the contractors. Then there's the electricians and the gas company hotshots with their attitudes. I just fix whatever needs fixin'. Like this fitting's gonna have to be re-soldered. The sooner it's done, the sooner we can inspect this trailer and release it. Everything else is done."

"Ain't them pipes supposed to be wrapped with friction tape?" Norm inquired.

"Ran out of that too," Lyman obliged.

Sal rose. "How do you keep track of everything?"

"It ain't easy," Lyman admitted. "And there's no sense tryin' ta inspect trailers till we get converters for the burners. Them six trailers down there," he declared, pointing to them. "They be needin' hookups to the water line that they're laying up there." He motioned in another direction, then eyed the ring of keys attached to Norm's belt loop. "Nice keys ya got there, brother," he announced in a new tone.

"Compliments of Lenny Norquist," Norm revealed.

"No shit?" Lyman remarked. "Lenny cut 'em at the office?"

"Yeah," Norm responded.

"Can I see 'em? Yours too, Sal?"

Though puzzled, both complied.

"Worthless," Lyman remarked, heaved them toward the woods, and they slivered through the leaves. "Roy just radioed. Lenny used the wrong blanks."

Sal and Norm broke up.

Lyman pointed to several trailers that Bob Updike and his crew were supposed to block, but no one was there.

"So where are they?" Sal asked.

"Saturday night's comin' up, man," Lyman replied. "People go out.

'Course, there ain't too many river joints open near the river since the flood."

A panel truck pulled up with the dapper Craig at the wheel. Exiting, he eyed several trailers, and he ran his comb through his thick hair.

"Ain't no skirts there, brother," Lyman commented. "Those trailers ain't even been inspected."

Sal and Norman laughed.

Craig approached and Lyman described the leak.

Craig shrugged off Lyman's demand for large crescent and pipe wrenches, levels, and long tape measures. "They're comin'," he promised and handed the threesome new master keys.

"These gonna work, man?" Lyman asked pointedly.

"Guaranteed," Craig replied.

"Yeah, like everything else," Lyman said with a laugh.

Skip and the others pulled up behind Craig's truck. Craig handed Skip the new keys and left with Lyman to inspect a trailer. The others cruised up and down the roads for two hours without doing anything, stopping whenever they met, as did Sal and Skip for the third time.

"Anything new?" Skip repeated like before and eyed Elmer fussing with his belt.

"No," Sal answered.

"Where's Lyman?"

"Not sure. But he's probably working somewhere."

"Tough job."

"I'll say."

Both departed in opposite directions. Minutes later, Sal observed another panel truck advancing toward him. Both vehicles slowed, pulled alongside each other, and halted.

Miles looked over. "What the hell 're we supposed to be doing?" he barked.

Sal analyzed Miles' high cheekbones set in a rigid, cheerless face. His tight skin seemed to be holding back a pressing skull. "Who knows? What 've you been doing?"

"Nathin'. How's about you?"

"Less."

"Where's Lyman?"

"I don't know," Sal varied.

"Geezus Krist," Miles stormed, smirked, and looked away.

"Might just as well tour the site again. Unless you've got everything memorized."

Possessing a scant personality and no sense of humor, much less Sal's facetious brand, Miles cursed.

Sal turned to Skip who halted behind him, exited, and sauntered over.

"Where's Lyman?"

Not again, Sal sneered. This is ridiculous. "Sounds like a broken record."

"Who the hell knows," Miles complained angrily.

"What're we supposed to be doing?" Skip quizzed.

Sal glanced at a bright, cloudless sky. "Not you too. Who knows? But it's a nice day for cruising around and wasting gas."

Lyman pulled up behind Skip's truck, jumped out and approached.

"Where the hell 've ya been?" Miles scolded.

Lyman evaluated Miles sternly. "Fixin' a leak," he snapped. "Why, you in charge?"

God forbid, Sal thought.

"Geezus Krist, ain't cha gonna tell us what to do?" Miles berated.

"Me?" Lyman protested. "I ain't in charge. Besides, what the hell do you care? You're haulin' in the bucks for doing nothing. What's your problem?'

"Yeah, but Geezus Krist," Miles grumbled, then, as if running out of words or forgetting the point, looked away indignantly.

"There's different holdups," Lyman barked, reiterated them again and shook his head exasperatedly.

"When 're we gonna take care'a all that?" Miles demanded.

"What, the water, electricity? What?" Lyman charged, and Miles fell silent. "Don't panic, man." Realizing that he was blocking an approaching propane truck, Lyman hopped back in his truck, drove off, and the others followed him.

Must be nice, Sal thought, spotting Roy driving a new 1972 government Chevy with a blue vinyl top.

Converging in a haphazard circle and wide area, all stopped, and Sal evaluated Roy wearing sunglasses (bothering him for suggesting that he hadn't been doing anything meaningful) and Craig sitting alongside of him. Wonder where the wonder twins have been hiding?

"What's going on?" Roy drawled.

Don't *you* know? Avoiding uttering nothing, since a negative response lacked value, he described the leak as if it were a new disaster.

Draping his arm across the steering wheel, Roy stared ahead as if he were pondering the profound.

He doesn't understand, is oblivious, or overwhelmed about so many problems. Or he's simply bored. Realizing Roy couldn't handle too many issues at once, Sal explained about the electricians threatening to quit for the day, and an unusually long pause unfolded. Hello. I finished talking. Your turn, Chief, he suppressed and swallowed down a laugh. "That's it."

Roy's head swung back. "Where's Lyman?" the small mouth repeated.

Hiding exasperation, Sal checked his mirror. "Here he comes now."

The panel truck halted. Stepping out, Lyman jogged over to Roy's car. "Bad news, Chief," he announced as all listened. "The damn electricians don't want to install the poles. In fact, they're haulin' out at twelve for the day."

Roy checked his watch. "Wot?" he commented, pretending he didn't know about it. Don't they know this is a a-emergency?"

Lyman shook his head. "We can release three trailers if we get electricity."

"Where they at now?" Roy asked.

"Follow me," Lyman answered, returned to his truck, and all complied.

Descending a hill, Lyman halted before a middle-aged couple standing in the middle of the road. The others stopped behind him and the woman asked if she and her husband could take a peek inside the *Majestic.*

"We don't have the key to *any* trailers, ma'am," Lyman enunciated. "Here's the boss, now," he announced, pointing to the Chevy. "Ask him."

The couple sauntered toward Roy whose elbow was protruding outside his opened window.

"Can you show us inside?" she shouted. "The *Majestic* is beautiful. How long is it?"

Lyman shook his head slightly.

"You a flood victim?" Roy inquired.

"Well, a, no."

"Sorry, ma'am," he answered and zoomed ahead.

"Why, how rude. Harry, do something."

Harry shrugged.

She walked imploringly toward Sal who followed suit politely and reminded her about the disaster.

Smirking annoyingly, she headed toward her parked car, and Sal sped after the others.

Suddenly hot-rodding out of a bumpy side road further ahead, came Miles who barely missed a backhoe backing into the road with a bucketful of dirt.

Braking, Sal watched him u-turn obliviously and speed away in the opposite direction. This is all so stupid, I think I'm going to puke. Stop killing yourself, his other self interceded. You can't control anything. Sighing, he caught up with the three panel trucks and the government sedan droning up the next incline. Here we go again, Sal groaned, observing Jill standing in the middle of the road waving frantically.

Roy stopped, as did the others.

Rushing to Roy's side, she complained vehemently and almost incoherently that a contractor had left a load of cinderblocks in the middle of the road.

The Chief stared obliviously ahead.

Undaunted, Jill dropped her hands onto Roy's car.

Like I'm watching a movie, Sal imagined, noticing Roy's head finally nodding, but weirdly, as if it were on remote control and Sal almost broke up.

"Attention all units in the Edgewood Court vicinity," Craig boomed over Sal's radio. "Discard the master keys I just gave you. They're the wrong ones."

Skip honked. Sal guffawed and Jill kept peppering Roy's immobile head abusively.

Craig repeated himself, then tactlessly blamed Roy for mistakenly leaving the good ones behind.

"Is anybody with authority listening to all this?" Sal mumbled.

"I am," Elmer insisted enthusiastically.

Sal looked over and grinned good-naturedly.

"Tools 're in," Craig announced, received another honk from Skip, and started unloading a long-winded dissertation about signing out for them. "Immediately, if not sooner."

Sal winced over the cliché. My ears.

"Tools are each man's responsibility," Craig belabored.

He must enjoy hearing himself, Sal criticed. About to shut his radio, he pictured blocking out a legitimate emergency, and changed his mind. So, where's the baseman? Maybe out to lunch like everybody else, he answered.

Roy's head finally turned to Jill who seemed momentarily startled into silence.

But words never unloosened from the Chief's thin lips, Sal observed and was surprised when Craig began inching ahead.

Jill started following sideways unperturbedly, as if her hands were stuck to the car. But when her lips switched to what Sal sensed was more complaining, Roy appeared to have had enough and honked once. Motors coughed into life as if responding to distress. He increased speed and Jill stumbled away to the sidelines, almost falling.

Shocked, Sal considered stopping in order to check if she had been hurt, but boxed in as Skip tailgated, he was forced to continue. Though Jill appeared to be all right, Sal had trouble steadying his shaking head.

Suddenly thundering out of a muddy side road came Norm, Terrance, and Dinger, like lost tanks rejoining their unit. Roy veered toward several heavy-set men heaving equipment into a yellow Electric Company truck, and he and the others pulled up and stopped behind him again.

The electricians took turns glancing at the odd motorcade, then menacingly at the exiting HUD men, especially Lyman who had parked ahead of them.

Standing inside the electric company truck's cab, a heavy-set man, smoking a pipe, eyed the HUD panel trucks briefly. He accepted a heavy spool of wire from an electrician and heaved it wickedly further inside to his helper who positioned it beside other loaded equipment.

Several more electricians, carrying wire, boxes, and tools, appeared from around a nearby trailer and headed toward their truck.

Undismayed, the HUD men shuffled over behind their leader dangling a cigarette from his lips. Wearing his usual denims, cowboy boots, and a colorful shirt depicting an elk, Roy resembled a country singer waiting to be announced on stage. He approached the converged electricians.

"A fight," Skip whispered.

"Far out, man," Dinger cried.

"Calm down," Norm warned.

"Who's in charge?" piped Roy's familiar, Southern drawl directed at the converged electricians.

Several of them scowled menacingly at him and the HUD men.

The pipe smoker accepted another spool and hurled it inside more furiously than before.

His helper wedged it between other paraphernalia, straightened, and folded his arms belligerently, as if he were a fighter waiting for the ref to announce him in the ring.

The pipe smoker removed his pipe contemptuously, tapped out the ashes on the truck, and slipped it inside his shirt pocket. "Who wants to know?" he growled and another electrician arrived carrying a meter box.

Roy adjusted his oversized, green sunglasses. "Ah do."

The pipe smoker grabbed the meter box and threw it recklessly inside atop a pile of conduit.

The pipe smoker examined Roy's name tag. "Hey Dutch. Some guy wants to see you," he bellowed.

Carrying a box of fuses, Dutch emerged from behind the same trailer. Scrutinizing the HUD faces, he shuffled toward them, looking away indifferently before arriving. "Yeah?" he growled. Avoiding Roy's stare, he settled his small, defiant eyes on the trailer across the road.

Roy squinted because of his smoke. "How come you guys is quittin' already? We needs them poles installed ta-day."

Wearing a long-sleeved shirt rolled past healthy biceps, Dutch turned to the yellow truck. "What poles?" he inquired, still without regarding Roy, and another electrician appeared shouldering an aluminum ladder.

"Poles for the alectric," Roy drawled sharply.

Dutch handed the box to the pipe smoker who tossed it into the cab.

The pipe smoker accepted the aluminum ladder, clattered it inside belligerently, and Dutch studied it lengthily before turning to Roy.

"We don't use no more poles, except short ones for meter boxes," Dutch snapped with fiercer indifference. "Gotta put everything underground now," he lied and turned to the pipe smoker. "Is that all of it?"

"Yeah," the pipe smoker replied. Deliberately settling on Dutch as if the HUD men weren't there, he began discussing the possibility of showers in the late afternoon.

"This guy needs punchin' out," Skip whispered and Roy turned to Craig who shrugged.

"They only work a half day on Saturday according to Jill," Lyman reminded Roy who frowned.

Another electrician arrived, slid a small box into the cab and hopped inside.

"Looks like somebody's puttin' somebody on," offered Dinger so slowly that he managed to ease some tension.

Dutch headed toward the driver's side. "We only work till twelve on Saturday," he confirmed.

Roy sniffed mockingly.

Sal surveyed the electricians. Talk about sinking to the depths of unconcern for the flood victims.

The sound of a distant dozer penetrated the uncomfortable silence.

Roy flicked his cigarette to the ground, mashed it, and turned to Craig. "Lemme see that thar thing," he ordered, pointing to Craig's radio.

Clutching the truck handle, Dutch paused to eye the radio curiously, as if he were wondering about its relevancy.

Roy flipped the switch, lifted the receiver to his ear, and stared with abandon at an empty, unblocked trailer in the distance. "Baseman, baseman, this is one," he sing-songed.

"This is base. Go, one," the same deep voice resonated.

"Clear all lines. I need yo best ears," he announced and hesitated dramatically as all watched and listened, including the electricians sitting on the equipment inside the bay. "On yo land phone, press the far button to the right—your direct line to the White House."

"Far out."

Staring, Dutch laughed derisively. "Who're you tryin' ta shit?" he scoffed but hesitated curiously before opening the door.

"Tell the man we're at Edgewood Trailer Court raght now," Roy resumed undauntedly. "The a-lectric company's giving us static," he drawled and Sal smiled about the pun.

Dutch shook his head sarcastically, jumped inside, and slammed the door behind him.

Sal edged closer to Norm. "Is Roy kidding?"

Norm shrugged.

"They wanna quit, and the day ain't even broke through yet," Roy practically shouted for Dutch's benefit. "Somebody ain't told 'em about the flood. Yo'all copy? O-va."

"This is base relay," baseman answered officially and repeated Roy's transmission. "Do I copy you correct?"

Roy answered affirmatively, shut the radio, and handed it back to Craig.

Dutch poked his head out of the opened front window. "Everybody in?" he inquired loudly.

"Yeah," the pipe-smoker responded.

Dutch sneered at Roy, started the motor and deliberately floored the gas pedal, kicking up dirt as he zoomed away.

"What do you want us to do?" a voice uncorked anti-climatically.

The men frowned at Miles Jankowski whose son, Wayne, one of HUD's personnel managers, had hired, Sal recently learned.

"Go play with your trains," Skip breathed quietly, referring to Miles' hobby, and the men laughed quietly.

"Hang in there," Roy cried, heading toward the Chevy with Craig.

"Can ya spell that out, Chief?" Skip asked beyond Roy's hearing.

"Geezus Krist," Miles barked, eyeballing the duo entering the Chevy which drove away, disappearing over a hill.

"Might just as well inspect some blocked trailers," Norm suggested.

"Yeah, goddamn it," Miles agreed impatiently.

Lyman glanced at the others and smirked. "What for? Contractors have to dig the ditches and lay the pipes. Plumbing and electric's gotta be checked after that. All that ain't been done yet, 'cept for a couple of trailers," he deliberately repeated for Miles' benefit.

"We can still inspect everything else," Miles maintained.

"Yeah," Skip sneered, slanting his flippant face at him. "Sinks and sofas could a fell out when they drug trailers over from the Fairgrounds. Why, just yesterday I almost run over a tub on Route17."

Observing Elmer's puzzlement during the laughter, Norm nudged Skip good-naturedly. "Somebody might believe that. Don't confuse folks any more'n necessary. Some people needs something to do, even if it's dumb," he contended with a grin.

An hour later, the HUD men were eating lunch in the empty trailer across the road when a vehicle appeared from over the hill.

"Roy," Miles gasped. Panicking, he rose and rushed to the front door.

"No it ain't. Slow down, Superman. Geezus Krist," Skip mimicked. "You're on your lunch hour. You ain't gonna get fired. You can even loaf on this job."

Seated inside an official-looking Electric Company car cruising into view were yellow helmeted men, all noticed from the front window. The "72" Chevy followed and both vehicles stopped where the confrontation had occurred.

"*That's* Roy," Norm specified.

"And this is lunch," Lyman emphasized. "Relax," he told Miles.

Both sedan doors opened almost simultaneously. Bodies exited. Four Electric Company officials conferred with Roy and Craig briefly. All reentered their vehicles and stayed put.

"Hey, lookie who just drove back," Skip announced dramatically, referring to the yellow truck. "I guess they miss us."

"Whaddaya know about that," Lyman contributed.

The truck bounded ahead of both cars and parked in the same spot also. Dutch and the electricians exited irritatingly and began unloading equipment.

"Well, I'll be darned," Norm declared.

"Guess Nixon was in," Skip commented.

"We better get out there," Miles resumed fearfully.

Skip gulped down his root beer. "Go ahead."

Lyman bit his sandwich and shrugged. "Suit yourself, man," he told Miles. "Maybe you can help them unload."

Miles sulked during the laughter.

Sitting on the floor near Sal, Elmer regarded Lyman. "Are you the boss?"

Lyman laughed. "Hell, no, man."

"Like, if we leave ta help them, we can't finish eatin', man," droned an unsteady voice from the kitchen, as if the owner were on drugs.

Several men turned to Dinger. Sitting alone at the table, he took a large bite of his third McDonald's hamburger.

"Yeah," Kevin and Terrance agreed almost simultaneously, breaking away from the window with the others.

"They ain't tol' us when to eat," Miles piped up again. "That's the trouble. They ain't never tol' us nathin. Ain't you goin' out?" he asked Sal.

The slim teacher shrugged. "I'm eating. I'll go out if they need me."

Miles' face turned stern.

Talk about paranoia, Sal left unsaid.

Skip studied Miles' taught face. "You're makin' this a career? 'Course, at the rate we're settin' up trailers, maybe you should check HUD's retirement plan."

The men laughed and Miles fell sullenly silent.

Finishing his hamburger, Lyman rose and eyed the messy kitchen table. "Make sure you clean up," he reminded Dinger about to leave his paper cup behind.

"No problem, man," Dinger answered.

Miles contemplated Sal. "You leavin' now?"

"Yes, because I'm done," Sal responded with a smile, grabbed his radio, and headed for the door.

"Damn good reason," Skip agreed and all followed suit. "Never seen such a frightened hen in all my life," he whispered to Sal. "When there's work, ya work. When there's loafin', ya hang in there, like the boss says."

Once outside, they approached Roy, Craig, and the officials watching several electricians and Dutch seething while unloading their equipment.

"They'll even work Sunday if you want," an official told Roy, and an electrician pulled off an armful of conduit pipe resentfully.

"That's all ah wanted to he-a," Roy replied and removed a pack of cigarettes from his shirt pocket. "Pleasure doing business with ya," he added and extended his free hand.

The helmeted officials took turns shaking it awkwardly and strolled back to their car.

Roy and Craig entered the Chevy. They cruised behind the Electric Company staff car down the road, and both vehicles disappeared over a hill.

"There," the facetious Skip announced, analyzing the hard, tight-skinned Miles resembling a helpless boy watching his parents drive away without him. "Was that worth choking down a cheeseburger for?"

Dinger ogled his cousin. "Nothing's worth that, man," he uncorked slowly.

"Do me a favor, Dingdong," Skip began, attracting attention, and he snapped his head. He evaluated Dinger's strange features, including his thick glass and long hair parted in the middle, and the group braced themselves. "Ask them electricians how long they plan ta work today."

"What for?" ·

"'Cause I think they'd really appreciate it," Skip stressed and the others smirked into laughter.

"How long's it gonna take them to hook up that electricity?" interrupted the nervous, impatient Miles.

"No harm in *you* asking them that either," Skip suggested and Miles cursed.

Lyman grinned. "We'll inspect whatever trailers have electricity."

About to leave with his radio, Skip turned. "What about hookin' up the water?"

"Pipes still gotta get laid, man," Lyman reminded him. Then, as if comprehending his allusion, grinned.

"No way am I gonna lay a pipe, man. My dick ain't *that* tough," Skip cried.

Lyman became serious. "We gotta use a special water key ta turn on the water in these trailers," he specified, referring to a long rod with a chuck-like head on the end. "They use them in my trailer park."

"And make sure ya turn on the water before ya turn on the electricity," Skip announced for everyone's benefit. The water heater could explode if it heats up with no water," he warned and flipped his hair in place.

"Glad somebody knows somethin' about somethin'," Norm responded jovially. "It's better'n knowin' nothin' about everything."

"We'll make sure heaters are turned off," Sal deliberately repeated for Kevin and Terrance's benefit, since both weren't paying attention. Like in class, he noticed.

Though vaguely remembering contractors activating the water with such a key before they opened the site, Jill and Shorty couldn't find one in their storage shed. Consequently, Lyman left to check his trailer park for one, wasted an hour inching along behind the long line of cars heading toward Elmira, and was unsuccessful. Deciding to check at the local water company, he found himself struggling to convince the officials who he was and why he needed one.

Meanwhile, Skip leaned back inside a trailer where the men had congregated, and the thin paneling squeaked. "Most of these trailers was made in the South for people living there," he told the group lounging in the living room chairs and on the floor. "Some ain't even insulated."

"Why didn't HUD buy them in the North where it's cold?" Sal admonished.

"Who knows? Maybe they're comin'," he offered. "But them gas burners is definitely too small to heat these trailers."

"How do ya figure?" Norm asked, sitting beside Sal on the couch.

"They're half the size of the ones that go into forty-two footers," Skip replied. "The victims better pray for a mild winter, or some balls are gonna freeze."

Norm folded his arms, leaned back, and yawned.

"HUD just put two old maids in a trailer downtown. Guess they got nothin' to worry about," Skip resumed.

All laughed except Dinger.

"Why?" Dinger bit.

Skip frowned. "Because they're movin' to Florida, dummy."

"Well, Geezus," Dinger whined. "How was I supposed to know?"

The front door opened a half hour later. "The key, gentlemen," Lyman announced dramatically, and clattered a five foot rod, a half inch thick, along the tiled floor. "Finally convinced the water company to lend it to us. You'd think they didn't know nothin' about the flood." He boosted himself inside, placed hands on hips and looked down at the rod as if it were a dead rattler.

Sal noticed his frown and approached. "Problems? It's broken?"

"Ain't that, man," Lyman confessed. "No way can we turn on any of the eight blocked trailers. Some dumb contractor had the toters park them on top of the receptacles. There's no room to get the rod in underneath, man, unless they're moved about three or four feet to the left or right. That'll take days. Bunch a nitwits," he derided and shook his head.

Derisive laughter responded from everyone except Sal.

Dinger swept aside the long strands of hair on his face. "Far out."

"How could they be that dumb?" Norm inquired.

"Geezus Krist," Miles swore.

"They were dumb enough to hire Dingalong," Skip declared. "Anything's possible."

Bend the rod somehow, Sal realized. But how? Without wasting more time? "How far down does it have to go inside the receptacle?"

Lyman appreciated his concern "'Bout three feet straight down."

"Cut the rod," Sal suggested.

"Can't. It wouldn't be long enough ta catch the groove below. Come on. I'll show ya," he offered and all followed him to the first trailer.

They crouched and Lyman crawled underneath the trailer with the rod. Locating the receptacle about midway under it, he brushed dirt off the cover.

"Hey, man," Dinger called very slowly. "Are you sure that's the water recepta– Whatever, man."

Lyman singled out the weird glasses and long hair from the many faces studying him. "Not really, man. But it says *water* on the cover."

"What?" Dinger asked.

"Busted again," Terrance ridiculed and smothered him with laughter, along with Kevin and the others.

Lyman removed the cover and demonstrated. "Get what I mean?" he announced and crawled out. He handed the rod to Sal, rose, and brushed himself off.

"Geezus Krist," Miles spat again.

"I gots an idea," Dinger began. "Cut a hole in the ceiling above it. Then we can stick the rod down from inside, man," he said boyishly and no one laughed except him.

"Got a better idea," Skip offered. "Cut a hole in your head and we'll siphon the water outta your brain."

Kevin broke up again with Terrance and Elmer laughed belatedly. "Busted even again."

"No sense wastin' more time cuttin' a second hole," Skip ruled out. "Just tilt his head."

Deciding to contact Roy, Norman radioed unit one but Lenny answered. Norm spent several aggravated minutes explaining the problem, but Lenny lacked the capacity to understand. Giving up, Norm told him to have Roy radio him and signed out.

Good luck with that, Sal kept to himself, rose, and analyzed scattered trees beyond a short field. "Bend it. It's the only way."

"Yeah, but how?" Lyman asked. "I tried with my bare hands but couldn't. We need a vice. You try. Maybe you're stronger than me."

"Yeah, sure," Sal responded, accepting it back with a laugh. "Thanks for the compliment."

"It ain't even ours," Miles reminded everyone.

"I've got an idea," Sal remarked, broke away from the group, and started descending the short embankment. The men followed him slowly and reluctantly, and then paused to stare curiously at him trotting towards the forest beyond a field.

"Where's he headin'?" Lyman asked.

"Beats me," Skip replied. "Maybe that's what happens when ya flip out. Ya run for the woods."

Striding through the field, Sal ignored the laughter. Singling out the right maple tree, he nestled the rod between two thick limbs growing upward from its lower trunk and began pulling the end of the rod.

Skip approached with the others. "What's he wanna separate them limbs for?" he teased.

"He's tryin' to bend the goddamn rod," Miles explained and spat.

"Thanks, man," Skip responded sarcastically as Sal strained. "I didn't know. So? We're gonna just stand here and watch?"

Taking the hint, several pairs of hands grabbed the rod below Sal's grip.

"Learned rod-bending at college," Sal confessed.

"Must've flunked," Skip cried and Sal laughed.

All pulled at the count and the rod bended.

"Decent," Kevin remarked.

Sal stared at the almost right-angle bend. "Not exactly where I wanted it, but not bad." Wiggling it free, he handed it to Lyman who studied it.

"Maybe it'll work."

Dinger checked the gash. "What about this tree, man?"

Heading back to the trailer with the others, Skip turned. "Take it along, cuz," he flung over his shoulder.

Miles eyed the rod. "What's the water company gonna say about us bending their rod?" he barked.

"'Ooo, you bent my rod," Skip dramatized. "Don't worry about it, man."

"He's right," Lyman agreed. "That rod might cost the government six bucks."

Nine odd men plodded back through the field as the sun began fading in the west. Lyman crawled back underneath the trailer with the rod. Reinserting it, he started wiggling it, but had trouble locking it into the groove, and cursed.

"Ought to move the trailer," Skip teased.

"How're we gonna do that?" Dinger unraveled slowly. "It's blocked, man,"

"So's yer brain. Just watch and take notes," Skip chastised.

"Can't," Terrance piped up. He had Mr. 'D' for a teacher. Couldn't learn nothin' off him."

"Speak for yourself, Terrance," Sal reciprocated. "You can't even catch keys."

"Can't move the trailer," Miles disagreed, as if finally catching on.

Skip nodded at Miles and turned to Sal. "Hell 've a crew, man."

He's worse than some of my bandits, Sal scorned. He's older, should know better, or just know something. And I'm paying his wages as a taxpayer.

Finally successful, Lyman turned the valve, and activated the water. He removed the rod, shot it out from underneath, and it landed in the soft sod. "Keep an eye on that weapon," he bellowed at Miles who quickly retrieved it before anyone could react.

Skip eyed Sal. "Let 'em hold on to it. It'll make him feel loved," he maintained quietly.

Sal grinned and the rest of the group stumbled inside the trailer in order to check for leaks. Skip, Sal, and Lyman inspected pipes under the kitchen sink, while Elmer and the others stood nearby and watched.

"Hey, there's a leak in the bathroom," Miles shouted. "I turned on the hot water, and there's a goddamn leak."

Eight men bounded down the hall as if their skills were needed to handle a major catastrophe. Arriving, they regarded Miles crouched under the sink, shining his flashlight on water spiraling down the main drainage pipe.

"Oh, for Krist sake, Lyman blurted, shutting the gushing faucet and pulling the plug. "What's wrong with you, man?" he accosted and heads shook in disbelief.

"Far out, man," Dinger cried during the gurgling.

Miles rose, and eyed the sink curiously. "No shit, the goddamn thing was leakin'," he insisted.

"So's yer brain," Skip uncorked. "Sometimes a sink overflows when ya ferget ta turn the water off and pull the plug, dipface. Ma learned me that when I was two." He turned on the shower and pointed to the nozzle. "Hey, there's a leak in the shower. Water keeps squirting outta them tiny holes."

Laughter filled the small room.

Miles notwithstanding, the men couldn't find any problems, and Lyman radioed Roy that the trailer was ready for occupancy.

Finally, Sal announced to himself and everyone stepped outside.

"No sense checking the other trailers that just came in," Norm said.

"We don't got keys. Or much tools, even if we could get inside," he informed everyone. "It's 6:30. How long are we supposed to hang out and do less than nothing?"

Lyman shrugged. "We could unpack furniture, put up storms and screens in the trailers. Even though it's the contractors' job now. That's what Roy told me."

Where the hell is wonder-boy and Roy, and what the hell are they doing? Sal repeated again.

"Let *them* do it," Skip told Lyman. "Them contractors 're gettin' three bills per trailer. Damn more'n I'll ever see," he grumbled, and flipped his hair in place.

"Oh, man, *I'll* take care of it. It's better than doin' nothing, man," Lyman barked, broke away, trotted down the embankment, and disappeared behind a trailer.

This is ridiculous, Sal mentalized. But deciding to help him, he spent twenty minutes descending and ascending embankments without finding him. Panting, he paused on firm ground and began tapping mud from his work shoes.

"Where the hell's Lyman?" a familiar voice snarled.

Sal noticed Jill sweeping refuse out of a trailer's side door.

"Something's gotta be done about the crap contractors are leaving behind," she fumed. "I'll be goddamned if I'm gonna sweep out every trailer. They walk in and out with muddy shoes. Look at this rug. It's gotta be vacuumed," she insisted, sweeping dirt into a neat pile.

"What happened to the plastic tarps?"

"Who the hell knows?"

"It's just a little dirt," Sal tried to console. "The flood victims won't mind cleaning up. They just want to move in. That's the least they can do for getting a rent-free trailer for a year."

The broom froze. "Are you kiddin'?" Jill practically exploded. "I can't get them to do nothin'. Last night, this woman bitches about no bathroom light. All she needed was a new bulb, a lousy twenty-five cents. So I get her one. Then she wants me to put it in, like she's helpless. Her husband's standing right there. Refused to do it. What's the matter with these people?"

"Did he say why?"

"Yeah, some crap about them not supposed to touch nothin', according to the lease. Hope they're gonna be that fussy takin' care of the grounds and their garbage after they move in, but they won't. They'll pile up junk and make a mess of things. And I'll have ta tell 'em ta clean up. Like I tell everybody in this dump."

Watching her resume sweeping, Sal shrugged. "Ah, maybe they'll be different."

The broom halted again. "Are you kiddin'?" she stormed. "You should see what they're doin' already. Was in a trailer last night. Some people live like pigs. In fact, pigs are cleaner. You wouldn't believe the crud."

Oh, wouldn't I? Sal disagreed, recalling renting his farmhouse to a welfare family (with ten children) who kept chickens in the house, clogged both toilets, and defecated out the windows.

"And kids 're bustin' windows, breaking paneling, and pullin' out fixtures. Shorty was up till two fixin' stuff."

Sal shook his head sympathetically and left. Hearing a distant door slam, he headed toward the trailer and entered through the unlocked back door. Lyman was standing on a kitchen chair, and Sal helped him tighten a globe onto a fixture. Working together, they repositioned a door-strike plate and replaced a faulty storm window crank. But once outside, they noted Elmer racing panic-stricken toward them, shouting incoherently about something not being his fault.

"I really didn't make a mistake," he insisted and mentioned something about "water all over the place."

"What do you mean? Show us," Lyman kept urging him, as did Sal, and they eventually quieted him.

Leading them over an embankment, Elmer headed towards Miles standing alongside a trailer.

Holding a rusty wrench, Miles was studying water gushing out from a pipe fitting under the trailer. "I seen some drops," he began as Terrance arrived with Kevin, then Skip from another direction.

Lyman stared at the gushing stream in disbelief. "Oh, for Krist sake. Gimmy that weapon," he ordered, grabbed the wrench, and Skip guffawed in disbelief. "Tol' you not to touch nothin'." He placed the wrench on the nut carefully. He tried tightening it, but the wrench slipped off and he looked away in disgust. "Released this trailer days ago," he sneered as water continued splashing out. "You stripped the nut, man. You over-tightened it. And don't tell me 'no,' because you did. Look at this nut."

"Already am, man," Skip remarked, studying Miles with his good eye."

Terrance and Kevin broke up and Lyman left to turn off the main valve.

"Elmer was helping me. Right, Elmer?" Miles blamed.

Staring at the accumulating puddle, Elmer began shaking his head negatively.

"Far out," Dinger contributed.

"We gotta turn off the water," Miles declared, unaware that Lyman had left to do so.

God, what a bunch, Sal thought and Lyman returned.

"Do me a favor," Lyman scolded. "Let me know when you think you see something leaking."

"Yeah, it's usually Dinger takin' one," Skip advised. "And read the maintenance manual about leakin' pipes."

"The goddamn thing was leakin'," Miles persisted.

Lyman shoved the wrench back into Miles' hand. "Take this cannon back to whoever you borrowed it from before ya kill somebody."

"What manual?" Dinger asked. "I never got one."

"They only gives it to guys what reads," Skip remarked.

Crackling gravel sounded and everyone turned to regard the blue Chevy pulling up along the road below. The passenger door opened. A tall, handsome figure with neat, swirling, blond hair emerged with a radio, slammed his door shut, and exited.

Trim and several inches shorter than Craig, Roy slid out wearing a colorful cowboy shirt with steer imprints above both pockets.

Craig accompanied him up the slight embankment toward the nine men.

"Got them master keys for the new trailers?" Norm hurriedly inquired as if worried that he would forget to ask or Roy would leave before he did.

"Nope," Roy responded simply, eyed the dripping pipe, and frowned. "Heard ya got a problem turnin' on water," he began and noticed the puddle. "What's this?"

"Dinger took a leak, Chief," Skip confessed so seriously that no one laughed for several seconds.

Roy placed his hands on his waist and smirked.

Lyman glanced at Miles who turned away disgustedly. "Just a small leak," he downgraded protectively.

"Looks big," Roy disagreed and crouched in order to examine the pipe.

"He had to go bad," Skip defended.

"All taken care of," Lyman assured protectively and described the problem with the eight trailers.

Rising, Roy gazed at them. "Who parked them that way?"

"Whoever hauled them here, the toters or the contractors," Lyman replied. "We could only turn on the water in the first trailer with a rod," he explained, but Roy kept studying the other trailers.

"Let's have a look at them," Roy responded and ten men processioned behind Lyman leading the way.

"We could use some tools," Norm repeated.

Why the hell doesn't Roy or Craig jot this stuff down on a pad and take care of it? Sal demanded.

Craig ran a comb through his thick, blond hair and glanced back. "Tools are in."

"Why didn't you bring some?" Sal accosted angrily but Craig was conferring with Roy and didn't hear him.

"So we could use 'em," Skip agreed, equally annoyed.

Norm sighed. "At least this beats sittin' around in the office," he hinted, but Roy didn't hear that either.

"Not by much," Sal retorted.

Roy crouched beside the second trailer with Lyman, Craig and the others, and everyone looked underneath the trailer for several seconds. Roy eyed Craig during the silence and shook his head.

What's to see? Sal wondered. "The receptacle is roughly in the middle." What's wrong with him? He's not too swift, he answered.

Roy rose. So did the others, as if they were following some kind of dance routine. Finally crawling underneath, Roy spotted the receptacle, removed the cover, and looked inside.

Sal smirked annoyingly. Why look inside? Parking trailers over receptacles is the problem. Trailers have to be moved or we need a shorter key that works better, hello. Maybe he's trying to show off how dumb he is.

Craig withdrew a small flashlight, turned it on, and tossed it to him. Roy seemed surprised that someone could have anticipated him asking for it or appeared to be weighing something else. Accepting it reluctantly, he kept turning it on and off.

That's a flashlight, son, Sal suppressed. Once they work, they usually work.

Pointing it inside the shaft, Roy stared for almost a minute.

This is too dumb for words, Sal concealed. "Why bother? Just try the rod out, " he finally verbalized quietly.

"Beats me, man," Lyman whispered. "Maybe he dropped something in there."

"Probably looking for a place to take a leak," Skip offered, also beyond Roy's hearing.

"Gimmy the key," Roy barked.

"The key," Skip relayed to the others.

"Where's the key, Dinger?" Lyman asked.

Dinger brushed aside hair from one eye. "Miles had it."

"I gave it to you," Miles disagreed.

Dinger denied it and they began arguing.

Oh, God, Sal sighed.

Skip shook his head. "The Gold-dust twins."

Terrance's laugh initiated the others.

Sal rose in disgust, found it in the grass, and brought it back. Crouching, he eyed Roy smoking a cigarette while Craig was conversing with him. Like a reporter interviewing a miner rescued from the mine, Sal reflected with annoyance and handed the key to him.

Exchanging hands, the key seemed to stop on its own, while the owner of the teardrop eyes, half-closed to avoid his own smoke, contemplated the bend.

Lyman explained how they had bent it and another pause followed.

"Now what?" Sal questioned Lyman quietly. "What's he studying? A bend is a bend is a bend."

Lyman shook his head and frowned. "The guy's thick," he muttered and Sal smirked.

Roy struggled to angle it inside, kept hitting the main steel girder above, and cursed.

"Could move the trailer," Skip told the others who laughed quietly.

"Could use a little more bend," Sal admitted but Roy ignored him. Remembering one summer when he was almost fired him for advising his foremen to use a crowbar as a lever to dislodge a boulder, he ordered himself quiet.

Roy paused to recheck the men studying him. "How many trailers is like this?"

You forgot already? Eight. Lyman told you before, Sal suppressed.

"Eight. We got water turned on in this one," Lyman emphasized. Frowning impatiently, he regarded Sal who shook his head.

Roy shot the key back to the men in disgust. "Damn."

Now we have to tolerate his childish reaction, Sal scorned and made a mental note of Craig leaning the rod against the trailer.

Silence followed, save for the sound of a small plane in the distance.

"Who the hell parked them like this?" Roy inquired.

Geezus, not again, man, Sal thundered inwardly. The toters or the contractors. What's the difference? It is what it is. Turn the page.

"Shorty and Jill," Skip whispered. "They drug them in themselves."

Muffled laughter followed.

"We should've been here guidin' 'em in," Norm muttered to Sal who agreed.

Roy emerged, and with everyone's help (except Lyman and the irritated Sal), spent ten boring minutes trying to figure out who was to blame. Finally breaking away, he and Craig entered the Chevy and left.

"Now what?" Skip asked. "Where're the hell's Abbot and Costello goin'?"

"Maybe to scold the toters," Sal contributed.

Lyman shook his head.

"Hey, this door's open," a familiar voice interrupted slowly from across the road. "We can go inside and turn on the water."

Heads turned to the obese figure standing before a trailer's door. His eyes looming large beneath thick, wire-rimmed glasses, Dinger spread his long hair apart.

"It ain't even blocked yet," Skip bellowed.

Heads shook disbelievingly.

"Forget about trying to fix the leak in the other trailer," Lyman told Miles. "Maybe the contractors might have another nut."

Skip eyed Miles. "Not like this one. He's one of a kind."

Laughter erupted.

Sometime later, all left to activate the water inside a trailer some distance away. To do so, someone would have to use a crescent to loosen a two-inch plastic nut behind the refrigerator. Since the group lacked one, Miles volunteered to borrow the same heavy pipe wrench from the same contractor, and he left to do so before anyone could stop him. He reentered the kitchen with it shortly afterwards, and the men stopped talking, smoking, and joking.

Miles adjusted the wrench's jaws as nine men watched inquisitively, including Lyman. Waving everyone away, Miles slapped it down on the nut which broke, scattering pieces across the floor.

"Oh Krist, not again," Lyman snarled in disbelief during the laughter. "Why'd ya have ta lay it on so hard? That's plastic. And we needed a crescent wrench, not a pipe wrench."

"They were usin' it," Miles defended, collecting the pieces.

Sal stared at him in disbelief. How could a grown man be that uncoordinated? How could his son have hired him? Surely he must 've known that he's totally useless. Maybe he felt sorry for him, his other self answered.

"Can't you tell the difference between a wrench and a hammer?" Skip asked.

"Now what? We can't release *this* trailer because of a nut," Lyman said.

"Which one?" Skip asked, leaning against the refrigerator.

"Must've been a bum nut," Miles explained.

"Now we gotta waste time trying to buy a two-inch plastic nut," Lyman declared.

Skip regarded Miles from head to toe. "Yeah. We can't even use Miles. He's six feet tall."

Studying the pipe under the sink, Miles shook his head. "They don't make nuts like they used to."

Skip reexamined Miles aslant with his good eye. "Wanna bet?"

Chapter 10

The usual chatter greeted Sal entering the office the next morning. Inhaling thick smoke, Rota's perfume, and a faint marijuana odor, he surveyed the conversers smoking, drinking, and laughing, and frowned. He opened several windows wider, headed for the kitchen, and joined a small cluster of men including Norm, Skip, and Dinger.

Lenny appeared and started distributing a stack of mimeograph sheets.

Regarding the cigarette dangling from Lenny's lips, Terrance accepted a sheet. "What's this?"

"Looks like a sheet of paper," Skip explained, "but I could be wrong."

Angling between the men, Lenny continued handing them out. "Tool boxes is in the back room," he announced almost inaudibly and the men cheered. "Ya gotta sign out for them. Make sure ya take only tools what's on the list," he instructed, his voice barely discernible above paper rattling and muffled voices. "And each man's responsible for anything he loses."

"Ya mean I can keep everything else?" Skip inquired.

"Go to hell," Lenny responded.

"Yeah, but what's this thing on the sheet?" Norm asked Lenny, pointing to a smudged fingerprint.

"Hey Lenny, couldn't ya pull your hand off the machine fast enough?" Skip asked.

"That's my trademark," Lenny breathed and departed.

"Could try washing your hands," Norm shouted to him heading up the hall.

"What for? They'd only get dirty again," he retorted, distributed sheets in the living room and returned.

"All day making one form?" Skip greeted. "Not bad."

"Whaddaya expect? Had ta replace the shocks on my car."

"Wouldn't doubt it," Skip scoffed.

"He would've run off more," Norm contributed, "but got tired pressing the *on* and *off* buttons."

Dinger frowned. "Don't it work by alectric?"

"No," Skip told him. "You should see the blister on his finger. Show 'im, Len."

Lenny gestured obscenely at him with his middle finger. "Least I don't sleep in trailers all day."

"How else can ya check out beds, right, cuz?" Skip asked, shoved Dinger good-naturedly, and grinned. Skip eyed Lenny folding his arms and arching his back belligerently. "Incidentally, none of them new master keys ya made worked."

"Don't be hard on ol' Lenny," Norm offered. "One set did work."

"Yeah, the originals," Skip obliged with a laugh.

"Far out," Dinger inserted.

"Let's face it, Lenny," Skip resumed, "as a master key maker–"

"He makes good coffee," Norm interrupted.

"Not really. Mine needed milk," Skip retorted.

Lenny grinned reluctantly and then became serious. "Okay, let's get them tools," he urged quietly, turned clumsily because of his bad leg, and the Edgewood group followed him into the second bedroom.

"But I ain't sure if I'm a main-ten-ence man or an inspector," Dinger reminded him sleepily.

"Neither does anybody else, Ding," Skip responded.

Lenny unpacked a large box. "Print your name on top and I'll collect the sheets later. Plenty a tools for all," he assured like a vendor. He started tossing hammers, screwdrivers, and pliers on the rug, near red toolboxes containing hacksaws, vice grips, socket sets, and other hand tools. "Just put a check in the box, next to whatever you take."

"What if I take an extra pair of pliers for my car?" Skip asked.

"No problem, man," Lenny answered. "Just check the box twice and mail Nixon a buck."

"Thanks," Skip replied during the laughter.

"This tape measure ain't even on the list man," Kevin criticized.

Skip banged his toolbox in mock disgust. "What the hell kind of a form-maker are you?"

"A poor one," Lenny admitted and grinned. "Just add it to the list," he obliged, and the men started carrying their tool boxes into the kitchen.

Lenny arrived last. Making his way to the coffee pot, he dropped his cigarette into a used paper cup and poured coffee into a new one.

"Man, we got no pens," someone declared. "Who's got a pen?"

"Whadaya think, this is, school?" Lenny asked.

"Forget the pen," Skip shouted. "The cup's on fire."

"Oh, shit," Lenny cried. Hurriedly activating the faucet, he doused the cup under the streaming water.

Dinger opened the refrigerator, stared at several six-packs of soda, and removed Rota's milkshake from yesterday.

"Hello, hello. Is anybody there?" a female's voice blurted over several radios that had been left on.

Hurrying to the counter, Craig activated his radio. "Hey, hold it

116

down, will ya?" he scolded as the men began dumping their tools onto the table (and scratching it, Sal noticed incredulously.)

Miles sneered, checked off a file, and clanked it into his box. "Geezus Krist what noise. How am I supposed ta concentrate?"

"I'd have problems if I had your engine," Skip remarked.

"What engine?" Dinger inquired.

Craig lifted the receiver. "Unit five. Over."

"That you, Craig?" the female inquired.

"Hey, hold it down," Craig repeated. "I'm trying to talk."

"Ain't cha learned yet?" Skip asked, checking off his tools.

Lyman shook his head.

"What's wrong?" Sal asked. "All this is too intellectual for you, brother?"

Lyman burst out laughing.

"This is Jill," Craig's radio's blared.

"This is unit five. Jill? Whose radio are you using? Over."

"Shorty found it on his car hood this morning," penetrated her voice despite several cut-offs.

"Break, break," baseman interrupted amid the noise and confusion. "All radio transmitters are requested to use code numbers. They should also be limited to–"

"When the hell are you guys gonna get down here?" Jill's voice cut back in.

"Break, break," the baseman panicked and Doris' telephone rang.

"Geezus Krist," Miles cursed. He rose, grabbed his toolbox in disgust and exited out the side door.

"Damn, I'm hungry," Dinger announced. He reopened the refrigerator, failed to find any food, and slammed the door shut, jolting Elmer leaning against it.

"The female trying to transmit, please discontinue," baseman's voice boomed through several radios.

Sal itemized a hammer and several screwdrivers. What happened to the gross of black pens we got from the Rand?

"I'll be right there to pick up the radio," Craig radioed and signed out.

Kevin made his way out of the kitchen, proceeded up the hall, and told Doris he was going home to get a pen.

Doris shrugged and several others joined him out the door.

"This trailer's got to be locked tonight. Because of the tools," Lyman told several faces.

"No problem," Skip responded. "HUD hired this guard, Charlie. He's going to be makin' the rounds. Met him yesterday."

"They make the best thieves," Lenny said.

"You should know," Skip replied with a laugh and Miles returned with his toolbox and sheet. "Too hot outside, man?"

Miles sulked.

"I don't know about you guys," Lyman announced. "But I'm heading up to Edgewood."

Miles banged his toolbox onto the table. "Who tol' you to go up there?" he barked.

Lyman laughed sarcastically. "Nobody. But one trailer still needs a nut, remember?"

Heads turned expectantly to Skip.

Checking off a pair of pliers, he flipped his hair back twice. "Ran out of nut jokes."

"Ah," Miles scoffed during the laughter.

"Master keys," Lenny announced breathily, and all regarded them in his extended hand. "Guaranteed to work."

Skip studied Lenny distributing them. "Why, you didn't cut 'em?"

Lenny smirked.

Lyman accepted his and left.

Sal expected Craig to order everyone there, but Craig leaned against the counter, ran his comb through his thick hair, and began chatting idly with the others. "What do you want us to do now?" Sal asked him fifteen minutes later.

"Keep leanin', keep drinkin', and keep bullshittin'," Skip provided.

"Ah, guess we might as well go," Craig consented.

"We can go home?" Dinger inquired. "Far out."

"To Edgewood," Norm clarified. "Ya never go home when you got a government job," he added whimsically.

"Wanna bet?" Skip inserted.

Several men laughed.

"Even when there's no work," Norm completed.

"Because taxpayers pays for loafin'," Skip explained.

"Keep your radios on in case I'm tryin' ta call you," Craig told the group that drove trucks. Reaching the highway shortly afterwards, they deliberately passed Miles, who ended up last in the seven-truck caravan. Minutes later, Miles' truck sputtered to a halt, and he stopped unnoticed on Route 17.

First in line, Craig turned into Edgewood. Although slowing, he spotted Jill waving her arms frantically, hurriedly u-turned, and backed out.

Six truck gears shifted into reverse and gunned after him in wild disorder.

"This is unit five," Craig boomed over the radios. "Where's Miles, over."

Silence followed and he ordered everyone to search for him.

Six trucks sent to find someone worse than worthless during an emergency? Sal objected. It's ridiculous. Why not one truck? It's deadwood racing after deadwood and I'm part of it.

Miles soon loomed into view leaning against his truck's door with defiantly-locked arms on Route 17. The caravan pulled over and the men piled out and converged around him.

"'Bout goddamn time," Miles greeted Craig. Goddamn battery's dead."

"So's yours," Skip remarked, stimulating the usual.

Craig asked for a volunteer to push Miles to a nearby garage.

Chirping birds appeared to respond during more silence, and Sal almost broke up. Oh, what the hell, he thought and agreed.

Craig radioed the others to follow him back to Edgewood.

Guess he figures Jill will be gone by then, Sal sensed with a laugh. He pushed Miles to a gas station with his truck, and the mechanic revealed that Miles' truck had run out of gas, though his gauge registered full.

"Ya got a bum gauge," the man explained.

"Didn't you notice that when you filled up?" Sal questioned Miles.

"I didn't fill up. This ain't my goddamn truck," he admitted while the mechanic waited impatiently beside the pump. "What's-his-face took mine."

Puzzled, Sal frowned. "What's-his-face? So, why change trucks?"

"How many gallons?" the mechanic interrupted.

"Three bucks' worth," Miles answered and paused to watch him start pumping it. "Got any goddamn money? I'm flat busted," he told Sal.

Sal stared at Miles' obnoxious face and frowned. "You're kidding. You use somebody else's truck and don't fill up which *you* should have charged? What if *I'm* broke?"

"The goddamn thing registered full, okay?" Miles barked.

The mechanic finished pumping. Miles tried to start the vehicle but clicking sounded.

"Dead battery," came the next verdict, annoying Sal further.

The mechanic regarded him and then Miles who stepped out.

When are you going to learn not to help deadbeats? Sal scolded himself.

The mechanic eyed Sal. "That's gonna be four bucks altogether. Three for gas, and a buck ta jump-start it. Unless ya don't want me ta jump it."

"We don't have much choice. Jump it," Sal agreed and the mechanic left to get his large battery. Sal eyed Miles leaning sarcastically with folded arms against the door. "I don't believe you."

"Just don't worry about it, goddamn it," Miles flung.

"What do you mean, don't worry about *my* money? Are you crazy?"

Miles sulked and Sal shook his head. He paid the man from his five dollar weekly pocket money, but was so annoyed that he forgot to take the receipt. They returned to Edgewood, pulled up behind the other trucks parked near the front gate and exited. Approaching with Miles, Sal noticed Bob Updike and the HUD men facing a crowd of flood victims. Most were begging for trailers. The handful fortunate to be housed in them complained that they were listing. One had almost toppled to the ground.

"Because of so much rain," Bob insisted. "That ain't my problem. That's an act of God."

"The hell it is," Jill disagreed.

Poor God. Gets blamed for floods, hurricanes–everything. Maybe God allows all that so we can learn how to get along with one another, Sal believed.

"No way am I payin' my men to re-block them," Bob refused, having recently signed a government contract to block a hundred trailers, Sal had learned. "Block is out of sight. Nobody's selling pipe according to government specs. And HUD keeps changin' the specs every other day. My man burned out a clutch trying to back in a trailer. Three trailers that I blocked can't pass inspection because I can't buy long enough heat tape nowhere. Who needs this?"

The flood victims, Sal suppressed.

"How long could it take a couple of guys to re-block a few trailers?" Lyman fired back. "Two hours? You're making good bucks," he insisted and Skip agreed.

"Ain't makin' enough," Bob responded angrily.

Enough for what? Sal disagreed. A bigger house, another car, a boat, pigging out at a more expensive restaurant? What?

Shaking his head, Lyman eyed Skip and Sal. "I radioed Roy. Here he comes now."

The blue Chevy hummed pleasantly to a halt behind the trucks. Wearing the same sunglasses, and smoking a cigarette, Roy exited unceremoniously, checked a tire, and scrutinized the distant trailers before checking the crowd. Craig gave his hair the once-through, slid out of the passenger's side and hurried to Roy's side as if he were his chauffeur or bodyguard. He strode ahead of the meandering Roy, soon managed to protect his boss from the victims' blistering complaints, but was running out of excuses. Roy placed hands on his waist, narrowed his teardrop eyes, and listened to more of the same that dwindled and stopped.

Settling on Roy out of curiosity, the victims seemed to be awaiting some comment, encouragement, profanity–anything from the Chief of Field Operations, but Roy simply stared at the horizon. An odd silence hung over the group, either out of expectation or exhaustion.

Maybe I should nudge him awake, Sal concealed.

"Roy's been watching too many John Wayne movies," Skip whispered to Sal who shook his head.

His eyes compressing further because of his own smoke, Roy turned reluctantly to the group. "Ma blockin' crew's comin' in ta'marra morning," he finally managed with tightly-closed lips without wobbling his cigarette.

What blocking crew? He's finally put one together? Sal questioned. It's about time even though it's more than a month too late.

The victims resumed bombarding Roy about how long that would take.

Would he do theirs first? insisted a pregnant mother. How about ours? inquired an invalid. So did several incapacitated seniors, a family of six, and other victims with similar problems.

Roy removed his cigarette and their voices dwindled slowly. "We'll re-block all trailers what needs it," he emphasized flatly. "Not you," he told Bob.

"Good," Bob replied. The crowd murmured approvingly, and Bob left.

Noticing the Chief heading back toward the Chevy, Craig lingered to satisfy more queries and complaints and Jill broke loose.

Overtaking him, she began pounding his blond head with similar complaints and requests. Ignoring her again, Roy opened the door, slid inside, and started the engine.

Having received false promises from contractors and Doris, the victims had second thoughts about Roy.

"Who the hell's he?" a man demanded.

Roy quickly rolled up his window.

To protect himself from Jill, Sal mused with a laugh.

Jill backed away fearfully.

Zooming a short distance ahead, Roy stopped.

"Chief of Field Operations," Craig answered the man.

"Yeah? How come he's in charge instead of somebody from this area?" asked another man.

"Because the South won the war," Skip answered, but unused to sarcasm and hardly in the mood for it, several victims frowned. Others regarded him curiously

"He's had experience," Craig defended. "He was in charge of something in the Rapid City disaster."

"They still haven't figure out wot," Skip uttered quietly to Sal.

121

"When Cleo tore up Corpus Christi," Craig qualified to an elderly woman. "He'll have the blocking crew up here in the morning," he promised so assuredly that Sal almost believed that Roy finally used the loungers to put one together.

"We've got lots of Southerners working for us," Craig answered.

Meaning they're more superior than Northerners? Sal protested.

Roy tooted his horn.

"Ooops, gotta go," Craig responded, broke away, and trotted toward the Chevy.

Glaring at the vehicle, Jill and the others lingered, hoping to rehash the same complaints with the HUD men, but they dispersed and started heading back to their trucks.

"Now what're we supposed do?" Miles grumbled.

"Not panic," Skip advised. "There's plenty a loafin' around fer everybody."

Problems hooking up gas, water, and electricity prevented Lyman from releasing more than two trailers that morning. Worse, one electrician accidentally loaded several large spools of badly-needed cable onto the wrong truck, and the driver was already speeding ten miles west of the flood scene in order to handle a downed wire.

Later that day, Bob fired his crew, not because of their poor blocking or their demands for time-and-a-half for working on Sunday, but because they blocked four trailers in the middle of the road where toters had parked them (and left for lunch) instead of the nearby area staked with red flags.

Sal learned that the only other contractor working at Edgewood until recently was a senior couple and their young grandson constantly rampaging through the empty trailers.

Two trailers suffered from leaky pipes, missing light bulbs, screens, and door handles which the small crew quickly remedied after lunch, despite Miles and Dinger's intermittent blundering.

The dangerous duo succeeded in screwing a fire extinguisher into the wall but only after Miles drilled six holes into the paneling while searching for the stud, all of which Dinger carelessly divulged to the others sunning themselves on the grass beside a trailer, except Sal, Lyman, and Skip checking out trailers.

"So, now what? What do we do about these holes?" Lyman demanded, "studying Dinger's art work," as Skip put it.

"Number 'em from one to six," Skip suggested. "Then sign 'Dingle' and 'goddamn Miles' underneath."

"I tol' you to stop," Miles stormed at Dinger regarding the holes belligerently with his tilted head. "He kept saying 'the stud's right there', goddamn it."

Lyman contemplated Miles' bony face, then stringy hair surrounding his counterpart wearing grotesque glasses. Regarding the holes, he shook his head as Elmer, Terrance, and Kevin watched with the others. "Nobody screws holes into paneling."

Skip snapped his hair in place. "They're almost in a straight line. You guys do nice work. Just lack experience. It really ain't hard ta find a stud," he presented as if he were addressing a child. "Ya tap the wall lightly with a hammer," he began, eyeing his cousin. "If it sounds hollow like your head, Ding Dong, ya ain't got the stud. If it sounds hard and solid like Killer, here, it's the stud."

Chapter 11

Sometime later, a male flood victim claimed that his oven didn't work. "Ya gotta light the pilot light first," Skip told him.

A woman victim complained that her air conditioner wasn't working.

"That's because these trailers don't have 'em," he pointed out.

Lyman intercepted Miles and Dinger about to disassemble a burner because it wouldn't start. "Gas ain't even been hooked up yet!" he bellowed.

Unstoppable, Miles eventually fixed a "broke" fan above a stove.

Investigating his achievement, the men were kind enough to praise him for untangling the chain.

Completing all possible inspections, the large group of men spent the rest of the afternoon lounging in trailers, resting in their trucks, or sitting on different cinder-blocks steps in order to absorb the pleasant sun.

Too dumb, Sal reacted when Craig arrived and decided to re-inspect sewer lines with Lyman and Norm. Once is enough for God's sake.

The men ate around 6:00 and loafed till 7:30.

The next morning a rather plump man in his twenties bustled inside the office trailer. Though exuding with officialdom and importance, he bee-lined toward the sippers conversing near the kitchen sink buzzing with the usual happy flies.

Nursing a cup, Sal observed him shake hands quite business-like with everyone without introducing himself. Roy's replacement? he speculated, studying an odd, triangular turf of hair hanging down from the man's forehead. You're fantasizing.

The man announced a meeting outside.

"Maybe we're finally going to see some action," Sal told Skip.

"Why, was there a disaster?" Skip inquired, carrying his cup toward those heading for the door.

"'Bout time," Miles grunted as if the man represented the victims' new savior or as if meetings solved everything.

Slanting his head, Skip studied Dinger with his good eye, then Miles. "Maybe he's goin' ta give us a lecture on how to hang fire extinguishers, he needled, descending the cinderblock steps. "Usin' you guys as examples."

"Let 'im, Miles growled. "I'll tell 'im who done it."

Shadowing them, Dinger almost stumbled. "Who's he?"

Halting annoyingly, Skip turned back. "Nixon in disguise. He's come ta check you out. Wait, man. You'll find out."

Terrance pushed Dinger. "He's some guy what's havin' a meeting."

Last out, Quincy paused on the top cinderblock step, surveyed the myriad faces in the cool, damp morning, and waited for silence that finally prevailed. "How're ya doing?" he began, an opening that always annoyed Sal for being trite, and the men howled enthusiastically.

Can't blame the vacationers for *that* response, Sal admitted.

Quincy waited for silence. "I'm kinda new, so I'd like you to tell me what's going on at Edgewood," he began innocently.

How can you be kinda new? Sal wondered. You're either new or you're not. It's like kinda felt, sorta ran, sat, or like being a little pregnant.

Sensing a threat to their loafing, the men unraveled such a barrage of complaints about no electricity, water, steps, and much more at the sites that Quincy seemed overwhelmed. Reaching up nervously, he fondled his turf.

"The guy calls a meeting, and doesn't even introduce himself," Sal grumbled, standing beside Skip in the crowd.

"Then you'd know who he was, man."

"We got lots a problems," someone's voice rose above the others, and a tumultuous surge exploded about badly-parked trailers, mud, electricians almost causing a brawl for refusing to work, and similar complaints.

Quincy kept nodding until the voices seemed to peter out from exhaustion. "Whatever you do, don't antagonize the contractors."

Sal eyed Skip waving away a mass of gnats. "How's that for being our top priority?"

Skip shook his head.

"Whenever they give you trouble, tell me," Quincy ordered.

"Tell you what?" Skip muttered.

"Tell him that they gave you trouble," Sal obliged.

Skip laughed.

"Are you our new boss?" Miles asked.

Someone sneezed and Quincy became stiffly grim. "Third in command," he said and cleared his throat. "Craig's second. Roy's in charge," he emphasized.

"In charge of what?" Sal verbalized quietly.

"He hasn't figured that out, yet," Skip answered.

"What's your name?" someone asked.

"Oh, sorry about that," he apologized, introduced himself, and paused to survey the group awkwardly. "We need somebody in charge of all the maintenance men. Since I don't know any of you, maybe you guys could nominate somebody."

"Dinger," someone shouted nearby and the men struggled to control their laughter.

Quincy searched for the speaker, couldn't locate him and gave up.

"Lyman," Norm recommended.

"He's got my vote," Sal recommended, attracting some head-turning.

"Don't know everybody yet," Quincy repeated.

Miles spat. "Ya outta know him. He gives orders like he's in charge."

Several newly-hired blacks jeered.

"Don't know nothin' about him," Quincy admitted.

Miles sulked. "The nigger."

"They appreciate being called blacks," Sal scolded.

Others turned to evaluate Sal's shadowy face and gold-rimmed glasses resting on a small bump halfway up his nose.

"He's probably already working at Edgewood," Sal scolded, implying that everyone else was delinquent including him. "He's the only guy who's really helping the flood victims."

Quincy shrugged.

What does that mean? Sal objected. I just nominated him, asshole. Don't you know anything about parliamentary procedure?

Someone asked who was supposed to set up furniture, HUD or the contractors. "Nobody seems to know."

Quincy frowned and shook his head. "The factory," he appeared to choose.

"What do we do with broke stuff?" inquired another.

"Send it back to the factory," Quincy declared, staggering Sal who pictured the logistics involved. "That's their responsibility."

"Not really," Sal countered. "Sometimes furniture and chairs in trailers get broken during transit." Or they're stolen, he suppressed.

"That's true," Quincy agreed. "These are the things me and Roy are ironing out."

"When's payday?" requested another.

"Soon as you start working," replied another and laughter tore loose.

"The second Friday of the month," Quincy announced. Similar questions and answers continued for a half hour and Quincy ended the meeting

Sal turned to Skip. "Do you realize how many man-hours we just wasted with all this nonsense?"

"I know. Thank God this ain't a disaster or I'd really be pissed."

Sal shook his head and everyone reentered the office for coffee. Torn between heading to Edgewood to help Lyman or complaining to Roy about the disorganization, loafing, and the bungling, Sal considered choosing the latter, though challenging authoritative males was still difficult since he hadn't had it out with his overbearing father yet. But observing Roy leaning against the kitchen refrigerator holding a cup and cigarette in separate hands, he pictured the suffering victims and became so annoyed that he forced himself to approach him. He described what befell Miles' truck and that HUD owed him four dollars, but Roy had trouble understanding separate matters. Desperately needing the money, Sal questioned how HUD would reimburse him.

"Re-im who?" Roy cried.

Several men laughed.

"How do I get paid back the four bucks I spent for gas?" he simplified but self-consciously because of so many eyes studying him.

"Got a receipt?"

"Well, no. I didn't bother–"

"Just get a receipt, Teach," Roy responded and grinned. "We'll take care a ya."

Famous last words. "Say, what the hell's going on here anyway?" he suddenly blurted, surprising himself.

Roy gazed languidly at smoke rising from his cigarette.

"When are we really going to start doing something?" Sal pressed.

"We are," someone responded from behind. "It's called loafin'."

The men laughed and a faint grin creased Roy's face, irritating Sal.

Though appreciating humor, Sal struggled to keep a straight face, then fought against Roy intimidating him as his employer. "All we do is hang around," he managed.

Voices suddenly dwindled and died, and several men evaluated Sal curiously again or perhaps with annoyance, since he was threatening the status quo.

"Do you realize how many people are without trailers? We're just hanging around," Sal emphasized.

Roy lifted his cup to several inches from his lips before drinking. "No need to get uptight, Teach. We're all tryin' ta pull together because of the flood," he muttered and the men agreed, upsetting Sal.

Horseshit, Sal exploded inwardly, regarding them standing about talking, laughing and sipping coffee. These guys are part of the couldn't-care-less generation, he started analyzing until his better sense intervened. It's not their fault. They're only human. It's not even Roy's fault. He is who he is. It's the jackasses responsible for hiring him.

Roy sipped noisily, wiped his mouth on his cowboy shirt sleeve and turned to Skip edging over curiously. "Ah want you and Sal ta go ta McArthur Park raght now. It's a new trailer court," Roy told him.

Realizing he might finally become seriously involved helping the victims, Sal cautioned against overreacting. "Where is it?"

"Don't you teach in this hick town?" Roy dug as if sensing that Sal had been challenging him.

"Haven't memorized every nook," Sal reciprocated, unaware how much he intimidated Roy as a teacher. "Besides, I live about thirty miles from here. It's probably not even on a map, since it's so new."

Roy positioned his cup under the spigot and filled it with coffee.

"I know where it's at," Skip assured impatiently. "Let's go."

About to follow, Sal hesitated. "What are we supposed to do there exactly?" he asked Roy.

"A bunch a trailers is comin'. Spot them as they come in. What else, Teach?"

What do you mean, what else? How the hell 're we supposed know what to do or that trailers are coming in, if you don't tell us, Commander? Communicate, damn it. The dumb never see their own stupidity. Besides, the flood's four weeks old. Where are they coming from, Alaska? They sell trailers right downtown for God's sake. Catching himself storming inwardly again, he stopped. "You can call me Sal," his other self seemed to intercede, and he smirked.

"You'll see the stakes," Roy ignored. "Ah might be down later."

Sal headed for the door. Having managed to complain, he almost felt satisfied, until he realized that he hadn't accomplished anything. Roy wasn't going to improve, he realized, stepping outside with Skip.

Thumping rock music caught their ears, and Sal eyed a suave man in his late twenties slouched in the driver's seat of a new Barracuda 400 parked nearby. Must've just been hired, he sensed, and headed toward Skip's panel truck that he was driving.

Reaching McArthur Park, they noted a bulldozer leveling several pads. Exiting, they eyed eight trailers staggered side-by-side like giant ice trays. Four more arrived and they parked them successfully in another area according to the stakes. When none followed after fifteen minutes, Sal radioed Roy but Craig answered.

"That's all for now," he confirmed. "Twelve more are coming soon."

Deciding to inspect those that had arrived, they were stunned. They were parked so closely to the stakes containing electrical receptacles that opening the front doors was impossible without banging them.

"Now what?" Sal asked. "How could they be so stupid?"

"They've had plenty of experience. Maybe these trailers is for three inch wide folks that can squeeze inside."

"Somebody doesn't know how to spot trailers."

"Yeah, ya gotta be at least retarded," Skip agreed, analyzing a distant dozer.

"Stakes weren't put in the right place, or trailers weren't guided in properly. Electricians couldn't have been that blind," Sal maintained and radioed Roy about it.

Leveling trailers with his "official blocking crew" consisting of four teachers that he had recently hired, Roy promised to check it out but didn't arrive until an hour later.

"Somebody made a mistake," Roy declared, banging one door after the other.

No kidding, Jack, Sal suppressed.

Roy began speculating who had been responsible, the toters, the electricians, his own men, or contractors.

Who cares? Let's do something about it, Sal grumbled.

Roy wasted another twenty minutes considering whether to have the Electric Company move the stakes or toters move the trailers.

Picturing the uncooperative electricians, Sal suggested the toters and Roy agreed.

Although Sal was relieved, Roy strolled back and began examining the same stakes again. "Is he for real?" Sal asked Skip beyond Roy's hearing.

"Probably ain't got them memorized yet."

"Maybe he's going to try pushing trailers away by hand."

Skip laughed.

Banging the last trailer's door several times against the stake, Roy stopped, lit a cigarette, and stepped back. He eyed the stake and door again and finally departed in his Chevy.

Thank God, Sal thought.

"Gas company's arriving at 9:30 sharp in the morning to install propane gas tanks," boomed Craig's voice over Sal's radio. "Keep an eye out."

Yeah, sure. I'll bet we can count on 9:30 sharp. Not today in this world, he answered.

The duo started inspecting one of the four correctly parked trailers. Sal assembled a bed frame in a small, paneled room and slid the box spring onto the frame while Skip inspected everything outside. But inspecting the electricity was impossible. No one thought about supplying fuses for the panel boxes.

Sitting on the bed, Sal wiped perspiration from his neck.

Since HUD had finally set up a charge account with Mathews and Loomis, a local hardware store, they decided to charge them there instead of wasting time radioing Craig or Roy for permission to do so.

Arriving, they noticed one of their panel trucks parked outside. Entering, they found Norm standing before the counter containing copper fittings, a soldering torch, and other supplies. They exchanged greetings, and

Norm briefed them about new problems at Edgewood.

A stocky-built salesman wearing a short-sleeved shirt returned with several pairs of long-nosed pliers, two large pipe wrenches, and Plastic Wood. He dumped them on the counter and planted his hands on his waist. "What else?" he asked and Sal glanced at a tattoo of a nude woman on the man's left biceps.

"Phillips screwdrivers," Norm responded. "We don't have enough."

Meaning they also disappeared along with so much else, Sal sensed accurately.

"How many?" the salesman inquired impatiently.

"A, let's see," Norm considered. "Oh, half a dozen."

The salesman shook his head. "All out," he snapped.

How can you be all out of screwdrivers during an emergency? Sal evaluated. It's like a restaurant running out of food.

"I think Lenny's ordered some more," Skip inserted.

The salesman sighed annoyingly.

"A can of putty for—" Norm attempted.

"Large or small?" the salesman interrupted.

"Large," Norm specified. "Some emery cloth and that stuff you use around threaded pipes."

"Pipe-dope cement," the man supplied. "Anything else in the pipe section, or are you gonna send me back there again?"

The pay's the same, Sal reminded him underground.

Reflecting, Norm turned to Sal. "The victims 've already plugged a couple of toilets. Sealer for plastic pipes," he told the man. "You know, that stuff that—"

"I know what it is," the man barked. "Large or small?"

"Large. Then I need some rubber plugs for bathroom sinks."

"What size?"

"The usual size."

"There ain't no usual size, mister," he enunciated sharply. "Inch, one and a quarter, what?"

What's eating him? Sal demanded.

"Half dozen of each," Norm decided. "Can you remember all that?"

"I can remember all that," the salesman snarled.

"And fuses."

"You, too?" Skip asked.

"What size?" the salesman growled.

"Not sure," Norm said. "It's for trailers we're settin' up at Edgewood."

The salesman slanted his head sarcastically. "What do you want me to do, run over there and check it out? Look, mister, come back when you know the right size."

"Forty amps," Skip interceded. "Same for us. They're about this big," he added, forming a "C" with his thumb and index finger.

The salesman exhaled in annoyance. "Wait a minute, I'll get a ruler."

Sal's head began shaking negatively. "What's the problem, man? The flood didn't come up this far?"

"Was I talking to you?"

Skip checked the man with his good eye. "We're all together."

"You're all goin' steady?"

Sal noticed Skip's irritated expression. He takes a swing and he'll land in jail, he pictured and rested a restraining hand on Skip's shoulder. "It's too much trouble waiting on us during a disaster? Are you the owner?"

"I could handle ya, if ya knew what the hell ya wanted."

"How about some patience? Got any of that? For a customer," Sal enunciated.

"It's for the flood victims," Norm qualified, smiling personably.

"I don't care if it's for the mayor," he responded.

Norm flashed disbelief at Sal and Skip.

"What about selling us another salesman? Got any of that?" Sal inquired and Skip and Norm laughed.

The man turned to an open doorway. "Hey Nelson," he shouted inside. "Wait on this bunch, will ya? Special customers," he announced and left.

"He won't get away with treating us like shit," Skip remarked. "Maybe Nelson's the boss."

"Forget it or we'll never get out of here," Sal said. "Do you realize how much merchants are profiting from the flood?"

Nelson arrived and surveyed their name tags inquisitively. "This stuff yours?" he asked, touching the pile.

Norm nodded and Sal complained about the previous salesman. "That's the way you people treat customers?"

Nelson shrugged. "Help's short because of the flood," he dispensed. "Anything else?"

"Yeah, get rid of the bum that waited on us," Sal recommended.

Skip and Norm burst out laughing.

"I don't do the hiring," Nelson answered, adding up the figures on the register.

"Are you the owner?" Sal asked.

"No. Is that it?"

He's probably in the Bahamas drinking margaritas on the beach, Sal protested.

Norm responded affirmatively, signed for everything, and the trio exited with their packages and boxes.

Pausing, Skip eyed Sal's tag above his shirt pocket. "Do you realize that they sell these at Walmart and K-mart? Any of us can charge whatever we want for ourselves. Who's checkin'? Shit, I'm runnin' out of space in my garage."

The others laughed.

"If the flood victims finds out who hired Roy to run the operation, they might hang 'im by you know where," Norm remarked and they parted.

Returning to McArthur Park, Sal and Skip worked well together, rectifying problems as a repair and inspection team.

"Can you imagine Miles handling this alone?" Skip commented. "He'd a yanked the toilet out, then maybe shut off the water, if he thought about it."

Sal installed an outside light. Skip removed an inoperable fluorescent bulb inside, changed faulty wiring, and applied putty to a leak in the kitchen sink. He was dabbing cement on another plastic pipe when Sal called him from the hall bathroom. Sal flushed the toilet, and Skip grinned when steam belched out from underneath the cover.

"They must a crossed the pipes at the factory," he diagnosed and removed the cover.

Sal visualized one of his couldn't-care-less males working at the factory. Doesn't surprise me.

"Have to, or some family's gonna be stuck with hot flushes."

Sal grinned.

Skip turned off the water under the toilet and they stepped outside. Skip removed part of the outside frame and paused to evaluate a mass of copper pipes. "They couldn't make the job harder if they tried." He found the faulty pipes, melted the solder with a propane torch, and re-soldered them correctly.

The gas men never appeared, preventing them from releasing any of the four trailers that they had readied for occupancy.

Annoyed, Sal radioed Craig.

"Eleven o'clock's their new ETA," Craig reported officially but they didn't show up then either.

Unbelievable, Sal smirked and radioed him again.

Craig promised that they would soon.

Sal also explained that they needed steps and that new pads had just been completed for more trailers. "Any more coming? Over."

"They're coming," Craig responded.

More delays. Can't do anything more until they do, Sal thought and shook his head. Stepping outside with Skip, Sal noticed four men working on a trailer some distance away. The blocking crew? Mr. Efficient must have just hired them, he surmised accurately. Approaching with Skip, Sal realized that they were young elementary school teachers that he had seen occasionally at teacher conferences but never met.

Crouched, one teacher with styled hair was watching a stout man with a black Santa Claus beard lying underneath the trailer struggling to wedge shims between the girder and a column of cinder-block. A third teacher had one foot on the yoke (like the famous picture of Washington crossing the Delaware, Sal almost laughed), and appeared to be waiting to operate the front jack. All were attacking the situation with an intensity that might have loosened a smile from the morose Miles, but paired off with Norm, he was arguing about who was the inspector.

"R-ready?" the third teacher shouted from the front and slapped a green fly attacking his disheveled hair.

"Wait a minute," the bearded man snarled.

A fourth teacher appeared from a panel truck parked nearby. Wearing a red hunting cap despite the heat, he was carrying a large crescent wrench.

"You know these guys?" Skip whispered.

"Seen them around. Good guys."

"Watch this," Skip added mischievously to Sal who appeared quite official wearing the inspector tag pinned to his shirt. "Don't say nothin'."

Sal smiled curiously.

Perspiring, the bearded man slid a small jack between a stack of cinder-block and a rusty girder.

"Is that your job, laying down?" Skip asked him, surprising Sal.

Looking up, the man rose, accidentally bumping his head on the trailer floor above him. Rubbing it, he read Skip's tag with irritation. "Why, you wanna give me another job?"

The man wearing the red cap approached, glanced at Sal, and regarded Skip.

The bearded man dusted himself off.

"Roy said you guys had blocking problems. That's why we're here," the man with the red cap defended amiably.

Skip eyed him, then the bearded man. "Yeah, but did he send ya here to work or lay down?" he pursued icily and jerked his hair back cockily.

Great acting, Sal conceded, struggling to keep a straight face. He even changed his voice and is pronouncing words correctly.

The man with the red cap stared at Skip, as though surprised about his complaint.

Skip's eyes narrowed fiercely at the man's long nose set against a dark, Latin complexion.

Beaming warmly, he introduced the bearded man as Phil (who resembled someone form a notorious motorcycle gang, Sal thought), Mike, who had been watching Phil, then himself as Vinny. Robert was operating the front jack, he explained, and flicked his smiling head at him. "We call him Rapid Robert because he's slow. Moves like a snail," he tacked on with a laugh.

Robert grinned but Skip's face remained fiercely rigid. Robert contemplated Sal's serious expression, suggesting that he was in authority. "Been working at Edgewood all morning," he shouted.

Placing hands on his waist, Phil stared menacingly at Skip."

Ain't that what Roy hired you to do, work?" Skip asked Robert whose grin disappeared.

Hope you don't get punched out, Sal worried and squatted to check the blocking.

Skip glanced at the stocky, bearded Phil standing off to the side glaring at him. "Who told you to block like that?"

"Roy," the bespectacled Mike supplied, wearing jeans.

"How else can you do it?" Vinny contributed curiously.

"By asking us first," Skip replied curtly and snapped his hair back.

"You guys are in charge here?" Phil growled.

Skip frowned sarcastically. "You see anybody else around?" he asked icily and squatted hurriedly also, as if to avoid getting decked out, Sal thought with a laugh.

Skip checked the blocking and Sal almost broke up.

Vinny crouched alongside Skip who glanced officially at his watch, then back up at Phil's beard.

"What time did you guys get here?" Skip asked Vinny, as if displeased about how little work they had done.

"Fifteen minutes ago," Vinny answered.

"Want us to finish blocking this one or start another one?" Mike asked.

Skip eyed Mike with fake anger.

Mike glanced away self-consciously and Robert finally sauntered over.

Glancing at Mike's warm, relaxed expression, Skip looked back under the trailer in disgust.

An uneasy quiet loomed under the bright sun.

Vinny read Sal's tag. "This is Sal D'Angelo," he introduced to Phil who barely nodded.

Skip regarded Phil who resumed brushing himself off. "Did I tell you to stop?"

Phil glared at Skip. "Stop what? We need four-inch block or

something to shove underneath," he barked and regarded Robert who nodded. "The jack's too short."

"Who's movin' the trailer once we unblock it?" Vinny asked Skip. The foursome scrutinized Skip, then Sal.

"Why didn't you measure the jack before, then prop something underneath if it was too short? You wasted a lotta time," Skip quibbled and shook his head. "This is what Mr. Brennig's been complainin' about. Why I was sent," he scolded, finally rose irritatedly, and Sal struggled to stifle a grin. "To stop all this goddamn goofin' off."

"We haven't been–"

"This is an emergency," Skip interrupted Vinny. "If you guys can't block fast enough," he snapped convincingly, "maybe we'll get guys that can. Get the picture?"

Sal was amazed how many people have natural acting ability.

Unintelligible grumbling tore loose from underneath Phil's formidable beard. "We just learned this shit," he barked.

"This isn't baby-sittin'," Skip resumed undauntedly. Slanting his head, he eyed each of the four frowning faces, one after the other, with his good eye. "This job requires long hours, hard work, and plenty of dedication."

"We can h-hack it," Robert stuttered.

Skip lectured similarly for several minutes. "Clear?" he concluded.

The men nodded, barely answered affirmatively, and Sal burst out laughing, surprising them.

"Sal D'Angelo," he announced and shoved a hand at Phil who almost refused it. "We're not in charge. I knew you guys were teachers. He's been putting you guys on. Smiling at their serious expressions, he failed to convince them until he mentioned that he taught at Southside.

The tension broken, the five exchanged notes about common teacher acquaintances, flooded-out schools, and the possible teachers' walkout. Questions then followed about the job.

Is Doris for real? Phil wanted to know.

"Absolutely," Sal returned. "A study in manners and refinement. HUD only hires the best."

"Unbelievable," Vinny contributed.

"Who's really in charge, Craig or that cowboy?" Mike asked and Skip and Sal broke up.

"Sometimes it's hard to tell," Sal obliged. Roy Nichols is, the cowboy. He's supposed to be officially. We're still trying to figure out what he's in charge of. He could just be in charge of hiring," he stated with a laugh.

"You got that straight," Skip agreed. "The roundup's next week."

Sal laughed again.

"The guy who barely showed us how to block and took off," Mike specified to the three other elementary school teachers' puzzled faces.

"Figured he was a flood victim," Phil remarked, "and got stuck up here from the South somehow."

"Close," Skip qualified. "He's really a leftover from the Corpus Christi flood."

The four teachers asked about hourly pay, quitting and eating time, and payday. Driving from one park to another all morning, they wondered if HUD intended to reimburse them for gas.

"You guys need private tutoring," Sal commented and answered more of their questions as accurately as possible.

Phil fingered his long, oval-shaped black beard. "We weren't told anything."

"Neither were we," Skip agreed.

"I never blocked a hat, much less a trailer," Vinny confessed.

Phil studied Vinny's red hunting hat. "I believe it."

"We're fast learners," Mike assured somewhat proudly. "Blocked four trailers in three hours before we came here."

"Without a level. S-saves time," Robert stuttered.

Skip and Sal registered amazement.

"Gotcha," Robert cried with a laugh. "We borrowed a contractor's level."

Laughing, Sal wondered why whoever ordered tools hadn't included levels.

Phil studied Robert. "Of course, it's tough working with an anchor."

"Yeah. Ca-can't you work faster?" he asked Phil, smirked into laughter, and turned his sharply-defined face to Sal. "These guys don't appreciate a highly-skilled blocker."

"We would, if you could only find us one," Phil needled back.

"What I've got to tolerate with three meatheads," Vinny took his turn to complain. "Thought teaching was hard."

Sal grinned. Noticing that they were using a car jack under the yoke, Sal and Skip shook their heads.

"A contractor's worker loaned it to us," Vinny clarified.

"HUD's got an account at Mathews and Loomis. Didn't Roy or Craig tell you?" Sal asked.

"No," Phil answered.

"You can charge levels there and whatever else you need," Sal explained. "We're trying to house the victims in trailers as fast as possible."

"Even though it's too late for that," Skip contributed with a laugh.

Assuming authority, Sal suggested that the four teachers unblock the eight trailers. They consented and all parted. Noticing a man bulldozing the dirt road, some distance away, Sal persuaded him to reposition them properly after the teachers un-blocked them and bill HUD. The man agreed and Sal radioed Craig that the gas men still hadn't arrived.

"They're a'comin' at three," Craig confirmed confidently, disturbing Sal.

An hour later, Craig radioed Sal to send the blocking crew to Edgewood because of the sinking trailers. Considering how much they had accomplished, Sal insisted that they stay put. "Explain that to Roy or have him form more blocking crews from the loungers," he insisted and they began arguing.

"Break, break," intervened base command. "Avoid excessive use of the radio. This is an emergency."

Shit, Sal gave in and signed off.

Finally arriving, the gas men discovered that the tanks were the wrong size, stunning Sal watching them hot-rod out of the park. Is everybody on drugs?

Skip regarded Sal. "At least they could've waved."

Sal exhaled with frustration. Inspecting the remaining trailers anyway, he discovered a cracked toilet bowl in one, which he noted on his inspection sheet. Finishing hours later, they were satisfied about having worked hard. Sal picked up the needed duplicate receipt from the gas station, parked beside the office, and both evaluated the slouched man inside the Barracuda.

"Must be some boss. None of us works that hard," Skip quipped. He pulled open the office door seemingly sucking out the usual dull roar and odors including perfume, and he eyed the loungers. Quincy was standing near Doris' desk talking to several men in a brisk, official manner. Dinger was perched on Rota's unoccupied desk, holding a sandwich in one hand, a stale doughnut in the other, and munching away noisily.

Don't they believe in fresh air? Sal objected and widened two windows. God, what a waste of manpower. But how could such a bizarre conglomeration have helped us at McArthur Park? he recognized, and he joined Skip maneuvering between the standees toward the kitchen. Entering, he attracted some sets of eyes glued to Rota's legs protruding down from a pair of rose-colored hot pants.

A sheepish smile adorned Rota's somewhat emaciated face, nor did she turn her head containing the usual large coiffure of auburn hair. She squeezed out the dishrag and shut the tap. She grabbed her coffee beside the sink and considered stepping between several men who hardly moved, apparently hoping for a breast encounter, Sal reflected with a laugh.

About to disconnect a cup wedged inside a column, Skip hesitated because of so many circling flies.

"Go ahead. Everything's clean," she advised and he did. "Oh, these goddamn flies," she complained, waving them off. "Bought a fly swatter. But if they think I'm going to start swatting, they're crazy," she insisted. "I'm no fly swatter," she said innocently.

Heads swung toward Skip who jerked his hair in place. "Could've fooled me."

"Thanks," she answered sarcastically and sipped.

Skip positioned himself nearby and slurped noisily. "Thought you wasn't gonna clean nothin' up no more."

Rota peered through the opening at Doris speaking loudly over the phone. "I wasn't. I thought *she'd* do it for a change, but no such luck. Couldn't stand the mess. Hey, you guys," she announced in a different tone. "How about keeping this place clean? Throw your paper cups away. Wash the dishes you use. How about it?" she demanded in a squeaky voice that would have had difficulty penetrating smoke, much less the surrounding chatter.

"Was you the one who cleaned up again?" Norm inquired.

"Yeah, but no more."

"Thought we had chamber service."

Rota smirked, and several men laughed.

"You do nice work, Rota," Skip insisted and Rota took another sip.

"I'll remind Roy about getting janitorial service," Sal offered sincerely.

Appreciating attention from so many fine, young stock consuming her breasts, Rota nodded appreciatively, and her mood changed. "If the phone rings again, let it," she chirped resolutely. "I haven't had time to eat. They bought me a roast beef sandwich. It laid on my desk all day. Finally gave it to Dinger."

"You don't like roast beef?" Skip asked.

Rota's expression suggested amazement that others hadn't noticed her situation. "When am I supposed to eat? Been busy all day with forms I don't understand, people who know less than me and others who don't take the time to explain anything. Contractors are constantly on my back demandin' I give 'em trailers. I don't even know how to fill out a dispatch ticket yet. Then guys complain about trailer problems I know nothing about. What's the tongue and a yoke?"

"Tongue is what tastes the yoke," Skip offered and laugher crackled sharply. "So, how're you getting along with the Thing?"

Rota took another sip. "No comment."

"What's the matter?" Norm asked. "Ain't Doris teachin' you nothin'?"

"She don't even know herself," Rota contradicted herself. "Or she starts to tell me, then stops to answer the phone or talk to a contractor, or she forgets. And I'm left hangin'. Then somebody starts talkin' to me. I forget what I asked her, and they wonder why we can't find contracts or inspection sheets," she continued and surveyed the many youthful faces contemplating her slyly. "And she's got her own filing system. How am I supposed to remember that every 050 number is part of a contract series beginning with a *three*? I think the nine hundreds are under, under– Oh, I can't remember. And she starts jumping on me because I file like normal secretaries, and everybody laughs, like I'm some kind of dumbbell. I've been filing 050 numbers under zero. That's why we couldn't find Lyman's inspection sheets last week. She files 970 as 1970 for God knows why, and all 088 inspection sheets are 6088 for another insane reason. Who knows what else she's doing?"

Evaluating her body and breasts, several men shook their heads in false sympathy.

"She started explainin' some of that stuff yesterday but she left with Roy. And I'm left alone to handle the contractors. I asked her three times to explain things. But she keeps saying 'later' because she's doin' reports or somethin'." Pausing to catch her breath, she glared through the opening at Doris still on the phone and turned back to reexamine her audience. "All other HUD numbers are filed as they are. I think," she told Norm. "How does that grab ya?"

Norm smiled. "Sounds organized."

Rota sipped again. "She throws me work like I'm a dog, and I mean throws it," she emphasized. "I keep adding numbers, separating inspection sheets, or filing yellow dispatch tickets, but I never understand why or see the overall picture."

"I'm takin' you ta lunch," someone announced, mimicking Roy, and laughter surrounded Rota who frowned in puzzlement.

"Hang in there, Rota," Skip encouraged.

Rota claimed she wouldn't know what to do if Doris got sick.

"She *is* sick," Skip confirmed and more men laughed.

Too frustrated and self-absorbed, Rota missed the humor. "Doris still hasn't showed me how to fill out the men's time sheets. I don't know how we're gonna get paid. Last week's time sheet still hasn't been sent out," she divulged innocently.

Silence appeared to spread in waves of horror. Finally armed with a legitimate excuse, the men stared savagely at Rota's breasts, is if to punish her for such terrible news.

"What?" protested Kevin.

"Our pay's screwed up?" objected another.

Like everything else, Sal scorned, leaning against the counter.

Skip turned his frowning face to Sal who shrugged. "You're puttin' us on," he told Rota and snapped his head unnecessarily.

"Not really," Rota answered.

"Maybe we need another secretary," Skip needled.

Missing the reference, Rota agreed wholeheartedly.

Sal grinned at first. But having experienced employers who paid late, inaccurately, or without regard for their employees who often desperately needed money for food and bare necessities like him, he started worrying because of overdue bills and limited money to feed his family. "Ask Roy to speak to Doris. He's the boss. The men have to get paid," he insisted kindly. Even for loafing, he suppressed, and all agreed somewhat angrily.

"Roy never scolds Doris about anything," Rota told Sal.

Constantly reviewing what late bills to pay at the end of the month, Sal struggled to remain calm.

"How come?" someone patronized.

Rota smirked, fell silent, and sipped noncommittally. "That I leave to your imagination."

Norm slipped his thumbs under his overall suspenders as if he were posing for a new photograph. "What's that supposed to mean?"

"They're shacking up," Skip provided.

"You said it, not me," Rota said and took another sip.

"You're kidding," Norm said. "And she's such a nice, sweet girl."

"What about him?" Rota disagreed like a true women's libber.

Doris' telephone rang. Answering it, she began shouting for Roy nestled in the far room.

"The vulture and the clam," Skip labeled, but apparently upset, the men hardly laughed.

A chair appeared to slide away from the desk in the last room.

"Telephone," Doris screeched with irritation.

Footsteps unloosed from under Roy's desk, and he headed up the narrow hallway. Once again, the overflow kitchen throng moved aside in order to allow what resembled a cowboy working his way between them, and he arrived in front.

"How come he doesn't answer her on his own phone? Sal asked Skip. "It doesn't make sense."

"He don't know how to work them buttons," Skip explained. "It's tough, man. Ya gotta be at least retarded."

"I better get back," Rota remarked nervously and left.

The four teachers returned from Edgewood and squeezed into the kitchen, hours later, as did Craig. Sweaty, muddy, disheveled, and tired, they began describing the sinking trailers with Craig, and Quincy appeared next.

Feeling slighted, Quincy began bullying into the conversation. Confused about who was really in charge, the teachers peppered both, and Norm turned to Sal. "Do we dare hang around for more of this?"

Sal shrugged. "It's part of the job," he explained and Norm laughed.

"What time are we supposed to *really* sign out?" Kevin asked Craig, capturing the foursome's attention.

"The usual," Skip provided and snapped his head. "Any time."

Norm inhaled and sighed incredulously. "Never had a job like this in all my forty working years."

"Could've signed out an hour ago, wrote down this time, and left. Nobody would a knowed," Skip answered and peered up front through the opening "In fact, anybody can sign out for anybody any time," he revealed (despite Craig and Quincy's presence), and he surveyed the men milling about in the living room. "We got more workers than flood victims."

"Makes you feel important, don't it?" Norm responded and chuckled good-naturedly, exposing his widely-spaced upper teeth.

"Roy don't even check the sign-out sheet," one of the men commented.

"No sense," Skip scoffed. "He can't read."

Exchanging similar observations, the kitcheneers eventually sauntered boredly into the living room, signed out and left.

The next morning, Quincy announced that Corning desperately needed him and ten others to help with operations. He would be gone indefinitely, he revealed and randomly chose ten loungers from the living room. He bade the rest goodbye, received polite applause, and left with them.

"Thought he was our leader?" Skip inquired back in the kitchen with the others. "Guess we overworked him."

"We should head for McArthur Park," Sal hinted to Craig. Amazing that I have to coax him into sending me there.

Engrossed in idle talk, Craig turned, holding a cup in one hand and a cigarette in the other. "Might just as well."

More amazing is his indifference. Mr. Couldn't-care-less himself, Sal labeled.

Skip eyed the refrigerator oddly because of his bad eye, and snapped his loose hair back on his sarcastic head. "Planning to send down any more trailers?" he asked Craig.

"Any more pads ready?" Craig seemed to counter.

"Pads' 're almost all done. We needs trailers, man," Skip returned.

"Why didn't somebody tell me?" Craig asked.

"I told Roy yesterday," Sal inserted.

"Never heard nothin' about it," Craig said. "How many more trailers will fill the park?"

"Sixteen," Sal responded.

"Good," Craig replied, reinserted his cigarette back, and inhaled.

Skip waited impatiently for Craig to exhale. "So, how many are ya gonna send?"

"None."

Skip laughed with several others and Sal sighed. "How come?"

"Ain't got none," Craig admitted and sipped again.

"What about the ones you said were on the way?" Sal inquired.

Craig shrugged. "Ain't never showed."

"This is stupid. Why not?" Sal demanded. "It's been about six weeks since the flood. Caravans of trailers should be arriving."

"They are," Craig said. "They've been shipped from all over. Thirty-six are comin' from one plant alone."

"How come they don't buy locally?" Skip interrupted. "There's trailer companies right down the street, for Krist sake. Talk about dumb."

"They did," Craig answered.

Skip whirled. "Really? Then where the hell are they? With all this help, we could push 'em ta the parks."

Craig laughed with the others. "We'll have more trailers by this weekend, than, than," he attempted and noted the sink. "Flies in this room."

Skip eyed them. "Don't get carried away. There ain't that many trailers in the world."

Chapter 12

Entering the office Thursday morning, Sal observed Roy standing near the couch holding a cup of coffee in one hand and his radio in the other. Making his way around the different circles of men, he approached him absorbing an earful from Doris about missing steps, re-blocked trailers, the gas company's mistake, and other problems. He appeared overwhelmed or bored, Sal realized, particularly when Rota started peppering him about forms she didn't understand.

Doris' telephone rang, interrupting Rota and Doris answered it. "Telephone," she shouted to Roy. "You answer it this time," she ordered.

The men moved aside so that he could pass. Roy complied and all paused to listen. A male flood victim, living in a church basement with a family of six, begged Roy to come up with a trailer. Roy promised he would and hung up.

Sure, ya will, Sal mocked. Approaching Roy working his way back to the same circle of men, Sal was tempted to accuse him of being incompetent, but Roy was listening to someone relating an obscene story, and Sal paused. Though finding an opening, he had difficulty attacking the man for the same reasons as before. In fact, broke, he asked Roy about his four dollars first, and the men seemed annoyed about the interruption, Sal noticed, disturbing him.

Roy frowned.

Does he know what I'm talking about? Sal wondered under the men's curious scrutiny. "I've got the receipt now," he threw in as a reminder.

"Hang on to it," Roy flung again, and his head swiveled back to the story-teller who resumed.

Some people need the money, Sal stormed angrily. "Take it to the Rand?" he suggested.

"Hang on to it for a while," Roy repeated without irritation or curiosity, piquing Sal even more. "I'll let ya know."

What's the use? Four dollars means nothing to some people. Heading toward the front door, he reached for the knob and the door almost opened in his face.

Skip stepped inside. "Need flashlights to check under sinks, man," he told Sal who nodded.

Overhearing Skip, Lenny disconnected from his small group and proudly angled his oversized forearms below rolled-up sleeves for all to see. "There's a box of 'em in the cabinet above the sink," he declared almost wispily, and both men followed him into the crowded kitchen.

Skip opened the first two doors and peered inside. "Got a flashlight? I can't see."

Lenny laughed. "They're in a box."

Opening another cabinet, Skip surveyed the empty shelves. "They must be invisible."

The next cabinet contained only a can of coffee and filters.

"What the hell?" Lenny breathed sidestepped clumsily because of his bad leg and looked. "Where'd they go?"

Skip grinned sarcastically. "Sucked away inside the jaws of Agnes."

Checking another cabinet, Lenny frowned. "Two sets of crescent wrenches were in here. Tools, screwdrivers and a toolbox," he emphasized dramatically. "All gone."

"Put the shit back, Len, and we won't turn ya in," Skip chirped.

Lenny opened two more cabinets simultaneously and evaluated a stack of paper plates, coffee cups, and napkins in one of them. "This pair of scissors is all that's left in this one."

"Shit, you must've missed that, Len," Skip cried, causing laughter.

"What's gonna wander away next?" Lenny asked.

"A trailer?" Skip suggested, unaware that one had disappeared days ago.

Lenny shook his head grimly. "Wouldn't surprise me none," he remarked quietly. "They dispatch trailers to any bum with a toter."

"Maybe they're in another room," Norm suggested.

"What? A trailer or a bum? Skip asked.

"Maybe the inspectors took all those tools. To inspect," Norm specified.

"Without signing 'em out on one of Lenny's forms?" Skip demanded. "Get serious. Old Len's too slick to allow that happen. Maybe we should check one of his forms." He glanced at the mimeograph machine and scattered papers on the table. "If only we could find the right one in his pile of shit."

"Go to hell," Lenny practically whispered, limped toward two cabinets above the stove, and checked inside.

Skip leaned against a counter and eyed him aslant. "Hey, Len, what the hell do you do all day?"

"Checks inside cabinets," someone contributed.

"Same as you, nothin'," Lenny replied and slammed both cabinets shut. "It's contagious."

"Can't you mind the house better'n that?" Skip pursued. "What's the government paying you for?"

Lenny paused to reflect. "Can't figure this out," he mumbled at the stove.

"Ain't nothin' new with you, Len," Skip dug.

"I'll buy another box of flashlights today," Lenny offered.

Skip laughed. "You'll buy another box? Get him. You mean you're gonna charge HUD for another box at Mathews and Loomis, plus everything else, so ya can sell the shit ta the bums ya hang out with."

"Fuck you," Lenny spewed.

That's enough of this, Sal dispensed, excused his way past the men, and Norm and Skip followed him into the living room.

Rota stared curiously at Doris ignoring her ringing telephone.

"Telephone," a veteran loafer cried. So did someone else near the couch.

Doris finally grabbed the receiver angrily. "We're getting trailers out as fast as possible," she stormed into the receiver above the talking that subsided. "Ya just gotta be patient," she screeched and hung up. "Damn people," she added, stunning Sal, particularly when several men laughed.

"Put in my hardest day sitting right there," Norm told several newly hired men sitting on the couch and they scrutinized him curiously.

Stepping outside with Skip, Sal eyed his inoperable truck and reentered. He approached Roy holding his cup while standing beside a group of men. "You might want somebody with a panel truck to tow my truck to the Rand," he presented and absorbed his stare. "Or have Tony send a mechanic here to check it out."

Roy produced his best stare yet.

Doesn't understand again or forgot, Sal realized. "Want me to call him?"

Roy agreed and Sal did so from Roy's office. But the Rand switchboard operator was tied up with flood victims calling about trailers, and he had trouble getting through.

"Yeah," a familiar voice finally answered almost ten minutes later.

"This is Sal D'Angelo. Tony Grannis?"

"Yeah."

Sal described his in operable truck and a long pause followed. "Did you hear me?"

"Yeah, I heard ya," returned that typically irritating arrogance and sarcasm that Sal disliked, especially because of so much incompetence and disorganization.

"The truck broke down last week, and you're calling now?" Tony barked angrily. "What the hell's the matter with you?"

"I told Roy, but–"

"HUD's payin' rent on them trucks. I coulda sent my man down to fix it. Trucks is scarce. You guys piss and moan about no trucks. It's your own goddamn fault," he shouted.

Sal extended the receiver from his ear.

"You guys sit on your ass while trucks is broke, then never calls."

And what the hell do you do? Sal concealed.

"Almost a week? That's bullshit. I'm wracking my brain looking for trucks. Guys breakin' my chops 'cause I got none. The company don't have any more because of the flood and you–"

"Slow down. I'm telephoning for Roy Nichols," Sal stormed back almost in equal volume.

"Hah? I told you guys to call me if and when a truck breaks down. Who the hell is this? Where's the goddamn truck? What's wrong with it? Maybe it needs gas. Krist, the other day I sent a man to check one that wouldn't start. How the hell can it start with no gas? Where's the truck now?"

Calm down, Sal ordered himself. No sense wasting energy on such an asshole.

"What's wrong with it?"

Sal explained again.

"You didn't try fixin' it, did you?"

"No," Sal responded. He can't handle the truth.

"Don't touch nothin'. My man 'll be up in an hour. Where're the keys?"

"In the truck."

"What?"

Sal smiled. "They've been inside since then. They would've gotten lost here in the office."

"Hah? Where? What office? Who're you?"

"Salvatore D'Angelo. I'm in charge of trucks ova he-ah," he dramatized.

"Yeah? You ain't never heard of cars stole out of locked garages?"

"Not if they don't run."

"Hah?"

"How's anybody going to steal a truck if it don't start?" he demanded mischievously again. "What's wrong with you, man?"

"All I know is one of my trucks was stole yesterday."

"Did you find it?"

"What?"

"You mean you forgot already?" And these guys get jobs? He's probably a G-13. "The truck you claimed somebody stole."

"Yeah, we found it."

"Where? In back of the Rand?"

"Hah? What're you, a wise guy? Who is this?"

"Sal D'Angelo. Because it could have been one of the trucks that we signed out for some time ago. Maybe it was the truck that you figured you lost. Hope you didn't take one of *our* trucks by mistake. Didn't you check with us here?"

"Hah? Your truck? What the hell 'er you takin' about? Hell no, I didn't check with you guys. I got enough ta do here."

Doing what, sitting on your ass? "How do you know ours wasn't the missing truck that you found, if you didn't check with us here?" he deliberately repeated as if he were stupid.

"Look, I know, goddamn it. Say, who're you? What's your job over there?"

"Fairgrounds supervisor," he said and hung up. Nice title, he announced with a grin.

Chapter 13

Driving home that night, Sal hardly had time to write out his bills, much less spend time with his family. I'll be getting home at eleven, he realized and struggled not to lapse into self-pity.

Dinner awaited him upon his arrival. Though Trudi never prepared anything heavy, he disliked retiring on a full stomach. Sparing her his frustration and boredom about the job, he had generalized about some of the incidents to her. A steadfast German, she was unaccustomed to such behavior even from the ignorant, uninformed, and the stupid. Had he described some of the incidents, she would have urged him to quit and look for another job. It could be worse somehow, he reasoned in bed, remembering how much money he lost to the rain working as a landscaper.

The following day at the office, Sal met Happy who had been lounging in the Barracuda. Having been sleeping overnight in his car, Happy had transferred his belongings into one of the office trailer's bedrooms, Sal soon learned. A Southerner, Happy was standing in the middle of the living room unleashing an explosive tirade against "the thief" whom he claimed had stolen his electric razor. He planned to catch "the bastard" and hang him by the testicles.

Where did they dig this mongrel up? The Okeefanokee Swamp? Sal berated, edging to the sidelines. Once again he felt like he was watching another stupid, unrealistic play.

Though Norm tried to help Happy remember where he "might have misplaced it," as Norm put it, Happy stuck to sensationalizing the thievery.

"The place is crawlin' with Yankee thieves," Happy insinuated.

Standing nearby, Phil fingered his black beard and glared at him. "I don't think so," he growled. "This is a public place. Don't be accusing us of anything. Shave at a motel or inside your Barracuda, not here."

"Hey, I ain't accusin' you, man," Happy moderated.

Craig entered, bee-lined toward the urn, and Sal asked him if the thirty-six trailers had arrived.

Craig reached for a cup. "No. Supposed to come today," he answered with familiar unconcern reminiscent of some of Sal's listless, apathetic students. Craig placed the cup underneath the stainless steel spigot and flipped the handle down. "They'll be here, Teach," he promised, as if he were doing Sal a favor and lifted his cup to his lips.

"When?" Sal growled. "Who told you they're coming? Why don't you *really* look into it? Like *call* them," he emphasized. "Who told you they were coming?" he repeated deliberately.

Craig maneuvered his lips as if he were removing excess coffee and worked his face into frown. "Doris or Roy. I forget."

"That's why there's so much disorganization and confusion. Nobody pinpoints anything. Nobody checks and nobody cares. Information seems to sneak through, gets exaggerated, and rumors abound like, like flies in this room," Sal finally unloaded sharply, pleasing himself.

Craig laughed.

He's like my scholars, Sal mused. "What the hell's so funny? Two days ago Roy calls a meeting outside at nine thirty in the morning, and he never shows up. Is he crazy?"

"He had to go someplace."

"Yeah, he had to go someplace. Wonder where *that* is?" Sal sneered. "So, nobody could let us know? One of you should have apologized. What are we, animals? It would have been good for our morale."

"Are you kiddin'? These guys never had it so good. They're getting paid for drinking coffee," he admitted, surprising Sal.

"Roy or Doris should be radioing the toters or the company about those thirty-six trailers. What the hell's going on? We're not running a mail-order business. We're trying to put destitute people into homes. Don't you get it?" he fumed, and several men turned to study him curiously again. "There's a lot of suffering going on out there."

Craig shifted weight to a different leg. "Hey, man, you forget. I ain't in charge." He laughed. "Whenever you guys don't know somethin', it's because of Roy, not me. He don't tell me nothin'."

Here we go passing the buck. "So, you ask him."

Craig nodded. "Think I don't?"

"So, what does he say?"

"Sometimes he tells me things; sometimes he don't."

Would complaining about Roy's indifference, incompetence, and stupidity accomplish anything except aggravate me further? In fact, what are you accomplishing ripping Craig apart right now?

"The guy's working under a strain," Craig answered. "He's got too much on his mind. Then there's Doris–"

"Bullshit," Sal barked angrily. "Look at all this manpower standing around doing nothing. He's just too dumb to figure out how to utilize it. He shouldn't be in charge," he stormed next. "That's the bottom line," he barked and more men stopped talking in order to regard him.

"Agreed," Craig replied without flinching and sipped again. So, now what? I can't fire him. No way am I gonna risk my job and bitch to him or Brennig. I don't have another job like you."

"So you'd rather tolerate the bullshit?"

"Let me put it this way. I'd like to keep this job for a while," he divulged mildly and paused. "Do the best you can at what you're doing," he recommended, unaware that Sal saw through the empty words and the man. "You're doing a good job at McArthur Park. You're puttin' in the hours. Don't fight it, man."

Whenever threatened, patronize, Sal criticized grimly. "Can't stand the incompetence. Especially because we're supposed to be helping the flood victims, damn it."

"Neither can I," Craig assured.

Bullshit, Sal raged internally this time. You're like the couldn't-careless bunch who only think about themselves in this damn, greed-orientated society, he reminded himself, broke away, and left with Skip waiting in his truck. You're using hardcore profanity now? he scolded while they drove to McArthur Park. It's got more power than proper English, he justified. And necessary to emphasize a point. Not that it had much effect on him, he sensed, calming down.

Arriving, they met Audrey, a pretty, young social worker, and Harley Bomark, a young, well-dressed, black counselor wearing a moderate Afro. Both had just settled four families in trailers. Realizing that they were waiting impatiently for more trailers "to be released," Sal and Skip hurriedly inspected and released another one after gas was hooked up.

Craig radioed from the Fairgrounds that ten of the thirty-six trailers had finally arrived.

Having heard too many false alarms and rumors, Sal wondered if this was finally the beginning of the "great influx," as some men had predicted.

News that the trailers were tying up local traffic had a way of seeping into taverns, bowling alleys and local golf courses. Recognizing the chance to tote trailers to the sites, independent toters of every kind started emerging from their slots for quick, easy money.

Where were these guys before? Sal contested. Waiting for enough trailers to arrive so they could make some extra bucks like now, he answered.

Trailers soon started reaching Edgewood and McArthur Park, although not without the usual problems. Though Sal radioed Doris that two more trailers would fill Mc Arthur Park, she sent three, surprising him. "How could Miss Secretary of the Year confuse two with three?" he demanded, standing with hands on his waist beside his radio on the ground.

"Simple," the indomitable Skip replied nearby. "They're the same according ta wonder girl."

And how come Craig isn't sending us some help, including himself? he suppressed.

Trying to convince the third toter, one of the regulars, to tote the trailer back to the Fairgrounds wasn't easy, Sal soon realized. Mistrustful–and who could blame him, considering so much confusion, Sal realized–the man refused to believe that another pad didn't exist somewhere, and even checked inside the park. Driving back, he also doubted that HUD would pay him for toting the unneeded trailer back to the Fair Grounds and threatened to leave it in the street. Not until Sal radioed Craig and Roy (who assured him that HUD would pay him), did the man consider leaving, and he threatened to "beat the livin' shit" out of Sal and Skip if HUD reneged.

"No problem," Sal agreed. "Actually, I wouldn't mind that happening," he told Skip as the man headed for his truck. "I'd be able to get rid of some of the shit I've been absorbing on this job."

Watching him pull away noisily, Skip guffawed.

"'Course, I can't blame the guy. I'm still trying to get my four bucks."

Harley and Audrey settled six more families into trailers. They handed the duo a list of problems, ranging from leaky faucets to off-track closet doors because of cheap hardware and/or sloppy installation, Sal sensed. One trailer's door wouldn't shut properly because of bad leveling that was obviously a blocking problem, both men knew. Another lacked hot water, and the two worked hard and late to correct such problems that were multiplying as more families moved in.

Amazing that neither Roy nor Craig is sending us help, Sal protested, perspiring while tightening a nut in the leaking drainpipe under a kitchen sink, and he warned against pitying himself or becoming jealous for working so hard while so many others loafed. "Try the water, now," was becoming his famous line.

Skip did. The drainpipe didn't leak and they left. Though dark, they decided to patrol the park in case of further emergencies. No one stopped them, so they returned to the office, signed out after ten o'clock, and headed for their homes.

Chapter 14

Saturday morning was hot and humid. Skip and Sal reached McArthur Park shortly after nine. Parking on a muddy road, they slid out of the panel truck with their toolboxes. They planned to resume inspecting further ahead toward two long, parallel rows of trailers already housing victims, when a young girl wearing yellow ribbons in her hair ran towards them. So did a short man from another direction. The door of the first trailer in the row also flung open, and an elderly woman wearing a blue bathrobe eyed them anxiously. Emerging, she had difficulty reaching the low cinderblock steps with her leg.

Sal and Skip paused curiously, and the young girl headed towards them.

"Are you the men from HUD?" she inquired.

"That's us," Sal responded and barking sounded.

"My mother wants to talk to you."

"Okay. What can we do for you?" Sal asked her.

"Are you the HUD guys?" interrupted the short man.

Two young, black teenage males loped into view from around the next trailer and approached.

Sal awaited the young girl's answer, and another door opened from further down the line.

"It's them, Ma," shouted another young girl, struggling to reach the low cinderblock steps also.

Out stumbled a middle-aged man from a trailer on Sal's right.

"Our toilet's leaking," the first young girl announced and another dog started barking.

Several other victims started surrounding the duo, and the woman wearing the blue bathrobe thrust her head near Sal. "Can you check our table. One of the legs is too short."

"Hey. We're missing a kitchen chair," the short man announced before Sal could answer her.

"We'll be right there," Sal heard Skip answer someone else.

"How come our couch don't fold into a bed like everybody else's?" the middle-aged man complained.

"It's them," a man in his twenties shouted.

"It's about time," his wife answered.

"How many chairs do you have?" Sal asked the short man.

"Hey, one of our windows is busted, man," one of the blacks insisted impatiently. "Are we gonna have to pay for it? We didn't do it."

155

"I can't find an outlet to plug in my dryer," inserted a young woman wearing a red bandanna around her head.

"Which trailer?" Sal heard Skip ask someone else as more flood victims arrived.

"When's garbage pick-up?" a male senior citizen badgered Sal about to answer the bandanna woman. "My wife wants ta know."

"I don't know," Sal responded to both. Removing his pad and pencil from his back pocket, he tried to jot down "dryer hook-up problem, #12," but someone kept tugging his arm.

"When are we gettin' regular steps?"asked another man while Sal explained to an obese woman how to operate the oven, and wolf-like barking joined the fray.

"Say, mister," Sal barely heard because of the barking

"Our toilet's leaking," the girl wearing yellow ribbons uncorked, and several others bombarded Skip similarly.

"Yo, hey man," the other black teen interrupted. "Can we put up posters? No tacks, just Scotch tape. Hey man–"

"You'll have to ask–" Skip attempted.

"Just a minute," Sal told the arm-tugger.

"Say," a tall man shouted, accidentally spitting in Sal's face.

"What about my dryer?" interrupted the red bandana woman.

Sal dropped his pencil. Stooping for it, he slipped it back into his rear pocket hurriedly, withdrew his handkerchief, and wiped his forehead.

"Are we gonna get phones?" a new female demanded.

"What about our table?' the woman wearing the blue bathrobe shouted to Sal wiping his face.

"Hey, I was here before you."

"Stop pushing," complained another.

"Six," the first man replied into Sal's distraught face.

"Six what?" Sal demanded. What the hell did he ask me before?

"Mister, what about our toilet?" the girl with the yellow ribbons insisted.

"Our kitchen faucet's dripping," a female interrupted Skip struggling to explain how to operate the blower.

"Hey, how about getting me another couch?"

"You have to open the blower door. There's a switch inside," Sal barely heard Skip explain.

"Where's the blower?" asked another.

"What's a blower?" a woman asked.

"Can you fix the leg?"

"What about gettin' us another couch?"

"Hey, wait your turn."

"What's your number?" Sal asked the man. "What's your number?" he shouted. "Why are you talking to him? Didn't you just– "Shit," he complained, accidentally dropping his pencil again, and the man frowned.

"We don't have a phone yet."

"What's your trailer number?" Sal questioned the blue-bahrobe woman standing beside him. Where the hell's my pencil?

"Damned if I know," Sal barely heard her reply.

"What about that busted window?" the black man persisted.

"Six chairs," the short man shouted as the barrage continued. "That's all we got."

"There's water all over the floor," the young girl insisted and pulled Sal's arm again.

"Can you get us higher steps?"

Sal looked down at the young girl exasperatedly. "What?"

"What about them posters, man?" the other black teen persisted. "Hey Sal," Skip shouted, edging away, and the crowd followed him. "Run for the truck!" he cried, absorbing a similar pummeling of demands and complaints. "Now!" he raged, but had trouble veering around the crowd.

Breaking away, Sal realized the crowd was following them, and burst into laughter. Spotting an opening, the duo sprinted beyond the mob, reached the truck almost simultaneously, and opened their doors frantically as the crowd closed in. They slid inside, slammed and locked them, and fists started banging the truck.

Panting and perspiring, Sal started the engine hurriedly. He backed up carefully between the pressing crowd. A hand fumbled for the truck's door handle, gave up, and the owner backed away as did the others. U-turning, Sal inched ahead slowly.

Several victims waved fists and ordered him to stop. Bypassing them, Sal accelerated along the dirt road. Obscenities followed and a stone hit the roof. Finally outdistancing them, he turned right. Reaching the main macadam road, he floored the pedal, and the truck droned belatedly ahead. "Unbelievable," Sal cried, eyeing them through the rear-view mirror.

Slouched, Skip erupted into more uncontrollable laughter, as did Sal. Consuming a half a mile, Sal pulled up alongside a curb, stopped, and they spent ten minutes recounting the incident. Then, like two mischievous boys, they slumped down and outlined their strategy: return and park some distance from the trailers, which they did unnoticed some time later.

Sal studied the gas men lazily installing another tank, crews blocking different trailers, and men macadamizing the road ahead.

Skip peered over Sal's lowered head. "Is it safe?"

Sal scrutinized the trailers. "Looks okay. I don't see anybody."

"What about them two kids over there?" Skip asked, pointing.

Sal checked one of them spanking a puddle with a hacksaw. "They're fine, but the hacksaw's taking a beating."

Skip laughed.

Sal started the truck. Driving back slowly, he halted and both exited. Sal knocked on the first trailer. Skip headed for the second one and neither of them had problems. The third trailer belonged to the woman wearing the blue bathrobe. Sal unloosened a screw in the table's leg and extended it. He gave her two missing light bulbs and left. The senior citizen in the next trailer asked about the garbage. Sal promised to check it out and jotted it down. The fourth trailer belonged to the black men. Yes, concerning Scotch-taped posters, Sal decided, noted down their broken window, and trotted away.

The woman in the fifth trailer opened the door and yawned. "Why the hell can't you guys come at a decent hour?"

"Sorry," Sal replied. Departing quickly, he arrived at the trailer containing a young couple that grumbled almost incoherently about nails in the bathroom. Following him there, Sal stared with incredulity at two brads protruding from a piece of molding. Talk about a serious problem, he snickered beyond their hearing and tapped them back into the wood with the end of his penknife. Returning to the living room, he frowned at the husband sitting on the couch beside boxes of household goods.

"No hammer," the man explained somewhat sheepishly.

"I didn't have one either. Anything else? A hair more serious?"

The man complained about a stuck window.

Don't get annoyed, Sal warned, undoing the lock, and opened it. They're human, just like you, he reminded himself and left.

Exiting a trailer across the street, Skip joined Sal and revealed that he had steadied a wobbly table by lifting a leg off a scatter rug.

Sal told him about tapping in the brads. "If they're going to be that helpless, we'll need a hundred men a day," Sal commented.

Pausing, Skip snapped his hair into place. "Almost what we got vacationing back at the barracks."

Sal knocked on the next door that shuddered open, and the short man complained about the missing kitchen chair.

Skip peered inside and counted them. "You only get six, plus the table, not seven."

"But we're seven," the man insisted, as if it were the standard family size. "Can you get us another one?" he asked Sal.

Shrugging, Sal promised to try and wrote it down. Recalling several extra chairs in the office, he asked if it had to match.

Offended, the man stared. "Can't you get one that does?"

"We'll try," Sal agreed again.

Both arrived at the eighth trailer belonging to the girl wearing the yellow ribbons, and Sal knocked.

Opening the door, the girl turned to her mother inside. "I told them, but they didn't wanna come, Mommy."

"I know," Mom answered while approaching. "Most men are mean like your father. That's why he's not allowed to live with us."

Drenched with perspiration, Sal frowned about the negativism she was instilling in her daughter about men.

"Water's leaking around the bottom of our toilet," the mother told the duo.

They replaced the seal and left. They were about to head for the ninth trailer when a male teenager intercepted them."Hey, man. Hey, man," he cried breathlessly. "In the bathroom. Water's overflowin' out the toilet tank," he shouted and ran. "It's all over the floor," he flung over his shoulder.

"This kid's suffering from flood shock," Skip told Sal trotting alongside, and the teen led them inside the trailer.

Entering the bathroom, they removed the tank cover, reinserted a plastic pipe into a metal tube, and replaced the cover. Skip flushed the toilet. It worked properly and they left. They deliberately ate their bagged lunches in the truck in case more problems arose, and when none did, they resumed inspecting.

Lyman joined them in order to help activate electricity, rather than bother the contractors and their crews to do it. He also fixed leaks and inspected most of the hot water tanks up the line. The threesome released more trailers in the passing hours. Shortly after eight o'clock, Sal and Skip were about to return to the office when a girl, about four years old, rushed over with her younger brother.

"Mister, ya gotta come to our house," the boy cried, looking up at Sal in the driver's seat. "Water's all over the floor and the shit–"

"Shhhhhh," his sister scolded him and both giggled.

"Oh, mister, please. Nobody's home," she said. "Please come."

"Now don't cry," Sal answered fatherly. "We'll come," he agreed, starting the engine. "How can parents leave two little kids at home alone?"

Skip shook his head.

Running ahead, the children kept looking back as Sal motored slowly behind them.

The children dashed inside their trailer, and the duo followed them into the bathroom. Wood shims, soap, toys, and clothes were scattered on the floor. Inhaling something putrid, they spied sausages of defecation lying in a puddle of brown water nearby, and froze. Standing beside the toilet, was a younger, scrawny, wet boy. He flushed the toilet with a happy smile and his sister screamed at him. Brown water rose, started overflowing the toilet, and his older brother howled hysterically.

"No way," skip announced, backing into Sal recoiling from the stench. "I'm outta here." He stumbled past Sal glaring at the children, and strode down the hall.

"What did you do?" Sal scolded, and the two older children blamed the younger brother who started squealing louder than his older brother. "You tell your parents we can't fix that. Where's your mother or your father?"

A car halted outside and the younger brother stopped screaming. Sal studied the three young children staring up fearfully at him. Tired, perspiring, and irritable, he broke away and bypassed Skip talking to the parents in the living room What a day, he groaned, and entered the truck.

Scolding sounded. Spanking followed and the children wailed. That's the wrong approach, the teacher in Sal addressed. Skip arrived, shaking his head and they drove away.

Chapter 15

Entering the office on Sunday, Sal made his way between the loungers. He entered Roy's vacant office and telephoned Audrey. She promised to handle the dryer hook-up problem and brief the flood victims about garbage pickup, when they were getting telephones, and more. Sal thanked her and entered the supply room for his radio that he had plugged in for the usual overnight charge.

Craig appeared holding his usual cup of coffee. "You'll be working with Miles at McArthur Park today."

Sal disconnected his power cord and tossed it on the cluttered bed. Surprise, he regarded Craig's pink, upturned nose. "What? Who says?"

"I say," Craig replied and grinned sheepishly.

Sal shook his head. "No way. The guy's creep city."

"Sal, you've got to," Craig whined.

"Why? Skip and I work well together. We accomplished a hell of a lot yesterday."

"I know. We appreciate that."

Yeah, I bet.

"I'm puttin' Skip with Dinger. They're going to Skycrest. It's a new trailer park. We need a good maintenance man like him out there."

Sal couldn't resist. "Who, Dinger?"

Craig burst out laughing.

"Come on, Sal. It's the only way. You were the one complainin' about the disorganization and incompetence."

Sal eyed the handsome face exasperatedly. "So, I get punished?"

Craig laughed. "Not really."

Scrutinizing the hall lined with loungers holding cups of coffee, smoking, talking, and laughing, Sal frowned disgustedly. "Geezus," why don't you grab a couple of those loose ends hanging around sucking wind? We handled all of McArthur Park ourselves."

"I know. We don't have time to break them in. You guys did a damn good job. Even Roy said so."

Sal smirked. "Yeah, sure."

"I'm serious. He did."

"Miles and Dinger are dangerous. They need constant supervision. Actually, they need each other," he modified with a laugh. "Put them together."

Craig laughed again.

"They're worse than kids," Sal maintained but refused to suggest firing them. They might need the money desperately like me.

"What can I say?" Craig cried.

Sensing that he had pushed enough, Sal sighed and agreed reluctantly. He followed Craig into the living room and approached Miles sitting on the couch. "All set?"

Miles looked up. "All set for what?" he snarled.

"Didn't Craig tell you?" He paused, as if expecting Miles to become personable but Miles simply stared up at him. "You're going with me to McArthur Park." He turned to complain to Craig for not informing Miles, but the tall man was already lost in the crowd. Singling out Roy holding a cup and laughing uproariously over another apparent joke, Sal considered complaining about the communication gap—the present incident an example, but Roy's blaring radio interfered. The Chief kept laughing for several seconds before answering it and Sal changed his mind.

"He ain't tol' me nathin'," Miles spat and looked away.

Studying Miles' scrubby, black hair, Sal waited for him to ask questions, but Miles remained fixated. "Is it okay if I dump my tools in your truck?" Sal asked friendlily. "We have to use your truck because mine broke down."

"I'm drivin'," Miles insisted without regarding Sal.

"Whatever," he returned and decided to punish such outrageous obnoxiousness. "Does it have any gas?"

"Yeah, she's got gas," Miles sneered.

She's? The truck's a she? It's going to be one of these days, Sal warned. Try not to let that happen, his better sense advised. "Okay, let's go," he urged enthusiastically.

Though Miles finally glanced at him while rising, he sulked.

Sal followed Miles' bobbing frame outside. Both entered Miles' truck. But unlike with the witty Skip, conversation was skimpy. Throughout the trip, Miles shrugged or didn't answer Sal's comments about operations, the flood, and related matters. Picturing Miles tinkering with his trains, Sal wondered how such men communicated with their wives, if at all. Maybe they don't and that's fine with both, he reasoned and they reached McArthur Park minutes later.

"Pull up by that second trailer over there," Sal mentioned casually and pointed.

"How come?" Miles disagreed, surprising Sal.

"That's where we left off yesterday," he explained simply. "Looks like the contractor just finished blocking that trailer. Not here, the next one."

Exhaling derisively, Miles motored ahead almost begrudgingly.

Geezus, man, driving an extra ten feet is no big deal, Sal concealed. Stepping out with his clipboard, radio, and flashlight, Sal observed Miles pouring coffee into his cup from his thermos. Oh, for God's sake. Sal eyed Miles staring ahead indifferently. And *he* was the one complaining about not doing anything, Sal sneered. About to suggest that they meet inside the trailer as soon as possible, he sensed that Miles was purposely ignoring him. Exiting, he headed for the yoke alone. Struggling to suppress his irritation, he copied down the serial number and then the manufacturer's name displayed near the door. He inspected the windows, outside metal, and the blocking. Expecting Miles any minute, he stepped inside to inspect further. He opened the cabinet door under the kitchen sink, turned on the water, and appreciated that nothing leaked. He slipped his flashlight back into his pocket, grabbed his clipboard and radio, and headed for the bathroom.

The water pipes weren't leaking, either. But he knew that one of them had to drain a full sink of water and flush simultaneously while the other checked the outside sewer pipe for leaks. So, where the hell is he? he grumbled, stepping outside. Tolerance, he warned, observing the empty truck. Oh, for God's sake, he smirked, spotting him crouched before a reclined worker tightening a large nut on a black plastic pipe under a trailer.

Sal sauntered over. "Need you to check the sewer pipe for leaks," he nevertheless reminded him cheerfully, realizing it was better to be hypocritically kind than sincerely mean. "When I fill the sink with water, unplug it, and flush the toilet," he delivered slowly. "Okay?"

Miles ignored him.

Impatient with the mundane, Sal had limited tolerance for the rude and the obnoxious and struggled to control himself. "As soon as possible," he forced himself to add cordially.

"They got a leak right here, goddamn it," Miles disagreed without taking his eyes off the fitting.

"*He* can handle that."

"How do you know?" Miles seemed to address a nearby stone.

"I don't. But that's the contractor's job, not ours."

The man glanced up at Sal holding his clipboard containing inspection sheets.

Miles spat. "Ain't it our job to help whenever possible?"

"You got that straight, but we need to do other things. I need you back at the trailer. You've got to check the sewer pipe for leaks while I fill the sink with water, unplug it, and flush the toilet," he repeated as slowly as before.

Miles glanced up at him without answering.

"We're not even up to this trailer yet. He'll have that fixed by the time we inspect it."

"What's the difference where we start, hah?"

Sal frowned. "I like to inspect trailers, one after the other up the line, if possible. It's easier and logical." Occasionally suffering from self-doubt and insecurity, especially in the face of others' defiance or disagreement with what he deemed obviously logical, he fell silent. Besides, Miles was ignoring him again. "Do you need him?"

Adjusting his pipe wrench, the man rechecked Sal. "Hah? No."

"Okay, let's go," Sal ordered Miles with finality and walked away. Consuming ten yards, he turned back and appreciated that Miles had risen, although slowly.

Miles followed him lethargically, jerked his head away self-consciously when their eyes met, and they reached the trailer.

"I'll fill the skink with water, unplug it, and flush the toilet at the same time, and you'll check the sewer pipe," Sal repeated still again near the cinderblock steps and awaited Miles' response.

"*I'll* take care of the sink and *you* do the goddamn pipe," Miles disagreed as if Sal had given him the harder job.

Talk about a child. "Be my guest," Sal obliged, stepped aside to allow him to ascend the steps and enter the trailer, and left. Walking around to the back, he located the sewer pipe exposed in an open trench some distance from the screened bathroom window. Crouching, he eyed the partly-opened bathroom window. "Okay, plug the sink, fill it with water, then let me know when you unplug it and flush the toilet at the same time," he deliberately explained carefully. "Understand?"

"Keep your shirt on," Miles barked from the bathroom and nothing happened for five minutes.

"Let me know when you flush," he called out, staring down at the pipe. "Did you flush and pull the plug? You have to let me know," he requested amiably. We're wasting time, he realized and rose. Walking to the window, he had trouble discerning Miles through the screen. Where the hell is he? Offer the child something, he suggested, almost breaking up. "The sooner we check these trailers, the quicker we can relax," he shouted inside.

"How the hell can I fill the sink if I'm taking a shit, goddamn it?" Miles exploded.

Sal exhaled, shook his head in disbelief, and saw red. "How the hell am I supposed to know you're taking a shit if you don't tell me?" Shit face, he withheld. "Why couldn't you go later?" Ugh, he winced, picturing finding a leak in the pipe *after* Miles flushed. "Why couldn't he fill the sink anyway? Sal also realized. Because he isn't too bright, he answered.

Waiting for him to the flush, Sal tightened a loose hexagon screw with his special screwdriver. Discerning splashing water, he assumed he never heard the flush and rushed to examine the sewer pipe. Crouching, he checked the fittings, but none leaked. Thank God, he sighed relievingly and trotted back to the window. "Nothing's leaking," he shouted inside. "Did you just flush the toilet and drain the sink at the same time?" he repeated in order to be doubly sure, deliberately avoiding the word *simultaneously.*

"I ain't even filled the sink yet, ya jerk. I just washed my hands."

Oh, God, Sal groaned, looking away. Now I'm a jerk. "Why the hell didn't you plug the sink while you were washing your hands, then pull it out when you flushed?" he told the window.

"Because I didn't fill it, goddamn it."

Hell of an answer. He watched Miles' hands lift the window higher, and his skull-like shadow appeared against the bathroom screen.

"You wanna run the goddamn show? Go ahead."

Oh, for God's sake, Sal bemoaned. He strode to the front and entered the trailer. He hurried along the narrow hallway and halted in the bathroom doorway. "What the hell are you doing?" he demanded angrily, observing Miles watching water splashing away full blast. "You need to plug the sink." Dummy, he suppressed.

Miles stared at the water without responding and Sal controlled an urge to shake him up. "Plug the sink first," he repeated still again. The guy's playing. A grown man. Or he doesn't understand, or, or– Breaking off impatiently, he stepped inside, plugged the sink angrily, and shut down the tap. "Now, I'm going outside to check the pipe. You need to unplug the sink and flush at exactly the same time. But you have to let me know, get it? Shout as soon as you do that, okay?"

Miles seemed captivated with the water and didn't answer.

"And what's this *jerk* crap?"

"You take care of your goddamn job. I'll take care of mine," Miles lashed out without turning.

"What the hell's that supposed to mean?" God, this is stupid.

"Go do your job, goddamn it and I'll do mine."

"I can't do my job without your cooperation!" Sal fumed.

Glancing back, Miles flashed indignation. "Just don't goddamn order me around."

"Nobody's ordering you goddamn around. We're supposed to work together, release trailers and not watch other men work. What the hell's wrong with you?"

Miles looked back. "Is that right?"

"Yeah, that's right. We're supposed to communicate," he emphasized. Probably doesn't even know what the word means. "That's how Skip and I released half the trailers here."

"Oh, bully for you. A, you wanna check the goddamn sewer pipe now? Or waste time bull-shittin'?"

"Listen, wise guy," Sal snarled. "I'm going outside. But you keep jerking my chain and I'll shove you inside the medicine cabinet, get it? he asked and left.

Crouching before the sewer pipe again, he signaled for the simultaneous flush and release of the sink plug.

"Leakin' any?" Miles shouted out the bathroom window.

I should play his silly game and not answer. "Did you pull out the plug and flush at the same time."

"Yeah, yeah, yeah. How about tellin' me if there was any leaks, so I don't have to wait all day, hah?"

Why? You can't tolerate your own stink? "Okay, no leaks. How's that? Okay with you?"

Miles fell silent, and Sal checked the appropriate box on his inspection sheet.

"You wanna be the goddamn boss, go ahead," Miles growled again but conciliatorily.

This is much too dumb. Refusing to be further intimidated, he wrote down the date on his inspection sheet, signed below, and approached the window. "Nobody's the boss. We're working together," he tried to repeat pleasantly. He broke away and met Miles stepping outside the front door. "Let's check the next one," he urged almost friendlily. "You want in or out this time?"

"Don't make no goddamn difference to me," Miles retorted contradictorily.

Sal glanced at him. This guy's dangerous. "In, then." The less responsible job.

But the two were destined to squabble. Heading for another trailer later, Sal waited for him to stop talking to several electricians erecting a meter box. "Why waste time asking how much meter boxes cost?" he demanded after Miles finally broke away. Frowning, Sal shook his head, strode ahead, and Miles deliberately lagged behind, upsetting him.

Later they argued about how to install an outside light. Realizing Miles had psychological problems, Sal tried not to humiliate him. But when Miles insisted on wiring two wires incorrectly, Sal had no other choice but to reverse them, solving the problem.

"The goddamn wiring was screwed up," Miles nevertheless insisted afterwards.

No kidding, Sal concealed. What if he eliminated *goddamn* from his vocabulary? He'd probably become a mute, he answered. Later, a woman entered a trailer that they were inspecting and complained that her blower wasn't working.

Miles promised to check it and the woman left.

Sal looked up from his clipboard. "Do you know anything about blowers?"

"Are we supposed to be helpin' 'em or what?"

166

This guy's got a doorknob for a brain. "Not if you don't know anything about blowers. You might damage it further."

"Who says I don't know nothin' about blowers? You says, not me."

"I need you here." Goddamn it, he considered enunciating sarcastically but decided to spare him. "Tell the gas men about it. That's their job, not ours."

"I promised and I'm going."

Sal's head shook negatively twice. Seventy-eight guys attracting dust at the office, and I gotta get stuck with Deadwood City, he sneered and glared at him. "Go. I'm through arguing. If Craig radios, I'll tell him we can't inspect anymore trailers because you're checking a blower."

"Tell 'im, goddamn it," he barked and left in a huff.

Sal exhaled with frustration. Though he inspected the rest of the trailer and two more without Miles, curiosity began to gnaw at him. Stepping outdoors, he scrutinized several dozen trailers, wondering which one contained the annoying Miles. He trotted toward the gas and electric truck parked beside one. Entering the trailer, he hurried into the kitchen and greeted two men. One was watching the other lying on the floor on his side checking the stove that they had moved several inches from the wall.

"Did a HUD man ask you how to fix a blower?" Sal addressed the man on the floor.

About to bend a piece of copper tubing, the man looked up. "No."

The other man turned to Sal. "What's he wanna monkey with a blower for? Them's already set. Alls you gotta do is turn 'em on."

Sal agreed and revealed all.

"You guys ain't supposed to monkey with blowers," the reclined man seconded indignantly. "That's *our* job. Wouldn't touch one 'less I knowed what I was up to."

Sal shrugged. "Tried to tell him that but he's thick. Worse, he doesn't know a blower from a toilet bowl. Maybe one of you guys could check him out before he blows up the park."

Both men laughed.

The reclined man's head and tubing disappeared behind the stove. "Check it out, Paul. I'm okay for a while."

Sal and Paul left. Both eventually found Miles in a trailer, sitting on the kitchen floor before the burner. Sal greeted a young woman perched on a nearby chair holding a baby sucking a pacifier. Noticing screws, nuts, and other parts scattered on the floor beside Miles, Sal frowned.

Having already removed the front plate, Miles was fumbling with something inside the blower.

"I smell gas," Sal announced and the woman rose fearfully.

"How's she commin'?" Paul nevertheless asked Miles cheerfully and the woman retreated to the doorway.

"Oooooo, gettin' there," Miles replied nonchalantly.

Sal pictured lying in bed in the hospital reading about barely surviving an explosion. Miles 'll have it beyond repair in a minute, ma'am, he suppressed, folded his arms, and joined her.

Paul crouched beside Miles. "Did you turn off the gas first?"

What for? Gas don't explode, Sal mimicked inwardly.

Unscrewing a nut, Miles gave Paul the silent treatment, and Sal had difficulty controlling a sarcastic laugh.

"Better turn off the gas," Paul persisted, pointed to something inside the stove, and the woman hurried into the living room with the baby.

Despite eyeing Paul's finger, Miles continued tightening the same nut.

"Wouldn't touch that if I was you," Paul cautioned.

Sal noted Miles' protruding tongue. HO-gauge would.

Miles tapped a screw. "Don't that regulate the gas?"

Sal struggled against shaking his head.

Why fuss with it if you ain't sure, Franklyn?

Paul laughed politely. "No, this one is, here." He pointed to it with his screwdriver and turned it off.

Thank God, Sal announced relievedly.

"Thought it was one of 'em," Miles confessed almost sheepishly, and an odd chortle stumbled out of his bleak face.

"Better put all this back and see what we got," Paul told Miles, eyeing the parts on the floor. Reaching inside the stove, Paul started finger-turning a screw.

Always put your blocks away after you finish playing with them, Sal directed at Miles.

Paul finished tightening it and tapped a plate with his screwdriver. "Never take this off. If anything ever goes wrong, it happens here," he explained, tinkling another area. "These burners are new and–" he attempted, but noticing Miles extending his screwdriver inside the stove as if he were about to stir a pot of stew, Paul broke off worriedly. "That's okay. I'll take care of the rest of it."

Miles began clanking a piece of metal with his screwdriver. "What's this here?"

Satisfied that Miles' screwdriver was behaving, Paul finger-tightened two more screws and reinserted the remaining parts. The blower had only needed minor adjustment, he told Sal and particularly Miles and all left.

Once outside, the twosome headed for the next trailer where they left off, and Sal calmly conveyed to Miles not to try fixing burners. "I need your help," he deliberately patronized him in order to avoid offending him unnecessarily.

"How else can you learn about blowers?" Miles persisted.

"By working for a burner company or going to school," Sal suggested almost kindly and Miles fell silent. "You shouldn't fool around with anybody's burner. And with a woman and a baby–"

"I wasn't *foolin'* around, goddamn it."

"That's what scares me. Gas explodes for God's sake. It's probably more dangerous than electricity. You wasted over an hour in there," he scolded, and noticed a woman approaching them.

She described a leak in a small outside pipe. "It don't bother nothin' in the trailer. But I thought you should know. Number eighteen."

Sal thanked her as if she were doing *him* a favor, promised they would check it, and she left. "We'll take the truck to save time," he told Miles and appreciated that he was following him toward the truck, despite his smirk. Sal hopped inside on the driver's side, but Miles refused to enter. Now what?. "I need the keys."

"*I'll* drive," Miles announced.

Sal shrugged. "I'm here now. It's no big deal."

"It's my truck."

God, what a child. "Not really. It's HUD's. They don't mind who drives."

Miles sulked.

"Okay, if driving a hundred feet turns you on," Sal consented and exited.

Entering, Miles stayed put. "You're such a goddamn big shot, *you* check it out."

I don't believe this, Sal kept hidden, eying him staring ahead. "You're kidding. *You're* the maintenance man."

"Not accordin' to you. Accordin' to you, I can't do nathin' right."

God, what I've got to tolerate in and out of school. About to open the back door for his tools, he suddenly realized that they were still in Skip's truck. Damn, he cried. Now I have to ask Mr. Charming for his. "Is it okay if I borrow your tools?" he attempted nonchalantly.

Miles folded his arms indignantly and slouched.

"Is it okay if–"

"Go ahead. *You're* the boss," Miles barked.

Tolerance, Sal reminded himself again and left with the tools. Walking around to the back of her trailer, he spotted water squirting from a copper fitting under the trailer and crouched for a closer look. Realizing that the fitting had been sawed and needed to be un-soldered and replaced, he noticed the same two small boys playing in the dirt with the hacksaw. Sal told the woman that *they* might have been responsible, and she promised not to have them play there again. "It might be a good idea take away the hacksaw," he also ventured and she agreed, although reluctantly, as if it were none of his business, he sensed.

Sal grabbed the propane torch and solder from the truck, but couldn't find the right fitting. Looking up, he eyed Miles talking to a middle-aged man standing before a ranch house across the street from the park. Spotting the keys in the ignition, Sal considered speeding off to buy the fitting at Mathews and Loomis rather than ask Miles to drive him there, but noticed the man gesturing at him.

"Hey," the man called.

Sal approached. Now what?

"Maybe you know," the man addressed him and Miles headed back toward the truck.

Where's Mr. Technician going, now? He needs more coffee?

"You look like the boss," the man resumed. "He says you are, anyway," he added, nodding at Miles entering the truck. "What about them trailers?" he whined angrily.

Sal surveyed several long rows of them parked parallel to one another. "What about them?"

"I'm gonna look at them all summer?"

What's he talking about? Sal pondered, trying to evaluate them from the man's standpoint. "They look okay to me."

"How long 're they gonna stay there?" He pointed what Sal sensed was his sedate ranch facing the first row of trailers across the street. "Why me?"

Surprised, Sal glanced at his house and shrugged. "Why anybody? You're not the only house facing the row. You're lucky you weren't in the flood." Maybe God's testing all of us to see how kind we are or aren't towards one another, he reminded himself again.

"Oh, I'm lucky I wasn't in the flood," he sneered. "No way, Jose," he scoffed and shook his head.

"What do you mean no way? You want us to haul them back out?"

"Why should I take this bullshit? I rack my ass for years– Look at my place." He gestured at the well-landscaped evergreens, rhododendrons, and flowers surrounding the front of his house.

Sal eyed a slate walk that bisected the front lawn tastefully and a yellow-leaved dogwood alongside. "Very nice." I'd trade my house for yours any day. How people could be sensitive enough to love natural beauty and not have compassion for others, slays me. Just like my father, he recalled, studying a beautiful Japanese maple and a ginkgo standing like sentinels on the lush front lawn.

"Yeah, very nice," the man mimicked, and both glanced at Miles taking a sip of coffee while staring blankly ahead.

"Thanks. So? I'm gonna have this shit in front of me? Brats running across my lawn? And what about the noise? 'Very nice'," he says. Hey," he announced in a new tone that seemed to wrinkle his broad forehead. "I don't give a shit about the flood victims."

"So I gathered."

"So you gathered," he mocked. "So, what the hell 're you gonna do about it?"

"What the hell do you want me to do about it?" You selfish bastard, he concealed. "Thousands of people lost their homes and belongings and you're bitching about–"

"You twenty-thousand-a-year men 're all the same," he interrupted.

"Yeah, twenty thousand a year. Sure." I don't need this, Sal sneered and walked away.

"Wait a minute," the man called angrily. "You sit at your desk, make with them big plans. Why the hell didn't you stick this park somewhere else? Like up your ass?" he barked and laughed.

Sal whirled. "What the hell 'er you talking about?" he blew up. "Twenty thousand a year? Don't I wish. Would you believe seventy-two hundred a year as a teacher? This is a part-time summer job paying three eighteen an hour which I took because I can't make it during the regular year. Not with a wife and four kids. You probably rake in twice as much without a degree," he enunciated. "What're you, an electrician, plumber, sanitation worker? I've got to teach kids not to lie, cheat, steal, and interrupt me before I can even *think* about teaching them English. Kids who don't want to learn because they hate school, me, and this lousy, competitive, greedy world, mostly because parents like you don't teach them anything. All you're worried about is the buck and material things like your house, car, and boat," he mocked, noticing it sitting on a trailer in the backyard. "You don't teach them about values, decency. That's what life should be all about," he fumed almost incoherently. "Yeah, frown. You don't understand, right? Nobody understands. I've got to get them to like me before I can convince them to read and write, which most of them can't do. I've got to be their father because parents like you don't teach 'em *not* to be mercenary, apathetic, and think only about partying and having sex. Drawing marijuana plants on their arms, books, and desk," he sneered. "Parents like you aren't teaching them to avoid drugs, much less that we shouldn't be killing one another off in this stupid war. Parents aren't teaching kids to be loving because the military keeps advertising on television and in the newspapers that they should sign up so they can fight and die to stop the threat of Communism. All bullshit," he stormed and broke away.

171

"Wait a minute. What's your hurry? You look like a Jew. Are you a Jew?"

Oh, now comes the anti-Semitism bit. Pausing, he turned back. "Why, what do Jews look like?" he growled. I'm going to hit this bastard, so help me, flashed a thought. Which wouldn't accomplish anything, he knew.

"Hey, you're funny, know that?"

"Yeah, I'm funny, just like you."

"Use your influence. Get them to move all this shit the hell outta here."

Is this guy for real? "*They* haul in trailers, block 'em, lay water and sewer pipe, put up poles and meter boxes, and you want them to pull out? They're for the victims."

"Yeah, I don't give a shit about them."

"I know. You told me. Stop bragging."

"I'm worried about me," the man barked, pointing to himself.

"No kidding? That's another major problem–selfishness, and it's worldwide. Capitalism teaches us to take, take, in a dog-eat-dog world. Never give, hell no. Giving contradicts business. No wonder the idealistic youth is rebelling against the establishment."

"What about the value of my house?"

"Didn't you hear what I just said, for Krist sake? Or am I talking to myself. Why, you're planning to sell it?"

"Not now, but suppose I want to next year? With this shit in front?" He nodding at the trailers. "That's what the house 'll be worth–shit."

"Did you ever do anything for anybody without getting paid for it?" Sal flung.

The man stared perplexedly at him.

He doesn't even know what I'm talking about. You're wasting your time, his other self interceded. "Those trailers will probably be gone in less than a year."

"Famous last words. How the hell do you know? How the hell does anybody know?"

"So, they'll assess your house for less and you'll pay less taxes."

"Oh, smart guy. Thanks."

"That's not much to ask considering–"

"And how come this trailer, this one goddamn trailer," he emphasized, referring to the one directly across from his house, "has to be parked so close to the curb across the street? It's practically on top of my house. Look at the next one." He nodded at it staggered in the next row.

"You're not putting yourself in *our* position. That was the only way to utilize as much space as possible. Can't you see that?"

"Yeah? But why start here with this one in front of my house?"

Selfishness is blinding your meager ability to see clearly, Mister. "Use your influence."

Sal regarded the man. "What influence?" he replied with disbelief. "I told you before—"

"That says 'inspector,'" he interrupted again, pointing to Sal's tag.

All isn't always what it appears, man, Sal concealed. "Yeah, but it's meaningless. You can buy these at K-mart."

"I seen you make with the radio. Go ahead. Make with the radio."

Sal shook his head. "Mister, I don't believe you."

"The name's Barry, Barry Perrano," he introduced, extended his hand and Sal regretted shaking it reflexively. "I phoned City Hall I don't know how many times," he emphasized but quieter and almost friendlily.

"Really," Sal responded. You think shaking hands makes us buddies? You're an asshole. Meaning, you've got a lot to learn.

"I even got up a petition. Those bastards won't even listen to reason."

This is too much. "I gotta go," he declared and walked off in disgust. Noticing Miles slouched with closed eyes inside the truck, he was in no mood to deal with him. He borrowed a fitting from a contractor, repaired the leak, and walked away when Craig pulled up driving a large truck filled with four-riser steps.

"We gotta replace all the steps. They're too low," he announced from the driver's seat.

Another real beaut. "You've *got* to be kidding."

"Not really."

"Who the hell made that stupid mistake? Didn't anybody measure how high they had to be? We have to waste time unloading these and loading the others. Geezus, I don't believe this."

Craig tapped the side of the truck impatiently. "What can I tell ya," he responded almost sympathetically, spying Miles heading toward them.

"Wait a minute. Wait a minute," Sal protested. "What do you mean *we*? What about all the deadwood socializing back at the hotel?"

"What?"

"Why didn't you bring along some helpers?"

"I just picked up these risers from a local lumber yard. I didn't wanna waste the time."

"What about how much time *we're* going to waste unloading and loading, just the three of us?"

"What can an I tell ya, man," he repeated, exiting.

"Why don't you just drive back to the office and pick up some of that driftwood."

"Ah, there was no sense. We'll have it done by then."

"I'll drive back with Miles' truck. We can fit three guys–" he attempted, but Craig started unloading hurriedly, and Sal broke off. What's the use. "Hold it a minute."

Pulling a riser to the ground, Craig looked up.

"Before we start knocking ourselves out, how about telling Miles what his job is?"

Craig turned to the teacher with the slim waist, and grinned. "What do you mean?"

Miles arrived and Sal revealed everything, including Barry's complaint.

Mostly laughing throughout, because of Sal's flippancy, Craig studied Miles. "You're not supposed to touch burners," he told him. "In fact Sal *is* over you," he agreed, despite several goddamns from Miles. "You're supposed to work together," he added throughout Miles' objections, and Sal exhaled relievedly. "Sal can't inspect nothin' 'til both of you fix all the problems. Stick close to Sal and don't do anything on your own, copy?"

"Miles grumbled incoherently.

What's HUD going to do with all those short steps? Sal wondered watching Craig drive away with them after they finished loading them.

Returning to the office, Sal broke away from Miles and approached Craig sipping coffee near the percolator. "That's it. Pair 'skull-face' with somebody else. The guy's nowhere, a total dud."

Craig burst out laughing. "That's why *you* 've got 'im. Nobody wants to work near him. Norm said he'd quit if he had to again. Even Dinger can't stand him."

"So, why me?"

"Because you're a nice guy."

"Thanks," Sal replied with a grin. "So, why are the good always punished?" And why do bastards get respect? Although not from the good, he reminded himself.

Craig laughed still again. "McArthur Park's almost done?"

Sal nodded. "Maybe in a couple more days."

"Stick it out with him," he encouraged congenially which always swayed Sal. "Then I'll switch you to Skycrest. They're spotting trailers there now. Water and electric should be in by then. Most of the guys 'll be there. It's a large park. Sixty pads."

"Good. Where will you be sending Miles then?"

"There, with you guys," Craig chirped.

Sal made a face and the handsome Craig guffawed. "Don't worry. He'll be lost with so many of you guys there."

"Good. If he never finds himself, it'll be too soon."

Craig laughed again.

Chapter 16

Capitalizing on his almost unlimited energy, the wiry Sal accomplished considerable work at McArthur Park, despite Miles' sluggishness and obstinacy. Craig sent Skip and Lyman to help them and they finished the park late that evening. Sal and Lyman entered the office, added themselves to the others lining up to sign out, and Doris screeched that Lyman had been promoted to a G-7, surprising him.

Since few knew how hard Lyman had worked on his own or cared, Sal attributed his raise to the usual white appeasement, especially since Lyman had been the only flood victim to receive a four-bedroom trailer. "Good for you," he congratulated sincerely. "You deserve it."

"You and Skip should get raises too, man. You guys took care of McArthur Park by yourselves," Lyman reciprocated kindly amid the noise.

"Thanks. But I'm not holding my breath."

"Maybe you should try working inside, man."

Sensing its advantages and having even considered it, Sal pictured Doris and winced, particularly because he despised paperwork. "Yeah, but doing what?"

"The office is a zoo, man. They could probably find something for you to do, maybe even give you a title."

Titles are neat, Sal sneered sarcastically, recalling the many worthless administrative positions in education.

"The government's forever makin' up new jobs for folks. Administrative coordinator or somethin', man. How about office consolidator?"

Sal burst out laughing.

"Maybe you could straighten out the paperwork," Lyman continued "Rota and Doris sure can't."

Maybe they could give me a back room, Sal evaluated, eventually signed out, and drove home.

The next morning, Craig announced in the living room that because many trailers had arrived overnight, he planned to break in more inspectors including the four teachers.

Congratulations! Sal announced sarcastically, standing alongside the others in the middle of the room. So, we're finally going to use the deadbeats almost two months after the disaster. But why break up a good blocking crew? Why change the lineup if they're scoring runs? Another explosion of unadulterated stupidity.

Craig ordered Sal and Norm to inspect as many trailers as possible at Skycrest. He told Skip and Lyman to correct several minor problems at Edgewood, and ordered Miles and Dinger to deliver two sets of steps to a family set up in a small, distant trailer park.

Sal appreciated distancing from both of them. Thank God, he controlled from uttering.

"We'll find it," Miles assured Craig after receiving scant directions, and the dangerous duo bolted out the door without bothering to ask for the address.

They'll take care of them for the day, Sal concluded with a laugh.

Craig caught them before they drove past Happy (sleeping in his Barracuda following a hangover the previous night), and gave them the address.

Reaching Skycrest with Norm, Sal parked between two rows of six trailers that a contractor and his crew had blocked. The first trailer passed inspection but they needed a different key to activate the water. Lacking it, they drove to the Water Board. Much to their astonishment, the water company refused to open earlier than 9:00, "flood or no flood," the Board's spokesman told them, stunning Sal, and they returned in order to inspect everything else except the water.

Though the first three trailers checked out fine, the fourth was completely empty, lacking furniture and beds–even the usual stove and refrigerator, plus the kitchen table and chairs. Recalling strollers examining unlocked trailers at McArthur Park, Sal suspected foul play and radioed Craig.

"You're kidding," he mistakenly transmitted back. Hurriedly correcting himself, he requested the trailer's number and its exact position.

Sal asked if the trailer had been fully equipped before leaving the Fairgrounds.

"Affirmative," Craig radioed back.

Sal had advised Craig to have a HUD employee sleep overnight as a guard in a trailer in each park. "Money well spent, instead of paying deadbeats to hang around doing nothing," he had added, nodding at the hippie-looking contingent still struggling to figure out if Sal were "cool" or part of the hard-nosed establishment.

"I'll mention it to Roy," Craig had responded.

Meaning that'll be the end of that, Sal sensed. "Of course you might have to worry about some of these guys," he had insinuated beyond their hearing.

Craig had looked back. "What do you mean?"

"Stealing has been rampant since the Sixties. Where've you been? Teachers can't even leave a ballpoint unattended on a desk without it disappearing," he had reminded him and Craig laughed.

176

Removing his handkerchief in the present, Sal picked up an orange and yellow capsule he noticed on the kitchen floor. You're a modern day Sherlock Holmes, he labeled himself with a laugh, then had second thoughts. That's for the police to discover, he reasoned innocently, dropping it back in the same place after examining it briefly.

Apparently comprehending the incident's potential for sensationalism, Craig radioed back and bubbled with repetitious, redundant questions which Sal answered patiently at first. But when more followed, including "What's your 10-20?" Sal had had it. Stepping outside for better reception, he squeezed the lever. "This is unit thirty," he transmitted as Norm approached in order to listen. "I'm at Skycrest, standing on the top step of a cinderblock that's two feet too low," he insinuated.

Norm smiled meaningfully. "Nice."

"I'm about twenty-six inches outside trailer number four, looking at one Norman Meriwether who's about fifty inches away, but I haven't measured the distance." He glanced up at several cumulus clouds on a magnificent, sunny day. "We're both approximately ninety-three million miles from one hot sun. Oh-va."

"Break, break. This is base relay. Cut the unnecessary chatter," the voice ordered during Sal's snickering, and Norm laughed.

Rarely catching Sal's facetiousness, Craig thanked him for the details and signed out.

Oh, no. Here comes Big Chief Redundancy himself, Sal labeled, noticing the blue Chevy bobbing to a halt in the dirt road ten minutes later.

His eyes looming an odd green because of his sunglasses, Roy exited. Having apparently heard everything over his radio, he approached the duo. "This ah gots to see."

What's to see? No furniture means nothingness, emptiness, man, Sal commented, following Roy and Norm inside. Times a 'wastin', man, he dramatized. Just call the police.

Roy surveyed the vacant living room like a cowboy version of Dr. Watson.

Don't point out the capsule, Sal warned, eyeing it nearby. He might be a druggy and save it for himself.

Roy placed hands on his waist and checked the walls, even the ceiling.

The furniture ain't up there, Chief. Neither is the thief, Sal reflected.

"Damn," Roy complained as if *he* had been robbed. "Nobody seed nothin' from them houses across the street?"

We seed in spring up north, man. "Didn't ask them. Maybe we should call the police," Sal hinted.

"Whoever it was, done thorough work," Norm offered.

The three continued into the living room and Roy turned to Norm as if he were surprised to see him.

Sal gazed at the slightly brighter floor tiles where the refrigerator had been, noted a second capsule near a dust wad beside the wall and almost panicked. If Roy sees that, we'll be here forever, he warned and looked away. That's *also* for the police to find, he told himself, and Roy's dallying annoyed him further. Sal offered to fill out a report at the police station and deliberately veered toward the front door.

Roy agreed, pleasing Sal, and all stepped outside. Sal followed Roy to his car. Sliding inside, Roy rolled down his window as if he were a priest about to hear Sal's confession.

Sal tilted his head as if to oblige, but Roy stared ahead and fell silent. That's it? You ain't got nothing to say, no input about a major theft? You got it, he answered and started elaborating about developments at McArthur Park. About to place his hands on the car, he remembered Jill and jumped away, suppressing a laugh. Though Roy had been nodding throughout Sal's dissertation about their accomplishments, nothing was getting through, Sal noticed, fell silent, and a long pause ensued.

Sleeping already? With eyes open? Hello. Anybody home? he cried, struggling to prevent laughing again. Pulling himself together during more silence, he casually asked if he could work in the office. "I could probably organize the paperwork," he ventured, studying Roy's rigid profile.

Another pause followed.

I'm finished talking. Your turn, man.

"How 're you with paperwork?" tumbled from the small mouth.

"Good," he nevertheless answered. Anything's better than tolerating so much bungling, even Doris, he assumed. The turkey's toying with the idea, he surmised accurately. Paperwork moves me, he teased. Crumpling rowdies' cheat notes is my forte. Majored in rewriting at college, he reflected, recalling how many rough drafts he wrote before handing in the finished product.

"How'd ya like tryin' ta straighten out the mess in the office?"

Didn't I just ask that? Sal questioned, squelching still another potential laugh with a grin and finally became serious. "But I'd have to be completely in charge," he announced. Do it my way. Like the song.

Roy fell silent.

Maybe I sounded too anxious and intimidating.

"I'm puttin' you in for a G-5," Roy suddenly announced, catching Sal off guard.

Sal's better sense warned him not to trust someone so unreliable, nor would he tell Trudi. Sounds too much like "I'm taking you to lunch," he reasoned.

"Got it wrote down inside, right here" Roy declared, tapping a file folder on the dashboard, attracting Sal's hazel eyes.

Really? Because good things don't come my way that easily and simply, he reminded himself somewhat cynically. Maybe it's written on some form. Wish I could see it, crossed his mind. "Thanks. Appreciate it, but what about Skip and Norm?"

"What about 'em?" Roy asked.

"They deserve raises too."

"Them too," Roy agreed but too quickly, Sal noticed. "Matter of fact, I'm headin' for the Rand ta handle that raght now."

Desperately wanted to believe him, Sal wished him luck, and Roy departed. Deciding to take action about the burglary, he drove to the police station with Norm. He revealed everything to the clerk who copied down the information, including the trailer's name, number, and Skycrest's location.

"You're gonna have to see Detective Gallagher or give 'im a call after two o'clock," the clerk barked officially.

Sal thanked him and returned to Skycrest with Norm. "Maybe the company sent that empty trailer by mistake. Or everything can be accounted for somehow," he told Norm, who agreed. But since thievery was widespread, they decided to check for witnesses before telephoning the company and knocked on the door across the street.

An elderly couple answered. They had noticed a truck beside the trailer but assumed people were moving in. Worried about a possible robbery so nearby, they started questioning them about it. Assuming he was overstepping himself, Sal answered guardedly and both men left. Sal telephoned the police station after two, but Gallagher wasn't in. A different officer offered to take the message which Sal repeated, and the officer told him to call back later. He did at five. Gallagher still wasn't in. Another officer asked if he could help. Sal revealed all, and was told to call back at six, did, but Gallagher still wasn't in.

"Can you describe exactly what happened?" a different officer asked.

Oh, for God's sake. Don't these guys write anything down or communicate with one another? No wonder people don't want to get involved. Hanging up, he finally reached Gallagher shortly after seven.

"Exactly what happened?" Gallagher inquired.

Sal almost guffawed. What 're you, a HUD worker in disguise? Or is the whole world like this? he evaluated incredulously and repeated himself still again.

Gallagher thanked him. "Could you meet me at that trailer tomorrow morning at ten sharp?"

Why? You're going to be there? he teased at first. Why should thievery go unpunished? "Definitely," he replied firmly.

"What's the exact address?"

I gave it to you, ran a thought, but he complied.

Shortly after signing in the next morning, Sal and Norm drove to Mathews and Loomis. Sal charged HUD for the fitting the contractor had given him, returned to Skycrest and the man was surprised when he gave it to him. Isn't that what we should do in the world? Sal reflected proudly and inspected trailers with Norm before leaving to meet Gallagher. He arrived before ten but Gallagher didn't show, nor at eleven or twelve. Meeting the other HUD workers for lunch in one of the trailers, Sal was so annoyed that he couldn't help revealing all.

"Maybe he's on a hot case," Skip defended inside the living room. "Heard two guys got nailed for leaning against a tree in Elmira last night."

Sitting near Skip, Norm un-bagged his thermos, unscrewed the cup, and laughed.

"Far out."

Sal shook his head before biting his ham sandwich.

"Sal's told the story so often, he's got it memorized," Norm contributed. "Should've taped it so you could play it every time you phoned them."

Sitting near the window, Lyman turned. "That wouldn't work. What if they'd ask questions?"

Skip looked over. "Hell, they've only asked one so far and that's 'What happened?' They've been giving Sal *their* recording ever since: 'Sorry, Gallagher ain't in.'"

Sal laughed with the others.

"Ah, maybe Gallagher works part-time or is on vacation," Norm conceded.

Skip flipped his hair in place. "Yeah, he's a druggy on the side." Several hairs slid down, and he snapped them back.

Chewing sounded so noisily during a lull that all turned to Dinger sitting across from Miles at the kitchen table. Aware of their eyes, Dinger tilted his head characteristically. "Somebody should call the police."

Cheers mixed with laughter and Dinger waited patiently for quiet.

"I ain't kiddin'" received even more and Dinger frowned at the laughing faces.

The men resumed talking with one another, and when Miles turned around to chase away a pesky fly, Dinger reached across, grabbed Miles' pickle and swallowed it whole.

Norm noticed. "How come you don't get fat?"

"He don't chew," Skip explained.

"Just swallows. Nothin' gets digested."

Norm squashed his brown lunch bag into a small ball. "Maybe we ought ta put Dinger on the case. We'd accomplish the same thing, nothin'."

Gallagher finally arrived at four in the afternoon. He located Sal inspecting a trailer further up the line and explained that he had been "tied up."

What can I say, Sal left unsaid and they entered the empty trailer.

Gallagher scrutinized the living room like Columbo, Sal mused. He's even got the right hunch. But where's the raincoat? he threw in with a laugh.

Gallagher turned to Sal. "Can you describe exactly what happened?"

You've *got* to be kidding, Sal objected but complied. Nice going, Columbo, he praised, pretending not to notice him picking up and analyzing the second capsule. But what about fingerprints? You just smudged them. What would Perry Mason say?

"Looks like a pep pill," Gallagher commented and slipped it into his pocket.

Take it with a glass of water and call me in the morning, Sal's inner self responded with a laugh.

Ambling down the hall, the detective glanced inside one empty bedroom after another. He repeated the desk clerk's questions and promised to have a police car patrol the park at night. He also inquired if the front had been locked, as he had several times before.

Sal replied affirmatively but the redundancy and incompetence was becoming unbearable, especially when the detective checked the ceiling also. "Obviously the stuff has been stolen," he announced almost angrily.

Caught off balance, Gallagher lowered his head, regarded the astute face behind gold-rimmed glasses, and nodded. "That's true."

Who's the detective here, you or I? Sal contested and both stepped outside.

"If you get any more complaints, let me know," Gallagher uttered carelessly.

Sal almost broke up. That's the wrong case, Jack. This was a robbery, man, not a complaint. "Okay," he nevertheless replied and Gallagher headed toward his car. "Aren't you going to check the people across the street?" Sal called, purposely excluding *even* for fear of embarrassing him.

"Oh, yeah," Gallagher agreed, again as if he suddenly remembered.

Oh, for God's sake. Maybe Dinger *should* handle this case, Sal jeered to himself and joined Norm waiting nearby.

Chapter 17

Shortly after the men signed in at eight the next morning, Roy ordered all maintenance men and inspectors–that is, the loungers–to the trailer parks.

Well, what do you know about that? Maybe he just learned about the disaster, Sal scorned.

Somewhat curious that Roy had ordered them there or perhaps welcoming a relief from so much loafing, the men piled into the panel trucks and even their own cars, undoubtedly a first, Sal reflected. Such numbers overwhelmed the blocking contractors who soon had trouble readying trailers fast enough for so many men.

Why in God's name didn't Roy do this before? Sal demanded, although, entering the living room where the large group had gathered for lunch, he encountered the same party-like atmosphere. Looks like all they did was change living rooms. Talk about absurdity. He stepped over several hippie-like bodies reclining with hands behind their heads on the floor and chairs. At least I don't smell pot, he thought thankfully. *Yet,* he added. Finding an opening, he slid his back down the paneling as if he were a little off the wall himself, and sat on the floor near Lyman leaning against the same wall.

Lyman yawned. "Ever have a job where you could sleep and shower on company time?"

"Yeah. I was in the military," Sal commented and several men grinned.

A knock sounded at the front door.

"Come in," Skip invited, elbowed to the floor nearby, and the door opened.

The upper torso of a middle-aged woman appeared. Apparently standing on the low cinder-block steps, she loomed surreal, like a midget or a puppet on strings, Sal imagined curiously. Ignoring the many long-haired men eyeing her inquisitively, she began surveying the combined living room and kitchen unconcernedly. "Oh, Susan, take a look at this. It's beautiful," she called and Susan arrived.

Eyeing Skip and the loungers briefly, she scrutinized the rooms. "Oh, my, Estelle. It's amazing what they're doing today."

"We just want to get an idea," Estelle apologized to Skip without regarding him.

But Skip and Sal had been complaining about similar onlookers all morning, several having even sneaked inside a trailer while both were struggling to start an inoperable refrigerator.

"Are you flood victims?" Skip demanded.

Talking faded into silence.

Looking deeper inside, Susan regarded the kitchen. "No, but we've never been inside one of these. Can we take a look?"

"You're already looking," commented a lounger quietly.

"No problem, ma'am," Skip answered. "We got a special man ta show ya around. Dinger," he beckoned.

Several unkempt heads turned, following the women's line of vision.

"Really?" Estelle asked.

A third face appeared beside Sue's.

"Oh, that's unnecessary," Estelle insisted, re-scanning the rooms.

Skip flipped his hair back neatly, and the toilet flushed down the hall. "Oh, I insist," he invited and they paused.

The bathroom door opened. Sluggish footsteps sounded. A figure arrived resembling a new version of Christ, save the hefty shoulders, tattered jeans, and thick glasses.

"What's up?" Dinger inquired.

"Nothin' much," the flippant Skip quipped almost boredly.

Guffawing tore loose and the group squelched them immediately.

Dinger took one look at the women and tilted up his head belligerently, as if he were allergic to any female resembling his mother.

Continued suppression became difficult. Norm pretended to remove fuzz from the rug. Lyman covered his mouth, and Sal kept staring at an outlet as if it were the *Mona Lisa* in miniature.

"Show these ladies around," Skip ordered Dinger politely, flicked his head at them, and flipped his unruly hair back.

Dinger regarded them again. "Around where?"

"Skycrest. Where else?" Skip inquired. "What's the problem, man? These women wanna check out trailers."

"But I thought–"

"Dinger, where 're your manners?"

Susan frowned suspiciously. "Never mind."

The faces disappeared. Skip kicked the door shut and laughter thrashed the walls savagely.

Chapter 18

F riday was the first payday. Though the pay-period only covered a few days for most men instead of the normal two weeks, the loungers arrived earlier than usual at the office and were in good spirits. But learning that the courier wouldn't be delivering their checks until ten o'clock, all left begrudgingly for various sites and more loafing.

Regrouped inside the same *Majestic* again, fast becoming a second office, Skip and the others decided to maneuver Miles and Dinger into returning to the office for one reason: wait for the checks to arrive and bring them back.

"Doris is so screwed up, she might even be dumb enough ta give 'em to you," Skip qualified.

But conveying the plan to the duo was difficult, especially about what excuse to give Roy, should he be there and somehow ask why they had returned.

"That'll never happen," Sal quietly confided to Skip standing nearby. "Why would he care about a couple of loungers hanging around. That never bothered him before."

Skip placed hands on hips. "Just make believe we ran out of inspection sheets and we sent ya back to get 'em," he reiterated to the duo loudly for the third time as the myriad faces—sporting long hair, beards, mustaches, cigarettes, and tattered work clothes—studied the two concernedly from every possible nook in the crowded room. "But you're really trying to get the checks, get it? Or at least find out if the courier brung them."

Dinger swept back his long hair as if he intended to enter a forbidden room, and he ogled Skip through his thick glasses. "What's a currier?" he mispronounced.

"Oh, man," Lyman protested, ushering in moans of indignation and annoyance. Clasping his neck, he leaned back on the couch.

"The guy that brings in all our paperwork and shit every morning," Skip shouted above the razzing. "Where 've you been?"

Talk about poor listening skills, Sal criticized, studying the duo from the end of the couch. They're not even paying attention.

Eyeing the sulking Miles standing beside Dinger spreading his hair again, he settled on his cousin. "I got it. You want us to get your check," he asked slowly and Miles sulked impatiently.

"Not just mine. Everybody's," Skip exploded. "They'll probably be in the manila envelope the courier drops off every morning," he reviewed exasperatedly. "If Doris don't give 'em ta ya, Rota might. But if she don't, ya might have to swipe it on your own, maybe when Doris or Rota ain't lookin' or one of 'em goes to the girlies' room."

Dinger parted his hair still again. "But what about inspection sheets? Don't we need 'em?"

The men groaned and complained even louder.

"It's a subterfuge," Sal ventured for a laugh.

Skip regarded Sal. "Geezus, man, you gotta be kiddin'. He'll never grab that."

"A what?" Dinger asked.

"You and Miles are really going to find out if the courier brought our paychecks," Sal simplified.

"We are?" Dinger replied.

"Oh, man," someone sighed.

Skip flipped his hair in place with increased frustration. "But you're *really* gonna try ta bring back the checks. That's all we need."

"Don't confuse him," Sal interceded.

"It's too late. He's been confused since birth. Ah, maybe it's hopeless," Skip conceded inaudibly to the duo and Sal shrugged.

"How else 'er we gonna get rid of 'em?" Lyman muttered.

"Let 'em go," Norm whispered to Skip. "The less they're here, the less chance a trailer's gonna explode."

Skip and several others agreed, and the duo finally left.

Several hours later during lunch time, stumbling sounded against the door.

"They're here," someone announced, silencing the conversing group and the door opened.

Miles boosted himself inside with his lunch box and thermos. Rising, he worked his way unceremoniously between the floor-loungers (eyeing him disbelievingly), headed for a kitchen chair, and sat, depositing both on the table.

"Is this guy for real?" Lyman inquired.

Hands on his waist and standing beside what resembled several beatniks, Skip glared at Miles. "Excuse me? Did ya get 'em?"

The stone face attached to an almost rigid body cleared his throat twice. Unscrewing his thermos cup, he clacked it back on the table and poured himself some coffee. "Dinger's got 'em," he managed with difficulty.

"All *right!*" someone exclaimed and cheering sounded.

Heads swung expectantly to the sound of approaching footsteps outside.

A chubby hand tossed a white lunch bag inside. Familiar-looking

186

mimeographed sheets followed. Two hands appeared to boost inside an odd body with an odd head containing streaming hair and thick glasses. The hands collected the white bag and sheets, and rose. Straightening, the body started angling unceremoniously between the men evaluating the sheets in Dinger's hand.

"What the hell?" Skip injected. "Where are you goin', Tarzan? Did ya get 'em?"

Heading for the table, Dinger paused. "No problem."

The men cheered again and Dinger handed the sheets to Skip.

"What's this shit?" he inquired incredulously.

Dinger brushed aside his hair. "Inspection sheets."

Laughter and complaints raged anew.

Skip underhanded the sheets to the floor in disgust and glanced at the ceiling in disbelief. "Not inspections sheets, dummy." He turned angrily to Miles munching away while staring ahead obliviously. "Miles, rest yer chops for a second, will ya? Where 're the checks?"

"What checks?"

Howling laughter battered the thin walls.

"Thought yuz wanted inspection sheets," Miles managed.

"Inspection sheets?" Skip remarked, slapped his head, and tossed back a trough of unruly hair. "The hell would we need them for?"

"The paychecks. We sent ya to get the paychecks," Lyman thundered amid laughter and moans of indignation.

"Tol' ya," Miles snorted at Dinger before taking another bite.

"Then how come ya sent us ta get inspection sheets?" Dinger asked lethargically.

"We didn't send ya ta get inspection sheets," Skip stormed. "The inspection sheets was just an excuse in case Roy asked ya why ya come back."

"Ooooooo," Dinger moaned, arriving at the table. "I was wonderin' why–"

"You didn't get the checks then?" Skip interrupted.

Dinger tossed his bag on the table and sat across from Miles. "No."

"Give up drugs," Skip shouted. "I keep tellin' ya."

"Did they say when they're comin'?" Norm asked.

Dinger opened his bag hurriedly. "Who?"

"Doris, Rota," several men shouted simultaneously.

Tolerating similar absurdities during the school year, Sal didn't think he could take much more. Shaking his head, he began eating his sandwich.

"Oh, I thought you meant–"

Norm sighed. "Shouldn't 've sent two boys to do a man's job."

Dinger's head tilted upward defensively.

Miles exhaled, lowered his sandwich irritably and turned to the group. "Nobody said nathin' about nathin'."

Receiving boos, he sulked.

Lyman evaluated both men. "Did you guys ask the women if the checks came in?"

Dinger unwrapped the first of several cheeseburgers and Miles sipped coffee. "Yeah," he provided cryptically and the smell of fried hamburger meat filled the room. "I think they're coming later," he revealed with a full mouth.

"What's comin'?" Skip asked.

Dinger frowned perplexedly. "The checks. Ain't that what you wanted to know?"

Cheers surprised him and he frowned.

Miles lowered his cup. "The courier's bringin' 'em in this afternoon," he finally divulged.

Sarcastic laughter erupted, mixed with applause, cheers, and more indignation.

Chapter 19

L ater that afternoon, the four teachers pulled into Skycrest with a load of steps. Parking, they entered the *Majestic*. Phil had stopped at the office in order to find out about the checks which hadn't arrived, and he announced that Roy had left to get them.

The large congregation became so annoyed about the delay that they stormed outside, headed for their trucks and cars, and sped back to the office in order to wait for Roy. Arriving in wild disorder, they swarmed inside. Filling the room, they seemed to attack the urn angrily, as if to punish whoever had been responsible for the delay. Grabbing cups or rinsing out others, they soon fell into the coffee-lounging mode.

Sal and the foursome unloaded the steps, returned hours later, and so did Roy shortly afterwards. Rarely smiling, Roy carried his blank expression inside the noisy room which suddenly quieted, as if the curtain had just risen on a new scene. Eyes contemplated him curiously, then defiantly upon noting that he was empty-handed. Ignoring them (and the usual contractors waiting impatiently for Doris' attention), he studied Doris who was on the phone discussing what bar she and Roy would be attending that night, pleasing Roy, Sal realized with more disbelief. Roy glanced back at the group and appeared to ponder which small cluster looked most inviting to join or perhaps what was the shortest way to the urn, and Doris finally hung up.

"How're them checks comin'?" someone flung recklessly.

Since blocking and much more had to pass inspection before Doris submitted the contractors' pay vouchers, several contractors began staring angrily at her. "How come they still ain't been inspected?" one of them complained, having blocked three trailers weeks ago.

Doris ignored him. "Did they come?" she screeched at Roy still standing mutely before her and Rota palmed her ears again.

Staring at Roy, the group appeared to anticipate that he wouldn't answer. Odds favored it. But had the head containing teardrop eyes just nodded or shaken negatively? Even Doris didn't know.

Hands on hips, Roy resembled a cowboy awaiting his turn to lasso the bull. Whispering broke the silence, petered, and died. Craig slyly disconnected from his knot of hairy joke-tellers and edged toward the loungers surrounding Roy.

Roy unbuttoned his cowboy shirt unceremoniously, reached inside and withdrew what resembled the usual manila envelope that the courier delivered.

Eyes appeared to widen. Mouths seemed open pleasantly.

Roy flipped it on the desk before Doris who grabbed it like a starving raccoon.

"Don't let nobody touch this but me," she shrieked at Roy.

The room suddenly came to life. Contractors moved aside as if to avoid flying glass and Doris began tearing the envelope open.

Paid separately at the Rand, Roy turned heel disinterestedly, practically stumbled into Phil and Vinny, and headed down the hall as if the bartender had just moved the poker game to the saloon's back room.

"About time, goddamn it," Miles blurted.

Doris began dumping the checks on her desk and Roy's door banged shut.

"Far out."

"Look fo' mine," Happy shouted, bullying his way past the others.

Unbelievable, Sal raged anew, standing near the cabinets. Where's *he* been all these days? he pondered incredulously, as Doris started pawing through the pile looking for her check.

"Aren't they in alphabetical order?" Phil inquired.

"Regular little beaver, ain't she?" Lyman contributed.

"More like a raccoon," Norm qualified from the end of the couch.

You're insulting the raccoons," Skip disagreed.

Finding hers, Doris held it before her face.

"Where's mine?" Happy demanded, squeezing ahead of several men, including the usual ignored contractors surrounding her desk.

"You owe the government for sleepin' on government property," Skip told Happy who ignored him.

"Two hundred and six?" Doris complained. "That ain't right. All that work for a lousy 206 bucks?" she objected, then grinned, suggesting pleasant surprise, especially about attracting so much attention.

"What work?" Lenny's breathy voice carried from near the urn.

Lyman rose and someone took his place.

"Is mine there, damn it?" Happy barked, finally breaking through to her desk. He picked up three checks, read the names, and dropped them disgustedly to the floor without bothering to pick them up.

Asshole, Sal labeled him from the couch and a contractor placed them on her desk.

"Meriwether, Norm," Doris called. "Eighty-six forty," she divulged, staggering Sal.

"Hey, you ain't supposed ta tell everybody what I got," Norm admonished, angling between the men who seemed reluctant to part. "Ain't you gots no sense? Them's personal."

"Get yo' filthy hands off," she scolded, slapping Happy's hand

190

angrily. She compared Norm's check to hers, dropped it on the desk, and another check fell to the floor.

"Mine ain't there," Happy exclaimed, fingering more checks and the same contractor stooped for the second check.

Phil shook his head.

"Can't expect ta get paid for listenin' to rock all day," Skip told Happy. "Classical, maybe."

Norm located his check. "Damn," he muttered disappointedly. "They screwed up. Can't they do nothin' right?"

"That's all of them?" Happy demanded.

Doris picked up another check. "Al-men-," she attempted, breaking off. "Allmendinger, Bruce. Dinger, is that you?"

"No, it's his twin," Skip responded and Doris burst out laughing about Dinger's name.

Dinger tilted his head indignantly and wiggled between the crowd.

Norm picked up a sheet beside the checks and eyed Doris. "Sign next to my name?"

"These all that come?" Happy interrupted.

"A dollar thirty-eight," Doris announced, reading Dinger's check, and she cackled into more laughter.

"A dollar thirty-eight?" Dinger protested near Craig.

Skip sighed. "They over paid him."

Several men laughed.

Frowning, Norm signed the sheet.

"That ain't right," Dinger objected, reaching for his check, but Doris pulled it away, still studying it.

"Well, kiss my ass," Happy declared. "I'm gonna see Roy."

"Why, he's a good ass kisser?" Skip remarked.

"What the hell am I supposed ta live on?" Making his way between several others, Happy headed towards Roy's office.

"Sell the Barracuda," Skip suggested. "Buy a tape deck. It's cheaper."

"Is this an office or what?" Phil asked.

"A *what*," Vinny clarified.

Norm pointed to the sheet. "Sign there," he told Dinger frowning at Doris still reading his check.

"Hey, gimmy that," Dinger demanded quickly in what Sal recognized was his regular voice.

My, what money brings out of us, he rebuked.

Mike adjusted his glasses. "Like, the guy can't even get his check."

"Goddamn it," Miles spouted.

"Don't read 'em. Just call names," Lyman insisted angrily,

191

seconded by the others.

"Don't get excited," she replied.

"Look who's talking," someone snapped during the sarcastic laughter.

Doris wrinkled her nose mockingly at the cluster of men around her desk, including the contractors eyeing her incredulously. She dropped Dinger's check onto the desk.

Hurriedly retrieving it, Dinger studied it carefully.

Norm turned to examine it and Lenny broke through to her desk.

"Your hours are wrong," Norm informed Dinger. "You worked more'n six hours, didn't you?"

"Not really," Skip disagreed. "Unless he got paid for him spreadin' his hair. Then it's about right."

"A dollar thirty-eight?" Dinger repeated.

A contractor squeezed through. "What about them trailers, damn it?" he reminded Doris impatiently but she resumed examining her check.

"And they took too much money out," Norm told Dinger. "Yours is all screwed up. So's mine."

Reaching the desk, Lenny started searching for his check, and Doris slapped his hand.

"Here's yours, Lyman," she announced and read the amount.

Lyman struggled through the pressing crowd. "Keep it to yourself, damn it, woman. Are you nuts?"

Finding his, Lenny lifted it up in order to study it.

Laughing, Doris snatched it out of his hand.

"Hey, you tore it in half," Lenny objected vigorously.

"That's all you're worth, half a check," Skip remarked.

"This is ridiculous," Phil commented angrily.

Lenny snatched his half back, jumped awkwardly aside with both parts, and attempted to fit them together. "You better hope I can cash it," he breathed to Doris.

Doris brushed the remaining checks into her lap. "Ah ain't givin' out another check till ya move back. Move, move, move."

"Where?" someone objected because of the surging crowd.

"Don't mess around, Doris, goddamn it," someone complained.

"Ah ain't foolin' around," she insisted.

Several men struggled to comply but the others refused to budge.

The same contractor glared at Doris. "Hey, Miss, what about them three trailers?"

"See if mine's there. And if you don't give it to me, I'll get it myself," Skip threatened.

Why isn't *he* interceding? Sal grumbled, observing Craig standing off to the side with folded arms.

"Goddamn it," Miles spouted.

"Try it," Doris warned Skip.

"Nah, I might dirty my hands," he answered.

"I done called off all who's getting' checks," she screeched but all stayed put, mistrusting her.

"Hey, mine ain't right either," Lenny complained in an almost falsetto voice. "They underpaid me."

"It's right then," Skip remarked.

"Are you gonna give me mine or what?" Lyman demanded, turned, and glared at Craig.

"Okay, Doris, that's it," Craig finally reacted, although as if he were scolding a mischievous child.

"Make 'em all get back," Doris raged at him. "Back, back, back.

How am I supposed to give 'em out with ya'all breathin' down my neck?" she shouted.

And you want to work in here? Sal asked himself.

"Ah ain't givin' out another one till ya move back. Move, move, move."

The men struggled to push the others back, but to no avail.

"What about them three trailers?" inquired a familiar voice.

"Who the hell does she think she is?" Vinny objected, ushering in similar complaints again.

Doris lifted up the checks in her lap. She called another name, read off the amount, and the men jeered angrily.

"Call Roy," someone urged.

"Call him what?" chirped a familiar voice.

"Don't give out the figures," Craig insisted but with a grin, Sal observed.

Shrugging, Doris finally complied.

Most of the other men received less than expected also, and complaining spread anew.

"Where'd them checks come from?" Norm inquired.

Returning from the bathroom, Rota headed toward several men who parted reluctantly while examining her breasts and legs.

"Louder, damn it," someone urged. "How come she's so quiet now?"

"Sal D'Angelo," Doris called.

Managing to reach her desk, Sal read $160.75 which seemed to be correct.

Obliging the oglers, Rota's legs appeared to assume a life of their own. Promenading deftly between hungry eyes, they reached her desk, and seemingly paused as if awaiting the body to slide onto her chair, or in order to give the onlookers a final eyeful. Folding, they finally disappeared underneath the desk. "Is mine there?" she asked quietly, as if suddenly realizing that it was payday, but few heard her.

Craig scrutinized the room. "Don't worry if your pay is screwed up," he shouted, having received his check. "They'll make it up on your next check," he assured officially.

How does he know? Sal demanded. Besides, why not get it right the first time?

Fondling the manila envelope, Doris looked up and regarded the men staring down at it with anticipation. "Y'all still here? That's it. There ain't no more checks."

Stunned, the men hardly moved.

Odd maneuvering through the crowd, like a mole making its way out of the hay, attracted attention, quelling voices.

Temporarily blocked, Roy forged ahead.

Several men including the contractors moved aside as he proceeded ahead. Heads turned to study him expectantly, and the Chief of Field Operations veered toward the front door. Opening it, he stepped deftly outside as if looking for his horse, banged the door closed, and laughter seemed to batter it.

"Where's he headin'?" Norm demanded.

"Outside. It's too noisy in here, man," Skip explained.

Several men cursed, stumbled out the door, and all departed.

Chapter 20

T hat night and during the next few days, two hundred and fifty trailers poured into the Fairgrounds. Lacking needed supervision, the toters parked them in several crooked rows beyond the office. Because of the increased number of inspectors and maintenance men, discrepancies were eventually rectified and 180 were ready to be toted to the parks.

Finally, Sal enunciated to himself and he left with the others for Skycrest.

Hoping the courier would arrive with the missing checks, many of the men returned shortly afterwards, including Sal who wasn't needed at the park.

Arriving later than normally, the courier absorbed pummeling from the men asking if their missing checks had arrived. "I'm only the courier," the black man defended as usual, and he handed Doris the brown portfolio. He removed his pith helmet, waited for her to sign for it, and yawned.

"Thanks for tellin' us that man," Lenny unfolded softly to him from several feet away. "We didn't know."

Bored, the courier tapped his helmet against his thigh and grinned reservedly.

"There ain't no checks," Doris shouted angrily and the men jeered and complained.

"Are you sure you ain't got mine?" pestered Happy as if the courier would know about his check in particular, and the courier's grin vanished. "Bernie Hills," he reminded him, as if he were an executive.

"Don't know nothin' about it, man," the courier responded.

Noticing Doris reading the HUD bulletin instead of signing for the portfolio, the courier shook his head and frowned.

"Sign on the back," he reminded her impatiently, and he glanced at Happy. "I tol' you guys before, man. I don't know nothin' about checks," he insisted and turned back to Doris. "Anything goin' back?"

"Yeah, Miles and Dinger," someone suggested.

"Oh, my God," Doris shrieked, startling the courier, several contractors, and Sal leaning against a cabinet. "We gotta move."

Skip eyed her. "Who, you and Roy?"

Norm burst out laughing.

"What do you mean?" a lounger asked. "By August 4th, next Friday."

Several men converged to read the bulletin in her hands. "We gotta clear outta here," one of them confirmed.

"What?"

"Move where?"

"How do you know?"

"Goddamn it."

"Anything goin' back?" the courier repeated worriedly.

"Roy," Doris shouted. "We gotta move all the trailers outta the Fairgrounds. They're gonna have a fair."

"We always have a fair every August," Phil explained.

Sal sighed. "Looks like the dopes in charge forgot about that, or thought we'd be out of here by then."

"Just sign on the back," droned the courier's voice. "I gotta blow."

The door opened in the far room.

Reading the bulletin, Skip backpedaled through the crowd, deliberately stumbled backwards onto an available space on the couch, and howled into laughter.

"What the hell's going on? What's all the hollerin' about now, woman?" Roy shouted, arriving.

The courier exhaled tragically and flipped his helmet back on. "Just sign right there," he said, pointing. "Anything going back?"

Skip sat up. "Yeah," he told him. "Two hundred and fifty trailers. Stuff them in your portfolio, man."

"Wonder who's paying for *that* mistake?" queried Norm.

"Who do you think?" Skip replied. Rising, he approached those surrounding Doris' desk.

"Check with Millie for me about my check, will ya, man?" Happy ordered the courier who smirked.

Roy edged ahead of several men standing before her desk, including the usual contractors waiting impatiently for her attention.

"We gotta move, Roy. It says so right here," Doris bellowed though he was only several feet away.

The face containing droopy eyes stared at her.

"I'm hungry," injected a familiar voice.

"Move back," Doris scolded the group again and Roy finally squeezed through.

Phil stroked his black beard. "I don't believe this."

Sal adjusted his gold-rimmed glasses. "Give yourself time."

Lenny turned to the courier. "You ain't expectin' her ta sign that thing today, are ya?"

Pain appeared to spread throughout the courier's already grim face. "Wouldn't mind if she did, man."

"Better men than you've died waitin' right there, man," Lenny breathed and scattered laughter engulfed them.

"Damn," Roy exclaimed.

The courier turned to Lenny. "Does she always let people wait like this?"

"Only durin' a disaster," Skip responded.

"Why did HUD pick this place? They must've knowed about the Fair," Norm objected.

Roy handed the bulletin back to Doris and several men stepped aside so he could pass. He veered toward the front door, opened it, and left, leaving eyes hanging there momentarily.

Noticing an opening, the courier strode closer to Doris' desk. He removed his helmet, slapped it back on his head emphatically, and eyed his watch. "Guess it's about time ta blow. Just sign on the back, and I'll be outta your hair."

Doris reread the bulletin and he headed for the door.

About to grab the knob, the courier turned. "Anything goin' back? I kept asking," he added, frowning offendedly.

"My reports," Doris shrieked. "You gotta take back my reports."

"Right," the courier agreed, almost charging back. "And ya gotta sign that ya got everything," he insisted and grinned optimistically.

"Where are we moving?" Norm asked Rota.

Doris finally signed the portfolio, handed it to the courier, and he flew out the door.

"The Holding Point, five miles away," Rota uttered in her usually quiet voice.

"Can ya hold it down, Rota?" Phil teased.

Laughter rippled across the heads.

"Do you realize the cost of moving 250 trailers?" Sal told Skip. "Probably twenty-five bucks a shot," he answered himself and paused to calculate the amount. "Over five thousand bucks, because dopes didn't have enough sense to choose the Holding Point in the first place."

"Unreal," Phil remarked.

Chapter 21

Word spread quickly that the government was paying *thirty* dollars per trailer to move them, and the next day, out of Elmira's depths and crevices and neighboring towns, appeared toters of every kind before Doris' desk: short, dirty, old, young, smoking, coughing, and possibly high on alcohol or drugs. Outside were their idling trucks, some in the same condition.

Once again, Rota offered to help issue dispatch tickets.

Once again from between slightly bucked teeth spouted Doris' refusal. "You don't know how," she belittled, attracting attention briefly.

Having just arrived from trucking all night, several of the usual toters grumbled about having to wait for her attention again. Unaccustomed to such a reaction, the local toters eyed them curiously.

Sal rested his hairy arm on top of a cabinet. "Teach 'er," he urged annoyingly again but she ignored him. Things 'll be different if and when I work in here, he vowed innocently.

Doris copied down a serial number on a dispatch ticket angrily.

"It's hard to fill 'em out," Skip needled. "Ya need basic kindergarten." He evaluated Doris' disheveled desk and turned to Rota's tidy version, then Rota sitting boringly behind it. "It's only offered in the South," he told her and noticed balls of paper surrounding Doris' overflowing waste basket. "Trash collecting is a prerequisite but she flunked it."

Sal laughed with Rota and the others.

A well-dressed toter asked Doris where he could park his idling vehicle and Doris scolded him for having filled out the ticket himself.

"You best not get involved with dispatchin'," Norm warned Rota congenially. "She'll be blamin' you for her mistakes."

"Doris never makes mistakes," Vinny contributed.

"Her parents did," Skip disagreed.

Wearing a dirty, long-sleeved shirt rolled up beyond his biceps, Lenny rocked awkwardly on the balls of his feet. "That weren't no mistake." Flashing his bulky, dirty, thick-veined arms, he inspected them slyly. "That was an abortion that lived."

A cup in hand, Craig laughed with Lyman and the others. He stepped between several frowning toters, reached Doris' desk, and encouraged her to teach Rota how to fill them out.

Doris showered him with protestations that she had no time.

Craig grabbed half of the tickets awkwardly, handed them to Rota, and received an ovation that drowned out Doris' objections.

"I'm tellin' Roy," she shrieked at him backing into his slot. "Don't forget to write in the correct HUD numbers," she screeched at Rota, then glared at the loungers and toters. Conditioned to such outlandish behavior at various truck-stops and bars across the nation, the new toters seemed unfazed. Half-nodding sleepily standing patiently in tight formation before Rota's desk, they seemed to be holding one another in place.

Skip eyed them ceremoniously and turned to the HUD men, including Sal. "Now, I ask ya," he began quietly. "Could ya find a more reliable-lookin' bunch than these bums?" he teased and several of them laughed. "Some of them look like they just rolled outta the Elbow Room," he uncorked, referring to a local tavern.

"Can you hold it down a little, fellas? While I figure this out?" Rota squeaked.

"And don't forget to write in the date and sign your name," Doris screeched at her.

"Rota's capable of handling that," Norm presented amiably. "Aren't ya, Rota?"

Rota shook her head. "Oh, please," she complained, palming her ears again while staring at a blank ticket. "I can't think."

"Neither can Doris," Skip remarked.

"Don't fight it, Rota," Lenny breathed encouragingly. "Just use trial and error. That's how we knock off everything here."

A bearded man began laughing and nodding as if he were insane, doing drugs, or both, Sal sensed.

"Take it easy," Craig told Doris, and several loungers watched Rota fill out her first dispatch ticket.

"They get the green copy. We keep the yellow," Doris bellowed at her.

"I know," Rota responded meekly and handed the green copy to a toter who thanked her.

"There," Skip remarked, referring to Rota. "That outta put Doris in her place."

Rota issued several more tickets. But despite Craig standing alongside or perhaps because of it, Rota forgot to sign some. Quietly admitting her mistake minutes later, she asked the loungers to stop the toters before they left.

Confronted with such a crisis, the HUD contingent merely stared.

Comprehending the situation, Sal dashed outside and halted all except one pulling away with a trailer. Watching from the window with several others, Craig was about to give up on him when the Barracuda thundered into operation.

Happy's experienced foot hit the pedal repeatedly, vibrating the office. Tires squealed. A cloud of dust followed. The vehicle zoomed past the office like the Batmobile. Catching up, Happy footed his brakes which screeched. The toter stopped and Happy persuaded him to return for Rota's signature.

Shortly after such mistakes were rectified and the toters left, Skip rose ceremoniously and made his way to Doris' desk.

Once again heads turned curiously. Voices dissipated and stopped.

"I got a question," he commenced as if he felt obligated to satisfy his audience. "Did ya ever think of askin' those guys for their license? Then checkin' the guy's face with his photo? And writin' down his license number? What stops 'em from signin' a false name on the ticket and just stealin' a trailer?"

"Stupidity," Norm interceded. "HUD officials think this is paradise."

The harmless banter continued for several minutes, until the front door opened. Talking ceased and eyes fell upon a lone toter. Having just pulled in a trailer from a company in Nebraska, he refused to reroute it to the Holding Point. "We ain't insured to go there," he told Craig standing alongside Doris' desk.

"Five miles, for crying out loud," Craig objected.

"Yeah?" the man retorted. "What happens if I get into an accident? HUD's paying? My orders says Fairgrounds. That's where I brung it. That's where she's stayin' unless my boss says otherwise."

Craig picked up Doris' telephone and handed it to him. "Call 'im."

"In Nebraska? That's long distance."

Because of so much wasted manpower, needless expense, theft, and much more, the men pummeled him with laughter, almost felling him.

"We can handle it," Skip assured the puzzled face."

The government pays its phone bills," Craig assured, having trouble running his comb through his thick, blond hair.

Skip snapped his hair back. "Yeah, they're just weak on paychecks."

"Oh, this is a government operation?" the man asked.

Lenny checked his veined arms below rolled-up sleeves. "Wouldn't be standin' around doin' nothin' unless it was."

Another round of laughter bothered the man. Accepting the phone, he frowned while dialing. All listened as he described the problem to someone on the other end. Answering affirmatively four times he hung up.

"Well?" Craig asked.

"They weren't in," Skip provided.

Laughter sounded sharply, then dissipated back to curiosity.

"They said no way," the man said. "I'm supposed to drive it back."

"You're kiddin'," Craig deposited with a frown and the man shook his head. "For a lousy five miles?"

"Didn't they hear about the disaster?" Phil insert like an old veteran.

"It ain't the miles. It's the principle of the thing," Skip provided with hands on hips.

"No way Jose–not even for three blocks," the toter said and left.

"During disasters," Skip announced, "this goes ta show ya what companies *won't* do to make a buck," he completed with a laugh and shook back his unruly hair.

Chapter 22

Appreciating the opportunity to earn extra money, the independent toters succeeded in moving all the trailers to the Holding Point by nightfall, including a new four-bedroom one for the office. Early the next morning the front door opened dramatically at the old office trailer before everyone had a chance to move. In stepped a cheerful, gum-chewing man wearing a khaki uniform. Surrounding his waist was a thick belt supporting a leather pouch containing special tools. "Telephone company," he chirped attracting the usual attention from those waiting to sign in, and he eyed Doris. "Where do you want the new phones installed?"

Uproarious laughter felled another innocent bystander.

The installer's face experimented with several frowns. "Something wrong?" he directed at Doris and checked his order book.

"We don't need a phone. We're moving to the Holding Point," Craig interceded.

The telephone man smiled self-consciously. "Didn't you want more phones here?"

"Yeah, eight weeks ago," Lyman said. "Where've ya been? We'll be needin' 'em at the Holding Point now. Just take 'em down there."

The telephone man twisted his lips grotesquely as if he had just been arrested and frowned again. "That's outta my district. Another guy 'll have to do that. Just sign here."

By noon, except for cases of canned goods that the Red Cross donated and never distributed to the victims for some unknown reason, the men transferred desks, tools, and other heavy paraphernalia to the new office, minus whatever never made it there for obvious reasons.

Had the astute Lyman not reminded Craig about the donations that evening, they would have been left behind in a horse stall.

Craig asked for volunteers to load as much as possible in their cars and drop them off at the new office before continuing home. "To save time and not waste manpower," he foolishly added to several inquisitive faces and was equally crucified with laughter.

Sal, Skip, Lyman, and the others volunteered. Since Rota knew which stall contained the donations, she led the way. Arriving, they watched her unlock the door under the glow of city lights. She swung it open, took one look at the darkness, and hesitated. "Anybody got a flashlight?"

Obliging her, the gallant knights turned heel almost simultaneously and hurried to their vehicles. Doors opened. Glove compartments were flapped ajar. Flashlights were removed and door slams disturbed the humid evening. Returning, the entourage flipped them on almost simultaneously. But spotlighting one another playfully, many discerned an unusual similarity of flashlights. If embarrassment were possible with such an array of manhood, some experienced it. Others merely frowned in wonder.

"Hey, in here, guys," chirped Rota as if she were competing for Prostitute of the Year.

One particular head, belonging to the most outspoken, snapped back fallen hair. "So that's where all the flashlights went."

"Where?" Dinger asked Skip while looking inside the stall. "In there?"

"I'll be damned," breathed a familiar voice belonging to another young man whose rolled-up sleeves bared thick forearms containing bulging veins, and he laughed breathily.

"I only borrowed mine," Norm conceded sheepishly and snickered self-consciously. "Was gonna return it."

"Sure ya were," Lyman said. "So was I, man."

"Hey, guys, shine it more this way," Rota squeaked from inside.

Sal checked his similar flashlight. "Huh. What do you know about that," he also admitted.

Lenny slyly illuminated his thick, veined arms proudly. "Bunch a thieves."

"Look who's talking," Lyman answered.

"You guys gonna stand around shining light in each other's lying faces or give Rota some light?" Skip barked.

Laughter rattled the calm night and Dinger stumbled inside with the others.

"Hey, food," he cried.

Lenny whirled awkwardly. "You were expectin' horse manure?"

Skip illuminated his cousin's face with light. "Who invited him inside? The Fair ain't openin' for another week."

Lyman lifted out a case of pickles. Skip grabbed a box of Kleenex, and Dinger paused to sweep back his hair.

Surprised about so much stock or perhaps sluggish from so much loafing, the men began carrying out supplies to their cars, slowly at first, deliberately leaving the heavier boxes behind for the others.

A change occurred minutes later, although, looking back, no one could pinpoint when it happened or who had triggered it. Insisting that the new office could never use so much Clorox, Rota could have been responsible. Or it could have been Norm who claimed that the Red Cross donated to the needy which he seemed to think included him.

Carelessly bragging that the Red Cross recently gave him a case of Coke free, Lenny might have been the culprit. His peculiar lunge for a spaghetti carton might have started the change, although many would have blamed it on his bad leg. After all, why would carrying out one particular item instead of another be more desirable?

Perhaps a strange burst of energy or quickly-moving legs heading toward a case of soda might have initiated the sudden change.

Whatever the reason, obviously fearing losing out on the choicest delectable for themselves such as spaghetti, canned soup, and soda, all seemed to have panicked simultaneously, and the pace of what was a begrudging chore suddenly became ugly.

Hands started hurriedly grabbing such boxes carelessly. Bodies "accidentally" bumped one another aside in order to grab them. Minor squabbles arose about who saw what box first or who needed a box of detergent the most, and so on. Stumbling back and forth to their vehicles, nobody even heard Rota.

"Can ya shine your light over here, fellas?" she repeated for the third time. In fact, she seemed to be addressing a large box of sanitary napkins or was simply talking to herself.

Even Sal pretended not to hear her at first. But although probably the most needy of all the scavengers, he was too noble to ignore any plea for help, especially from someone so fair, and he carried the box to her car. Aware that being poor often brought out the worst in humans including him, he suddenly felt ashamed. "What are we doing?" he announced loudly, though secretly scolding himself and the others ignored him.

How could so much be taken home–that is, stolen for themselves– without anything being dropped off at the Holding Point? all suddenly seemed to sense simultaneously. To cover themselves, they started setting aside large cases of worthless cornstarch, mustard, matches, and similar undesirable items for the new office.

Arriving there twenty minutes later, the men appreciated that according to Doris, Craig was sleeping with a divorcee he had met at Edgewood. The large, unwanted boxes were stacked in the fourth bedroom, and the men left for the night.

Making the rounds at 11:30 that evening, Charlie, the night watchman, found Lenny inside. He accused him of planning to rob the place, including what he assumed was worthwhile Red Cross merchandise and food. Disagreeing vehemently, that is, breathily, Lenny accused Charlie of stealing hand tools, a chain saw, two radios and much more from the old office. The two were close to blows when Craig returned (for what reason, nobody knew that either) and separated them.

Evicted from his apartment for owing three months rent, Lenny explained that he planned to sleep there that night, but to no avail and early the next morning Craig announced plans to fire him.

Discussing the incident near the kitchen sink during Craig's absence, Norm offered a different motive. "He wanted to wash his hand with Red Cross soap."

"He'd need more than an overnight's lodging for that," Skip disagreed and the usual banter followed and continued until all left for Skycrest.

Charlie revealed all and more to Millie who told Craig that Lenny had been indicted for drunken driving some time ago and Craig fired him the next day.

Consequently, HUD promoted Charlie and permanently transferred him to a desk job with them at the Rand.

I guess Charlie must have done some heavy police work worthy of ol' Gallagher, Sal reflected sarcastically.

Friday morning was payday again. Anticipating their checks, the men were still discussing Lenny while lingering inside the living room in the new office.

Skip jerked his head, though his hair was in place. "You can loaf, be half-retarded, not know a screw from a hole in the wall, but if ya have a police record, you're dead," he unloaded sympathetically or perhaps cynically. Several men agreed, including Sal who had urged Craig to give him another chance, but he was unsuccessful. "Ah, he got the short end. He's just been discharged from serving in Vietnam, has a bum leg probably from getting wounded," he speculated, "and now he's unemployed. That's what ya get for fightin' for America."

Meaning he's probably no better or worse than half of these dilettantes, Sal concluded, especially since they surely signed for whatever they wanted for themselves. Nevertheless, because of the usual hookup delays and whatnot, releasing trailers was slow anyway, despite the increased manpower from the dedicated few that included Sal, Skip, Lyman, ant the others. In fact, many loungers sneaked back to the office in order to sniff around for their paychecks, including Sal.

The courier arrived. Wearing his notorious pith helmet, he dropped his portfolio on Doris' desk, then, as if anticipating her explosions, jerked away and covered his ears playfully. Hardly missing their cue, the men attacked Doris' desk in noisy waves again as if *they* were the delayed explosion.

Doris defended herself well against such frantic hands. She grabbed the portfolio. She sat on it, told the worried courier that nothing was going back, and signed appropriately.

Stunned with surprise, he shot out the door.

Doris ordered them to back off as before and the men grumbled back to their crevices like lions for their stools, and she removed the precious envelope. Withdrawing the checks, she called names like a sergeant announcing mail and once again revealed amounts like an auctioneer at a cattle sale.

Fierce indignation broke out almost immediately again, although not because she refused to stop, but because checks were missing again, wrong, or amounts were low.

Talk about incompetence in Washington or wherever, Sal suppressed, standing nearby.

Craig shouted for quiet and the assemblage eased it back begrudgingly. He slyly whispered something in Doris' ear about going to see Millie about the problem and slipped out the door unnoticed.

Guardedly hoping for a raise, Sal was willing to settle for the correct amount. Accepting his check, he discovered neither. Paid about half of what he had estimated like many others including Happy, he soon learned that because of a mechanical breakdown, all overtime reaching one hundred hours for the two-week period had somehow reverted back to one hour.

Angry pandemonium soon broke loose and eventually dwindled into idle speculation.

Though the men blamed the IBM machine for the mistake at first, they appeared to chose fleshier stuff– that is, an unsuspecting female keypunch operator in Washington D.C., according to Happy who denounced her. In fact, he had seduced her, although only after a second date, and mostly because he provided "good stud service," as he put it.

Who cares? Even if it's true? Sal objected, leaning against his favorite cabinet. "The guy's a real ass," he whispered to Norm who agreed, sitting on the end of the couch.

Skip angled his head in order to evaluate Happy with his good eye. "How come she didn't make sure *your* paycheck was right, hotshot?"

Sal grinned appreciatively.

"Ah, she probably don't work there anymore," Happy scoffed. "Met her when ah had this job in Washington."

"After Rapid City or before?" Skip pressed mockingly.

Ignoring him, Happy described having an affair with another woman and this episode captured more attention because of volume and because the new men weren't convinced that he was a fake.

How could anybody spout off that much without having some pull? Sal nevertheless considered curiously.

Happy finished with a declaration that every secretary in Washington was either a prostitute or a senator's call girl.

Though hardly a feminist, Skip eyed him sarcastically. "If bullshit was water, we'd have another flood."

But considering so many incorrect checks, including Sal's, the men stampeded out of the trailer angrily.

Chapter 23

Despite Norman's belief that given enough time and men, things could be bungled into going right, another telephone man appeared with an order to "replace black phones with colored ones."

Now there's a real top priority during a disaster, Sal kept hidden.

"What black phones?" someone inquired. "We just moved in."

"Cool it," Norm scolded. "He's just trying to add some color to the crisis."

Despite similar comments, the man installed three phones in frightening speed, surprising everyone, but a major problem soon arose.

Because complaints had become so numerous at the Fairgrounds–every third call either coming from a flood victim living in a trailer or at the Armory, church, or school–Roy requested an unlisted phone number for them, stunning Sal again.

That 'll cut off communicating with contractors, toters, and companies. Plus flood victims. Geezus, can it get any worse?

Roy might have gotten away with such brilliance had it not been for Hugh Brennig who demanded to know via the courier "why the hell" Roy changed their number. When no one responded, much less Doris, Brennig sent another note via the courier (standing like a cadet at attention before her) demanding to know "What the hell is your new number?"

On Thursday, the courier delivered another note from Hugh who asked "When the hell am I getting your new number? How the hell can I telephone you people?"

"Ah don't know," Doris actually verbalized, reading the note to Roy standing before her.

Watching Rota type, the courier turned back to Doris. "You don't know wot? I didn't say nothin'. Anything goin' back?"

Doris looked up. "Tell Mr. Brennig we'all will let him know."

"Let him know wot? I'm only the courier."

"Anythin' come in about ma check?" popped a familiar voice from deep inside the throng of coffee-cup clutchers.

"I don't know nothin' 'bout your check, Happy," Doris spat.

"What about the rest of us?" queried another.

"Shut up, all of you. Ah gotta phone the Rand and give 'em our new number," Doris shouted.

Nor was Roy aware that half the men already knew the new number, including Melissa, Craig's girlfriend and Audrey. So did Rota's hair dresser, her mother, and her husband still confined to sleeping on their porch. Though Doris had been telling contractors that only Roy knew it, several contractors "had the nerve," as she put it, to copy it down from where she had written it on a piece of masking tape attached to her phone.

The Employment Office knew it somehow. So did the base operator. Millie gave it to the Rand switchboard operator who began divulging it to everyone who requested it.

Also managing to get it, Mrs. Newhouse, a flood victim, telephoned describing herself as anemic and suffering from heart disease. "Can you please, please help me get into a trailer?"

"Hold on a minute," Doris snapped, having the decency to put her on hold. "Telephone," she screeched to Roy hooked to a coffee cup. "It's Mrs. Newhouse. She wants ta know about a trailer."

"Dang," Roy complained.

The men stopped talking and laughing in order to listen.

Disconnecting from his coffee-sipping platoon, Roy approached Doris. "You ain't gived out the new number to nobody, have you?"

"No way," she replied.

"I'll talk to her," Happy interfered. He took two giant steps from his small circle of professional loungers, waltzed over, and slid atop Doris' desk.

Doris pressed the proper button and handed him the phone.

"Good morning, Mrs. Newhouse. What seems to be the problem, ma'am?" he drawled loudly and paused to listen. "You're living in your sister's basement?" he inquired and covered the mouthpiece. "That's a dumb place to live," he told his audience and several men cackled appreciatively.

Sal frowned. It's not funny, asshole.

Happy removed his hand. "Not sure when you're gonna get a trailer fer sure. We're working on yo' case raght now," he uttered into the mouthpiece and winked at his listeners. "Of course we are, ma'am. Would ah lie to you, ma'am?"

Have you ever told the truth? Sal wondered irately.

"Ah know all about your problem," Happy continued. "Mr. Nichols done told me. We're doin' everythin' humanly possible, ma'am. "You'll get took care of immediately, if not sooner. Who is this you wanna know?" he asked incredulously and surveyed the men. "Mr. Hud in person."

Laughter responded and he hung up.

Chapter 24

Holding a cup of coffee Friday morning, Craig dispatched Lyman, Skip, and Norm to Skycrest. He ignored the rest who left to do as they pleased as usual and Craig stopped Sal about to follow those heading for Skycrest.

"You're working in here today," he announced.

Sal glanced at Roy continuing to his office with his cup. "Really?"

"Didn't Roy tell you?"

Sal almost laughed. "No. What will I be doing?"

"Whatever Doris tells ya I guess."

"Are you gonna be working in here, Sal?" Doris screeched, rattling him.

Maybe I shouldn't, he reconsidered, shrugged, and the few remaining men still nursing their coffee stopped talking in order to listen.

"Roy, is Sal gonna be working in here?" Doris screamed down the empty hallway.

Oh, God, Sal moaned. Talk about lacking tact. Grin and bear it, his other self ordered. Maybe you'll get a promotion. I sure as hell could use the extra bucks, he answered.

"Hey Roy?" Doris shouted again, then, as if remembering, reached under her desk. Sharp buzzing sounded in the far room, and she lifted up the phone.

"Yeah?" Sal barely discerned from Roy's far room and Doris repeated herself into the receiver.

"Yeah," Roy answered indifferently.

"Good," Doris barked.

Really? Sal wondered. He was about to walk back to discuss the job with Roy, when Doris clunked the receiver down noisily.

She touched a stack of yellow dispatch tickets. "You can have Lenny's job. Start loggin' these in," she ordered Sal brusquely.

I don't think so, he objected, eying the stack. Excusing himself past a few onlookers, he headed down the hallway.

Doris glared at him. "Where ya going? What about these dispatch tickets?" she demanded, but the telephone rang, distracting her. "Telephone, Roy," she shouted and buzzed his telephone.

Reaching Roy's opened door, Sal stared at the man's embossed leather boots lifting onto the desk.

Roy leaned back in his swivel chair as if he were a company executive. "Is that raght?" he answered disregarding Sal. Joking with Juan

Martinez, Chief of Field Operations at Corning, Roy seemed to come to life initially, Sal noted. But when Roy started discussing how alcohol had affected their dart games at a bar last night, Sal had trouble controlling his irritation.

He's deliberately making me wait, doesn't know any better, or is really that much of a jackass. Probably all of that and more, he stormed underground. Blow up and you'll get nowhere, he warned. Maybe even ruin the opportunity to help the victims and even yourself.

Roy hung up and regarded Sal. "Yeah?"

"Craig said you'd like me to work inside," he baited vaguely, hoping Roy would agree and clarify his duties, maybe even label them officially. He also pictured Roy clearing his throat, apologizing for not communicating with him all along and beginning with something like, "I've been meaning to talk to you." But reality seldom imitated fantasy, he knew.

Clasping hands behind his neck, the real Roy galloped into Sal's mind. "Yeah," he grunted dispassionately without removing his boots.

I think you've just been belched into a new job man, Sal announced. Absorbing Roy's empty stare, he decided to speak, lest he remain forever lost inside two droopy, expressionless eyes. "What will I be doing?"

"Helpin' Doris."

No kidding, fella. But can you be a hair more specific?

Roy studied a Phillips screwdriver on his desk, as if it were the solution to the disaster.

Realizing that was it–the depth of Roy's ability to communicate–Sal almost pitied him for being so meekly endowed. Suddenly remembering how badly Doris filed, Sal almost choked. "Fine, but if you want me to run the office," he deliberately added, hoping he would confirm the idea, "I'd like to run everything my way." Like the song, he revived again. Evaluating Roy's thick growth of thin hair, he almost smiled. If he can't tolerate me coming on strong now, forget it. I'll go back to inspecting.

Gazing at several pencils whose sharp points suggested little use, Sal vowed to keep quiet and stay put until Roy answered. You could be here all day, his other self reminded him. That's okay, the pay is the same, he answered with a laugh. How's my raise coming? he was also tempted to ask but decided not to confuse him with too many issues.

Roy yawned, as if equaled to Sal's challenge. "I'll let you know," he uttered without changing his expression, nor did he remove his feet. Bored, he looked up the hallway.

Did you really expect much more? Sal asked, considered throwing in a *when*? but recalled the gas receipt and removed it from his wallet.

"How do I get paid for this?" He deliberately extended his hand half way, realizing Roy would have to unclasp his hands, remove his boots, and sit up in order to reach it. That's your punishment for having bad manners, among other faults man, he reflected and controlled himself from laughing.

Roy responded reluctantly, then began studying the receipt too intently for the impatient Sal.

That's a receipt, man. "For the gas I paid for," Four bucks, remember? Don't they give receipts to folks back at the Swamp? Nothing's on the back, man.

"Hang on to it," Roy uttered, tossed it on the desk, re-clasped his neck, and leaned back, squeaking his swivel chair.

Thanks for spearing me you boots, man. Ya got fast hands, but a slow brain, Sal kept underground, but he was too annoyed to mellow. "That's what you said six weeks ago," he flung, noting Roy's sleepy face. "Why don't you take care of it now?" he pressed. No need to be a phony, he ordered, noting his smile. The guy's a jackass, whether he can help it or not, he moderated.

Roy swung his eyes disinterestedly to the left and Sal pictured dumping him until he reminded himself that this was the real world, not the movies, nor was he John Wayne.

"Hah?" Roy asked.

Sensing Roy might be trying to even the score in what was developing into a psychological exchange between two opposites, Sal repeated himself firmly, calmly, and patiently. "I could use the money," he hinted, partly out of desperation, exasperation, and boredom. But he stopped short of blaming his need on his wife and four children. "Four bucks is four bucks."

Roy uncorked another king-size yawn.

Pulled into viewing molars again, Sal smirked. Pressing further would be as pointless as asking why the Holding Point wasn't chosen as the original staging area, he realized.

Roy snapped his head, yawned, and complained about being tired.

Stop bar-hopping, minimize fucking, and retire early, professor. Exercise, eat well, and give up television. Sharpen your mind with reading anything, even comic books, and you'll be fine, he rambled inwardly. Reading comics behind my parents' backs as a child is how I got my first start with reading, man, he mellowed with a laugh. Regarding Roy's tan cowboy shirt during another pause, Sal caught himself side-tracking another chance to complain about the lounging.

"Doris 'll handle it, Teach," Roy barely responded.

Frustrated and annoyed more with himself than Roy, Sal picked up the receipt. "Okay," he agreed in order to hide his embarrassment about how desperately he needed the money. He slipped it back inside his wallet and headed up front. *This job's getting to me*, he realized, sensing that he should have been more demanding about the money, taken initiative about his new job, and confronted Roy about the renewed loafing.

Getting this clown fired would be a blessing. Any replacement would be an improvement, Sal assumed innocently. Lingering in the living room, he felt out of place and was torn between attempting to communicate with Doris or loafing with the others. Noticing Craig and the usual toters standing impatiently before the impudent Doris, he settled on the slightly bucktoothed woman nervously filling out a dispatch ticket, and winced about working within sixty feet of her.

Maybe I can really be useful in here, speed things up, do everything possible to help the victims, he tried to reconsider positively. But momentarily giving up speaking to Doris, he deposited his lean body on the couch. *Organize the paperwork somehow*, he encouraged. *Maybe I could maneuver myself into making decisions before it's too late.* Rising, he approached Doris' desk and studied her pretty green eyes. But noting her filling out another dispatch ticket without acknowledging him, he wasn't sure where to begin. His first attempt to discuss how to help her received a small blow–Doris actually slapped his hand when he reached over to study a dispatch ticket, and laughter sprung from the knot of men surrounding her desk.

"Nobody touches dispatch tickets," she snapped and Sal smirked.

Tolerate the shrew or forget about working inside, he warned again. *But how?* he asked, almost shaking his head about the absurdity of it all. "Just trying to help," he offered defensively. Having heard something about a log, he asked what it was and where he could find it.

But Doris had difficulty handling two different matters also. "Somewhere," she replied, handed the dispatch ticket to a toter who excused his way past the group, and left.

"Where?" Sal pressed and the telephone rang. *Good luck*, he told himself. "What does it looks like," he squeezed in before she answered it.

Doris leaned back with the receiver, began chatting idly with Tammy, and Sal asked Rota.

Involved with her own paperwork, Rota became flustered. "Just a minute. I don't want to make a mistake with this."

Sal waited several minutes.

Forgetting Sal's question, she started joking with Craig about where he had spent the night again, annoying Sal further.

"Rota, the log," he reminded her.

"Oh, right, but I can't right now, Sal."

You were just able to talk to Craig, damn it, he grumbled. Blow up at her and that would have the same effect, even get you fired. Thank God, I have a job as a teacher. Or do I? he worried because of the possible strike and flooded-out school.

Rota noticed his expression. "Ask Doris."

Sal eyed Doris holding the phone between her ear and shoulder while writing a dispatch ticket for another toter. "Doris is out to lunch."

Rota frowned bewilderedly.

"Don't fight it," seemingly puzzled her further, and he turned back to Doris.

Still on the phone, she frowned annoyingly at an angry contractor who had been waiting to speak to her.

Noticing Sal's situation, Craig walked to Doris' desk, slyly removed a clipboard of papers, and handed it to him, surprising him.

The log, Sal recognized, thanked Craig with a nod, and eyed the front page's caption. *Lenny*, he labeled, noticing mimeograph smudges and he shook his head. One year of English with me raised him to this level of sloppiness, he varied with another laugh. Turning pages, he sighed about the dirty sheets and illegible handwriting. Neatness counts, damn it, he believed, recalling his class lectures about how sloppiness invited disregard about everything in life.

"Lenny's been loggin' in dispatch ticket information," Craig explained.

"Could 've fooled me," Sal answered.

"You might be getting his job."

Sal pictured the trouble Lenny had with the mimeograph machine. No thanks, Sal hid. "Whatever," he answered. "But why not file the dispatch tickets alone, instead of transferring that same information to a log? It's unnecessary and wastes time."

Craig shrugged and slurped his coffee. "That's why they hired Lenny, to handle the wasted time."

Everything's a joke, Sal kept to himself. "He's got *that* job under control. And these guys got loafing by you know where," he added beyond their hearing.

"Tell Doris."

Sal couldn't resist. "About the loafing?"

Craig laughed.

Noting her still on the phone, Sal smirked. "She's trying to figure out what bar she and Roy are going to tonight."

Craig accidentally spilled coffee on himself while laughing.

It really ain't that funny, Sal dramatized to himself again. "Pull yourself together, man."

"Ask Rota."

"She might collapse from the question's pressure," he commented, also beyond her hearing.

Craig laughed again and Doris finally hung up.

Sal complained to her about the log's redundancy.

"Oh, Sal, don't worry about it. We just log the damn stuff in," she dispensed without looking up from filling out another ticket, and Sal studied her childishly large letters. "You Yankees is all the same. Bitch, bitch, bitch."

What's that supposed to mean? "It's got the same information."

"We file dispatch tickets too," she insisted angrily, still without regarding him.

Calm down, woman. I don't know what's worse: your disposition, bad manners, or the overwhelming incompetence. Calm down yourself, he also ordered.

"Do whatever you want, Sal," she stabbed as if she were trying to satisfy a pesky child, and she practically flung a ticket at a third toter.

That's the problem. I really can't. "Don't shout. I ain't that far away, woman," he dramatized calmly again and she started filling out the fourth dispatch ticket.

The first toter reentered and positioned himself politely or perhaps reverently before her desk.

Doris eyed him. "You still here?"

Hands on his waist, the toter frowned with irritation.

"What do *you* want now?"

"There ain't no 050s out there," he grumbled.

"Did you look everywhere?"

"Yeah," he answered and the telephone rang.

Exhaling, the toter exchanged a sympathetic glance with Sal. "Hey, I can't hang around here all day," he told Doris. "I gotta get back on the road."

"Hello? Hang on," Doris told the caller. She pressed the hold and the usual furious buzzing sounded in Roy's office again.

"Who is it?" Roy shouted from the far end again and Sal shook his head.

"That guy from Metropolitan Propane," she screamed back at him. "Nick something." She turned to Rota. "Is he gonna work for us? He's cute," she stated quietly but Rota was too preoccupied to answer.

Peering down the long, narrow hallway, Doris frowned because of the standees blocking her vision. "Is he gonna work for us?" she repeated louder.

The woman's insane, Sal concluded inwardly.

"I don't know," Rota responded.

Doris' phone buzzed. She pressed another button, started disagreeing with Roy, and the toter exhaled disgustedly.

I guess the cowboy finally figured out what button to press. And they're discussing me, Sal sensed accurately. She doesn't want me working in the office. I guess I can't blame her, picturing himself criticizing her for being sloppy, rude, disorganized, and much more.

"Ah'll go back to West Virginia," she threatened indignantly and a pause followed.

Familiar shuffling sounded, and Sal spotted Roy working his way past the kitchen overflow.

The Chief halted before Doris' desk. "Doris," he announced dramatically, capturing the loungers' attention. "I'm takin' you out to lunch."

Scattered laughter seemed to pull an aggravated sigh from Sal's glum lips.

"It's 10:30," Doris exclaimed through her bucked teeth. "Nobody eats lunch now."

"Ah gots something ta discuss."

"Maybe he wants to propose," Sal muttered to several standees who guffawed.

Veering toward the front door, Roy turned.

Doris rose obediently with folded arms, ambled around her desk, and almost bumped into the first toter.

"Hey, you forgot me," he snarled angrily.

"And me," the second toter complained and all of them glared.

"You left that propane guy on hold," Sal reminded her.

Doris dashed back to her desk. Reaching over it, she pressed the button and lifted the receiver to her mouth. "Roy Nichols done left for lunch," she barked, hung up, and Craig laughed with several others. Remembering, she turned to Sal. "Ah'm done with them dispatch tickets. You can log 'em in."

"What about the 050s?" the first toter demanded and Sal quickly grabbed the log before she changed her mind.

"I'm on my lunch hour," she snapped, trudged behind Roy out the door, and the toters grimaced.

"What the hell's going on?" the first toter asked Sal gathering the clipboard and loose tickets.

"Things are a little disorganized," Craig interceded before Sal could answer. "We just moved in over here."

Eyeing the first toter, Sal couldn't resist. "Come back later when the confusion is more thoroughly organized," he deposited and turned for Rota's reaction.

"Hah? What? Not now, Sal. Got to get these reports done."

Heading for an unoccupied spot on the couch, Sal broke up. Sitting, he opened the log and noticed that important headings were missing such as the trailer's serial number, where it arrived (whether at the Fairgrounds or the Holding Point), when, number of bedrooms, and much more. Resolved to question Doris about such omissions since most of that information was available elsewhere, he knew, he reminded himself to ask Roy about the log's purpose. I'll get some answers if and when I'm in charge, he vowed and turned to Rota. Aware that she was struggling to read the men's signatures on the employee list, he offered to alphabetize and retype them on file index cards, despite anticipating their poor handwriting. "It'll ask them to spell their names if I can't read them. I took Hieroglyphics I and II at college."

"Oh, really?" she responded, taking him seriously. "Thanks. I never get around to doing such stuff."

An hour later, Roy reentered with the sulking Doris. Ignoring Sal typing the cards on a small typewriter desk beside Rota, Doris sat behind her desk. Angling between the men, Roy headed toward his room without regarding Sal either, irritating him.

Did you really expect anything different? Contemplating the pouting, arm-folded Doris, he wondered how many humans had died throughout history because of similar childishness, particularly during a disaster. Finishing the cards, he strode down the hall, entered Roy's office and started explaining what had been omitted in the log's headings.

"Yeah," Roy was already agreeing before Sal could finish. "Just fill in whatever you want."

No kidding, he thought. "But where can I find all that missing information?" Pray tell, man.

Roy stared self-consciously at the kitchen overflow.

"From the dispatch tickets?" You ain't gonna learn yourself nathin' if ya keep suggestin' answers, man, he scolded playfully again and squelched a smile.

Roy whipped out another small *yeah.*

Choice, Sal teased himself sarcastically, borrowing the word from his male students. "Why have a log at all?" he ventured next. I sound like a broken record.

Roy countered with a blank face.

"Why not just file the dispatch tickets and be done with it?"

"Ask Doris."

"Doris doesn't want to talk to me," he uttered gravely and scolded himself for sounding like an offended child.

Struggling to discern her beyond the kitchen overflow, Roy

narrowed his eyes. "Wot? She don't?"

"No."

Roy glared back at her. "Dang."

It's probably your fault, Daddyo. You probably don't communicate with her either. "Still want me to run the office?" Sal flung recklessly since Roy had never officially told him so. God, it's awful struggling to be needed or wanted. Blessed are those who are loved, wanted, or appreciated, even if they don't realize it, or they take it for granted when they do, he philosophized. How's she going to take orders from me if she doesn't from her employer she's shacking up with?

Roy sighed and frowned.

Suspecting that his relationship with her was stressing him out, Sal had no sympathy for anyone allowing someone with so many faults to dominate them in a relationship, even for sex. God, does she have much to learn about life and human relations. What about people like Roy? It's probably hopeless if they lack the capacity, he answered. Recalling Audrey's account that a flood victim had hung himself recently, Sal resolved to wait for Roy to speak once again, that is, arrive at a decision, ask something, make a suggestion–anything–no matter how long it took.

"Just try and help her out," Roy finally deposited. "We're getting a new girl tomorrow."

"You're replacing Doris?" Sal precluded without thinking. Like what Adam should've done with Eve? he pondered playfully.

"Wot?" Roy asked, surprised. "No, no, no. Another girl."

Sal placed hands on his waist and stared at the blond head and sad eyes. "How's the new girl going to learn anything from Doris who doesn't relate or communicate with anybody?"

"Hah? Wot? Can't hack them big words, Teach."

Oh, God, Sal almost moaned aloud.

"Ah, Doris ain't that bad. She's just in a bad mood, ta-day," he drawled.

Yeah, sure, Sal uttered to himself. He returned to the living room. He corrected the men's illegible signatures with their help, finished typing the remaining cards, and handed them to Rota who thanked him. He considered sitting on the couch, but three long-haired men were occupying it. Is this a Jesus look-alike contest or are you mongrels awaiting the next Woodstock concert? he teased, grinned, and one of them smiled back, as if he had read Sal's mind.

Sal removed the log on Rota's desk unnoticed and carried it into the kitchen. He excused his way past the men, pushed aside crumpled papers, mimeograph stencils, and whatnot on the table, and sat. Opening the log, he stared at the headings and had second thoughts again.

219

Is doing meaningless work better than loafing? Probably, but not by much. He decided to devise a new log that included the vital missing information that he could glean from dispatch tickets and inspection sheets. But since such sheets were scattered atop cabinets and the two women's desks, he knew the task would be difficult. Worse, since the inspection sheets weren't numbered, he would never know when he had them all, and left to ask Doris where he could find more. But arriving, he hesitated to question her because of her terrible disposition.

The telephone rang again. She answered abruptly and was short with another flood victim apparently begging to know when he could move his wife and two small children into a trailer, Sal caught. "I got no idea. That ain't my department," she responded and hung up.

Happy appeared and slid a paper plate of chicken and fried grits before her.

She grabbed a leg and started nibbling it. But eyeing Sal, she rose. Storming past him, she wiggle between the throng and eventually bullied through the kitchen overflow. She opened Roy's door, entered, and slammed it shut.

Guess they're still arguing about me, Sal realized.

"Any resemblance between this place and an office is purely coincidental," Vinny told Rota who laughed.

"Hope you take over, Sal," Rota uttered confidentially.

"Thanks, but I don't think Doris would agree. Much less take orders from me."

Happy grabbed Doris' plate. He angled between the men, passed the kitchen overflow, and entered Roy's office.

"Guess they're having a private meeting," Sal told Rota evaluating a group of men milling near the dining room sink. But what does Happy have to do with it? crossed his mind.

Rota touched her long, fluffy, auburn hair. "Don't know who's worse, her or Roy. Some bunch. I ought to quit but I need the money."

"Shouldn't work so hard, Rota," Norm commented sincerely from the couch, and she regarded him briefly. "You hardly take time to eat. Take off for lunch. Get away from this place."

"Oh, I should," Rota replied. "But I never do. Last night I didn't get home till twelve trying to straighten things out. I've got an eight-year-old son. I only see him at night. I peek in his room while he's asleep." Momentarily less nervous because of Doris' absence, she laughed. "If it wasn't for my mother who takes care of him, I wouldn't–" she attempted and halted. "This job's getting on my nerves. Reports for everything–even reports for reports."

"That's like the Army," Norm inserted.

"Lost five pounds last week. I just can't eat. I'm takin' all kinds of pills," she continued, but heard Roy's door open, and she stopped fearfully.

The kitchen standees squeezed inside when Doris approached, and they shuffled back into the hall after she left.

"Here comes the queen," Sal announced.

Rota laughed again. "I can use you in here just to make me laugh."

Her arms folded, Doris flopped into her chair.

"Everything settled?" Sal needled, unaware that he was intimidating her.

Doris looked up as though noticing him initially. "Been to the Fair? Don't go," she warned before he could answer. "It stinks."

Sal couldn't resist. "You've got to avoid the pigsties."

Though she ignored him again, he revealed his intention to rewrite the log. "Mostly because someone didn't keep track of dispatch tickets and especially the information on inspection sheets," he insinuated, referring to her.

"I ain't the only one handlin' that, ya know," she sneered and flicked her head at Rota.

"Any more inspection sheets floating around?" Sal inquired. "Maybe in your apartment?" he dug again when she disregarded him again.

Doris looked up. "What's wrong with you Yankees anyway?"

Sal examined her protruding lips because of bucked teeth. Now what? "Same as what's right or wrong with anybody or everybody in the world at any given time. Why?"

"Know why that guy quit Metropolitan Propane to work here?"

"Not really. What guy?" he pretended, as if to punish her once again for the same reason.

"Tsk. The one on the phone before."

"The one you hung up on," he replied, deliberately referring to the flood victim.

"Hah?"

"Forget it. What about him?"

"He was a big shot with the company, district manager or somethin'. The company always give him ten bucks extra for every tank of gas that got installed in his area, no matter who done it. Until the flood. When they tried Jewin' him down ta payin' him for only five, 'cause of all them trailers getting tanks, he quit. Now he's working for us."

"What else is new?" Sal asked. "People 've been reneging on promises, contracts, and treaties, since the beginning of time."

"Now don't go dishin' out them big Northern words," she contested. "Or try learnin' me nothin', 'cause I ain't learnin'."

"Wouldn't think of it none," he worded playfully. "But folks can't stop learning no matter how hard they try," returned the serious teacher in him again.

"Hah?"

God, what focusing. Turn up your hearing aid, woman. "Nothing. But five dollars apiece is better than nothing. If the company only installed two hundred tanks, that's still a quick two hundred bucks for doing nothing." Wish I would have been slain with that deal. He also could've sued them, especially if he had a contract."

"He done right quitting," Doris disagreed.

Sal shrugged. "Sure, now he's got a brilliant future working for HUD during cleanup operations. For maybe another couple of months tops, provided we continue loafing at the same pace."

Rota and several other listeners laughed.

"But what if these guys stop loafing and start working? Hell, he could be laid off in a couple of weeks."

Unaccustomed to such wit, Doris stared blankly at Sal, and her bucked teeth emerged slightly above her lower lip.

"What's his job going to be with us anyway?" Sal inquired inquisitively.

"Ah don't know. Roy says coordinator or somethin'."

Here we go with the titles. "Sounds official enough. What's he going to coordinate, confusion with disorganization? he concocted, sensing she probably wouldn't understand.

"He's gonna be a G-9 right off," she revealed, then sneered childishly, as if she were jealous.

"Is that all?" Sal responded and Rota laughed again.

"He's supposed to make sure trailers get gas and electric," Doris added.

"Hell, we've got plenty of guys to do that. They're called inspectors. Ah, but I'm sure he'll catch on to our loafing. Our boys are experienced. They'll show him."

Rota laughed still again and Doris regarded him curiously.

"Now, do I have all the dispatch tickets?"

"What're you, a G-4 or G-5?" Doris sidetracked.

None of your business, Sal almost retorted. Oh, what the hell. She can't help who she is right now either. "Roy promised me a raise. I'm supposed to be a G-5. Now about those–"

"Hey Roy. Did you make Sal a G-5?" she shouted down the hall, practically flooring him and a lounger shook his head.

"Doris, for heaven's sake–" Sal cried and checked down the hall. Well, I'll be damned flashed a thought, discerning Roy reading a comic book at his desk. The ol' boy's trying to get educated.

"Don't you wanna know for sure?" Doris inquired.

"That's okay. Let it go."

"Hey Roy," she shrieked again. "Did you give Teach a raise?"

"Yeah," Roy shouted back but too casually, Sal noted.

"There," Doris told Sal. "Now you can sleep."

Grinning disbelievingly at her, he glanced at Rota who frowned sympathetically. "Now, what about the dispatch tickets and inspection sheets?"

"What about 'em?" Doris retorted and the telephone rang.

Oh, God, not again, Sal groaned. "Do you have any more?" he asked hurriedly.

She answered another distraught flood victim curtly and Sal smirked.

Doris covered the receiver. "Check in the cabinet below the Xerox machine," she stormed.

Realizing he hadn't looked there, Sal nodded, left, but decided to check the second bedroom first. Unbelievable, he remarked, finding a small stack underneath a tray on a shelf. He added it to his growing pile, returned to the living room and chose not to waste time and energy asking Doris if she knew about them. He found more on top of a filing cabinet which Rota admitted that she was unable to file, because she couldn't understand Doris' filing system.

The bathroom, Sal announced, remembering seeing some on the toilet tank for days. Picturing inspectors leaving them anywhere, because nobody told them to turn them in, he found another small pile. Returning to Doris' desk, he was about to urge her to remind inspectors to give them to him when her telephone rang again.

"Telephone," she deliberately announced in order to distract Sal, he realized, and she grabbed the receiver hurriedly.

Two contractors entered. Both took one look at Doris and fell into the "obedient dog" mode before her desk–that is, rocking back and forth on the balls of their feet while standing impatiently before her.

Rota had sense enough to ask them if she could help them and directed them to Roy who they wanted to see.

Giving up trying to talk to Doris, Sal left. He found more of both on a closet floor and spent two hours copying information from them at the kitchen table. He was about to put the dispatch tickets in numerical order and the inspection sheets according to the date the trailer was inspected when Doris appeared. Veering between the usual coffee-cup bearers, she tossed more dispatch tickets on the table and started breaking away.

Sal eyed the low numbers in disbelief. "Wait a minute. Where'd you get these?"

Doris laughed like a mischievous child, paused before a man sporting fanned-out hair, ala Dinger, and turned. "What the difference?" she dismissed and the men ogled her breasts as she headed for the doorway.

Sal followed after her up the hall angrily. He zigzagged between the men and arrived before her sitting at her desk. "If you want my help," he purposely implied, "you're going to have to cooperate," he ordered sternly, struggling not to get upset. "Is that all of them now?"

She refused to answer and he had had it. Racing back down the hall, he entered Roy's office which the contractors had just left.

Clipping his fingernails, Roy looked up and Sal complained about her not cooperating.

"She's like that sometimes. Can't learn her nothin'. Believe me, ah tried."

"She should be fired," Sal barked, unaware how upset he was.

Calmly pocketing the clipper, Roy leaned back (squeaking the swivel chair), massaged his chin, and barely opened his mouth. "Just do the best you can, Teach."

Inhaling and exhaling, Sal pulled himself together. *I should just beat the shit out of* him *and call it a day.* "I can't help much if she doesn't cooperate."

"Ah got all the rest of the tickets," Doris shouted from her desk.

"Check that out, Teach," he dispensed, glancing self-consciously at him. "Just hang in there. You'll be all right. When Craig comes back, you and him's pickin' up a couple a desks. One fer you and the other fer the new girl what's comin' in ta'marra."

Overwhelmed by such an outpouring, Sal stared at him momentarily. *You mean I'm going to have my own room?*

"Plus a typewriter fer you. Fer the one we lost in the movin'," he added, astonishing Sal, particularly because Roy was indifferent about it.

Either it was stolen or it's still resting at the old office, Sal scorned sarcastically, but decided not to pursue it for fear of distracting Roy from possibly announcing that he was in charge of the office.

"We'll put you in the first bedroom," he declared, mellowing Sal. "That'll be yo' office. Even get you a telephone."

Not too bad, Sal admitted. *I'd have some privacy. But is this true or the usual bullshit people like Roy love to dish out?* "Thanks," he answered, returned to Doris' desk, and accepted the pack of tickets as Rota watched. "Is this all of them now?"

"Yeah. Ah done checked everywhere," Doris responded.

Good, but is that *true?* he questioned, aware how often certain people lied. He stared at several flies parading up and down the partly-eaten chicken leg on her desk. *Ugh,* he reflected, waving them off. "You're eating that despite the flies?" Mind your own business, his other self scolded.

"How come you gots so many flies up North?" she needled.

"They migrate up from the South," he quipped with deadpan seriousness, and Rota and several others burst out laughing. "I'll throw it out," he offered, afraid that Dinger might eat it.

"Whatever turns ya on," she agreed, surprising him, and she began filling out a dispatch ticket for the toter standing before her.

Sal grabbed her paper plate, but spying wads of paper beside an overflowing waste can behind her desk, he hesitated. "What about this waste can? I think it's full," he understated and the toter laughed. "Where do you empty it?"

"*You're* gonna empty it?" Doris inquired.

"Isn't that what folks do when they're full? But I hope I'm not being too technical for you."

Rota laughed again.

"Emptying waste cans is easy. Learned that when I was four."

"Ah don't know where ta empty the dang thing. That ain't my job," Doris retorted.

Sal dropped the plate inside the can and stooped for the wads. "Ya finds out, woman," he dramatized again.

Rota giggled. "You can empty mine too," she chirped, watching him pressing down the trash with his foot.

You've just been demoted from hypothetical head office man to office boy, he announced, observing Rota's full can. "You women are allergic to emptying waste cans?"

"That's men's work," Rota responded.

Sal paused, holding Doris' can. "Really?"

"My husband does that in my house," Rota added.

"Ma brother does it back home," Doris sing-songed.

Sal regarded one face after the other. "What're you, female chauvinists? If that's true, then how come washing dishes *isn't* female's work then?"

Rota laughed, assuming he was teasing them.

"There ya go with them big words," Doris said.

Sal grabbed Rota's can and one of the men opened the door. "Thanks." Probably more work than he's done since he was hired. He emptied them in a dumpster outside and returned.

"Put mine raght back where it was," Doris ordered.

"Mine too," Rota requested gentler.

Kindness breeds contempt, Sal reminded himself. Complying, he returned to the kitchen. Looking through the opening, he noted Craig heading for the urn.

Craig grabbed a cup. Holding it underneath the spigot, he flipped the spigot down, but nothing happened. Tipping the urn, he cursed. "Don't nobody make coffee around here?" he asked but not loud enough to interrupt the girls typing furiously, as if they were attempting to outdo each other, and he eyed Sal through the opening.

"I haven't been assigned that job, yet," Sal answered, rose, and approached the opening. "I would've made some, but I hate to work near the maggots."

Craig removed the urn's cover and glanced at the flies buzzing around paper plates filled with chicken bones, ketchup, and stale fries. "Who belongs to this slop?"

"The flies," Sal answered.

Removing the coffee basket, Craig shook his head.

"Know why we moved?" Sal presented. "Nobody wanted to clean the other trailer."

Craig finally laughed. He turned on the tap, dumped the grains down the sink, and washed out the stem.

Wonder how long it'll take before the drainpipe clogs? Sal questioned, "Soon as I get finished doing nothing, I'll start doing a hair more, like swatting flies. Where've *you* been?" he accosted.

"Around," Craig replied, filling the urn with water.

"Wide area."

"Yeah," Craig admitted.

Did it include the flood victims? Sal almost asked, but picturing the loungers, considered Craig less guilty than they. Men radioing the office often provided a clue about their whereabouts, he knew. "Just left the office" or "I'm on Route 17" usually meant that such individuals were to their respective parks for the usual loafing after attending to their personal affairs.

Craig eyed the counter containing streaks of sloppily-wiped milk, donut crumbs, and smudges buzzing with flies also. "This place is startin' to smell already," he admitted and started searching for coffee in the cabinets.

"We should get cleaning service. The government can afford it," Sal reminded him again. "It would be money well spent," he urged, then scolded himself because of so many other more important concerns.

Opening a cabinet door, Craig eyed chicken bones, leftover fries, and a crumpled napkin on a paper plate. "Looks like Happy's garbage." He opened another and peered inside. "Where *is* he?"

"Not in there. He's probably listening to his rock tapes. Second from the left," Sal obliged.

Craig opened the door. "Two cans? Where'd the others go?"

"The way of tools, chainsaws, flashlights, pens, beds, and countless other things which now includes an IBM electric typewriter."

Craig grabbed a can and froze. "A typewriter? Since when?"

"This morning, I hear. No problem," he sing-songed sarcastically. "Roy said you and I could get another one from the Rand when we get the desks."

"What desks?" Craig asked, searching for the can opener.

"Roy didn't tell you?"

"No."

"Communicating *isn't* his best suit," Sal stabbed and they eventually left for the Rand. But checking the Rand's secretaries, they soon discovered that none knew anything about the desks. "Didn't Roy Nichols call about them?"

"No," all agreed, hardly surprising Sal.

One woman referred them to a Mr. Davenport who told them to wait nearby for a Mr. Swenson who might know about them.

What's going on in the world, Sal wondered when he didn't show after they waited twenty minutes. Deciding to discuss the paycheck foul-up with Millie, he soon learned that she had flown to Washington D. C. about it. Who paid for *that* trip? Who do you think? he answered. She couldn't handle that over the phone? What? and miss a paid vacation for God knows how many days? Get serious, man.

He checked with the same secretaries about his four dollars and they referred him to three different HUD employees. He finally located the right person, but she had gone to lunch, and Sal carried his frown back to where he was before. How come employers don't have employees lunch one at a time, so somebody is left to mind the fort, particularly during a disaster? he grumbled.

Gazing languidly, six desks ahead, he spied Tony Grannis laughing and chatting with a disinterested secretary. My truck's still at the Fairgrounds, man, Sal reproached, which he ruled out reminding him in order to minimize stress. He grabbed *The Star Gazette* from a nearby chair, started reading about a flood victim's attempted suicide, and Craig arrived.

He led Sal to two unused metal desks and they carried the first one down a long hallway. Reaching the loading platform, some distance from their truck, they were perspiring heavily. They stopped to catch their breaths and noticed a man leaning against a Bobcat loader, sipping coffee.

"Where 're ya headin' with that?" he interceded.

"How about giving us a hand with your bobcat?" Sal requested since several parked semis prevented them from backing their truck up to the platform. We'd appreciate it. We've got another desk still inside."

The man stared at him.

227

"It's for the flood victims." Indirectly, he revised.

"Can't. Union rules."

Oh, another hard-nosed rule-follower, Sal concealed and surveyed the surrounding area flippantly. "There's nobody around but us."

"We won't tell," Craig contributed with a grin.

The man shook his head. "How do I know you guys ain't from the Union?"

"How do we know Jesus Christ hasn't risen from the dead?" Sal reciprocated. "Don't we just know that?" Besides, people don't usually get in trouble helping others, he concealed Yeah, sure, he responded cynically.

The man frowned. "Sorry. Gotta follow Union rules."

"Forget it," Craig told Sal who agreed with a smirk.

Tilting the desk, they struggled to slide it down the platform as the man watched.

Why didn't we bring along a couple of deadbeats to help? Sal scolded. They carried it toward their truck, a good hundred feet away, and both paused to catch their breaths. Because we didn't anticipate not getting any help, he answered.

Eventually loading it into the truck as the man continued studying them from the distance, they were exhausted and perspiring freely, more so by the time they arrived with the second desk. Taking a rest, they reentered the Rand, inquired about a typewriter, but no one knew about that either.

Noticing one resting on an unused desk, Sal unhooked the plug. "Let's go," he announced, lifting it off and Craig laughed.

Heading back to the office, Craig stopped to let Sal check how badly the flood had damaged Southside High. Entering the school, he heard loud bulldozing and descended into the cafeteria. Inhaling old plaster, mildew, and dust, he observed Mr. O'Reilly and a helper watching a bucket push a pile of plaster, tiles, wood, and similar debris toward a large hole punched out of the band room wall.

Wearing shorts and boots, Mr. O'Reilly removed his cigar. He greeted Sal, shook his hand, and described what six feet of dirty, turbulent water had caused. "We're going to have to brown bag it for months before we get the school back in shape," he shouted above the dozing. "We'll make it," he predicted, typical of a new optimism sweeping the area.

Sal pictured teaching again. That's a relief.

"New books are coming. School 'll be open on schedule. Unless there's a walkout. But I think they're going to settle," came more enthusiasm, as if Sal were a fellow administrator or friend. O'Reilly started coughing because of the dust and Sal left.

Craig began their slow journey behind the usual line of vehicles creeping along Main Street leading toward one of two semi-operable bridges. Though the Sanitation Department had cleared the major debris, signs of the flood still remained on both sides of the muddy single lane.

They soon observed a man emerge from an unlit store, dump a box of debris atop a pile of junk, and walk back. Like an ant returning to its hole, Sal thought. Further ahead, workers were installing new plate windows in Miller's Drugs, Martin's Hardware, and Sam's Bar.

Reaching the Holding Point, Sal entered the office hoping to find a lounger to help them with the desks, but it was empty, except for the women. Worse, the desks were too wide to fit in the doorway. You mean nobody checked? What about you? he scolded. Were I in charge, this wouldn't have happened, he assumed and measured the opening. Returning to the Rand, they found two young workers who helped them carry them back inside. But finding two narrower desks was even more difficult.

"At least they're lighter," Craig declared once they did, hours later and the same men assisted loading them inside the truck.

Chapter 25

arly Wednesday morning, Carmela Powers entered the office. She introduced herself as the new secretary which Rota and even Doris repeated several times, Sal heard from his office. To prove to themselves that they accepted her for being black, Sal sensed, hearing them patronizing her excessively. I guess it's better to be hypocritically kind, than sincerely prejudiced, he varied.

Though nepotism was supposedly forbidden, HUD also hired Carmela's husband, Dexter, as the new watchman.

Nick Maturo, the ex-Metropolitan Propane man, arrived later that day. Smooth-faced, insecure, and in his early thirties, he caught on quickly–to a cup handle. Despite being neatly dressed, he had no problem fitting in nicely with the shabbily-attired loungers, Sal realized with a laugh.

Quincy Howe also returned for good from Corning. He too snagged a cup and met Sal in the living room. "Hear ya got your own office."

Sal glanced at the man's slight potbelly and the odd tuff of hair pointing down from his head. "Just an ugly rumor."

"Let's have a private talk."

Now what? Sal thought, unsure whether it would be informal or official.

Quincy entered Sal's office first, continued around Sal's desk and sat in his swivel chair which squeaked.

Surprised, Sal sat in one of two metal chairs beside a wall of shelving.

"Guess you know I'm over you," Quincy began, catching Sal off guard.

"Oh?" Who cares? What's that got to do with helping the flood victims, even if true? he reflected and Quincy started opening drawers, looking inside, and closing them. Find anything interesting? "You mean *you're* my new boss?" he enunciated, sensing Quincy was improvising. Regarding the odd tuff resembling a wide brush lifted out of a can of paint, he struggled against breaking up.

Eyeing Sal's typewriter, Quincy started fondling the tuff into a sharper point which Sal found boyishly ridiculous.

"Something like that," Quincy answered.

You mean you don't know yet? "Okay, I'll play your silly game."

Wrinkles formed under the tuff, and Quincy flopped his heavy, bare arms on both sides of the typewriter. "It ain't no silly game. We gotta start movin' more flood victims into trailers. Too many guys is just hangin'

231

around."

Sal laughed sarcastically. "No kidding. Didn't think anybody noticed. So, why tell me? Tell Roy. Are you over him too?"

Twisting his mouth grotesquely, Quincy analyzed his bare arm protruding out of his short-sleeved shirt. "His assistant."

Tolerance, Sal ordered. So, I guess you promoted yourself. But pray tell, how did you manage to sidestep Craig? Or do we have two assistants?

Quincy observed Sal's frown. "Think I'm kiddin'? Ask him."

Sal noted scattered pockmarks in the man's slightly baggy face. "What were you doing in Corning if you were the assistant here?"

"Helping," he responded unconvincingly. "Juan never ran an office. He can't hardly read English."

"Sounds like a perfect man for the job. Neither can Roy and he's an American."

"What Juan don't know about paperwork could fill a trailer."

Now *that* sounds like a good quality. Paperwork be damned during a disaster, Sal raged. The male ego, he answered, and I'm forever placating it with guys like Quincy. "You're Craig's boss too?" he finally questioned.

"Yeah," Quincy confessed. "He's only a G-7. I'm a G-9. I'm over Happy too, only he don't know it. Don't tell him."

Why? because you're bullshitting me? he concealed but was curious about how far the absurdity went. "I thought Happy was a G-72 the way he handles his Barracuda. Why, you should have seen him zoom out of here and rescue a toter who forgot to sign a dispatch ticket the other day. It would've curled your hair."

"Ranks don't go that high," Quincy replied, taking Sal seriously.

Sal sniffed into a smile. "And this new guy, Maturo? Heard he's a G-9 too."

Quincy glanced past Sal's face. "Don't know nothin' about him."

If we can't get the best people to lead during a disaster, how can we in government, much less the presidency? Sal reflected and shrugged. "Okay, I'll follow your orders if it turns you on." But only to a point–not where intelligence leaves off and stupidity begins, he vowed.

"It ain't that," Quincy hedged indignantly. "I wanna start organizin' the men."

Sounds reasonable–even intelligent, Sal agreed, unaware how sarcastic he had become. "Good idea."

"Keep some control," he insisted. "Gonna have a meeting tomorrow."

Oh, good. When in doubt, meet. How we love meetings. They offer us a chance to socialize with coffee, doughnuts, and sometimes delicious cake. Of course, it *do* reduce the need for paperwork, he added playfully again.

"Want you to tell the men. It'll be in the morning, eight sharp."

"Are you coming?" Sal dug. Noting Quincy's indignant frown, Sal mentioned the morning that Roy called a meeting that he never attended.

"I'll be there," Quincy announced dramatically, as if he were McArthur's reincarnation, and he started fingering the typewriter keys that began striking the roller, annoying Sal.

Don't do that. It's not a toy. You're ruining the roller, jackass.

"How's your typing?"

"Hit in the low sixties sometimes, but my game's been a little off lately. Why?" Quit it. You're ruining the roller, Andrew.

"I want you to type three different forms."

Sal almost choked. Oh, God, maybe I won't play your silly game.

"One each for the maintenance men, inspectors, and contractors. and Xerox oh, about a dozen of each. Can you do that?"

Oh, God. Don't fight it, man, he ordered internally with a frown. "I think it's within the realm of ability. What do you want for the headings?"

"Don't know yet. Can you get me some paper?"

Sal glanced at an open ream on the shelf behind him. You're crippled? he inquired but rose, removed several sheets, and handed them to him.

"How about a ruler and a pen or a pencil?"

Hands on his waist, Sal frowned at Quincy inserting a sheet between the roller. I've been demoted to a servant now? "How about it?"

"Come on, Sal. I wouldn't know where to look."

"Geezus, man. There's a pen on my desk right in front of you." Annoyed, he left to ask Rota for a ruler. Why do some people believe in stupid paperwork? he continued grumbling, borrowed it and returned. Maybe to prove they're above manual labor, he answered, placed it on the desk, and Quincy eyed it while typing.

Watching boredly, Sal heard someone enter the radio room. Appreciating an excuse to leave, he excused himself, stepped inside the passageway separating the two rooms, and observed Carmela trying to figure out how to operate the Xerox machine. Surprised upon noticing inspection sheets in her hand, he approached. "Need copies of those?"

She smiled pleasantly and Sal regarded her pretty, young face. "Yes. Two of each."

"Two of each?" he repeated incredulously, accepting the stack. "Since when? Who said? What for?"

"Doris. She just got the word from HUD at the Rand. Came in with the courier. They're supposed to get two copies of every inspection sheet from us from now on."

"For God's sake, they come in quadruplicate already. Who's getting the extra copy, Nixon?"

Unsure how to accept such indignation from someone who might be in authority, Carmela shrugged.

Shaking his head he considered questioning Doris about it and peeked out the doorway. But noting her fuming about a report while several contractors stood impatiently before her, he changed his mind. What's a little more meaningless paperwork anyway? he conceded until his whimsical self kicked in. But that's how paper epidemics start. An extra copy here, another one there–and suddenly civilization collapses from tons and tons of– Catching himself, he stopped.

Carmela reached behind the machine, withdrew a small pile of dispatch tickets, and handed them to him. "These too."

"Oh, God," Sal cried, accepting them with dismay. I think I'm going to have a coronary. Frowning, he placed an inspection sheet under the cover, pressed a button, and the machine cranked into operation.

"Me and Rota are trying to straighten out the files," she explained, assuming he was in charge, he sensed.

"We're *already* making copies of dispatch tickets."

"Doris has more dispatch tickets on her desk."

"What?" he demanded, then calmed himself. "Today's?"

She shrugged. "I'll do them after I get done with these."

The machine stopped and he started copying the next sheet. "Oh, Carmela?"

About to leave, she paused curiously by the door.

Sal placed another sheet under the cover, pressed the button, and turned to her. "Good luck with those files."

Having witnessed several of Doris' temper tantrums, Carmela grinned guardedly at another strange white man.

"Do you mind some advice?"

"No."

"Keep away from Doris as much as possible."

Carmela's lips parted interestingly.

"She's insane," he deposited and turned back to the machine which grabbed and swallowed another sheet.

Smiling curiously, she frowned. Staring at Sal engrossed feeding copies under the cover, she seemed to have difficulty determining what looked more incongruous: an indifferent machine accepting papers from a trim, slightly-graying, bespectacled creature or the creature removing them. Not only did she appreciate his playful smile but she seemed relieved.

Minutes later, a red light appeared against a black background and the machine stopped working. That's it? He read "Replace the web."

What's that? You mean I overstuffed you? Nice going, he scolded himself and entered Roy's office. "What's a web?"

Roy literally rose to the occasion without answering and withdrew a small box from Sal's closet. He lifted up the machine's lid with savage confidence, opened a side door deftly, and snapped two metal clamps together, as Sal watched. He removed two cylinders connected to a dirty, cheesecloth wrapping which Sal sensed was the defective web and dropped it into the waste can. He shoved the cylinders in place and fitted the new web neatly between two small rollers–all in one operation but much too quickly for Sal to remember how he did it.

No wonder they're paying you eleven bucks an hour, Sal suppressed. "The large cylinder goes on top, the smaller, below," he muttered for future reference and Roy shut the side door. "You're tough."

Missing more sarcasm, Roy seemed to move faster. He grabbed a stirrer from inside the machine. He opened a cap, poured black powder inside a container, and stirred it.

"Nice style." Too bad you can't handle men like you do machines.

Assuming Sal was serious, he continued checking the machine's parts like a teenager tinkering with a hot rod.

"What did you just stir?" Sal asked, though bored whenever forced to fix anything mechanical.

Roy was too busy manipulating and cleaning a part to answer.

They've got to make machines talk someday, Sal began. Especially because of mute folks like Roy Rogers here in this dimension.

Roy closed the main lid and grabbed a paper towel from the roll on the floor. He wiped his hands, paused cockily, and eyed Sal.

You're expecting applause? ran a thought. You need to do something more meaningful than that before you get mine. Like really help the flood victims, Superman.

"Fire away."

"Good, thanks," Sal nevertheless responded and Roy left. Sal finished running off the inspection sheets that he had left on Doris' desk while she conversed with Tammy on the phone, and he returned to his office in order to add the new information to his log.

Quincy entered with three new forms he wanted Sal to type and duplicate.

Sal studied *Parts* and *Labor* heading one of them. More nonsense, he labeled. "We're going to start charging flood victims for service calls?" he suddenly comprehended.

Quincy pulled up the metal chair before Sal's desk and sat. "No, that form's for the trailer companies."

Disturbed about the man's enthusiasm about paperwork, Sal

lowered his arms on the desk and sighed.

"We're gonna charge them for what's *their* problems, like leaky pipes and bad electrical work *we've* been fixin'."

Scanning the second sheet which was for inspectors, Sal accepted the idea initially, then had second thoughts.

"From now on, inspectors are gonna report how many trailers they inspect, release, and what they call in to us. So we can tell HUD at the Rand," Quincy continued.

Smirking, Sal finally blew up. "That's ridiculous. We should handle those problems ourselves, like we've been doing. Picture the complications, man. Companies blaming the toters for breakage, toters blaming us, HUD blaming the company. It's too much trouble. And why bother inspectors to call us and report this information? It's dumb. Whose idea was this? We're going to need another secretary to fill out reports, bills, and whatever we send to the companies. Meanwhile, victims are suffering during all this bullshit."

"We got a new secretary, Carmela,"

Sal frowned at the pouchy face with the weird hair combed into a point. "Carmela's going to be helping Rota and Doris."

"Don't worry. I got you, don't I?"

Oh, shit, Sal thought and grimaced.

Noticing his expression, Quincy laughed.

"Anyways, I think Hugh Brennig's wife's gonna start working here too."

Sal sensed more nepotism. "What? She needs a job? Hubby doesn't make enough? Why not hire a flood victim, for God's sake? Who's making these stupid decisions?" Them in power–which you ain't, he dramatized again.

"I hear she's bored," Quincy responded. "She's tired of swimming and sunning herself all day in this house they rented."

Sal sighed. "Poor thing. How did they fill her pool? With flood water?"

"Hah?"

"Never mind."

Quincy leaned forward. "Couple a other things. I think a shipment of lumber is suppose to be comin' in today. We're gonna start building our own steps ta replace cinder-block. Roy just hired a carpenter. Him and a crew is gonna work around the clock."

"Funny place to work," Sal inserted impudently. "You sure we need *that* many steps?"

"We need two for every trailer. Four thousand trailers is gonna be set up by the end of August. Don't laugh. That's the word from Brennig."

"Maybe he's got the wrong word."

"We gotta start shakin' ass," Quincy persisted undismayed.

"Why, we're expecting another disaster?" No, two is enough, he answered. The one outside and the one in front of me.

"The government's flyin' up some guy named Floyd Rorick. He's bringin' up tractor trailers, trucks, toters, flatbeds, men–the whole nine yards. He's big in the South, a millionaire. And he don't fool around. Ever hear of him?"

I know a guy named Joe from Los Angeles. Ever hear of him? he almost asked. "No."

"The government gave him a contract to set up four hundred trailers."

"We don't even have that many in the field."

"We will. They're on the way."

"Heard that before. Besides, not enough parks are open. Half the contractors are just sitting around now."

"Two new parks are openin' soon. They're workin' on more. Most of the other contractors is gonna handle private sites anyway. That's where Happy and his crew comes in."

"Happy? I assumed Roy hired him just to listen to rock and roll in his car. What's going on? *His* crew? He's in charge of the freeloaders in the office here." *He's* got a crew?"

"Yeah, the flyin' squirrels he calls 'em."

Now there's a name. "You mean Happy's going to start working? Or flying?"

Continuing to take Sal seriously, Quincy nodded officially. "He'll be working when there's work."

"Really? Then how come he isn't working?"

"He's gonna make sure sites is ready–clear trees and shit before trailers comes in."

Folks are shitting at the sites? You're kidding.

"He just left with his crew to buy rakes, chainsaws, axes, shovels, and other shit.

You mean more stuff is going to disappear?

"We gotta start hustling," he cried eagerly and grinned. "We're hiring another girl, puttin' her in the bedroom next door. That's gonna be the official radio room." He nodded at the passageway. "She's gonna be the only one ta answer the radio and take messages–just one person instead of everybody and anybody answering all the time, get it?"

"Not all of it. Guess I should be taking notes."

"Come on, Sal. Don't fool around. Everybody and his brother answers important messages that come in here from inspectors and even maintenance men. Or we lose 'em or they forget to tell Roy or Craig, you name it. Doris don't even have a radio."

"Thank God."

"It's ridiculous,"

"Almost as ridiculous as Doris."

"Once I get started, I don't fool around," he emphasized and paused for Sal's reaction.

You'll go crazy if you don't join him like you do your bandits, Sal reminded himself. At least he has got plenty of enthusiasm for stupidity. Just love the boy a little, he relented. I think I'm really going off the deep end, he scolded, catching himself smiling sincerely.

"The other day somebody took a message in the john and left it on the toilet tank," Quincy resumed. "It was something about Brennig tryin' to get us to telephone him."

"We usually try to keep important matters secret."

"Another thing. I'm gonna be gettin' a trailer for my office. They're gonna move it in back a this trailer."

What? No. I can't take it. "Are you serious? Why not give it to a flood victim?"

"That's right."

"You've *got* to be kidding. What're you planning to do, open up a business? Run off inspection sheets and sell them?"

"We're gonna move a lot of tools and shit over there. Give us more space here."

"Yeah, the loungers keep bumping into one another."

"Incidentally, three toolboxes was settin' on the floor in Roy's office."

Did they hatch anything?

"Now there's only one left. Know anything about it?"

"What, the one that's there?"

"No, the two that's missing."

"Well, I was never good with math, man," Sal continued facetiously. "But if you subtract *two* from *three*, that leaves *one*. That's correct because, well, *two* from *three* has always been *one*."

Quincy finally laughed. "Seriously, though."

"Okay, seriously, Roy ought to lock his door."

"Can't. They only lock from the inside."

Sal shrugged with incredulously. "So? You buy a lock and install it on the outside. Maybe one of the seventy-eight workaholics inside could help. Never mind. I'd install it, if Roy gave me permission." God what trouble we have thinking, much less doing, he reflected, but warned himself against pulling out his pad. Quincy could get a heart attack. "Maybe we should stop rationalizing so much–pretending we can't do things when we really can, because of our great technology. We can even undo others' mistakes if we really wanted to. The trouble is, we're constantly producing only for profit or for weapons to kill."

"Hah?"

"Nothing. Forget it. Thinking aloud again. It's a habit. Sorry to interrupt," he said almost sincerely and almost shook his head upon catching himself philosophizing again.

"The government don't want nothin' defaced."

Sal pictured Miles' holes in the paneling, Doris nailing notices on the wall behind her desk, and the scratched kitchen table and sink. "Then how come we keep defacing everything?"

"Who knows? Well, I gotta blow. Gotta start gettin' my shit together before my trailer comes in. If the lumber comes and I'm tied up, have 'im dump it somewhere in back."

Sal nodded, and Quincy left. Sal spent twenty minutes Xeroxing more inspection sheets and dispatch tickets. Logging in the information at his desk, he heard a large truck pull up in back, and rose.

Realizing Quincy had disappeared, he stepped outside with his radio.

What the hell are we going to do with all that? he contested, observing 2 x 10 x 16 foot lengths of wood stacked eight feet high on a large flatbed. Build a house? Who could have been dumb enough to order that much wood? And what about two by fours and other thickness needed to put steps together? Don't fight it. Leave it to the knuckleheads to figure it out. Catching the driver's attention, he pointed where he wanted the vehicle parked and unloaded.

The driver backed up, stopped, and a slim senior citizen possessing a medium build hopped out. Wearing a thick t-shirt and a skullcap despite intense humidity and heat, he handed Sal a copy of the invoice, fitted the original between his teeth, and grabbed the truck's steel brace with youthful exuberance.

Talk about enthusiasm, Sal reflected admirably.

But pulling himself up into a small space in the bay, the man almost fell.

"Easy," Sal cautioned.

Righting himself, he began hurriedly struggling to pull off several sixteen-footers at a time.

The company couldn't afford to send along a helper? flashed a thought. "Wait a minute. Wait a minute."

The man paused awkwardly, accidentally dropped the boards, and scolded himself.

"What are you doing?"

The man removed the invoice from his teeth. "Unloading."

"Unloading? You mean this isn't a dump truck?"

"No."

Sal exhaled in disbelief. "You've got great spirit. But where's your helper?" he inquired, computing holes in the man's t-shirt without really eyeing them. "Your helper. Where's your helper? Don't you have a helper?" he shouted. Better yet, where's your hearing aid?

"Hah?"

Oh, man. "Who's going to help you unload?" he enunciated.

The man stared perplexedly at Sal.

"You expect to unload this yourself?"

The man grinned, exposing missing front teeth. "Yeah," he assured and spat.

HUD ought to hire him and fire the deadwood, Sal sneered with a laugh. "You'll be here all day."

The man frowned.

Help's scarce, Sal reminded himself sarcastically.

Grabbing several boards anyway, the man struggled again.

"Wait a minute. How come they only sent one man?" he shouted.

The man frowned again.

HUD hired all the available men to loaf for us, Sal responded with another laugh and repeated himself louder.

The man appeared to study Sal's clean, short-sleeved shirt. "Shit, alls ya need is one good man," he chirped and spat again.

"When's he coming?" Sal teased.

The man swung the boards aside so he could grab them easier. "Hah?"

"You'll be unloading for hours, even with *my* help," Sal practically bellowed.

"Shit," he sneered. Withdrawing cement-crusted gloves from his back pocket, he fitted them on quickly, as if wasting time or resting was unthinkable. "Have 'em drug off 'fore you walk back to the trailer."

Yeah, but will you be still alive by then? Grinning, he lowered his radio and pulled out several boards that clattered to the ground.

"Done twice as much myself last Saturday," he quipped and pushed several boards aside for Sal to pull out which Sal did.

No way am I going to let him kill himself. "I don't want you to get a heart attack working so hard," he shouted.

"Shit, already had four and I'm still kickin'." He paused to regard Sal shielding his eyes from the sun. "Hah?"

Sal smiled. "Nothing. I didn't say anything," he shouted.

The man struggled to push aside more boards but lost his balance and nearly fell.

"Hey, forget it," Sal insisted but the man didn't hear him.

"I'll feed 'em. You pull 'em off," the man offered, grinning happily.

"Wait. Hang on," Sal bellowed.

The man regarded Sal. "What fer?"

Talk about a character, Sal suppressed. "I want to talk to you."

Moving closer to Sal, the man evaluated him curiously. "Hah?"

Sal placed a hand on the man's bony shoulder.

The man frowned perplexedly.

"You can use some help. It's too hot."

"Hah?"

"You'll get sun stroke working in this heat," Sal shouted.

"Nah."

"Wait. Don't do anything." I've gotta shake a few loungers loose from inside. "I'm getting help," he verbalized loudly and appreciated that the man stayed put. About to hurry back inside (lest the man resume trying to unload again), Sal remembered something else. "Nails," he roared, eyeing cars whizzing back and forth along Route 17 in the distance. "Did you bring any nails?"

The man squinted, frowned, and his mouth twisted open. "Nobody said nathin' 'bout nails."

"Doesn't surprise me." ·

"Hah?"

"Nothing. No sense unloading, now," he yelled. "You might have to go back for nails."

"Hah? I ain't unloadin'," he mistakenly assured.

Breaking away, Sal strode toward the office and entered. Oh, for God's sake, he moaned, noticing only two young men sitting on the couch besides Happy leaning over on Rota's desk, writing down the women's orders for lunch. Even the kitchen's empty, he observed, glancing through the opening. "A truck of wood just pulled in. Need your help to unload it," he told Happy and glanced at the others who looked away.

"Hey, I don't unload trucks," Happy declared without regarding him.

"What *do* you unload?" Your own bullshit?

Happy ignored him and he soon learned that the two men were waiting for their contractor to return from buying piping. He asked them to help unload the wood, throwing in that it was indirectly for the victims, and they stared at him. Help's scarce, Sal considered adding. They exchanged glances, shrugged, and rose, surprising him. All walked in back and Sal persuaded the old man not to help and the threesome started unloading.

Oh, no. It's form man extraordinaire, Sal winced, observing Quincy trotting toward them.

Quincy eyed several sixteen-footers that Sal heaved onto a pile.

"How're you doing?" Sal greeted friendlily.

"What're ya doing? Who ordered *that much* wood?" he demanded.

"Roy's building a house for his mom. Who knows?" he remarked, watching the two men pull out several boards. "I agree. That's a lot of wood just for steps."

Quincy shrugged. "Oh well. The government's paying, so who gives a shit?"

"I do. Because I'm a taxpayer." I ought to tape my response and sing it whenever I hear those familiar chords.

Quincy took his turn assuming Sal was joking and laughed.

That's the problem. Everybody thinks conserving is a joke. "Don't we need nails?"

"What do you mean?"

You don't know what that means? he hid and checked the invoice he had stuffed into his pocket. "Whoever ordered all this, maybe Roy or somebody from HUD, forgot the nails. You need nails to hold wood together."

"Are ya sure?"

Is *he* serious? Slow down. *Think* before you speak, Quincy. "Yeah. I've been nailing wood together all my life." Even loose deadwood from some of my classes.

"How do you know they didn't order nails?" he queried as if he were trying to catch him fouling up, Sal sensed.

Oh, man, Sal frowned with irritation. "Because I'm psychic."

"What?"

"Because nails weren't on the order and they weren't loaded on the truck because of some stupid mistake." Hello.

"Lemme see that."

Oh, for God's sake. He handed it to him as the old man watched the two young men pulling boards off in slow motion.

"Oh, Krist, guess somebody screwed up," Quincy admitted, and trotted back to the office with the invoice.

Sal resumed typing. One way to get rid of him. Hope the pest stays there.

Minutes later, a flatbed pulled up with Vinny at the wheel, Phil alongside, and Dinger, Mike, and Robert standing in the bay.

"How much for the wood? I'm building a house," Phil teased and the old man's face almost went berserk.

Perspiring, Sal clattered several more boards onto the pile and laughed. "How about giving us a hand?"

"No problem," Vinny replied and exited with Phil.

Dinger swept back his hair and ogled the group through his large, thick glasses. "What house?"

"Forget it, Dingle," Mike responded, jumped off with Robert, and Dinger frowned as if he were allergic to physical labor.

They were almost finished unloading when Quincy raced toward them. "They sent the wrong size," he shouted. He removed a tape from his belt, measured a plank, and shook his head. "They're suppose to be eight inches wide accordin' to the specks, not ten."

Everyone burst out laughing except the old man who started pulling out a board until Sal settled him down and explained.

Lowering it, he lifted up his weathered, wrinkled head. "Hah?"

Having removed his shirt, Phil's bare chest resembled a blanket of black hair matching his beard. He paused to examine Quincy's pock-filled face, grimaced about the news. Dinger finally jumped off, pocketed his hands and assumed the watching mode.

"What the hell's the difference?" Phil protested.

"Two inches," Mike teased, and the old man settled on the pleasant, young face.

"What?" Dinger contributed.

"No big deal," Sal agreed. "Wider steps are even better. People will be able to step down easier."

"Not accordin' to HUD's specks," Quincy disagreed and absorbed the old man's puzzled face.

"Hah?"

"What?" Dinger asked.

"The hell with the damn specs," Phil barked. "The flood victims won't mind."

"That's for sure," Sal agreed.

Dinger swept aside his long hair again. "What?"

The old man swung his head to him.

"Dinger, is this your old man?" Vinny asked.

Dinger regarded the old man, then Vinny. "Whadaya mean?"

"You keep saying *what*, and he keeps saying *hah*," Vinny clarified. "Thought you two were related."

All laughed except the old man and Quincy who insisted that they return the wood. "Ta keep things straight."

Sal and Phil disagreed vehemently along with the others. The twosome started arguing with Quincy and the old man kept regarding one after the other.

"We're only going to waste time," Sal maintained.

"Hey, I'm over you guys," Quincy countered.

Tired, Sal simply shook his head.

The men started reloading. The old man climbed back into the truck confusedly, and they finished sometime later.

"Shower time," Phil announced. "See ya later," he told Sal and headed for his car, as did the others toward theirs.

Can't blame them a bit, Sal thought, sensing that they were heading home, and the old man drove away.

Chapter 26

The next morning, Quincy ordered the men outside for a meeting. But talking and drinking coffee with one another in their usual circles, few responded, and he repeated the announcement several more times before they started bouncing out.

Quincy positioned himself on the top step as if he were Khrushchev reviewing the troops below. He discussed his three new forms for ten minutes and then complained about the dirty bathroom and kitchen sink. "Some guys aren't working to their fullest potential," he also scolded, loosening some sarcastic laughter from the men, most of whom were pocketing their hands because of the cool, damp fog. He answered several stupid questions and admitted knowing nothing about the check fiasco. Catching sneezes and yawns, he was about to end the meeting when Dinger raised his hand. But jumping him, Phil and Mike pulled him to the ground unnoticed and Quincy adjourned the meeting.

Quincy pulled open the door, and the usual scent of fresh coffee flavored with cigarette smoke and touches of marijuana appeared to wake the crowd stumbling noisily inside. All bee-lined towards the urn and percolator and they lingered despite Quincy's complaint. In fact, appreciating such good-natured camaraderie and conviviality, Quincy even joined them.

Chapter 27

The following morning, out of the debris of characters entered Wally Ingram. After signing in, he attached himself to a cup of coffee, joined the lingerers, and announced that he was the head carpenter. Married, middle-aged and rather handsome, except for bad front teeth that he kept trying to hide, he sported a ponytail held by a ring. Mustached with a hundred or so curly whiskers struggling to become a Fu Manchu goatee, he wasn't quite a professional carpenter, as he had apparently told Millie, Sal sensed, listening to him describe himself, but puttered around his house like millions of home owners, Sal recognized

Therefore, he deserves to be a G-7 and titled "head carpenter" by whatever intelligence decided so, whether it was Millie, Roy, or Craig? Sal addressed. Don't fight it, he answered and tired not to care, since he would be quitting soon.

Wally soon abandoned the coffee-clutchers and conferred with Roy in his office. Reappearing, he selected from HUD's finest, eight of the most promising apprentices, that is, assistants to help him construct the steps out of the wood. "Young bucks," he labeled them during Rota's furious typing. "Meet me outside for a meeting in ten minutes. Gotta take a quick one," he told them and left. Returning, he was stunned upon not finding any of his young bucks and naively questioned Doris about their whereabouts.

"Not now. I'm busy," she responded from her desk fronting the usual knot of contractors and toters complaining about her inattention.

"Maybe his young bucks left to look for some young does," Skip commented from the couch.

Yes, fine young bucks indeed, Sal agreed, sitting alongside. The kind that sleep in class whenever they show up.

"Be right back," Wally felt obligated to inform Doris smirking at the man before her whom she ignored. Checking the parked cars that often thumped with rock, he reappeared with seven smiling culprits that he caught playing poker in a trailer. They had even laughed, he complained to Doris who folded her arms belligerently at the same group.

Wearing a skimpy halter, Rota telephoned the young buck who claimed that he had gone home after getting sick, she relayed to Wally and handed him the phone.

"Probably sufferin' from loafin'. It's contagious," Skip commented as all watched and listened.

"Why didn't you let me know?" Wally kept hammering away into the receiver and eventually hung up. Surveying the loungers, he chose one

Andre Daniels as his replacement, and invited him to join the rest of his select group near the urn.

Bespectacled with disheveled black hair and a receding chin, Andre seemed pleased. But although also groggy and sickly-looking, he possessed enough energy to stare at Rota's breasts.

"If they fall out, every man for himself," another apprentice commented and the others laughed.

Andre was wearing the same blue Chicago Bulls t-shirt for weeks, despite the heat, Skip told Sal who apparently hadn't noticed him amongst the crowd. "He's been warming that same chair over there since he was hired," he added beyond Andre's hearing and pointed to it. "Actually he was sittin' there when they brung it over from the Fairgrounds."

Sal laughed. "Wouldn't surprise me a bit."

"A contractor fired him, I heard," Norm explained, standing nearby.

The reality was that Roy had stopped for gas at a convenient store where Andre often lingered in order to socialize with his girlfriend who was a cashier. Possessing a keen eye for quality workers, Roy had scooped him up on the spot, Sal soon learned and suddenly recognized him as a former student.

"He's part of the Sixties' residue," Sal told Skip and Norm. "The kind they drop out of school for barely showing up once a week. McDonald's usually fires them for getting in the way."

Andre soon found HUD equally as boring as school. According to those still trying to figure out why Wally picked him, Andre loomed odd standing with pocketed hands near the urn. Vacuuming in large portions of foul air through wide-spaced nostrils, he was the only one who wasn't smoking, drinking coffee, or talking.

Obviously as gifted as Roy for spotting quality workers, Wally designated him as his assistant for another unknown reason.

After the meeting, Wally left for Mathews and Loomis with his capable assistant and several other "apprentices." Returning, they reentered the office carrying hammers, skill saws and screwdrivers, plus a splendid assortment of nonessentials that included clamps, vices, and several chainsaws.

Just nice to have and hold at government expense, Sal mocked, looking up from behind his desk as they passed in and out of the bedroom where tools were stored, fondled, discussed, and often dropped. For me to discard the broken pieces, he grumbled, but appreciated that Wally had enough sense to order other wood needed for the steps which arrived shortly after the men signed in next morning.

Sal was Xeroxing inspection sheets when Wally and his group entered the tool room and left with many of the tools. Soon to fade away into somebody's house or get sold for drugs, Sal sensed, since no one kept track of them or anything else. Gathering originals and copies, he peered boredly out the hall window from behind his desk and noticed the group heading for the lumber beside a single set of four-riser steps that Wally had charged locally.

Wearing a fine carpenter's smock charged at Mathews and Loomis, Wally approached the steps before his eight "apprentices" who surrounded him in a circle. He boasted that he could duplicate it, plus many more "with no problem" but chose Andre to be the first "to take a crack at it," as he put it, especially since Andre mumbled that it would be "a piece of cake," as *he* put it.

Why bother making them when you could save time and money buying them from wherever you got that one?

Wally plugged a long extension cord into the outside outlet, and Andre kept checking various circular saws strewn in the grass, apparently for the one possessing the best grip, since there was no other reason to do so, Sal concluded wondrously. Finally selecting one, Andre plugged it into the extension cord. Squeezing the trigger, he gave the surroundings a few blasts, and removed a long plank from the pile.

Though Sal had left for the bathroom, missing the incredible moment, it proved to be beyond belief especially since Wally had lectured the men about the importance of safety, the day before. But according to what the other apprentices spouted or what spewed from between Wally's rotten teeth, Andre had penciled the board for a cut. Holding the activated saw, he stumbled on a rock or rolled off a beer bottle although no one knew for sure.

The saw jammed and Andre started shrieking that he had cut off his leg.

Rushing over, Wally kept shouting to the seven others, "See what can happen if you're not careful?"

Such shrieking could only be a dog, Rota had insisted to Doris and a handful of experienced loafers.

Wally soon stormed inside raging incoherently about blood all over him and the ground. "More than ya could shake a stick at," he kept repeating, frightening Rota. Fortunately, Sal had just exited during the confusion. Possessing eleven years of quality experience deciphering all kinds of mutterings, outbursts, and profanity, he understood Wally's ranting immediately and persuaded Doris to stop chatting with Tammy on the telephone and call the ambulance.

Stirred (or perhaps annoyed about the interruption), the loungers wandered outside with their coffee, including the dedicated Rota. The ambulance arrived, departed with one less lounger, and the loungers stumbled back inside in order to finish eating doughnuts (which Rota had bought) and drinking their coffee.

The incomparable Skip Reynolds was about to discuss the incident when Phil opened the forum before a circle of men standing near the couch. "How the hell can you be dumb enough to cut your leg with a circular saw? It's impossible. They shut off immediately."

"And why try cutting a plank while holding it on your leg?" Vinny injected.

"Maybe he never heard it," Norm flung from a crevice between the cabinets.

Regarding him, several men waited for the punch line. "Didn't know the thing was turned on," he clarified.

Skip clasped his neck and leaned back against the wall. "*He* was turned on," he enunciated. "The guy was so stoned, he smelled like a Colombian marijuana field on a rainy day."

"Yeah, but even when you're stoned, ya got sense enough–" Vinny attempted.

"Hell, half of these hombres are stoned right now," Phil muttered quietly beyond their hearing. "Never saw such a bunch of misfits in my life, except my third-period retards."

"I still say there was something wrong with the saw," Norm maintained.

"Yeah, it got stuck with a bad operator," Skip provided.

"Maybe it never turned off when he let go," Norm announced during the laughter.

"Maybe the thing was defective," Vinny offered.

"What, the saw or Andre?" Skip inquired.

"Can ya hold it down, fellas?" inquired a quaint voice belonging to a petite woman talking on the phone to Andre at the hospital. Hanging up, she attracted immediate attention. "His leg needed twenty-two stitches but he's all right."

The men cheered.

"He said he's gonna sue HUD for millions. Maybe even Black and Decker," Rota told her audience.

"Who's they?" Dinger asked.

"Two guys in Wally's crew," Skip answered. "Pay attention."

Rota waited for the laughter to subside. "HUD promised him a lifelong desk job," she added and the episode ended Andre's sawing career.

Chapter 28

As a result of the incident, the hall window became Sal's favorite vantage point for catching similar occurrences, especially since it was directly in his line of vision from his the desk. The next day, he observed Wally sitting on the planks like a grand duke barking orders to his young, valiant knights and encouraging them to produce what Andre failed to accomplish. Consequently, screeching saws and thumping hammers soon disturbed the countryside with such frightening enthusiasm that Doris stormed outside to complain about the noise, adding that she wouldn't mind if they got lost in the next town.

Although Wally settled for twenty feet further away, Sal appreciated that he still could see him and his apprentices clearly.

Though his group managed to pound out several steps in the raging hours, their concoctions were lopsided, uneven, or wobbly, failing to meet Wally's high standards.

Working alone like the Wright brothers and somehow resembling them, two silent, industrious "carpenters" labored hard, long, and with care. Completing an unusual version, they placed it before Wally for his approval.

Resting beneath the afternoon sun, the set loomed odd, particularly because it led nowhere. Wally must have had the same impression, Sal figured, because, staring down at it, he frowned with curiosity and wonder.

Hopping off the planks in order to examine it or perhaps even test it, Wally adjusted his black ponytail and brushed himself off.

Saws and hammering stopped. The "carpenters" paused to watch him, including Sal.

Wally approached the two gifted men wearing brands of off-color jeans adorned with patches of unmatched material. He studied the risers carefully and nodded. Placing his foot on the first step, he reached for the railing but pulled too hard. The railing came off in his hand and he fell backwards, landing on the ground. Hammering and saws resumed immediately, as if to protect their boss from some embarrassing laughter. Though the noise obliterated Wally's voice, he rose quickly.

Sal noticed Wally's mouth opening and closing, and his ponytail bobbing up and down to the rhythm of his jerking head, suggesting that he was tongue-lashing the two gifted men staring at a cluster of buttercups near the planks. It's like watching a silent scene on television, Sal criticized with a laugh.

The saws finally stopped. The men converged before Wally who had shouted for another meeting, Sal realized, glancing out of the same window while running the Xerox machine.

Wally announced that the group was about to watch a man make a fine set of steps, obviously meaning himself, Sal realized, since someone responded with "Where?" which Wally apparently never heard. Wally removed his own favorite weapon from its fine case. Carrying it to a new location in the tall grass, again for some unknown reason, he clicked it on and, like his men, gave the surroundings several machinegun blasts.

Logging in dispatch tickets at his desk an hour later, the curious Sal rose and walked to the hall window for a better view Wally's concoction.

Having almost completed his steps, Wally attempted to remove a bent nail with his hammer's claw while his "young bucks," encircled him in order to watch. Bending down, he pulled too hard. The hammer went west. Wally went east, and the master carpenter fell back again, this time momentarily disappearing in the weeds. Stumbling to his feet, he blamed one of his men for having handed him the wrong nails, although they only had one size. Disgusted or perhaps embarrassed, Wally gave up. He relegated his unfinished piece to a man with shoulder-length hair, and hammering and banging resumed. Wally reentered the office, poured himself some coffee, and flirted with Rota for the remaining day.

Chapter 29

The next day a toter moved and positioned Quincy's forty-two foot trailer about twenty feet from the office without blocking Sal's view of the carpenters. Thank God, Sal appreciated, listening to the whining saws from behind his desk. A man needs some kind of entertainment.

The four teachers blocked Quincy's trailer quickly and Roy arranged for HUD to pay a backhoe operator to dig a trench for the septic tank. Norm, Skip, and Lyman laid the sewer and water pipes and transferred the office's tools into one of the three bedrooms. Quincy drilled holes on the jamb for a large padlock he charged at Mathews and Loomis and spent the remaining day loading his belongings into another bedroom. Since Sal seemed to be officially working in the office, Doris constantly shouted down the hall for him to answer incoming radio calls, especially since Rota refused, having only recently learned that the "little black boxes" the men carried weren't regular radios, as Skip had teased her into believing. Consequently, unless Roy, Craig, or others happened to be in the office to answer such transmissions, Sal did, including when he ate lunch in the car or carried his radio into the bathroom in order to relieve himself. God, what dedication, he praised himself. If they only knew, he added with a laugh.

The plump, pretty Pam Meadows arrived that morning. Sitting at his desk, Sal heard Roy announce in the living room that she would be the "head radio operator," as if he had just conceived the idea, Sal sensed, having adopted that very title himself in order to boost his morale. Hearing the front door slam behind Roy's exit, he suddenly realized that *he* would have to brief her about operations or she would never answer transmissions intelligently. Accurately picturing Doris ignoring her standing before her, he walked to the living room, introduced himself to the woman who was in her early twenties, and accompanied her past the gawkers. "This is the kitchen," he announced, feeling like a tour guide

Both paused to look inside and Pam eyed the numerous flies making their usual sorties from bones, unwashed cups, paper plates, and plastic utensils left beside the sink.

"Everybody waits for somebody else to clean up, and it's usually Rota," he explained. "Sorry about the noise," he commented, referring to the hammering and screaming saws outside.

Passing Sal's office, they entered the radio room that was empty, save for the Xerox machine, a few metal chairs, and a sophisticated microphone resting on an old, scratched, wooden table. Reaching down,

Pam wobbled it as if it were a piece she had just noticed at a garage sale.

Sal eyed her long, fanned black hair, dimples, and scattered freckles. "Probably pulled out of the Chemung during the flood."

Pam giggled.

"Sorry about that. I'll get one of the carpenters to cut–" he attempted, fantasized them shaving the legs down until they disappeared completely, and broke off. "*I'll* take care of it," he emphasized and she eyed him curiously. How come Roy didn't have us get her a regular desk? he reflected while describing operations. "Don't listen to what you might have heard on television. Imbeciles have been running this operation because imbeciles hired imbeciles which they're still doing, believe it or not. Trailers should have been brought in six weeks ago. The odd cowboy up front isn't a spillover from the Fair but the king of field operations. Doris, the young woman sitting closest to the front door, is the queen."

Unaware how to evaluate him or assuming he was joking, she struggled not to giggle.

"Rota's the other woman. She's nice. Neither one, especially Doris, is too heavy on manners or they would have introduced themselves to you." Complain too much and she'll quit, he warned but couldn't resist continuing. "And you might've seen the guy who constantly parts his long, shoulder-length hair. The one wearing weird glasses. He's Dinger. He isn't part of the Fair either. Just another hippie. Or a nut pretending to be one. He's mostly on drugs, like half of the raccoons inside. They're heavy on lounging and socializing. Actually Dinger was one of my students. That's how *my* students get after they have me for English at Southside."

Apparently suppressing more giggling, Pam bit her lip. "Oh, you teach there?"

"No, I'm just the babysitter. One of the best."

Pam giggled quietly.

"You'll get to meet all the other weirdoes soon. Inspectors are supposed to make sure doors close, tables stand, and rugs lie." Be serious, he urged but couldn't help mocking Miles' and Dinger's antics without naming them. He described what maintenance men did besides drinking coffee. "Were it not for guys like Lyman, Skip, Norm, and a handful of others (like me, he was too modest to include), the entire operation would be even further behind because our supposed leader–and you'll probably get to know him–doesn't know what to do with all the fruitcakes inside." He flicked his head toward the living room. "Except to let them stand around, tell jokes and drink coffee."

Identifying with Sal's personality, appreciating his wit, and feeling comfortable with him, she giggled freely.

"And that's only half of the men. The rest sign in and usually rush out to the parked trailers so they can sleep, play cards, or drink beer. You name it. Some play golf, go home, or whatever, but they always return to sign out at night so they can get paid for doing nothing."

"Are you serious?"

"Yes. Occasionally, somebody like Craig kicks them out or sleeps in one of the trailers himself, if he isn't shacking up with his girlfriend. In fact, Roy still hasn't figured out what is going on or what he's supposed to do. He keeps hiring men as fast as they disappear."

Pam frowned.

"You wouldn't believe how long we were using rusty tools," he revealed, as if he were describing the original pioneers of America. "Maintenance men were borrowing them from the contractors for weeks, even from the flood victims."

Assuming Sal was exaggerating, Pam regarded Sal's deadpan expression and giggled louder.

"You might think I'm kidding but I'm not. Struggling to be serious but failing, he poked fun at Wally's supposed carpentry skills, Quincy's concern about paperwork, and Doris' contemptuous attitude toward everyone, especially contractors and toters. "She even hangs up on victims calling up about trailers. You'll find out." Finally realizing that he was bombarding her, he stopped. Both entered his office and he handed her an updated list of everyone's radio number.

"How come so many numbers have been crossed out and changed?"

Sal couldn't resist. "Some guys like different, more exciting numbers. Can't say I blame them. Who likes a boring *nine* or a *twelve*?"

Pam giggled again.

Sal soon realized that she was intelligent, had an organized mind, and she learned how to operate the radio quickly. But left alone to answer calls in the succeeding days, she needed his help to learn where trailers' identification numbers were on yokes, if a pay-loader could squeeze between two trailers ten feet apart, and if the flying squirrels were capable of sawing down an obstructing oak at one particular site, all good questions.

One of her faults was that if she wasn't giggling about Sal's persistent facetiousness or mutterings about the obvious incompetence, stupidity, and the temperamental Xerox machine, she was constantly moaning about missing her husband who was fighting in Vietnam.

Most contractors accepted her immediately because she was pretty. So did Tony who apparently assumed she was because of her beautiful speaking voice, Sal realized. Treating all women sexually, Tony flirted with her whenever he radioed, as did many others. Nor did the baseman interfere. Because she was a woman, several HUD men and some contractors (who sometimes used HUD's radios and answered messages occasionally) refused to accept that personnel had really hired her to handle the radio or that her information was accurate, until Sal verified both, irritating him.

Sal answered the radio on one occasion when Pam left for the bathroom and the baseman transmitted "Thank God."

Sal considered protesting with "Break, break" and lecturing him about male chauvinism, but lacked the audacity and didn't want to tie up the radio.

Carrying the Xerox machine's overflowing waste can up front the next day, Sal noticed Carmela copying down information from an inspection sheet, and paused before her desk. "Excuse me," he began without sounding sarcastic, and he smiled friendlily. "What are you doing?"

Having witnessed his grumbling sarcasm constantly directed at the "incompetent hire-ups," Carmela had adjusted reasonably well to his odd personality and idiosyncrasies. In fact, she considered him gentlemanly and often smiled at him. "Logging in released trailers, why?"

"A second log?" he inquired and a lounger's horse-laugh distracted him momentarily.

"There's two more around here someplace besides the dispatch log."

"You're putting me on," he responded, lowered the can, and stared disbelievingly at her. Isn't one or two pieces of crap enough? he spared her.

"There's even two more around here beside the dispatch log."

"Five logs?" he emphasized. "You can't be serious."

"Uh huh."

Glancing at Doris, Sal struggled to keep calm. "Why do we need five logs?"

Carmela shrugged. "Doris just say to log these in."

About to question Doris about it, Sal noted a tall, handsome, elderly man standing before her.

Floyd Rorick had just arrived from the airport in a rented car, and Sal overheard him ask her where he could find reasonable motel lodgings for him and his men.

Her arms folded and upper teeth protruding slightly, Doris shrugged. "How should I know? I don't live around here."

Sal watched him frown in surprise.

"Could you check the *Yellow Pages*? Ah'd sure appreciate it."

Smirking, Doris paused before reluctantly giving her desk drawers a loud workout. Finding the phone book, she thumped it on the desk with annoyance.

Welcome to the club, Sal squelched, eyeing him staring curiously at her.

Floyd started flipping through the *Yellow Pages*.

"Mind if I check that log?" Sal resumed with Carmela.

"No." Handing it to him, she rose. "I'll look for the others."

Sal scanned the listings under the different headings and frowned. Carmela returned with two more–a delivery log and the fifth–a feeble conglomeration of poorly-organized, duplicated information.

"This is overkill–ridiculous. My master log's will include all of this information."

Carmela nodded politely and sat behind her desk.

Sal shook his head and thanked her. Eyeing Rota typing furiously, he observed the well-groomed, suave Floyd lower his tanned head, and he peered out of the window behind Rota's desk.

Floyd watched his driver carefully back a flatbed (supporting a large bulldozer) safely between two trucks parked near a cyclone fence. He turned to Doris, and a disturbed expression changed his classically-chiseled face. "It was ma distinct understanding with Mr. Nichols," he began without regarding her, and paused momentarily because of the loud hammering and sawing, "that you folks were going to reserve fifteen motel rooms for us," he drawled heavily and glanced at Sal. "Had I known you couldn't handle that, ah'd a made arrangements ma-self. You say he's not around?"

"Who?" Doris asked.

Feeling silly holding the logs, Sal felt sillier about Doris' answer. Roy, who else, girl?

"Roy Nichols," Floyd seemed to protest, regarded clusters of men standing about chatting and laughing, and several looked away self-consciously.

"Ah don't know nothin' about all that," she returned curtly.

This might be interesting, Sal sensed, deciding to linger.

"You're the secretary, aren't you?" he asked, glanced at Rota and then Sal who nodded at Doris.

"Ah don't keep an account of every place he goes, ya know," she offered saucily.

Smoke that in your Southern pipe, man, Sal mused.

Floyd glared at her momentarily. Wearing a sports' jacket and a dressy, white shirt opened at the collar, rare for contractors, he checked his watch, then Sal again.

Hi, Sal mused, almost succumbing to laughter again.

"Ah was supposed to meet him at two," he told Doris. "We just flew up from Mississippi." He checked his watch. "It's two forty raght now."

Wait 'll you meet ol' pun'tual, man-of-his word Roy, Sal reflected playfully again, shifted the logs to one hand, and stepped forward. "Sal D'Angelo," he introduced amiably, extended his right hand, and Floyd shook it.

Obviously appreciating that Floyd stopped questioning her, Doris began rummaging through some papers. "I ain't got that one double-wide contract," she barked at Rota, and Floyd glanced back at her. "Ah needs you ta find it."

"Maybe I can help you," Sal offered Floyd.

Hammering and sawing stopped abruptly and Wally started barking orders.

"Where's the damn contract?" Doris shouted at Rota and Floyd winced.

"Let's go to my room where it's quiet," Sal suggested, deliberately avoiding saying *office*, because he didn't want to sound pretentious or mislead anybody into thinking that he had authority.

"Fine," Floyd responded appreciatively.

"Sal, where ya headin' with them logs?" Doris blurted above the resumed sound of hammering and sawing.

Both men paused, turned, and wrinkles deepened those already etched in Floyd's forehead.

"We'll talk about them later. We just don't need that many," Sal told her.

"Ain't nothin' to discuss. Leave 'em here."

Stay calm, Sal insisted. "You're repeating information."

"Sal, don't mess with nothin' you don't understand," she warned and Floyd stared at her.

"I'm not going to argue," Sal retorted, and Floyd followed him heading for his office.

"Ah need 'em now," Doris bellowed.

Floyd glanced back incredulously.

Rota placed a paper on Doris' desk.

"That ain't the contract. Can't you read?" Doris scolded above the outside noise and Floyd looked back still again before entering Sal's office.

"Sal, gimmy them logs," Doris shouted.

Irritated and embarrassed, Sal offered Floyd a seat politely and appreciated hearing Doris' telephone ring. He deposited the logs on his desk, walked around, and sat.

"Is that gal always like that?"

"Only when she's in a good mood."

Floyd smiled, then shook his head. "She should be fired."

Tell me about it, Sal agreed and shrugged. "I don't have that authority. I'm just helping in the office," he presented amiably again. He offered to try and find lodging which was scarce because of so many displaced victims, he explained. "There might be some where I live. But that's over twenty miles away."

"No problem about the distance, as long as they're decent. We could use about a dozen rooms. Appreciate anything you could do," he added congenially.

Quincy entered with his head bowed, observed Floyd, and slowed. "Want you to give me a hand in my office," he told Sal who introduced Floyd to him. "How're ya doing," Quincy flung and looked back so quickly at Sal, that he never saw the Southerner rise to shake hands and Floyd sat back down awkwardly, Sal noticed.

"Got a ton of inspection sheets and dispatch tickets what needs sortin'," Quincy addressed Sal.

"Mr. Rorick just arrived," Sal hinted politely, feeling embarrassed again. "He's going to be providing large-scale help for the flood victims," he emphasized. And deserves more than just a glance, he kept hidden, hoping Quincy would improve his manners. "He's trying to get situated."

Quincy caressed his tuff and gave Floyd a good-for-you look. "HUD's been hollerin' for copies of inspection sheets all day. We're way behind. Looks like you got a ton of Xeroxin' ta do. Come over as soon as possible."

Watching him leave, Floyd turned to Sal. "Are they all like him and her around here?"

No way am I going to defend such a bunch, Sal decided. "It gets worse before it improves."

Floyd smiled politely, then frowned. "How about this Roy Nichols? Where's he at? I need ta contact him."

Now's your chance to crucify him, despite risking getting fired. But that would be tactless and inappropriate right now and accomplish nothing, Sal reminded himself. He'll find out anyway. "Actually, he's constantly on the go and hard to find," he responded sincerely, promised to radio him and briefed Rorick that Doris dispatched trailers.

"Where can ah get cinder-block?" Floyd asked.

Several saws seemed to dwindle and stop, as if the operators wanted to hear Sal's answer.

"Ah didn't see any when ah arrived."

"There's several companies in town."

"In town? *We've* got to order 'em?" he protested with astonishment. "You mean block aren't here already? Ah thought this was an emergency."

So did I, weeks ago, Sal concealed. Having suggested to Craig and Roy to order block and store it near the office before prices rose higher, Sal inhaled and exhaled. "I'm not in charge of anything," he repeated, almost self-pityingly this time.

"It ought to be piled ten feet high close by. Have like an open warehouse with a block lifter. What about sewer pipe, copper, and other materials?"

Sal shook his head.

Floyd's frown returned.

"What can I say?" Wait till he learns that Doris' incompetence and indifference causes trailers to crawl out of here like molasses. He might pack up and leave. "I think some big company's planning to set up a warehouse in back," he admitted in order to remain reasonably positive and honest. "You'll have to ask Roy." Powers that be are still negotiating about it, his facetious self injected.

Floyd shook his head. "It's almost two months since the flood. Nothing's set up."

Feeling personally responsible, Sal felt embarrassed once again and shrugged. Here's another chance to belittle Roy, he recognized, but pictured sounding like a disgruntled employee who disliked his employer and fell silent. Besides, all this sounds too much like fiction anyway, he rationalized.

"How much 're they getting for block around here?"

"It's gone up because of the flood. Thirty-four cents for eight inch, twenty-eight for four."

Floyd grimaced. "That's highway robbery. What's wrong with them?"

They're suffering from a serious disease—greed for the buck, he suppressed, and the saws and hammering resumed. How come Thou Shouldn't Be Greedy wasn't included in the Commandments? Plus so much more?

"They're taking advantage of the emergency."

"They don't care. A buck's a buck. They've raised the price because of the demand and they're getting it." That's the capitalistic way nowadays, even when people are suffering, Sal concealed.

Floyd glanced out the hall window as if the noisy saws and hammering had distracted him. "Hell, ah might do better ordering from Mississippi. Trouble is, travel time and expense trucking a flatbed of block up here would prob'ly cost about the same."

"Possibly I can get you a better price near where I live. Companies might be too far away from the disaster to take advantage of it. They might even deliver."

Floyd rubbed his eye, sighed, and regarded Sal. "Ah've got to check my vehicles, and ah got forty-eight other things to do. Ah'd be most appreciative if you'all could look into it. If you get a better price, maybe you could order me, oh, say ten cubes of each.

"I'll definitely look into it."

Floyd thanked him, rose, shook Sal's hand, and headed for the doorway. Pausing before the side window, he eyed the carpenters curiously, as if wondering what they were doing, and resumed up the hall.

Though Quincy was the only one available with supposed authority, Sal felt uneasy about assuming so much on his own. Ah, but Quincy's not the type to deal with somebody like Rorick, his other self justified. Besides, he's too preoccupied with stupid paperwork.

Sal arrived before Doris, and she snatched the logs out of his hand angrily. Shaking his head, he left to tell Pam to radio Roy that Rorick had arrived. Annoyed about lacking a phone in his office since he had repeatedly asked Roy and Craig to have the telephone company install one, he entered Roy's empty office and slumped into his seat. He phoned several dealers in his area, found one who charged less for both sizes, and ordered five and two cubes of each, all they had, which they promised to deliver tomorrow. Another dealer charged about the same price. He was about to jot down the information when Quincy entered.

"Comin'?"

"In a minute."

Quincy plopped into the nearby metal chair. "Who're ya callin'?"

Sal explained everything.

"Oh, Krist. Let him order his own shit. That ain't your job."

Here we go again. "Are you serious? It's for the flood victims," he barked.

Quincy glared. "It still ain't your job," he enunciated.

Go to hell, imbecile. "I'll be over when I'm done," he insisted angrily and Quincy registered annoyance.

Doris' phone rang and she buzzed Roy's phone. Sal pressed the flickering red button and answered. Another dealer offered to match the price for both sizes and Sal ordered more of the same from him.

Quincy waited impatiently as Sal flipped through the *Yellow Pages* again. "Now what?"

Almost seething, Sal repeated belligerently that he was trying to reserve motel rooms for Rorick and his men, and started dialing.

"Screw that. We gots work to do."

The line was busy and Sal hung up. Should I unleash a "Fuck you?" and possibly get fired? he considered again and reminded himself to be tolerant. "This is for the flood victims. Indirectly," he added once more because he prided himself about being as accurate and honest as possible. What I'm trying to accomplish supersedes *your* horseshit. "It won't take long," he insisted and checked more listings.

Quincy frowned. "The hell with Rorick. I need you now, not later."

"I promised to call and that's it," he declared firmly, dialing. "Slow down. It's just paperwork."

"Roy just radioed me from HUD down at the Rand. They never received copies of the last batch of dispatch tickets and inspection sheets. They want 'em on the pronto."

Sal saw red and hung up. "For God's sake," he exploded. "The hell with that bullshit. Stupid paperwork ain't gonna help the flood victims, man," he dramatized. "What the fuck is wrong with you and everybody? Are you crazy?" He glared. "What I'm doing is more important than what you want me for."

"You wanna tell that to Hugh Brennig?"

"Tell him. I don't give a shit. And I'll tell him what's *really* going on around like the loafing in what has become a hotel for them. And that this is the most disorganized, blundering bunch of assholes that I ever met. It's worse than how the military sometimes operates, and worse than any of my worst students ever behaved."

Quincy stared in surprise.

"In fact, Rorick might be more important than Brennig." He grabbed a copy of Rorick's contract with the government that described hm delivering and setting up a hundred trailers. "The White House sent him here," he lied. Sometimes you have to–in order to benefit the innocent and the suffering, plus get the jackass off your back, he stormed inwardly, then ordered himself to calm down. "We could've treated him a little more politely." What's this *we* baloney?

"Who didn't treat him polite?"

"You." You've got no conception of politeness and manners, he suppressed and snapped his head up the hall. "And neither does Thing behind her desk."

Quincy glanced at Doris and turned back. "She treats everybody like shit," he agreed, studying Sal's dialing finger. "Just hurry up," he added and finally left.

Hope you still have a job, Sal reminded himself again, realizing that he could work six more weeks before school started. He eventually found reasonable enough motel accommodations near his home and entered the radio room. Eyeing the table wobbling from Pam's hand feverishly copying down a radio message on a large yellow pad, he frowned. "Did you get Roy?"

"Just a minute." Finishing, she looked up. "Roy who?" she teased, having heard him arguing with Quincy.

"Oh, God," Sal moaned, sending her into uncontrollable giggling.

"Pam, I've gotta go. Stop giggling and tell me."

"Yes," she answered between gasps.

"What did he say? Nothing, I suppose. That's all he ever says," he grumbled and she resumed giggling.

"Pam, it's not even funny."

"Yes," she finally managed. "You're right. He didn't say anything."

"Good. Three cheers for consistency. So, where *is* the turkey?"

Eyeing his expression, Pam burst into giggled, finally stopped, and told him.

Heading up front, he found Floyd standing before Doris' desk, and briefed him about the reasonable block prices and motel accommodations. Floyd thanked him, and despite his revulsion about paperwork, Sal decided to help Quincy as promised. Stepping outside, he absorbed a full blast of sawing and hammering. When the hell are they going to have enough? he reflected, observing the carpenters busily putting together a reasonable version of the original steps near several very large piles. Entering Quincy's trailer, he located him sitting before a makeshift desk in a small bedroom, leafing through inspection sheets on his lap.

Wonder where they picked up that bomb? Probably washed up in the flood, he answered. "How're you doing? Told you I'd be back," he worded congenially, although not because he feared getting fired, but because he saw no reason to treat him badly.

"What the hell took you so long?" Quincy greeted without looking up from eyeing the top sheet in a pile on his desk.

This guy's developing into a professional pain in the ass. "Had things to do."

"Each Xeroxed dispatch ticket goes with the same Xeroxed inspection sheet according to its HUD number," Quincy began. "Trouble is finding them ta match together," he added and giggled.

Easy, Sal warned himself. He's just another child.

"I'm puttin' the dispatch tickets in numerical order," he announced and smiled proudly.

Sounds exciting, Sal struggled to suppress also, unaware how intolerant he had become.

"Why don't you start with them inspection sheets?" he inquired, nodding at the pile.

I don't know. Why don't I?

"Better yet, go back through the files and start Xeroxing every dispatch ticket and inspection sheet that ain't been done."

Are you kidding? he balked, picturing how long that would take, even without Doris interfering with him rummaging through the file cabinets. Watching him sort papers, he considered revealing his master log. Maybe paper mâché will help. The new log could be succulent, right up his alley. But sensing Quincy wouldn't appreciate taking orders from him, he remained quiet. He studied the sheets Quincy was tossing onto different stacks, realized Quincy would probably pester him until he complied, agreed to do so, and left. Reentering the office, he headed for the front cabinets.

"What the hell do you want?" Doris greeted, jarring him and silencing several of Wally's men sipping coffee.

"Some people have spiders on their pianos," Sal retorted, part of an old joke. "We've got mice in our cabinets," he modified, pulling out the first drawer, and studied inspection sheets in a file folder. "Just checking the traps I left here last night."

Rota and Carmela laughed along with several men.

Transcribing information into a log, Doris glared. "Don't touch nothin'."

Sal removed two file folders. "Why, there's been another robbery?".

"Where ya goin' with that?" she shouted. "Sal?"

"The bathroom needs new wallpapering," he responded over his shoulder. "Don't panic. I'll bring 'em right back." Veering into his office, he remembered Pam and entered the radio room through the passageway.

Pam yawned. "Oh, is this job boring. Wish I could telephone my husband."

"How about doing something for me?"

Pam giggled coquettishly. "Why, what do you have in mind, honey?"

Tuning in to a screeching saw, Sal smirked good-naturedly and she giggled anew. "I'd like you to start Xeroxing inspection sheets and dispatch tickets. Quincy's orders," he revealed sarcastically and she giggled louder.

"Know how to operate the machine?"

"No," she managed.

"Good. Want to learn?"

"No," she responded.

His smirk returned and so did her giggling.

"Good, I'll show you," he said, did, and gave her two different piles to Xerox. Free to battle Doris about the single log, he concluded that copying trailer information onto file cards would be simpler, quicker, and neater, and therefore much more efficient. But transferring so much information onto them would consume time. I'll have to access the files and logs, he realized, but wasn't anxious to go through Doris again, much less appear obsequious before one so unbearable. Returning, he pulled up a chair near the filing cabinets, glanced at Rota thumbing through papers, and sat.

"Where are ma file folders?" Doris snapped without looking up.

Stay calm, he ordered himself. "Pam's Xeroxing them," he uttered pleasantly.

"Pam?" Doris objected. "If she screws 'em up, *you're* responsible."

They're already screwed up, he squelched and finally proposed the file card system.

"Not now, ah'm busy," she snapped.

"No, not now, later. There 'll be a card filed numerically for each trailer." Down, boy. You're starting to sound like Quincy. It's contagious. "Using HUD's numbers, each card 'll contain such information as–"

"Yo'all can blabber all you want. Ah ain't listenin'. Ah'm busy."

". . . the date the trailer arrived," Sal deliberately droned, "where it was set up, by whom and–"

"Sal, will you shut up? You're botherin' me."

Standing nearby, a contractor raised his eyebrows in surprise.

". . . when it was released and– Doris, will you listen?"

"Ah done tol' you before. Ah'm busy."

Sal turned to the contractor. "She's busy. Don't know what she does, but it never ends."

Thumbing through papers, Rota bit her lip sympathetically.

"It would eliminate unnecessary logging, like the inspection sheets you're logging in right now. You're probably duplicating information."

"Do it yourself, then, goddamn it," she ordered and shoved the log into the inspection sheets before her.

"What I'm suggesting is for your own good," he scolded without getting upset. "You should listen. I'm only trying to help."

Doris folded her arms indignantly. "Ah don't have to listen to you. You ain't my boss. Roy is."

Sal glared. "Maybe I should talk to Brennig about all this," he threatened but regretted immediately.

"Go ahead."

"You don't know where some trailers are because you keep bad records," he flung. "You're completely disorganized, inexact, and have a bad system."

"Wanna take over, Sal? Make out dozens of reports, do all the loggin', filin', typin', plus dispatchin' and everything? Go ahead. Ah'll go back to West Virginia."

Fine, he almost reciprocated. But picturing inviting a major confrontation, plus her possibly walking out in a huff because of him, he controlled himself, especially since he believed in kind, intelligent persuasion. "I suggest a file index card system that would–"

The telephone rang, interrupting him.

Doris pounced on the receiver like she did before. She discussed a contractor's contract with Millie and deliberately talked longer than necessary in order to annoy him, Sal realized. Finally hanging up (unaware that rebuking her seemed to calm Sal therapeutically), she pulled the log back without regarding him. "Are you still here?"

Sal couldn't resist again. "No, I left ten minutes ago. This is my shadow."

Scattered laughter surrounded them.

"So, what about it?"

"What about what?"

"The card filing system."

"Sal, ah don't give a ripe diddily what you do. Have yo' little 'ol card filing system, if it turns you on."

"Good. That's all I wanted to know. As long as you don't interfere when I want to use the logs or file cabinets."

"Ah never give nobody a hard time."

The men laughed heartily and she sneered at them.

"They give *me* a hard time."

Renewed laughter irritated her further.

"Ah'm gonna quit this job one day. Then you'll see what trouble yo'all is gonna have tryin' to run things."

"We're all going to be quitting some time. If *you* quit, the problem will be trying to figure out your filing system."

Applause and cheering surprised him. Flushing, he walked back to Roy's office. He telephoned the Rand and asked a HUD secretary for 3 x 5 index cards and a container for them, but they had neither, surprising him. How can a large office not have file index cards? It's like a convenience store not selling milk or bread. Still annoyed about not getting reimbursed for the four dollars, he rejected buying anything with his own money which was nonexistent anyway except for change.

"How about 5 x 8 cards that come in a nice, brown filing box," she offered playfully. The courier could deliver it. He's just leaving."

Too large, he first reacted. "Okay, send me the 5 x 8's in your nice brown filing box," he repeated facetiously and she laughed.

If I can't use it, I'll give it to Trudi to use for recipes. Having telephoned three times about his four dollars, he decided to ask her.

"The voucher's just been typed. You can pick it up anytime."

"You're kidding. You know about it?"

"Of course," she answered, suggesting that she communicated with HUD employees which Sal doubted.

"Great, but what about the money?"

"Pardon me?" Unaware that he was teasing, she paused and hammering and whining saws became noticeably discernible.

They're starting to drive me crazy like everything else, Sal groaned. Because the best laid plans of mice and men sometimes go awry, he considered voicing about the reimbursement. "Will you put the money inside the voucher?

"Pardon me?"

"Just kidding."

"A voucher enables you to get reimbursed from petty cash," she explained, taking him seriously, and he eventually hung up.

Unbelievable, he reflected, surprised about experiencing some joy about finally receiving the money, since he was hardly money-hungry, and he pulled himself together. Time to keep the elephant off my back before I pick up those big bucks. The longer Quincy doesn't know that Pam's helping me like a secretary, the better, he concluded and left out the side door. Eyeing the carpenters hammering and sawing away, he entered Quincy's trailer, spent a yawning hour matching and stapling inspection sheets with corresponding dispatch tickets, and returned to his office. Well, what do you know? he announced, noticing a dozen packs of 3 x 5 file index cards on top of a truly nice, brown, 5 x 8 filing box on his desk. Somebody was just too lazy to look for them, he sensed accurately. Ready to transfer information to the cards, he walked back to the front and heard Doris belittle another flood victim. How long is she going to get away with that? He thanked Rota for dropping off the cards and filing box and opened a file cabinet drawer.

Doris filed trailers according to HUD's contract with the manufacturer *or* by the yoke number, Rota told Sal.

The world had to figure out which one she was referring to, he realized, and was so irritated about such stupidity and incompetence that he pounced on her after she hung up. "In other words, if nobody can figure out who you're referring to, such files are worthless, damn it."

Carmela and Rota stopped working in order to listen appreciatively, Sal noted.

"*Ah* know which is which," Doris defended.

"But nobody else does. Don't you understand? How about joining the world?"

Nodding grimly, Rota stapled several papers together.

"If you can't find the file, yo'all needs ta keep a'lookin' till ya do."

"Are you serious? Do you realize what a waste of time that is for everybody?"

"Just 'cause you're too lazy ta keep a'lookin', don't mean everybody else is."

"*I'm* too lazy? At least I have enough brains to follow a universal system, not my own," he retorted and withdrew all the file folders from the top drawer.

"Make sure ya put 'em back in the same place," she stormed and rose.

"Don't worry."

Clunking around her desk, she handed Sal a piece of notebook paper. "That's a list of all the trailers according to HUD contracts and company names."

Sal thanked her and returned to his office. He began typing 3 x 5 cards by the trailer's number, manufacturer, and other pertinent information whenever possible and left enough space to add other important data that he hoped to glean from dispatch tickets later. "Oh, for God's sake," he muttered, finding two trailers with identical numbers in different parks and asked Doris about it, but she was busy writing dispatch tickets while arguing intermittently with several contractors including Rorick.

"Let Rota dispatch some dispatch tickets so we can get the hell out of here," suggested a contractor, seconded by the others .

"Ro-ta, Ro-ta," some loungers started chanting, surprising Floyd, and the men broke into laughter, then quieted in order to listen.

"She still don't know how," Doris barked. "Move back," she ordered the contractors.

"Yes I do," Rota squeaked.

"You tell 'er," a contractor told Rota.

"Just shut up or ya'all are gonna have to wait longer," Doris threatened the contractors.

"What's so hard about writing a dispatch ticket?" Sal asked Rota.

Rota sighed and frowned. "Nothing. She just wants everybody to think it's hard," she explained beyond Doris' hearing

"How come he gets three trailers and me only two?" complained a contractor.

"Ah owe it to him," Doris scolded and Floyd frowned again. "Now shut up or you get none."

"Who the hell does she think she is?" the first contractor complained and Rorick shook his head.

"Goddamn bitch. Had enough'a her shit. I'm gonna talk to somebody at the Rand tomorrow," the contractor threatened and two other contractors agreed to do likewise.

That could develop into something even *more* interesting than anything, Sal sensed.

Doris handed Rorick a dispatch ticket, and Sal mentioned finding the duplicate inspection sheets.

"Not now, Sal, ah'm busy," she retorted as usual.

"Wasn't just now. It was before," he needled and several contractors snickered.

"Move back and wait your turn," she ordered them again but few complied.

"What should we do about it?" Sal persisted. "I've got to know."

"Shut up, Sal," she snarled as if suddenly remembered that he was there.

Rorick asked her to give him ten trailers to block, since those he had ordered on his own hadn't arrived yet.

"Are you outta your cotton-picking' mind?" she shouted, jarring him, and they began arguing. "Ah don't care if you can block twenty a minute and you got a ten million dollar contract," she stormed, filling out another dispatch ticket. "You're lucky to get three."

Since she's the dispatcher, HUD entrusted the enormous responsibility of distributing trailers–the essence of the entire operation–to an incompetent, spoiled, erratic brat, a teenager. Too unbelievable for words, Sal reminded himself. And you just slowed her down even more, he realized and returned to his desk. Maybe file cards aren't such a good idea, he vacillated, realizing that the brown box was too large for them. Picturing them fitting in an empty shoebox, he jotted it down on his pad to bring one from home. A shoebox in an office? How unprofessional can you get? he nevertheless scolded himself.

Sal found more duplicates, noted them also and carried the rest of the inspection sheets to Quincy who accepted them almost gleefully.

Whatever turns you on, Sal kept to himself.

"You're staying late. We gotta finish these," he announced, sorting inspection and maintenance sheets (which the men had just given him) into separate piles.

"What do you mean late? It's already late. You mean later. I hardly get home before 10:30 as it is."

"Shit, I used to put in fourteen hours a day helping Juan at Corning."

You drank that much coffee over there? Sal almost verbalized. "That's all right for you, but I'm married."

"So am I," Quincy countered. "Really? Your wife's up here?"

"Shit, no. She's in Georgia."

"That's not a marriage. That's like a separation."

"What?"

"So, with your wife down there, you're really not living like a married man like me."

"You're gettin' paid, ain't cha?"

Oh, here we go with the money factor again. "Money doesn't justify everything. In fact, it hardly justifies why we're on this planet. I'm only doing this because I have to. I've got a wife and–" Realizing that he was about to blame them, he stopped. "I wouldn't have become a teacher had I been concerned about the damn money."

"Well, ex-cuse me."

Sal evaluated the triangular-shaped hair that seemed to be pointing to Quincy's nose. "Besides, I haven't even gotten a full paycheck yet."

Quincy fondled his tuft of hair. "Who has?"

"Millie flies to Washington to straighten out the checks, and the damn payroll clerk is on vacation. It's too stupid. How come she didn't telephone first? D. C. has great sights. So, I guess she took a vacation. Guess who paid for it?"

Sorting papers with a fervor that continued troubling Sal, Quincy shrugged. "What the hell do you want from me? You'll get your money, don't worry."

"Everything's done carelessly and sloppily around here and nobody gives a damn." Realizing its therapeutic value–that unloading his grievances was helping him survive one of the worst experiences of his life, he began tearing Doris apart fault-by-fault and discussed her atrocious filing system. He condemned the wasted manpower and the stupidity and expense of moving 250 trailers to the Holding Point. "And a trailer-load of guys are standing around sucking wind. Or they're lounging in the other trailers." he specified, catching Quincy's curious glance. The guy doesn't even know what I'm talking about or cares, he sensed.

Sal stormed about the lack of organization and leadership, the truck fiasco, the dozens of steps that were built too low by mistake, the botched pay checks–everything and anything that suddenly stampeded into his zigzagging mind, including even Barry Perrano. "There isn't anything about this entire operation that was handled right or smoothly from the beginning." Except what Lyman, Skip, and a few others accomplished at Mc Arthur Park, (plus me, he concealed because it would have sounded like bragging and seemed too insignificant compared to what could have been accomplished sooner had the overwhelming manpower been utilized.) "And the victims have had to suffer because of it," he enunciated.,

"Don't worry about all that shit," Quincy dispensed. "We gotta rewrite this form to stop guys from handin' in maintenance and inspection sheets every day. Understand?"

"No. That's too difficult for me to grasp."

Quincy laughed. "Once a week should be cool. Then I need your help to figure out some new forms."

Oh, God, Sal sighed with a frown. What's the use? "I could've told you so. But you wouldn't 've listened. The trouble with this operation is that nobody tunes into intelligence." And intelligence runs the universe. "And we keep wasting time."

Quincy looked up. "Chill out, man," he urged, but as if he were fearful of losing Sal's assistance, Sal realized. "What the hell's the sense a gettin' all bent outta shape? Ya die young."

Realizing that he was taking his frustration out on someone else other than Roy once again, Sal felt more helpless than ever. Agreeing to stay late, he telephoned Trudi and didn't get home until eleven thirty. Tossing and turning in bed, he had difficulty negating inspection sheets, dispatch tickets, and file index cards from his mind. When Doris' face appeared and even lingered, he rose dazedly and took two aspirins. He slipped into a nervous sleep around one and dozed until the clock radio staggered him at six. He reached the office at 7:45 a.m. and felt he hadn't left. Observing all the men lingering outside in the dense fog, he parked, exited, and approached Skip, Norm, and the others amid what sounded like angry hammering and saws raging behind them. "What's up? They ran out of coffee?"

Norm laughed.

A slight breeze nudged a strand of hair across Skip's bad eye, and he shoved it back. "Everybody's gotta stay outta the pool. The flyin' squirrels is cleanin' up the barracks."

Wearing neatly ironed coveralls, Norm eyed the office trailer like a farmer studying his sagging barn. "She's gettin' the old G.I. treatment."

"Huh," Sal remarked, pocketing his hands. Tired, he wanted to sit but accepted the situation almost humorously. "What for? Because of the rotten food on the counters? There's only about an inch of crud on the floor? Hell, the bathroom doesn't even stink," he lied. "Roy's idea?" Probably not, he answered, recalling that Roy ignoring his suggestion about getting janitorial service, claiming the place would only get dirty again.

Norm inserted a fat thumb underneath a suspender. "Dignitaries are in town I hear. Governor Romney and the troops," he added cheerfully.

This guy ought to pose for *The American Farmer*, he fancied. "Amen for Governor George Romney and the troops," Sal dramatized, parroting Flip Wilson, a television comedian. "Probably the only way to get the office cleaned. Too bad they didn't visit us at the Fairgrounds."

Skip jerked back his hair. "Roy didn't want them to pass out."

A vacuum cleaner started up inside, obliterating some laughter.

Sal reexamined the trailer. "But why the flying squirrels? Aren't they just supposed to clear out sites?"

"They volunteered," Norm replied.

"Just like the youth," Sal remarked. "Always trying to clean up the older generation's mess."

"They even bought fly swatters," Skip contributed.

A saw started up, whined to a halt, and raged back to life. "Must be hard cleaning with them," Sal contributed.

The door opened, and the group regarded a male "squirrel" carrying out a box of garbage.

"Breakfast, Ding," Skip called and laughter spanked the surrounding fog.

"Ain't ripe enough," Phil said as the "squirrel" headed for the disposal canister near the carpenters.

"How's working in the office?" Norm asked.

Sal sighed. "Could be worse. I just don't know how."

"You and Doris hittin' it off?" Skip queried and the "squirrel" reentered the office.

"Absolutely," Sal dramatized. "Fine young woman. Good breeding."

"That reminds me," Norm said. "Forgot to hand this in yesterday."

Sal waved off the inspection sheet. "It's redundant. Like everything else around here. Quincy's making up a new log."

The door opened and a "squirrel" motioned them inside.

The group entered boisterously, headed for the urn and percolator, and Sal carried a smirk halfway down the hallway. Entering his office, he glanced through the passageway, and noted Craig sitting before the microphone. Where's Pam?

Craig rose, entered Sal office through the passageway and intercepted Sal before he sat. "Pam called in sick." He reached into his back pocket for his comb and began running it through his hair. "You're handling the radio because of your knowledge of operations." He pocketed his comb and leaned against the passageway's jamb.

Sal regarded the upturned nose with a suspicious smile and sat. "That's what I mostly do anyway," he reminded him.

"The pay's the same," Craig retorted with a grin.

Eyeing a stack of dispatch tickets and inspection sheets on his desk that needed Xeroxing, Sal exhaled. "What pay? They still owe me for two weeks. Got a ton of things to do and Pam's got to be sick."

"Good. Knew I could count on you," he responded with a laugh that renewed Sal's smirk. "Me and Roy 're leaving for a new trailer park. We also gotta look for new sites and other shit."

Oh? You're gonna be shacking up that long? "HUD's still looking for sites? No wonder we aren't dispatching trailers fast enough."

"It's the town officials. They're still arguing about where to HUD should put them. People don't want them near their homes."

"So I heard," he responded, picturing Barry Perrano, and Craig left.

Since most calls were for the office, Sal felt like a kangaroo hopping back and forth between both rooms every few minutes in order to answer transmissions and work on the cards. Transferring Pam's radio into his office was out. He would have had to disconnect an antenna that Skip spent hours installing in order to improve reception. Nor could he fit the typewriter and cards on her small table. Picturing the grief involved trying to find another desk at the Rand and transferring it over, sent a pang of stress into his abdomen.

Minutes later, Wally entered, exhaled exhaustedly, and sat beside Sal. He started boasting about his assembly-line crew which was so good putting "quality" steps together that they were now able to work independently without him.

Sal ruled a line on one of Quincy's new forms. Meaning you can get some heavier loafing in. "You're nothing but a modern-day Henry Ford." And you're nothing but a hypocrite for patronizing him. What else can I do at this point in my life? he answered.

"They're turning out them steps by the ton," Wally muttered through his rotten teeth.

Amazing how much praise some grown men need for accomplishing nothing, Sal criticized and glanced at Wally's smooth skin and narrow mustache. God, how people love to follow styles, no matter how dumb they look, he entertained, realizing that Wally's whiskers had hardly thickened to a goatee. "Nice going," he nevertheless obliged, hoping to satisfy him.

Wally folded his hands behind his neck, stretched his legs, and slouched. "You know, I never was the boss over nobody. Now look at me."

Sal penciled in another line. "You've risen to great heights." Contemplating Wally's flat head because of his ponytail that seemed inappropriate for his age, he suddenly had an idea. "Ever run a Xerox machine?" How to kill one pest with one bat, he concluded and controlled the urge to burst out laughing.

"Why, whaddaya need?" Wally bit.

Sal told him about the inspection sheets and dispatch tickets.

"You never seen such a Xerox operator like me."

"Really? You don't look the type. Xerox men are usually short and stocky." Will you quit it? he scolded again. That's the only pleasure I have, he answered.

"You're kidding."

"Yes, I'm kidding. But anyway, let's see if you have any talent."

Both entered Pam's office, but in the ensuing minutes, Sal couldn't decide what was worse: radio calls interrupting him from trying to teach him how to operate the machine or Wally barely knowing that copy paper was white.

"Unit fifteen," the baseman's voice boomed again.

Sal strode back, grabbed the mike, and observed Wally

repositioning himself behind the machine like a teen about to lever up the next ball.

You ain't even got the right stance, dude, Sal declared and struggled not to laugh at his own sense of humor.

"Unit fifteen, this is base relay."

"Now, I turn the knob to two because you want two copies, right?" Wally mumbled.

Oh, God. Answering the call, he copied the message on the yellow pad, glanced back at Wally, and sighed. Can't back out now. He'll get insulted. Signing out, he rose.

"Unit fifteen, this is base relay."

"Oh, for God's sake," Sal cried, rushed back and reactivated the mike.

"I think I got it now," he barely heard Wally emit through his half-closed mouth.

"Unit fifteen here. Over," he answered and grabbed the pencil.

"Unit fifteen," the baseman began. "The Rand wants to know the exact number of two-and three-bedroom trailers on hand. Unit ten wants to know if you got keys for trailer 974-38 and 974-40. He's waiting. Unit twenty-four wants to know when trailer 960-36 at 14 Gray Street is gettin' gas and electric. Do you copy? Over?"

"This is unit fifteen, no, not everything. Run all that by me again, over."

"Hey, what does replace web mean?" Wally chirped.

Oh, for God's sake, Sal protested, feeling his pencil seemingly trembling while he rushed to copy the repeated numbers.

"What 'cha up to, man?" Sal heard Quincy ask Wally.

Oh, God, no. Quincy left his lair, Sal realized, perspiring.

"Helpin' Sal. That radio's got him goin' bananas."

Thanks for telling him, Wally. You're worth something. Maybe it'll slow the paper maniac down. "This is unit fifteen. I copy. Gotta get back to you on the keys," he transmitted and repeated the trailer numbers for verification. "About the trailer count, tell unit twenty-four to contact unit sixty, Nick Maturo. He's the official gas and electric coordinator, over." Where the hell is *that* bird? He's slicker than Happy and twice as invisible.

"That's a Roger, fifteen. They want that trailer count info on the triple, over."

"Will do my best," Sal responded, signed out, and strode back to the Xerox machine.

Quincy eyed the yellow pad in Sal's hand. "Where've you been?"

"What's a web?" Wally interrupted.

Sal exhaled exasperatedly. "It means forget about Xeroxing, until

274

I replace it."

"What is it?" Wally persisted.

"It's where spiders live," Sal answered.

"Where've you been?" Quincy pressed.

"Right here. Where do you think I've been? I don't take breaks," he cried, proud of his almost inexhaustible energy. "Only the beatniks inside do. They get tired from standing around in the office. That's why they leave. To rest up inside the trailers."

"Need you in my office," Quincy ordered.

"Everybody needs me," Sal retorted and caught Quincy's frown before he turned to Wally. "The machine won't run unless I install a new web," he advised him and jerked his head back to Quincy. "Cover the radio for a minute while I go up front," he ordered back and dashed out of the room. "We're unit fifteen," he shouted to him from the hall.

"You got one a them webs?" Wally called.

Sal turned.

"Maybe I can install it."

Yeah, sure. Just what I need. But could it be possible? He about-faced, and trotted back curiously. "Ever put one in?"

"No," he replied, sounding stifled because of his rotten teeth.

"Then forget it. Put that thing down," he ordered Quincy fussing with the mike. "It's not a toy."

"Unit fifteen, this is base relay," Sal discerned, striding past the kitchen. "Unit fifteen, this is base relay."

"Answer that," he shouted to Quincy "Unit fifteen. That's us. I told you." Maneuvering between the men, he headed towards Doris' desk, and barely heard Quincy comply above the droning voices inside and the sawing and hammering outside. 'Bout time you're doing something constructive.

Arriving in front, Sal noticed the loungers giving Rota's breasts the once-over as she peered over Doris' shoulder. He withdrew baseman's message from his shirt pocket. "Doris, do you know how many trailers are out there in the field? And the Rand needs a two and three-bedroom trailer count. We also need keys for trailer 974-38 and 40," he read.

"I'm busy," returned the usual without her glancing at him.

"So am I. But that's life. *HUD* wants to know," he emphasized, hoping it would have more impact.

Finally regarding him, Doris frowned as if she were struggling to remember his question. "Ah don't know how many's out there. Ah done never counted them."

Several standees laughed and she glanced up at Rota. "And will ya stop standin' over ma shoulder? It makes me nervous."

"Sorry," Rota responded and hopped back to her desk like a

wounded peacock.

Carmela offered to try and find the keys.

"Thanks," he responded, handing her the sheet. "I'll need that back when you're done."

Carmela nodded and Sal turned back to Doris. "Don't you keep a record of what the hell's out there?"

"Ah can't worry about that dumb stuff."

Tell them exactly that, Sal's other self suggested.

"Here's the keys to 974-38," Carmela announced minutes later and handed him a small, sealed, tan envelope and his yellow sheet. "Can't find any for the other one."

Sal thanked her and headed back to the radio room. Hearing the baseman call their unit again, he broke into a trot. "I'll take it," he shouted and entered.

Quincy rose and lumbered slowly toward Wally still standing before the machine.

"Unit fifteen, unit thirty-two needs six four riser steps to replace some *threes* at Skycrest," baseman's voice boomed again.

"We got 'em," Wally announced proudly to Sal hurriedly scribbling down the message.

Sal repeated it back, mentioned having only the one set of keys, and the baseman asked for the trailer count.

"Doris doesn't have that info, over," Sal replied militarily.

"This is base relay. Stand by, fifteen. Will contact HUD and convey that transmission."

Be my guest, Sal kept underground, heard him do so, but couldn't hear the other person's reply.

"Unit fifteen, this is base relay."

And this is stupid, Sal squelched. "Fifteen, here, go."

"HUD's transmission is, quote, 'Why not?' over."

Sal almost grinned. "They'll have to ask Doris, but she's busy, over."

A short pause followed. "Unit fifteen, this is base relay. Should I transmit that exactly? over."

"Absolutely, baseman, over."

"Roger, fifteen, base clear."

"Fifteen clear," Sal replied and lowered the mike to the table which wobbled. Gotta fix that, he reminded himself. "Now for the web."

"You comin' over when you're done?" Quincy asked him.

Wally studied the English teacher. "Need me anymore? Gotta check them steps."

Sal replied "yes" and "no" respectively and appreciated when both left. Hurrying into his office, he grabbed a web and returned to the machine. Perspiring heavily, he glanced helplessly at "replace web" and strained to remember how Roy inserted it. "If he hadn't tried to show off, maybe I'd know," he muttered with aggravation.

"Unit fifteen, this is baseman, over."

"Damn," Sal protested, rushed back to the desk, and answered.

"HUD wants the trailer count even if somebody has to count them in the field," the baseman declared and suggested that Sal find someone as reliable as he to do so.

Sal appreciated the compliment. But picturing the loungers in the field fooling around, missing trailers, losing the count, and so on, he rejected the idea involving anyone of them. None of them can count that high, he reflected. "Will do it myself, over."

"Good," baseman answered. "Just don't have the same guy take over the radio. Whoever he is, don't know nothin'. Over."

"Roger," Sal replied, then scolded himself for sounding so militarily. So, who's going to answer the radio while I'm counting trailers? he analyzed and chose Happy almost belligerently. One way to put a professional loafer to work.

Stepping outside into the lifting fog, Sal headed toward the sound of hard rock thumping above the pounding hammers and squealing saws. Reaching the Barracuda, he eyed Happy's reclining body. "How about turning that down a decibel?"

"No problem," Happy responded, surprising Sal, then again when he agreed to handle the radio.

"But do you know how to work that kind of radio?"

"Do ah know how ta handle that kind of radio?" he sneered, leaned back, stretched, and clasped his neck.

"But I need you today. Like right now, because I can't leave the radio unattended for long. HUD wants to know how many trailers we've got. Just remember, we're unit fifteen."

"You got it," Happy remarked and stepped out, revealing his shabby, lived-in jeans.

Sprinting around several piles of steps, Sal arrived in the field. Dopes, he rebuked, noticing them haphazardly parked. Why couldn't the toters or someone else have parked them in neat rows for everyone's benefit? And how come they're still here instead of at the sites?

The easiest and most logical way to survey them for an accurate count, was to stand on top of the first one, he concluded and borrowed a carpenter's ladder. Peering through patches of fog, he followed the different crooked lines with his eye and counted 243 trailers twice. Trotting back with the aluminum ladder, he heard raucous laughter, slowed before a trailer's opened door, and considered peeking inside.

You know what's going on, he reminded himself, accurately picturing a group of loungers drinking while playing cards amid beer cans and trash strewn about throughout the floor. Why aggravate yourself further? Moving on, he returned the ladder, reentered the office and paused before Doris' desk. "How's Happy been doing with the radio?"

"Do me a favor, Sal," she sidetracked.

Not now, I'm busy, he considered reciprocating. "A personal one, no," he nevertheless responded coolly. "For HUD, maybe, depending how stupid."

"Tsk." Doris smirked and the other women laughed.

"Ask Homer ta gimmy the numbers at the front gate," she requested casually while contemplating papers on her desk, and two hammers started pounding in unison outside, as if the wielders were fooling around.

Sal stared bewilderedly at the pretty face with slightly bucked teeth. "What numbers? What are you talking about?"

"Numbers. Numbers," she barked nervously. "Don't 'cha know what numbers are? *One, two, three, four,*" she rattled off, laughed at him, and Sal saw red.

"What the hell do you mean?" he shouted angrily. "What numbers? Who's Homer? You're forever inexact, vague, and cryptic. How am I supposed to know what the hell you're talking about? Even *you* don't know or you'd be able to explain it."

Rota and Carmela stared at him.

So did Doris. "Gol-ly, Sal," she scolded.

"You never explain anything," he stormed, barely discerning footsteps approaching from down the hall. "Which front gate? We've got three," he bellowed. The hell with him, he dispensed, assumed it was Roy, and he refused to look back.

"You're stupid. Know it, Sal?" Doris deposited calmly, infuriating him further.

"What's the hell's the matter with you?" he raged, feeling blood rushing into his already crimson head. "*I'm* stupid? You're stupid. You're the dumbest person alive. You're disorganized–"

"Hey," interceded a male voice from behind. "Knock it off," Happy shouted, striding toward him.

"And they put you in charge of, of ensuring that flood victims get into trailers? An imbecile like you? It's a disgrace. And you're forever asking others to get this or that because you're lazy, rude, thick, and inconsiderate–"

"Ah said knock it off," Happy barked.

Sal whirled back. "Mind your own damn business. I'm not talking to you." He turned back to Doris. "You dirty the place and expect others to clean it up for you," he stormed, momentarily losing his breath. "What're we, your servants? You come up here from the South, put signs up in the bathroom, and think we're dumb. Who the hell do you think you are?"

"You're stupid, Sal, know it?" she merely repeated.

"You're stupid, Sal, know it?" he mimicked in a high-pitched voice and Rota laughed. That's all you can say? Give me a break. Look at your desk. You're nothing but a slob. No wonder you never know where anything is, shacking up with a married man," he sneered. "What numbers?"

"All right, Sal, you're fired!" Happy exploded. "Clear out. Get your ass down to the Rand and tell Millie Jackson."

Infuriated, Sal barely heard him, unaware that he was also satisfying deeply-accumulated stress from eleven frustrating years struggling to teach uncaring, misguided, selfish, and party-happy misfits. Though somewhat relieved from finally telling her off, he pictured asking Homer for numbers anyway, though he didn't know what she meant, that is, as if he were *really* stupid. In fact, despite his present mental state, he still believed he could help the flood victims.

About to depart, he felt a stern hand on his shoulder and whirled back. Deliberately aiming below the face, he swung, striking Happy's large belt buckle. Rota screamed and Sal recoiled from the sharp sting. Cocking his fist again, he braced for Happy's response.

But doubled over, Happy had already reeled backwards. Losing his balance, he fell against Carmela's desk, jolting her. Grabbing the end of it, he struggled to get his wind and righted himself.

Sal wiped his bleeding knuckles with his handkerchief. If he swings, I'll destroy him, he vowed and hurriedly stuffed the handkerchief inside his back pocket. "Cover the radio," he ordered him. "And I mean now. I've got something to do. You want to tell Millie about me? Go ahead," he raged. "I'll tell her that you moved from sleeping all day in your car to sleeping all day in the office," he enunciated. "You want back pay?" he sneered. "You ought to pay HUD for letting you live here." He turned for the door and stepped outside. Although he absorbed a full blast of screeching saws and thudding hammers, the fresh air soothed him.

Fabulous, he soon scolded sarcastically, comprehending the significance of his action while heading for his car, and he pictured getting fired and possibly sued. Dumb, he added. He opened the door, slid inside, and checked his serene, bespectacled face in the mirror. What if he would have swung? Broken your glasses? How would you have paid for a new pair? Take out a loan from Beneficial Finance at twenty percent a shot?

He started the engine, backed out between a row of parked cars, and almost hit a stack of steps piled ten feet high. He eyed Wally talking to one of Rorick's men, then the carpenters hammering away or sawing with circular saws.

A respectable English teacher losing control? he berated himself further, driving ahead. Violence at your age and supposed maturity? What if Romney and the troops would've walked in with reporters just then? I would 've still bopped the punk, he answered. Sometimes it's hard to climb out of your own stupidity, his poetic mind embellished.

Reaching the front gate, he spied a young man looking up talking to a driver sitting in his idling toter hooked to a trailer.

Holding a magic marker in one hand and a clipboard and cigar box in the other, Homer signaled the driver on and slipped the marker inside the box.

Sal approached him, introduced himself, and they shook hands.

Homer removed a pen from his short-sleeved shirt pocket. He notated something on the clipboard and the diesel motored slowly and noisily ahead.

"Doris told me to get some numbers from you–whatever that means," Sal began.

"We don't let toters give us serial numbers," Homer sidetracked in a deep, nasal voice. Holding the box awkwardly, he copied down information from a paper the toter had given him. "And we count trailers as they come in."

What's that got to do with what I just told you? Why is he telling me this?

"Some of 'em can't even write. Or you can't read their handwriting. So George gives 'em temporary numbers ta stick on the trailers." He reopened the cigar box containing an assortment of red numbers printed on white squares about half the size of a 3 x 5 index card.

This guy's rambling. "You're numbering trailers as they come in?"

"Yeah, just up to a, how many the company sends over. I mean when a driver pulls in from a different company. Then I start over again. It can be a bitch when trailers comes in from different companies. And it's hard to keep track of the two-bedrooms and the three." He laughed oddly, as if he had acute sinus.

Sal studied him briefly. What's so funny?

"And we ran out of *nines*, so–"

The wind shifted and Sal sniffed sniffing asphalt. "Excuse me. I'm supposed to get numbers."

"Oh, twenty-six come in altogether. Twelve two bedroom and, a, a, what's that? a, a, twelve from twenty-six is, a, a–"

This kid's on drugs! Sal exclaimed inwardly. "Fourteen."

"Oh, yeah, right, right."

"Is twenty-six one of the numbers I'm supposed to give Doris?"

"Oh, yeah, right. Tell her twenty-six. How much is that? Twelve two bedroom and, a . . . . What did we say?"

"Fourteen three bedroom trailers."

"Oh, yeah, right."

About to leave, Sal turned. "You're numbering trailers consecutively from *one* to whatever, according to how many trailers a toter hauls in from his company? Then you start all over with *one* when a toter arrives from a different company? If you duplicate numbers, how can the office know how many trailers were delivered from any particular company?"

"Hah?"

Sal repeated himself.

"Hey, that's *their* problem, not mine."

Oh, God, not again, Sal groaned. "You mean it's *our* problem. Wouldn't it be simpler to copy down the trailer's company name, serial number, and how many trailers each trucker delivers from whatever company, so we can keep our records straight?" he deliberately reworded.

Unsure who Sal was or how to respond, Homer shrugged. "What do you mean?"

What do you mean what do I mean? I mean what I just said, he suppressed. "How does the office get to know how many trailers arrived from each company?"

Homer shrugged again. "She gets this copy," he explained, rattling the paper in his hand. "I think."

Sal frowned. I give up.

"Don't ask me. I only work here."

Maybe I should ask somebody who *doesn't* work here.

"A, yesterday Doris needed, a, twenty-six three-bedroom trailers and er, twenty-eight *twos* in a hurry, fifty-four altogether, all under sixty foot. So, me and George go gallopin' through the fields checking trailers to see how many bedrooms is out there."

Who's George? Forget him. He's immaterial. You're thinking like Homer, he almost guffawed. "Doesn't Doris keep a record of that?"

"Of what?"

Not again. You mean you forgot what I just said? "The *twos* and the *threes*."

Homer shrugged still again. "Took me and George an hour. Then Craig radios and tells us he just needs a, a *forty*, man. Ain't that a kick in the ass?

I'll say. I can almost feel it, Sal thought.

281

Homer reexamine his clipboard.

Don't fight it. Join them or go insane, he reminded himself. "Sounds like a HUD worker."

"Shit like that happens all the time."

"That's true," Sal agreed, almost guffawing at himself again. But surveying the trailers in the nearby field, he felt stupid, like whenever he agreed with an unruly student's stupidity in order to save time and the energy he would have needed to correct him.

"Remember me radioing about them trailers?" Homer suddenly digressed boyishly, interrupting Sal's thoughts.

Which ones? Sal teased. "You're unit sixty-seven?"

"In person," Homer honked straight from the nose.

Recalling hearing that same tone of voice, Sal finally laughed about more absurdity. "I'm unit thirty," he introduced and they shook hands. "Pam Meadows is the new radio person now, unit fifteen," he specified. I was filling in today because she's sick." Why are you telling him this? he scolded. Because I'm trying to avoid going insane, he answered.

"How many trailers ya need? *Two* bedroom or *threes*?"

Sal shook his head. "She didn't say. I don't even know what this is all about."

Both studied a toter circling slowly around the asphalt road while heading toward the trailers parked beyond the office.

"Can't spare that many anyways. Just er, a, four of each," he revised. "That's half."

What in God's name is he talking about? Spare them? There's plenty out there. What's the dumb system? And how come with all the available manpower, Homer and George are the only ones assigning trailers to the toters, if that's really what they're doing. "Okay, good," he nevertheless dispensed. Removing his pad, he copied down the twenty-four trailers' serial numbers, drove back to the office, and was relieved not to see a patrol car in front. Parking, he eyed the carpenters banging away amid the usual screeching saws and entered the office. Several contractors were staring at Doris as if she were a new female species. Pleased that the women were typing unconcernedly, Sal waited his turn. Doris finished treating both men gruffly, and he approached her. "Sorry about shouting at you before." I should've been quieter, he suppressed with a laugh.

Typing, Doris threw him a glance.

"Here's the exact serial numbers of twenty-four trailers that just came in." Why aren't we dispatching the trailers that are already out here? he demanded again but refused to verbalize, once again in order to minimize stress once again. He tore the sheet out of his small notebook and put it beside her typewriter, and then placed his hands on his hips. That's your napkin, sweetheart. I'll bring out the main course later.

Doris stopped typing and the saws and hammering seemed to become more audible. She reexamined his numbers, as did two contractor peering over one another's shoulders. "Ah don't want them numbers. Ah wanted the numbers of *twos* and *threes*. Homer knows that. Didn't you ask him?"

"Those are the exact serial numbers of all the trailers you can dispatch," he offered almost scholarly. "Can't you deal with a little exactness?"

"Sal, ah don't even know what you're talking about."

Rota stopped typing in order to listen and Sal broke away.

"Ah want different numbers," she shouted to him proceeding down the hall.

Rota regarded Doris. "You could've explained what you wanted a little more thoroughly," Sal heard her admonish. "You don't explain things. That's your major problem."

Doris disagreed and they began arguing.

If that were her only problem, she'd be human, he stated, paused before the side window and stared briefly at carpenters banging away enthusiastically. About to veer into his office, he remembered Happy, entered the radio room, and observed him slouched in the chair reading one of Roy's comics. "Any important messages come in?" he asked, curious about how Happy would respond following the incident. Probably hurt myself more than I did him.

Happy glanced at him. "Just these." He handed Sal the large yellow pad, and Sal struggled to decipher bad grammar and poor penmanship.

Another illiterate, Sal labeled. How do they fill out an application? "Unit seventy-five says there ain't no trailer at that address."

"What address?"

Happy rose, leaned over to show him, and Sal backed away because of his body odor.

"That address right there, man."

Don't these guys use deodorant? Better yet, don't they wash? "Where?"

"There," he insisted and pointed.

Sal analyzed familiar-looking hieroglyphics that his students often blamed on limited time or that they were in a hurry. "That's an address? Looks like chicken scratches. Tolerance, he warned himself again. "Can't figure it out." Though I've been deciphering Egyptian cuneiform for eleven years. "How about rewriting it?" he asked patiently, like he often did in class.

"You got it," Happy y responded with hypocritical enthusiasm, and he accepted the pad. "And you're supposed to call base relay about a trailer count." He rewrote the address hurriedly and handed the pad back to him.

Sal studied the same illegible handwriting. You're kidding. "I already told HUD hours ago." What's the matter with them? About to ask him whether a *three* was a *five* or an *eight*, Sal looked up and observed an empty room. That's your first brush with work since you arrived, Happy. Looking out the window, Sal spotted a carpenter playfully holding a two-by-four before another man threatening him with his live circular saw near his face. And probably your last. Radioing baseman, he repeated the count and answered two more transmissions. He approached the Xerox machine, carefully analyzed how to replace the web, and ruined two trying to do so. Finally, he announced when the red light disappeared after his third try. He started Xeroxing inspection sheets, but recalled Quincy's forms, and frowned.

Carmela dropped off more dispatch tickets and inspection sheets on his desk and started walking away. "Carmela, would you mind learning how to Xerox copies?" he called, realizing that he would need help if he wanted to resume working on his log.

Pausing in the hallway, Carmela approached him standing before the machine.

"Because I'm swamped."

She agreed, although mostly because she assumed that he was in charge.

A familiar figure approached while he continued explaining. Oh, God, not again.

"Comin' over?" Quincy interrupted.

"Be right there." Sal lifted up the cover, placed an inspection sheet on the glass, and closed it. "If you start getting blank paper, it probably means a paper jam," he told her. "Here's how you fix that. Remove this front tray and–"

"Done with them forms?" Quincy interrupted again.

Sal regarded Quincy's pock-filled face and the odd bang that appeared to be off-center, pointing to his cheek.

"I put an inventory form on your desk," Quincy resumed. "Type it up like it is and run me off, oh, say, about a dozen copies."

Yes sir. "Okay." He turned back to Carmela but Quincy lingered. Suddenly comprehending Quincy's request, Sal turned back to him. "An inventory form? Are you serious. What for?" I don't think I can tolerate that, he cried, unfolding more teasing.

Evaluating Carmela's shapely breasts, Quincy burst out laughing. "You never heard of taking inventory?"

Taking it where? "Of course," he scoffed, apologized to Carmela for ignoring her, and rechecked Quincy staring at him. "Inventory of what? What's that got to do with helping the flood victims? Who said?"

Leaning against the jamb, Quincy slyly analyzed Carmela's shapely legs. "You realize how much stuff's been ripped off?"

Sal tuned in to the monotonous thudding and several screaming saws. Always fight stupidity with intelligence first. If that doesn't work, beat the shit out of them. "Taking inventory isn't going to improve anything. We need tighter security. Nobody's keeping track of anything, from trailers down to tools."

"That's why they wants us ta take inventory. Then we'll know exactly how much stuff's been ripped off."

Sal stared at him in disbelief. "Then what?"

"Whadaya mean 'then what?'"

"What 'er you going to do, call the police, the FBI, Gallagher?"

Quincy glared in annoyance at him. "Who's he?"

"Mr. and Mrs. Gallagher's son."

"What?"

"Nothing. Forget it. The point is you'll never find out what's missing."

"Why not?"

"Let's say we have a half a dozen circular saws right now. We don't even know how many we were issued, much less what everybody charged at Loomis and Mathews and are *still* charging." And taking home, he suppressed.

"Man, you think too much."

"Yeah, it's one of my faults."

Carmela laughed.

"Man, don't worry about it."

"Don't worry about it?" Sal sneered. "Hundreds of victims are without homes. They're trying to get into trailers, and you want to take inventory? Why continue watching television, if the house is on fire, get it?"

"What?"

"In other words, don't try doing anything stupid during a disaster."

Reevaluating Carmela's breasts, Quincy looked back at Sal. "I think ya ought ta start doin' what I tell ya," he requested but somewhat meekly, Sal caught.

"Geezus, you haven't even finished installing the padlock on the bedroom in your bungalow. Your tool room, that is," he specified, noting Quincy's puzzlement.

Carmela smiled reservedly.

"Haven't had the time."

"Haven't had the time," Sal sneered. "Take a break from handling so much paper work. You'll cut down on your calluses. And buy a lock for us here. Every once and a while I notice one less chainsaw."

Quincy frowned.

"Then ask Roy to put somebody in charge of giving out tools from here and your bungalow and who's buying what and when at Mathews and Loomis' gift shop. We're also missin' two radios."

"Oh, they're out there."

"They're out where?" Sal sneered again. "In somebody's home or they've already been sold to buy drugs." Sensing that he was becoming upset and not getting anywhere, he finally agreed, hoping that Quincy would leave, but he stayed put, annoying him further. In fact, he continued eyeing Carmela sexually as Sal resumed explaining to Carmela how to run the machine. "The trick is fitting the tray back in afterwards."

Carmela nodded and Quincy finally left but entered Sal's office.

"Which isn't easy. IBM gives a raise to whoever can invent the hardest machine to run."

Carmel laughed again.

Because, despite our genius, we don't always think things through carefully enough, he knew, recalling how long it took before one company put the match-strike tab on the opposite side in order to prevent accidentally igniting the entire book. Passing through the passageway, Sal eyed Quincy sitting impatiently with an annoyed expression at his desk and struggled to suppress his own irritation.

"How come you ain't typed my forms?" Quincy shouted to him. "They're still on your desk."

Lowering the tray, Sal watched Quincy fuss with his bang. Humor him. "Not because I haven't been doing anything," he answered and scolded himself for sounding hypocritically friendly again.

"What?"

"I'll be back a little later," Carmela suggested.

I guess she's worried that I might turn violent again, Sal sensed with a laugh and noticed Quincy fussing with something on the desk. "I've been busy." You sound like Doris, he scolded himself. It's contagious, he answered.

"With what?" Quincy persisted.

Oh, for God's sake. With all the coffee-slurpers sucking wind inside, I've got to justify that *I've* been working? Sensing that Quincy wasn't really his superior, nor would he have cared if he were at this point, Sal turned to Carmela. "Excuse me. Be right back," he told her and entered his office. Sitting in the metal chair alongside the man, he deliberately began a wordy, detailed explanation about his front-gate errand, his struggle to handle the radio during Pam's absence, the new log, and Doris' unbelievable behavior during the disaster.

Satisfied, bored, or overwhelmed, Quincy rose and left.

And that's how you avoid that knot in the deadwood, Sal repeated, a tactic he often used in class in order to suppress his rowdies. "Sorry about that," he told Carmela, rejoining her at the Xerox machine and he resumed struggling to reinsert the tray. "Now don't breathe. The least distraction upsets me. Only seven people in the world can do this. Six are dead. I'm the only left who knows how to do it."

Carmela laughed somewhat freely.

Struggling to catch the rods on opposite sides, he missed twice. The tray slipped out of his hands during the third try and clattered noisily to the linoleum floor. "Damn."

"I'll never be able to do that," Carmela admitted.

"What? Drop the tray? It's easy," he said, stooping for it. "You'll get the hang of it. It just takes time."

Carmela laughed uninhibitedly, and he finally wiggled it into place successfully.

"Just let me know whenever anything jams. And I'll call the company to get someone to help you."

Nodding, Carmela laughed, started Xeroxing inspection sheets, and Sal returned to his desk. He finished all the forms an hour later, including Quincy's. He was about to resume Xeroxing inspection sheets when a voice blared "Unit fifteen, this is unit one hundred, over." Curious about the odd number that he never heard before, he dashed back inside the radio room, grabbed the mike, and responded.

"Get somebody to relieve you and bring over them forms on the pronto, over."

This is just too much, Sal groaned, realizing it was Quincy. They outta nail down loose radios. "Okay, over and out," he quickly agreed, lest baseman realize that two employees were tying up the radio from thirty feet apart. Picturing someone radioing his unit while he left, he hurriedly raced over to Quincy's trailer with the forms and entered the bedroom. He's like a little boy with a new stamp album, he concealed, sidestepping numerous piles of paper on the floor, and he handed him the forms. Hands back on his waist, he wondered how anybody could be so preoccupied doing something so meaningless during a disaster. I guess it beats being the disaster yourself, he reconsidered, picturing Miles and Dinger.

Quincy looked up. "Finally got me a radio." Reaching down, he patted it several times, as if it were a new dog.

"So I gathered when you radioed me," came a deadpan reply.

"Notice my message? Purposely made it sound important."

"Caught that immediately. You're sly."

"Because we're not supposed to radio anybody unless it's important," Sal thought, imagining himself a priest about to hear Quincy's confession.

I understand, my son. "You broke one of HUD's rules. Unless you really believed it was an emergency. Then they'd forgive you."

"I grabbed that radio off a contractor," he pursued. "They ain't got no business having them."

Sal surveyed Quincy's pock marks. True. Why would *they* need a radio in order to radio us? Except to help set up trailers for the flood victims. Better in your hands, so you can radio me about forms. "Is it turned on? Somebody might want to radio *me*."

"Oh, it's turned on."

Yeah, but are you?

"I see you changed a heading on the inspection form."

"*Location* is better than *park* because it includes private sites."

"I don't know about that," Quincy disagreed.

Sal remained adamant and Quincy gave in reluctantly, pleasing Sal who was anxious to get back to working on his master log. "I'd help you sort, but I want to finish Xeroxing all your forms." More lying, he scolded incredulously. "Bring everything over. We'll sort them out together in the radio room," he deliberately offered, sensing Quincy would be too lazy to do so.

"Nah, that's okay," Quincy obliged.

The more Sal kept insisting, the more Quincy refused.

Decent, Sal praised mimicking his students with a laugh, realizing that Quincy would stay put. That's how you bypass still another knot.

Remembering Pam's wobbly table, he glued several pieces of cardboard under the leg which steadied it, and cut off the excess edges. But if he wasn't typing, he was hurriedly filing dispatch tickets up front, dashing back to answer the radio, or Xeroxing inspection sheets and dispatch tickets, until the machine refused to print anything, despite where Sal set the knob. Appreciating no red light, he struggled to fix it between answering more radio transmissions. Unsuccessful, he telephoned IBM's repair department from Roy's empty office and was put on hold. Why does practically all of America assume that everybody likes rock? he grumbled, holding the receiver away from his ear. And when am *I* going to get a phone?

Sal explained the problem to a secretary who promised to send a service man there as soon as possible, and they hung up. Quincy's just going to have to suffer through this tragedy. Soaked with perspiration, he resumed typing his log.

Still typing three hours later without a break, Sal became so stressed out that he started toying with several mental images. One portrayed himself revealing the incompetence and stupidity to Governor Romney and his assistant, and he pictured their aghast expressions. Another had Romney's assistant hurriedly whisking the Governor away while Sal complained savagely about the loungers. The final one depicted Craig, Quincy, and Roy struggling to fit Sal into a waiting ambulance as he ranted insanely about the incompetence, bungling, and mismanagement.

That's it, he announced, checking his watch. Time to journey between the woods and sign out. The usual men were already swarming back, including Terrance and Kevin who nodded at Sal lining up behind Skip. "So, did the Governor arrive?" he asked Skip who nodded. "So, what did he say?"

"About what?" Skip teased.

Sal grimaced and Skip broke into laughter. "Nothing, man."

"Didn't they check the trailer parks?"

"They didn't come here to check what's *really* goin' on, man. Hell, they posed for pictures right here at the Holding Point. It's less muddy than the parks."

Surrounding laughter enveloped Skip and the trim English teacher.

"They'll probably go in the family picture album. For the grandchildren," Skip added and Sal shook his head. "What's wrong with you, man? Got a problem with grandchildren?"

Norm turned to Skip. "So, why didn't *you* tell Romney what's *really* been going on?"

Skip flipped his hair in place. "And spoil the guy's vacation? Are you serious?"

Sal noticed the dapper Nick Maturo laughing his way inside the office with several others.

Have a hard day? he mocked, signed out, and drove home.

The following morning, Sal and Skip signed in almost simultaneously. Both sat on the vacant couch, and Skip picked up *The Star Gazette.*

"HUD PRAISED FOR EXCEPTIONAL JOB," the headlines read, and he started reading the write-up aloud. "Trailers have been installed in record time, alleviating thousands of suffering flood victims."

Laughter broke out.

Skip waited for it to subside. "Romney and the troops must a checked the wrong disaster."

Sal rose and headed for his office in disgust.

"Hi, I'm back," Pam chirped from the passageway and waved girlishly at him.

Looking up from his desk, Sal smiled. "You're good news."

"Really? You missed me?"

"I'll say," he admitted friendlily and resumed typing.

"Anything exciting happen while I was gone?"

"Nothing ever does. The Xerox machine broke down, if you call that exciting."

"It won't run?"

"Doesn't even walk."

Pam commenced giggling.

"The repairman's coming today. How about doing some Xeroxing for me after he fixes it? Assuming he does."

The giggling increased.

"Of course, if the machine needs parts, they might have to be shipped from Ethiopia for all we know."

Biting her lower lip, Pam back-pedaled into the radio room. She poked her head back through the passageway fifteen minutes later. "Lisa Brennig just arrived."

"Show her in," he responded, typing.

Pam suppressed more giggling. "She's looking for something to do. Have anything?"

The English teacher with the stylish, gold-rimmed glasses stopped typing and lifted his head containing swirls of wavy black hair mixed with gray. "Give 'er a fly swatter."

Pam giggled again.

Sal reevaluated her. "Are you kidding? Hugh Brennig's wife?" he inquired and waited for her to stop giggling.

"Yes. Go check. She just arrived. She's sitting next to Doris."

"That's stupid. Doris won't teach her anything."

"I know. Sal, I'm serious. She's just sitting there waiting for Doris to tell her what to do. It's so dumb."

"About as dumb as seventy-eight guys standing around doing nothing. Or sleeping in trailers," he threw in, stimulating more giggling. "Wait till Doris peppers her with doorknob silence, then she's *really* going to grab dumb. Tell Lisa this is Act I, the coffee hour. Oh, what the hell. So, she'll get paid for sitting in a chair. It beats Quincy. He gets paid for warming it."

Pam giggled unrestrainedly for several seconds. "She looks so dumb though," she repeated between gasps.

Curious, Sal walked up front. Angling between the usual knots of coffee-sippers, he introduced himself to her standing alongside Rota's desk.

Attractive, well-tanned, and in her mid-thirties, Lisa wore simple clothes. Possessing bleached blond hair swept back and held together glamorously, she was intelligent, pleasant, and unpretentious, Sal noted appreciatively during their small talk.

"Lisa needs somethin' ta do," Sal heard a familiar male's voice drawl and Roy broke away from a small group and approached them.

"Yes," Lisa agreed enthusiastically.

Doris suddenly began arguing with a contractor about who had been responsible for sending him to the wrong address, him or her.

Surprised, Lisa looked over inquisitively at the slightly buck-toothed woman who possessed pretty green eyes and long brown hair.

Talk about being oblivious. Wait till Lisa reports your behavior to hubby. Guess you don't care. Will hubby? he wondered. And did he get wind about me clouting the barracuda bum?

Arriving from the hall, Roy checked Doris, then Lisa. Sipping noisily, he turned to Sal. "Got anything for her to do?"

Give him back his own medicine–the silent treatment, Sal considered. Then you'll be just as bad as he is, he answered and rejected the idea.

"Got anything for her ta do?" Roy repeated and Lisa eyed his light blue cowboy shirt inquisitively.

Keep scrutinizing him, Lisa, Sal suggested during the squealing saws and hammering. He's got more to offer than meets the eye. "That's fine. I could use her," he answered sincerely.

"Great," Lisa responded eagerly and Roy wiped his mouth on his sleeve.

Nice goin', hombre. Got anything else to offer, like some fresh stupidity? Because of Lisa's presence, he divulged the new log slowly, carefully, and almost indifferently to Roy, like a fisherman passing a fat worm before a large bass.

Lisa praised its merits.

Thanks, babe, Sal thought.

Doris resumed typing, leaving a contractor's mouth in the opened mode, and Roy mumbled louder than usually.

Not bad, Sal responded, appreciating that they were behaving normally and suppressed a laugh.

Sal handed Lisa inspection sheets and index cards and showed her what to transcribe. Rota agreed to let her use her typewriter and Sal swung it around. Then, like a bubbling maitre'd, he asked a lounger to give up his chair which he did reluctantly and Sal slid it in under Lisa. Comfy? Need a menu? Noting Roy watching dully, like a manager breaking him in as the new waiter, Sal struggled against laughing.

"Thank you," she uttered with a smile and sat.

"My man is waiting for me to call him," the contractor resumed angrily.

Lisa began typing and Doris leered at the man.

"His trailer's parked in the street. He's waiting," the man protested as Sal lingered. "Where the hell do you want him to haul it?" the man grumbled with irritation.

"The city dump," Skip suggested, standing before the others near the couch. "Them trailers is junk anyway."

Lisa smiled during the laughter, then frowned, Sal noted.

"I told you. Nineteen River Street," Doris shouted above the raging saws and banging hammers.

Lisa adjusted the typewriter's margin for the next index card and looked up.

"And I tol' you. It's the wrong address. There ain't enough room for a trailer there," the man complained. "Gimmy another site, damn it."

"There ain't no more private sites right now," Doris boomed, rattling Lisa who eyed her curiously this time.

Act II, folks. Wait till the curtain lifts for more of this Madhouse Matinee. Surely Lisa will want to share this performance with hubby. Now there's a curtain-puller Sal thought, eyeing Roy staring mutely at the wall. Finally heading down the hallway to his office, Sal heard someone following him.

"Did you Xerox them forms?"

Oh, for God's sake, give it a rest, man. Good morning, he provided for Quincy. Sal flopped into his squeaky-swivel chair and Quincy arrived, sitting beside him. "As many as I could. The machine broke down."

"How come?"

Sal couldn't resist. "It wanted to. That's the way some machines are. Most of them don't care about people. It's a disgrace."

"Come on, Sal."

"I don't know. You never heard of machines breaking down? They're temperamental. Some are worse than folks."

"Can you fix her?"

"I doubt it. I'm not too mechanical." Since when is a machine a female?

"Are you sure?"

"No. But I'm not going to waste three hours trying to fix it and ruin it beyond repair," he deliberately enunciated.

Giggling sounded.

"I called IBM." What did you call them? he teased, almost guffawing.

"What time 're they coming over?"

The guy's really tweaking my tolerance. "Twenty-one minutes after ten."

"Really?"

Pam's giggled uncontrollably.

"No. But I was hoping that would satisfy you."

Quincy checked the passageway.

"Relax, the repairman 'll be over. Sometime this morning." Then you'll be able to play games again,

"They said that?"

"No. They really don't care if you play games. Yes, sometime this morning," he repeated, noticing Quincy struggling to read the top index card upside down near the near the typewriter. Give it up, Ralph. You probably can't read right-side up.

"What're you doing now?"

"Talking to you."

Quincy frowned. Fresh giggling erupted from next door and Sal revealed the new log.

"You're makin' up a new log? How come?"

Sal couldn't resist again. "Because logs rot when they get old."

Pam burst out laughing and Quincy frowned at the passageway.

"The old one's been lying in the woods too long. They decay, man. Didn't you know that?"

"Hah?"

Pam reacted similarly.

"Nothing, forget it," Sal quipped and purposely began elaborating about the new log in boring detail.

"Roy said it was okay?" Quincy interrupted, and the baseman began calling unit fifteen.

"Yes. Want to help me work on it?"

Sensing Sal would probably be too preoccupied with his own paperwork to assist him, Quincy leaned back disappointedly. "How many forms did you run off?"

Sal glided his squeaking chair to the left. He opened a drawer, removed several stacks, and handed them to him. "Except for the contractor's form you've got enough of everything to keep you busy for a week. Unless you spend too much time gulping coffee. Then it 'll take a mite longer, man."

"Unit fifteen, Over," Pam answered.

Counting the stacks, Quincy looked up. "The most important one."

"Oh, man, come on."

"And you only Xeroxed a couple dozen inventory forms."

"How many do you want? We don't even have that much inventory since the men have been helping themselves. Unless you want to count the loungers, then I'd have to print a ton more."

Giggling during the radio transmission, Pam apologized.

"I need you to help me take inventory?" Quincy pressed.

"Hate to refuse," Sal responded sincerely because he generally enjoyed helping others. "But I want to work on these cards." You play with your toys. I'll play with mine, Nigel.

"Roy told you to do that?" Quincy repeated.

Sal almost smiled over the ironic turn of events. "Yes."

"Fuck the cards," Quincy barked, surprising Sal.

Down, boy. Easy. Fuck Roy too? "That's impossible. Cards don't like to get fucked."

"Come on, Sal. What time 'er you getting done?"

"With Lisa's help–she's typing them inside–maybe next Friday, a little after lunch."

Pam signed out. Having struggled not to giggle while writing down the information, she broke loose, coughed, and almost choked.

Quincy glanced at the passageway again. "Lisa who?"

"Lisa Brennig." Will this pest ever leave?

"She's related to Hugh Brennig?"

"No, just his wife," he replied impatiently.

"No kiddin'?" he sing-songed. "How come she's working here?"

"Doris needs secretarial help. She's having trouble figuring out how to foul up on her own."

Despite pulling herself together momentarily, Pam giggled steadily.

Unaccustomed to sarcasm, Quincy frowned perplexedly.

"She's running out of ideas."

Quincy smiled, but so awkwardly that Sal knew that he was hardly listening.

"Lisa's tired of swimming in their pool all day," he imparted for Pam's entertainment. "Look, I've got to get back to these cards," he announced, pulling his chair up closer to the desk.

Quincy adjusted his tuff, though Sal thought it was pointing nicely at his nose. "So, you're not going to help?" Quincy responded boyishly,

"Geezus, Quincy. I can't figure you out. Eighty guys are on vacation inside and you're bugging me. Get one of them workaholics to help you."

"You're already here and you know what's happening."

You mean because I'm easy, cooperative, and literate, Sal revised amid the giggling. "After I do these cards, I'll help you with anything," he promised sincerely. "I'll even do windows," he offered and resumed typing.

Quincy inspected the forms again, rose, and left. About to proceed up the hallway, he about-faced, passed the office, and wandered into the radio room. Tinkering sounded and the Xerox tray clattered to the floor.

Sal grimaced. What the hell? He shook his head and entered the radio room through the passageway. "What are you doing?"

Standing before the machine, Quincy loomed like a mischievous boy, and Pam was already giggling out of control. "This thing fell off."

"You mean you pulled it off," Sal scolded, accepting it with a scowl.

"I hardly touched it," Quincy whined and glanced at Pam. "What's eatin' her?"

"She's reading a funny novel. Do me a favor. Keep your hands off the cookie jar, okay?"

"What?"

"Don't touch the machine, man, okay?" he sing-songed and Quincy left with a shrug.

Sal fitted the tray back, returned to his desk, an attractive brunette entered shortly afterwards.

"I'm Jackie Palmer from IBM," she introduced amid the usual screaming saws and thudding hammers outside. "I'm the repair lady."

Really? A female? Rising, Sal accepted her business card. What's this world coming to?

"I can only make very minor repairs."

With a shape like yours, nobody 'll mind. Down, boy, yourself, he scolded.

"What seems to be the problem?"

Sal told her.

"I might be able to explain how to handle those problems," she offered with a smile.

"Oh, good."

"But I'm really not a repairman. Or repair woman," she revised with a smile. "I'm here to demonstrate how to use the machine. Do you people need a demonstration?"

Sal rechecked her card. Where were you when they delivered the machine weeks ago? "Yes. But can you demonstrate honest work? The guys inside don't know what that is."

Giggling tore loose and Jackie eyed the passageway curiously.

"Sorry about that. She's reading a funny novel. "Yes, *I* could use a demonstration," he admitted sincerely, accompanied her into the radio room, and introduced her to Pam.

Though Jackie started showing Sal how to remove a web and dislodged paper, Doris' shrill blasts at the contractors kept jarring her. Nor did Sal help by asking questions between intermittent innuendoes directed at Doris, including that she was mentally ill, sending Pam giggling to the bathroom again.

"Stirring the ink improves copies," Jackie nevertheless resumed along with other hints, made several adjustments and eventually left.

Sal wandered up front to check how Lisa was faring sitting so close to Doris. "You're fast and accurate," he praised, amazed how many cards she had completed. Wonder if she notices all the deadwood?

"Used to be a secretary," she revealed with a smile. "These are duplicates I found. Is Doris always that loud?" she whispered near his face.

Sal couldn't resist. "Only when she isn't wearing her hearing aid. Just kidding."

Lisa smiled during some laughter and Sal left for his office.

Oh, for God's sake, he complained, finding Wally sitting at his desk. If it isn't one piece of redundancy, it's another.

Eyeing him, Wally began bouncing up and down on the seat, which began squeaking louder than ever, as if in protest. Wally stopped to pat its leather arms, as if to calm it down and rolled the chair from left to the right. "This feels nice."

Sal contemplated the man's hair flattened on his head. "It's just a chair."

"Wanna sit here?"

"No, I'll just sit on the floor. Swing the typewriter around. I probably can type from there if I have to," he actually uttered sincerely and Pam responded similarly.

Assuming Sal was sarcastic, Wally laughed self-consciously, rose, squeaking the chair as they changed seats, and Sal resumed typing.

Wally leaned forward. "We're really turning out steps."

Sal glanced out the side window. You've certainly got some serious professionals," he commented, observing two carpenters playfully raising hammers at each another. "But it sounds like you guys are building trailers."

Wally forced a laugh through his almost closed mouth. "We're building a big cover for the wood."

Sal almost choked. "Run that by me again? You're doing *what*?"

Wally checked the passageway during more giggling, repeated himself, and covered his awkward smile with his hand.

What the hell does that have to do with helping the flood victims? Sal concealed. He stopped typing, reexamined the men, then Wally. "A cover? Out of wood?"

"Part wood and part plastic. It's gonna be cool."

"What for?"

Someone radioed unit fifteen during a pause. Picturing Sal's surprise, Pam struggled to contain herself while writing down the information.

"To protect the wood from the rain."

"Are you serious?" Sal protested incredulously and Pam giggled uncontrollably.

Quincy checked the passageway. "Yeah, man. I'm serious."

That's what scares me. "Wood can stay out in the rain, man. Don't you know that?" I can't take it.

"The cover 'll protect the nails and tools then."

"You mean you just decided that?"

"Not really."

"Can you *really* tell me, *really?* "

Pam's giggling caught Wally's attention again.

"You're making a cover out of plastic to protect the wood?" he repeated in order to appease his sanity.

Looking back from frowning at the passageway, Wally laughed belittlingly. "Outta *part* plastic and furring strips, Sal. Geezus, man. We're not that dumb."

Don't underestimate yourself, son. "You've been leaving tools outside overnight? In this day and age?"

"Ah, just a few screwdrivers and hammers," Wally scoffed. "We're gonna be puttin' 'em underneath the cover after it's finished."

Thieves *can't* crawl underneath? Sal considered asking, but wanted to avoid getting further upset, especially because another thought interceded. "You can trust the guys in your crew not to steal the tools?"

"Shit yeah."

You're kidding.

Pulling his chair up closer, Wally flopped his hairy, sunburned arms on the desk, scattering his sawdust.

Who brushes that off, you or I? came another squelched objection.

"You gotta see it, Sal," he muttered confidentially. "It's a masterpiece."

I'll bet.

Wally almost smiled, despite his bad teeth.

You ought to check out my file index cards, man. They're fabulous. I might even Xerox the best ones and hang them up in my bedroom.

Wally analyzed Sal's thoughtful expression, the slight bump on his nose, and his bloodshot, hazel eyes. "Ya really can't see it from here."

"You mean I can't get the full blast looking out the hall window?"

"That's right," he remarked proudly.

"You're going to shingle it?" Sal threw in and braced himself.

Wally laughed. Then, as if remembering, hurriedly covered his mouth again. "We're not making *that* kind of a top, man. You gotta see it,

Sal."

"You're demolishing trailers?"

Wally stared perplexedly. "What do you mean?"

"I was worried that you might be chopping up trailers and using whatever wood you might need like two-by-fours or the siding." I think I'm going off the deep end.

Pam appeared at the passageway. "I'm heading for the girly room," she barely managed, holding a handkerchief to her mouth. "Be right back. Can you take calls?" Noticing Sal's strained expression from the passageway, she strode through his room and almost stumbling into the hall.

"What's wrong with *her*?" Wally asked as both studied the doorway for several seconds.

"She's got incontinence. It makes her laugh."

"What's that?"

"I don't know," he answered, frowning with a shrug. There I go lying again, he scolded.

"Hear that hammerin'? We're tackin' the plastic down right now," Wally expressed happily and rose. "Come on, I'll show ya."

Oh, why not. I need a break from all the bullshit, even my own. He followed him outside. Inhaling sawdust amid the raging saws and hammering, he approached the lopsided thirty-foot square cover held together with double furring strips. Swarming around it was Wally's select crew and several familiar-looking loungers tacking, measuring, sawing, fooling around, or arguing.

Where's Candid Camera? crossed Sal's mind. Shielding his eyes from the blazing sun, he noticed someone dangling upside down on a crosspiece, like a chimpanzee. "When're you going to finish it? I know a nice family that wouldn't mind living inside instead of suffering cramped up in the Armory basement." Talk about wasting time, energy, and money.

Wally grinned awkwardly again.

Oh, God, Sal remonstrated, observing thick veins, dirty hands below rolled-up sleeves, and the upside down head. What's he doing here?

"How're ya doing Sal?" the mouth articulated impudently.

Sal grinned incredulously at Lenny, and a saw screeched to a halt, as if it were jammed.

Lenny swung around and sat upright on a sagging crosspiece. "Surprised?"

"I'll say."

"Got my job back," Lenny breathed almost inaudibly.

"So I see. Did you wash your hands?"

A saw's sound wound down, stopped, and a piece of wood clunked to the ground.

"Washed the wood," Lenny breathed. "It's easier."

Sal sniffed into a grin.

"Whaddaya think, Sal?"

"You're right. It's a masterpiece. What did Roy say?"

"He liked it," Wally insisted happily.

"He said that?"

"It's almost done. You know, I think I could even build a house. Be a contractor or something."

You're already something, man. Any change would be an improvement.

Wally shouted several orders, smiled proudly, and hid his teeth.

Sal frowned. He's really harmless, he kept repeating for the same reason as before. But what a waste of manpower, materials, and lack of concern for the flood victims. "Don't work too hard," he deposited and reentered the empty office save for the women and a well-dressed man holding a folder while standing beside a pulled-out cabinet.

Middle-aged with thick, curly-black hair, Marcel Cardenas slid the folder back and closed the drawer. He exchanged nods with Sal and headed down the hall. Noticing him veer into the kitchen, Sal approached Doris pouring herself a coffee near the urn. "Who's that man?"

Turning, Doris spilled milk on the counter that Rota had apparently just washed. "See what ya done made me do?"

"*I* did? Are you crazy? You did that yourself. I only asked you if you knew him."

"How should I know?" she sing-songed, once again as if he were stupid. "Ah never saw him in my life."

"How should *I* know that, since you never told *me* that either?"

"Hah?"

"Nothing. Never mind."

She grabbed a crumpled napkin impatiently and wiped the counter carelessly, leaving a streak, Sal noticed.

"Marcel somebody," she nevertheless revealed contradictorily. Calls hisself a expediter or somethin'," she divulged just as sloppily.

Sal studied her taking a sip. "Really?" The worm's starting to turn? Looking through the opening, he spied him conversing with several coffee drinkers standing awkwardly in the middle of the kitchen. Where were you a month ago? Had you been here then, you might have alleviated some unnecessary suffering.

The hammering and sawing ceased and a heavy silence prevailed, except for what sounded like a crackling fire when Doris struggled to remove a stale cookie from inside a cellophane wrapper.

Short, stocky, and seemingly Mexican or Spanish, Marcel smiled sardonically, Sal noted.

Doris took a bite, chewed, then sipped. "Roy says he's supposed to be somebody or somethin'."

We're all somebodies or something. "Was Roy in full uniform?"

"What? What er you' talkin' about?"

"Nothing. Forget it."

"Ya better watch him. Ah think he's got pull or somethin'."

"*I* better watch him?" Sal couldn't help enunciating disbelievingly. You're so out of it, you probably wouldn't understand his significance even if you could pronounce *expeditor*. "Watch him do what?"

Doris shook her head and scowled.

Marcel stepped into the hallway, returned, and stood before the same cabinet without eyeing Sal.

Deciding to linger near Doris out of curiosity, Sal poured himself a cup of coffee.

Marcel lifted out another folder as Lisa continued typing. Opening it, he flipped through pages, then studied one briefly. "Doris," he called urgently.

Doris sneered, broke away, and approached him with her cup.

Trying to appear casual, Sal eyed the counter containing less flies since Rota, wearing polka-dotted hot pants, hopped about swatting away despite resolving not to do so. Sipping bitter coffee, he analyzed Marcel's quick, narrowing eyes suggesting intelligence.

Marcel uttered something firmly to Doris, and she answered immediately and obediently, Sal noted. Looming serious, confident, and purposeful, yet calm and patient, Marcel asked Doris to repeat herself, then consumed every word she appeared to utter reluctantly and painfully.

Doris has finally found her master? Sal poured his coffee down the drain and discarded his paper cup along with Doris' crumpled napkin into the overflowing garbage can under the sink. Returning to his office, he typed for about an hour, checked in front, and Marcel was gone. Sal collected more cards from Lisa, fitted them into the empty shoe box he brought from home, and resumed typing.

"Got a minute?" interrupted a voice hours later.

Looking up, Sal observed Bob Updike and stopped typing. "Sure." What else is new? Sal questioned, listening to him denounce Doris for five minutes.

"She ain't been sending blues ta the Rand after our trailers pass inspection," he specified. "That's how we get paid. Half the time she forgets. I saw a couple a blues stickin' out from some of the shit on her desk. What the hell's going on?"

Sal regarded Bob's rugged, tan face beneath his slick black hair.

Why does everybody complain to me? "Did you tell Roy?"

"Yeah. He's another grand turd. Either he ain't around, or he don't say nothin' after ya pull him away from the coffee pot. Or it's 'hang in there,' and nothin' happens. The guy's a piece of work."

"Tell me about it."

"He's about as helpful as guys callin' in sick when I got extra work. I've set up over a hundred trailers. That's a lot of bread. I gotta pay my workers."

Plus yourself, Sal suppressed, aware that Bob partied heavily and was part-owner of a local nightclub where Sal once played solo piano.

"So, what about them blues?"

I don't know anything about anything. I just work here, he considered responding with a laugh. "I think some of them weren't separated from the inspection sheets."

Bob turned grave.

"When they were filed in the cabinets."

"What?"

"Unless they're lost."

"Lost? How could they be lost?"

You're opening up a can of worms, Sal warned. Why not at this point? he reminded himself. "Are you kidding? In this zoo?"

A frown distorted Bob's normally placid face. "Now what?"

"I don't know."

"Unit fifteen, this is unit five. Come in, fifteen," the radio blurted next door.

Bob glanced at the passageway without seeing anyone, and looked back. "Can you look for mine?"

Despite hoping to finish the log, Sal agreed and both arrived in front. Glancing at Carmela and Rota working on papers, Sal decided to speak to Doris about it. Maybe I'll bring out more of the beast in her, for Lisa's benefit, he schemed. Approaching her desk, he glanced at Lisa's fingers typing furiously. "Mind if I check the files for blues?" he asked Doris.

Filling out a report, Doris glanced up. "No way."

Act III, Sal announced. "Whaddaya mean no way? Why not?"

"Nobody's allowed to take nothin' from the files," she stormed.

Rattled, Lisa glanced at her in surprise.

"Who made up that rule, you?" Sal asked.

"How're we supposed to get paid?" Bob demanded. "HUD's suppose to get them blues. They shouldn't even be here."

Doris shrugged impertinently. "That's your problem, not mine," she uncorked without looking up.

Lisa stopped typing and evaluated her lengthily.

"What the hell?" Bob steamed and whirled back to Sal who shrugged. "What are you talking about?"

"Roy told me nobody's allowed in them files," Doris shouted.

"We don't really want to climb in. We just want to get Bob's blues and everybody else's," Sal retorted.

"Very funny, Sal. "Well Roy ain't here, so there," she sneered curtly like a child.

"Oh, I wouldn't say that," Sal disagreed. "He's here in spirit."

Rota and Carmela laughed along with several loungers standing nearby.

Bob placed his large hands on his thick waist. "No way am I leaving without 'em."

Doris threw her pencil down. "I gotta have quiet to figure this out," she shrieked, startling Lisa about to resume typing.

"Stop shouting then," Sal recommended and Rota laughed.

"Doris, my goodness," Lisa scolded.

"If you think ah'm gonna waste time goin' through goddamn inspection sheets, you're outta your cotton-pickin' mind," Doris fumed.

Oh, *that's* it, Sal realized. "Who said anything about *you* doing anything?"

A giggle popped loose from Pam standing outside the radio room listening.

"You ain't in charge, Sal," Doris repeated. "Roy is."

Really? Could've fooled me. What's he in charge of? Bungling? "May I use your phone?" he asked Rota.

"Certainly," she responded, although not to spite Doris, Sal realized and she pushed it toward him.

"What're you doing now, Sal?" Doris screeched, jarring Lisa again. "Don't you know dialing when you sees it?" he dramatized.

"How can anybody work in an office like this?" Lisa asked Rota who shrugged.

Giggling penetrated from down the hall.

"Millie Jackson," Sal deliberately announced into the receiver.

"Go ahead," Doris snapped. Folding her arms, she sneered and settled back into her seat. "Ask her. See if I care."

The operator put him on hold.

"Hope she keeps ya'all waitin' for an hour," Doris spat, surprising Lisa still again, and the front door opened.

Great timing, Sal thought, eyeing Roy entering with the well-dressed Floyd. How about being your old, reliable, bedpost self one more time, pal? Hanging up, he turned to Roy about to veer toward the hallway with Floyd. "Is it okay to give Bob Updike his blue forms?" Sal deliberately popped with savage nonchalance this time, aware about Roy's unfamiliarity about such matters.

Pausing with Floyd, Roy looked back lazily, then eyed Bob in puzzlement, as if he had never met him.

"That's how contractors get paid setting up trailers," Sal explained almost merrily as all watched and listened.

"Yeah," tumbled from Roy's lips, and he continued down the hall with Floyd.

"Ah don't want nobody messin' up my files, Roy Nichols," blurted Doris, disconcerting Lisa still analyzing her astonishingly.

Halfway down the hall, Roy and Floyd stopped and both turned.

"Get yo' self ready," Roy shouted to Doris. "We're goin' ta dinner in ten minutes," he barked and shuffled ahead of Floyd. Living room laughter responded, plus muffled giggling from inside the radio room.

Nice going. Both of you couldn't 've performed better had I written the script.

Roy closed the door behind himself and Floyd, and Sal sauntered to the cabinets with Bob.

"Ah 'll get even with you, Sal," Doris vowed.

Nice retort, Sal remarked and pulled out the second drawer. Numerous inspection sheets were carelessly shoved behind one another or between folders, as if the perpetrator were sloppy, in a hurry, or both, he noticed and handed a batch to Bob. "Somebody is going to have to go through all these," he admitted grimly to Bob who started fingering several, and Sal turned to Doris. "Most blues haven't even been separated from inspection sheets."

"Geezus Krist," Bob complained.

"Just don't worry about it," Doris snapped.

"I'll start checking through them now," Sal assured Bob who handed them back to him. "But I can't promise when I'll finish. That depends on—"

"You ain't gettin' my help," Doris warned without looking up.

Lisa shook her head and resumed typing.

"Thank God," Sal answered Doris and Laughter encompassed him and Bob.

Doris began buzzing Roy's telephone erratically again. "Ah can't leave till this report's done. Ah'm seventeen trailers off," she raged into the receiver.

"Hell, that's close enough," Sal turned back and responded while, heading down the hallway with Bob.

Laughter mixed with familiar muffled giggling.

Bob followed Sal inside his office and Sal placed the pile on his desk. "I'll try to round up some help with these. After imbecile leaves."

Bob placed hands on his waist. "Good enough. How do you tolerate her every day?"

"She grows on you–like cancer."

Bob shook his head and eventually left. So did Floyd, Roy, and Doris out the front door.

God, could I use a phone, Sal thought, contacting Millie inside Roy's office, and he inquired about the blues.

"Of course they get the blue copy," she responded, surprised. "How else can they get paid?"

"That's what I tried to tell Doris," he tantalized without elaborating.

"You mean contractors haven't been getting blues all along?"

"Many of them haven't. I found a bunch still attached to inspection sheets in a cabinet."

"What's going on over there? Let me talk to Doris."

Answer honestly and don't bury her, even though she's not worth protecting, Sal ordered. "She isn't here right now."

"Where is she?"

"Out to lunch." In more ways than one, he suppressed and eventually hung up. Enlisting Pam and Lisa's help at the kitchen table, he began removing and alphabetizing the blues from hundreds of inspection sheets. Wally wandered in from underneath the sun and Sal trapped into helping, despite Wally's insistence that he was a carpenter.

"And I should be teaching because I'm a teacher," Sal retorted. "That's life."

Lenny also limped inside. Apparently heading for the bathroom, he asked what the group was doing and Sal quickly scooped him up, dirty hands and all.

Returning alone sometime later, Doris sulked back to her desk.

Word spread so quickly about the undistributed blues that contractors started stumbling inside asking for them before the group finished separating them.

"See what ya done," Doris protested to Sal handing them out to those in front as the other women paused to listen. "Ya done give us more work."

"That's true. I ended up helping others. Sorry. Guess I sinned. People need to get paid so they can eat, pay bills, and keep the wolf from the door," he scolded her in a new tone.

Doris ignored him and he regarded the contractors. "You guys might speed things up if you take those to Millie Jackson. She works for HUD down at the Rand."

One contractor thanked him but the rest started grumbling about not finding theirs, as Sal had anticipated.

"We're not done sorting them," he explained. "Some inspectors might not have turned in theirs or what you set up hasn't been inspected yet." Why not? popped his other self, as if he enjoyed stressing himself out. Because some inspectors also lounge, socialize, and drink coffee.

"Any way of hurrying them?" another contractor asked in somewhat of an annoyed tone.

Hide the urn and percolator, Sal concealed, refusing to blame them. "I'll see what I can do," he responded, removed his pad, and jotted down the request.

"That's it?" another contractor asked.

"That's it," Sal declared. "I'll have more later."

A contractor admitted receiving two blues for the same trailer.

"How else can ya get paid twice for the same one?" a fellow contractor asked and Sal accepted their sheets during the laughter.

"We appreciate your honesty," Sal told him, as if he were a dedicated HUD official. "Probably inspected twice. Or you mistakenly wrote down the wrong number."

Other problems were more complicated. Bob accused a contractor of getting a blue for blocking one of his trailers which the other contractor denied, and they started arguing.

Another man complained that he never ever received a blue, though he and his crew blocked more than a dozen trailers. Sal wrote down his name, plus others with similar complaints and they finally dispersed.

Returning to his office, Sal finished the enormous task of typing cards for every inspection sheets that he had collected. He alphabetized them inside the shoebox which he left on his desk, and exhaled relievedly. Despite his aversion for paperwork, he felt somewhat proud considering so many obstacles and interruptions, particularly because he knew that the information was as accurate as possible. "Everybody's free to check the cards," he announced to the women. Even you, he mentally included a bearded lounger studying him curiously.

Carmela and Lisa thanked him.

"Not now, Sal," Rota replied, typing furiously, and Doris sneered contemptuously at him.

What, no roses? Sal queried, aware that the cards had already provided useful information to contractors, toters, Millie, and even Doris who had hurriedly copied down information according to Pam when Sal went to the bathroom.

Chapter 30

Entering his office Saturday morning, Sal slowed because of a pipe-smoking stranger sitting behind his desk thumbing through the cards. He's another HUD official? I'm getting fired for punching Happy? A lawyer? The police? What?

Annoyed about the man's audacity, Sal barely heard him introducing himself as an "assistant professor," much less the name of a remote college somewhere in Missouri.

"I'm writing a doctorate on various types of floods and how they're controlled," he quipped with a pretentious cockiness that disturbed the straightforward Sal. Smiling, he shook Sal's hand without rising.

Sal suddenly comprehended the man's reason for the visit. You've *got* to be kidding. "Don't you think this is the wrong time–"

"This is just a study," he interrupted, further irritating Sal and he asked several questions about the flood.

This guy ought to take a course in humility, Sal thought. Patiently listening while standing in the center of the room, he soon had had enough. "How about letting me sit behind my desk?" he added, staring incredulously at him.

The man rose and left in a huff.

And that's the end of *that* tune, Sal concluded again.

Sal solved the duplicate blues afterwards. He filed the correct inspection sheet in the front cabinet, took care of other contractors' problems, and returned to his office.

Noticing Marcel Cardenas entering in front with two others, the kitchen loungers stumbled out the side door hurriedly. So did the living room loungers the moment the trio passed and proceeded down the hallway. Sorting inspection sheets according to contractors' names at his desk, Sal looked up, and the trio entered. No wonder the vacationers abandoned the ship so suddenly, he realized and squelched his usual urge to burst out laughing during such outrageous moments.

Marcel introduced himself as HUD's expeditor and the others as HUD officials.

Nice to meet civilized people for a change, Sal reflected, shaking hands.

The trio conferred amiably but reservedly with Sal about operations, left for breakfast, and reentered the office afterwards. Passing Sal's office, they took turns eyeing him typing more information onto cards, and walked inside Roy's office. Emerging with Roy sometime later, they gave Sal the once-over, and the front door closed behind all of them, except Marcel.

He talked to Doris for a spell, returned to Sal's office, and sat in the metal chair across from him. "How're things going?"

Since they had already conversed, Sal sensed a deeper implication. "Improving."

Marcel studied him piercingly. "Meaning?"

Oh, one of these guys. "Meaning I'm finally making progress getting things organized." With stupid paperwork, he omitted.

Marcel moistened his lips. "Really?" he answered sarcastically, bothering Sal who thought his response had been reasonably accurate and fair considering the situation.

Sal regarded the man's dark hair, piercing eyes, and slight sneer. No, I'm lying.

"From the condition of the files, I'd have to disagree," Marcel disagreed coldly.

Fighting chaos and disorganization was bad enough. Getting no recognition for struggling to organize matters was worse. Accepting an innuendo of blame for a fraction of others' carelessness and disorganization was injustice sublime. No way am I going to protect her now. Not the way she's treated me and especially the others. "I don't take care of the files," he reciprocated just as coldly. "Doris does." Why can't people do their homework before trying to fault others? Who the hell do you think has been trying to straighten everything out? he demanded, then regretted not uttering. "She set up the files long ago. I suggested some changes after I started working in the office," he varied. "But it's been hard getting through to her."

Marcel nodded, which Sal accurately interpreted as comprehension –not agreement, understanding, or appreciation.

"I told her to arrange everything according to the exact trailer number, not the contract number." He paused for the man to digest the fact. "Sometimes she did; sometimes she didn't."

Marcel smiled. "So I've noticed. Any reason for so many logs?"

Caught off balance, especially since Marcel seemed to be uttering Sal's exact words, Sal was so surprised, that he squirmed briefly, as if he were on trial and hurriedly pulled himself together. "They were using those logs before I started working in the office," he imparted firmly.

"I see," Marcel returned with the same quick smile. A saw started up and stopped. Marcel looked out the window and turned to Sal. "But you didn't answer my question. Any reason for so many logs?"

"No. That's why I put all the information on cards. To eliminate so much redundant information included in so many logs." Sliding over the shoebox, he pictured the many victims still packed in the Armory and other places, suddenly felt silly, and flushed.

Marcel barely evaluated it, as if he had better use for his eyes.

"HUD didn't have a 3 x 5 metal box," he attempted to defend. Should've bought one with my own money. "I asked Roy to buy one, but–"

"What is it?" he interrupted, rattling Sal.

I just told you, jackass, he concealed and repeated himself almost verbatim.

Marcel's raised and lowered his bushy eyebrows while thumbing through the box. "A lot of work," he seemed obligated to admit politely, Sal sensed. "Do this yourself?"

The correct answer was "most of it," but Sal refused to promote himself, considering the victims. "With Lisa's help," he admitted but not casually enough to imply that he had done most of the work.

Sudden hammering caught Marcel's attention. This time he stared out the window before regarding Sal. "Oh, Hugh's wife. Yes," he said, implying a close relationship with the couple. "By the way, what do *you* do?"

Damn. Rattled and irritated, he was convinced that whatever he said would sound silly. "Roy wanted me to help out in the office," he chose, then regretted because it sounded vague. "Doris was having trouble keeping things organized."

Marcel nodded but as if unconvinced, Sal thought.

Bastard. Why do men love to belittle other men? he assumed because of insecurities traceable to his domineering father. The ego factor, he answered. "I also run the Xerox machine," he threw in, then regretted uttering for sounded even sillier. "And I help Quincy."

"Who's he? What does *he* do?"

Get in my way, he almost responded flippantly. First, this hombre challenges me. Now I'm supposed to define another employee's job? Talk about irony. Sal deliberately coughed so he could think. Quincy's the official form manager, his other self teased. Deciding not to defend or exaggerate Quincy's job, he saw no reason to belittle such a harmless soul. He'll find out. "I'm not too sure. He's just one of the workers," he offered vaguely and Marcel seemed to have trouble nodding again. "He's taking inventory right now," he couldn't resist, because he hated stupidity more than being mistreated like his father did during Sal's youth.

Marcel eyebrows pinched together during a frown. "Inventory? Of what?"

"Stock," he simply stated. What else? Talk about irony, he repeated, realizing that he sounding like he was defending taking it.

Marcel registered incredulity. "Where is he now?"

"In the other trailer."

"What other trailer?"

Sal told him.

Marcel shook his head. "We're not setting up trailers fast enough."

No kidding, Stonewall. Never said we were, Sal reciprocated but underground. "HUD had trouble getting enough sites from the start. We had to buck City Hall. And we were slow preparing the ones we eventually got," he oversimplified protectively again, recognizing that he was an employee defending himself against an employer. What's this *we* stuff, Buster? he scolded himself again. And where's my union lawyer?

Marcel became grim. "It's more than that. What's in here?" he asked, opening the 5 x 8 box, and Sal flushed.

Forget about the others' stupidity. *Your* dumb for leaving the thing on top of your desk. Can't win them all, he defended. "Vital information." The cards fit nicely–he almost teased, sensed Marcel wouldn't appreciate it, and stopped.

Marcel began flipping through the cards. "What're you doing now?"

Sal rattled off several more chores including transforming information to the 3 x 5 cards, and Marcel rose.

"Okay," he seemed to concede condescendingly and entered the radio room through the passageway.

Hearing him laugh idly and informally with Pam, Sal struggled to shrug it off. How come we're so lovey-dovey with women? Why *wouldn't* he be with a pretty woman? Especially since she's been handling the radio well, he replied, annoyed at himself for not conveying what was *really* going on, much less how hard he had worked with Skip at Skycrest. He was also angry at Marcel for not asking what the loungers were doing, much less catching on to their loafing. Staring at the shoe box, he couldn't suppress feeling offended until he remembered that he would be teaching soon. Thank God. I'll take my bandits any day compared to all this grief.

Marcel exited out the side door and Sal watched him eye the steps briefly and then the carpenters who were taking a break.

Sal observed him veering toward Quincy's trailer. That's it? You're not asking them what the hell *they're* doing either or checking out that stupid plastic top? Another nincompoop.

Wonder how he'll react after arriving at Form City? He questioned, picturing the forms scattered on the floor and on Quincy's desk. Wait 'll he finds out that ol' Paintbrush even *lives* there, he enunciated but suddenly felt sorry for him.

Marcel returned through the side door, glanced at Sal filing dispatch tickets in the 5 x 8 box and entered Roy's room. Departing sometime later, he passed Sal's doorway, stared curiously out the side window at the carpenters hammering and sawing in full bloom, and headed up front.

"Somebody done took two contracts I had laying on my desk," Doris screamed.

I guess Marcel's gone, Sal chirped inwardly.

Chapter 31

The next morning, Sal joined the group near the percolator and learned that Lisa had quit. Norm deposited a dime in a sticky jar on the counter, ventured a doughnut from a box, and Dinger watched him like a starving raccoon.

"Surprised she lasted this long with Doris," Norm commented.

Skip turned to the trim, bespectacled English teacher. "Sal overworked her."

Sal grinned and the saws and hammers cut through the rising voices in the kitchen.

"Wonder why she quit?" Norm asked.

Sal pushed off the counter adroitly. "Guess she needs to get her tan back," he obliged, pulling several laughs, and maneuvered out of the packed room. Transcribing more information to the cards back at his desk, he missed Lisa's help.

Marcel arrived with the same two men. Passing his doorway, each eyed him typing away.

Now what? Sal wondered, hearing them enter Roy's office.

Emerging afterwards, Marcel returned to the office, sat, and the others headed up front.

Sal stopped typing and looked up. "Good morning."

"What's good about it?" Marcel stabbed and immediately recommended a book-type log using legal-sized paper, stunning Sal.

Sal frowned in disbelief. Is this bird for real? Redo everything I just finished?

"It'll open horizontally like a loose-leaf. Write captions across the top like yours. I'll want trailers listed numerically according to HUD numbers."

"You're kidding,"

A saw blade pinched. Silence followed and it restarted. "Not really."

Sal evaluated Marcel's hard-nosed face containing thick eyebrows. "Mine *has* all that information. Why replace it?" he tried to unfold nonchalantly. Intelligent jackasses are always worse than stupid ones.

"Because I'm telling you," Marcel ordered with a smile.

Sal touched his shoebox. "I put a lot of man-hours into this. Yours doesn't improve mine at all." It's stupid, he kept underground.

Marcel refused to look down and they exchanged eyeballs.

More game-playing. The male ego, Sal reminded himself. Sensing the absurdity of it all, he looked away first, was about to add, "Why waste all that work and effort?" when Marcel interrupted him.

"You don't really have to," he conceded sarcastically, smiled icily, and the sound of a piece of wood clattering to the ground penetrated into the room.

Agree or call him HUD jackass number 356 and get fired. So, we'll go on a picnic, Sal considered, referring to his family. On the other hand, there's nothing wrong with acting tactful. "My cards are just as good, maybe even better," he nevertheless persisted. But as a permanent HUD employee, Marcel couldn't allow a part-timer to prevail, Sal sensed.

Rising disinterestedly, Marcel headed for the door. "Do it my way," he turned and remarked from above his shoulder.

Like *my* song, Sal mused. Having pushed enough, he wanted to punish Marcel just a little, even at the risk of absorbing a scolding or getting fired. "Okay, if it turns you on."

Marcel paused at the doorway and turned. About to respond, he seemed to consider something else. "Make up headings that include everything on your cards."

Whatever you say, Chief, Sal finally conceded.

"But don't type up the form until I check it." Proceeding into the hall, Marcel stopped before the window. He gazed briefly at the carpenters again, continued ahead, and the side door slammed behind him.

The episode deserved a shake of Sal's head. But seemingly all shaken out, at least for now, he studied the doorway briefly. His only consolation, though small, was that he had slapped an obvious superior lightly and survived unscathed or seemingly so.

Wally appeared minutes later. He exchanged glances with Sal, entered the radio room, and began flirting with Pam. Sal started devising Marcel's suggested headings for the new log when four contractors including Bob entered. Although some of their blues were still missing, they helped him correct certain mistakes, including their misspelled names, wrong addresses, and more.

"This delay is a real pain in the ass," Bob grumbled again which the others seconded. "I've had to pay my workers out of my own pocket."

Must be nice to have such a loving pocket, Sal considered verbalizing, but simply apologized sincerely. "We're still trying to get organized since we moved," he tried to justify, as if he were protecting his fellow employees again including himself.

"We can appreciate that," one said, folding his arms. "But when's all this straightening out gonna end?"

Sal pictured Marcel's new log consuming much of his limited time. "Soon as possible," he offered, rather than blame Marcel.

The foursome handed Sal a list of trailers they had set-up and blocked and once again asked him to help hasten their inspection. He told them he did, promised to remind them again and they departed after thanking him. Pam slipped into Sal's office after Wally left, and Sal likened the contractors and Marcel to actors who had just finished reciting lines in an imaginary play.

Moaning again about missing her husband, she soon complained that Wally had made a pass at her. "And he asked me to go for a ride with him."

Sal studied her fanned-out hair. "Who, your husband?" he teased.

Giggling briefly, Pam became serious. Wish it was. No, Wally, and he's married."

"So? You'd go out with him if he wasn't?"

Pam frowned. "Of course not."

"You shouldn't be surprised. Married men have been making out with married women for centuries and vice versa."

"He's a creep."

Struggling to change his own chauvinistic upbringing, Sal mistakenly suggested that she might have led him on.

"Encouraged him" Pam protested and rearranged her long hair streaming down her back. "A simple conversation encourages a guy? I didn't invite him in."

"Maybe it's how you talked, what you said," Sal replied, cornering himself further, he sensed.

"Friendliness is an invitation? I can't be friendly? Give me a break."

"What can I say? Sorry I misjudged you."

"Wish my husband was home," she sighed and left.

Lyman entered Sal's office. They greeted each other, shook hands, and Lyman sat across from him. Exchanging small talk, Lyman explained the reason for some duplicated trailer numbers in the parks. "Homer uses a magic marker to mark trailers with temporary numbers as they arrive. George parks 'em, then pastes on the numbers."

"So Homer told me," Sal inserted.

"Except ol' George screws up. He don't always paste on the right numbers."

Sal's head began swinging back and forth in negative protest. "You've *got* to be kidding."

"Wish I was. Yesterday I relieved him because he had a dentist appointment. That's how I found out. He had a hell of an excuse. Because, and I quote, 'We was running low on *fives* and *threes*, so I used whatever number was handy.' Would you believe that?"

Sal sniffed into laughter. "No, I refuse to believe that, man."

"Trust me. It's true. Either he's too dumb or too lazy to look for the right number or just doesn't give a damn. Take your pick, man."

"Several times I called HUD asking them to send up more numbers with the courier."

"What did they say?" Lyman asked.

"'What numbers?' Several different times."

Lyman laughed.

Leaning back, Sal squeaked his swivel chair during more giggling, and grinned.

"Had to let Homer know what George was up to, man," he seemed to confess, as if he too disliked informing. "It was just too serious."

Sal sighed. "Can't blame you, man."

"So, Homer and George are marking incoming trailers with different colored magic markers. Green for one company, orange for another, and so on for other companies."

"Don't they run out of colors?" Sal inquired incredulously.

"Not really, man. They're using magic markers," he enunciated.

Sal and Pam burst out laughing.

"Do they keep track of which color represents what company?" Sal asked.

"Who knows, man?"

Sal's lips thinned into another smile of disbelief. "What if either one of them gets sick?"

"They're both sick," Lyman maintained, heightening more giggling. "Oh, man, this place is so screwed up, I can't wait to quit so I can do some normal protestin' at college."

Sal's laughter seemed to incite more giggling. "If we ever get done."

Grinning, Lyman leaned forward. "Have you checked out what Wally's up to?"

"You mean the plastic cover he's making?"

"That too. He's got different teams building steps."

Sal eyed him suspiciously. "Is this another one of your puns, man?"

"No, man. Whichever team builds the most sets of steps in an hour gets a half an hour off."

"Off what, loafing?" Sal retorted, and Pam didn't disappoint him. "You mean they can loaf a half hour more or less? What?"

Lyman laughed freely. "They get free time off for punchin' out three sets, more for four, and so on up the ladder."

"Don't you mean up the steps, man? So this *is* another one of your puns."

Lyman laughed again along with Pam. "Wally just sits on the planks watching them with a pad, pencil, and a stop-watch."

Visualizing Wally's tight mouth and quaint hair tied behind his head, Sal struggled not to shake his head, and his upper torso stiffened oddly. "This place is just a continuation of high school with mostly goof-offs goofing off some more."

Phil entered. "Something's in the wind," he announced dramatically, resting inspection sheets on Sal's desk. "Hurry, take a look."

All looked out the side window at the large, boxy, plastic cover which a gust of wind had started tumbling slowly toward the office. The carpenters raced panic-struck after it, shouting at one another to stop it, but to no avail. Picking up speed during increasing wind, the cover began to lift slowly off the ground, only to drop back down when the wind slackened. It flattened out momentarily until a minor gust started somersaulting it toward the office.

"Brace yourself," Phil teased since it was too flimsy to cause much damage. "We're gonna get hit."

More wind lifted it several feet off the ground, as if it were a huge kite. It traveled gracefully toward the back end of the office, dropped gently to the ground, when the wind died, and thudded softly against Roy's outside wall, snapping several of its furring strips.

Nothingness followed briefly, save for Wally cursing the men for not catching up with it in time.

"Too incredible," Sal commented, laughing with the others.

Chapter 32

Because of unusual demands, the Keely-Justin Block Corporation, largest in the area, agreed to institute around-the-clock shifts in order to produce large quantities of block (which Sal accurately suspected was uncured), and sell at what were outrageous prices. They also consented to maintain a temporary warehouse near the office trailer, and flatbed loads of four-inch and eight block arrived later that day.

Daryl, a young, independent contractor, desperately needed to get paid for blocking three trailers at a site because he barely had enough money for food which reminded Sal about himself. Consequently, he was first to arrive shortly after the company opened at nine the next morning. Living inside a dilapidated van and working alone, he bought four cubes of both sizes which Sheryl, a young, flirtatious loader, deposited on his truck, and he sped to his site. Most of the block started crumbling after he blocked the first trailer. The same problem befell Floyd and several other contractors. Returning almost simultaneously before three o'clock that day in order to replace them, all were stunned. Lingering employees explained that company executives had closed in order to allow employees to patronize the restaurant an hour earlier than the usual four o'clock Happy Hour.

"Wonder how both sides arranged that?" Sal asked, watching from the side window (along with Skip, Norm, and several others), contractors, including Floyd and his men, and all dispersed in disbelief and anger.

"Who knows? Probably free drinks for free rooms," Skip speculated accurately.

Floyd and his driver drove to the main plant, located some distance away, and were surprised to discover that it was also closed. They returned at 8:00 a.m. the next day and learned that the warehouse wasn't opening until 9:00, irritating them further.

Other contractors were milling about angrily near the warehouse for the same reason. Sheryl arrived at 9:15. Wearing tight short shorts and no brassiere, she soon complained that the loader wouldn't start. Disregarding their annoyance about the faulty block, the disgruntled group offered to help. So did several of her co-workers and a half a dozen of the office's coffee-tilters swarming all over the machine under a hot sun, according to Skip and others relaying the proceedings to Sal.

Nodding at her sunny ramblings, Sheryl's rescuers seemed more interested in inspecting her see-through blouse and shapely legs, than solving mechanical problems until Daryl returned. Hopping off his truck, he began complaining to Sheryl about his defective batch. Accidentally leaning against the switch, he activated the loader, and the men cheered.

Sheryl kept insisting that company rules prevented her from replacing Daryl's second batch (with more faulty block, she didn't say), unless he returned the first load, annoying Daryl, and they continued arguing.

Loading the faulty pieces and trucking them back would "waste more time and money, causing the flood victims to suffer even more," he protested, surprising and pleasing Sal for his concern for them.

Captivated by Sheryl, or perhaps suffering from the heat, most contractors sided with Sheryl which hardly surprised Skip. In fact, most contractors appeared to forget why they were there, except, perhaps, to consume Sheryl's splendid limbs and analyze whatever scenery they caught through her blouse.

Sheryl and the others remained firm, and Daryl left in disgust. An hour later, he returned with the evidence, but Sheryl seemed to have second thoughts. She told Daryl to take his "bitching" up with several company officials (who had also been mentally undressing her from the sidelines), and he did.

Sheryl was in charge of everything, they insisted, although no one knew for sure if that included the gaping, Skip told Sal, which initiated the usual giggling.

Daryl eventually made peace with Sheryl, and he and the contractors trucked out more uncured block—possibly because of Sheryl's sales pitch, her breasts, legs, or something in between—nor could anyone attest to any of that either, and the loungers retreated to their familiar slots.

Chapter 33

L ater that morning, Lenny entered Sal's office. He sat down and started rambling about various incidentals, and his past success working for Wally until he finally admitting that HUD had fired him again "for no reason." Presently working for a contractor, he had become an "expert blocker," he bragged, eyeing Sal reviewing the headings he had written on a separate piece of paper before typing them in the new log.

Sal considered inquiring how he could become an expert so quickly without having ever blocked before, but once again decided to save energy and minimize stress. "So, how come you're not working now?"

"Taking a break," he breathed and the usual giggling tore loose from next door.

Picturing Sal's expression, Pam giggled louder.

Frenzied hammering caught Sal's attention and he realized with dismay that the carpenters were feverishly reconstructing Wally's plastic cover by replacing furring strips with what was stronger two-by-fours.

"Anyways, Sheryl quit last night. Took off with some contractor and a shitload of block," he practically whispered. He laughed insinuatingly and forgot to fold his thick arms, vein-side up against his dirty t-shirt for Sal's benefit.

"With good block or the crumbling variety?" Sal inquired and Pam broke up.

"Shit, how should I know?" Lenny scolded in annoyance, also taking him seriously.

"Are you serious?"

"Who do you think helped him load his truck?"

Sal evaluated him savagely. "You?"

"Yeah," he breathed proudly, as if stealing were commendable. "So did a lotta contractors who got screwed. Even some who didn't," he seemed obligated to qualify with a grin.

I need a break, Sal thought but decided to challenge Lenny first. "You mean they just helped themselves and left? Nobody saw them? No officials? Come on."

"I shit you not," Lenny breathed.

Nice phrasing, Sal commented.

Pam responded to an incoming caller blaring over her radio.

Lenny leaned forward. "Shhhh," he cautioned, eyeing the passageway to ensure that she wasn't eavesdropping. "They were pissed because they got bad block."

"Oh, really?" Sal asked sarcastically. "I didn't know."

"And the company's pullin' out. They don't wanna be bothered about all that shit."

"Very compassion of them during a disaster. That doesn't mean you're telling me the truth. First you tell me that a contractor's paying you $4.50 an hour for doing nothing."

"Right."

"What contractor would be dumb enough to do that? Then you say some Russell somebody is working for HUD and your contractor at the same time without either of them knowing it and getting paid for both jobs."

"You got it," Lenny insisted wispily. "He's picking up two paychecks for sittin' on his ass."

"Then you brag about stealing three hundred bucks worth of tools you charged at Mathews and Loomis'."

"Right," Lenny agreed proudly.

"Then, according to you, some contractor takes off with Sheryl after you help him steal a load of block."

"Yeah."

"No, Lenny," Sal objected. "My ears just aren't that porous. No way." Why bother getting involved with all this nonsense? Because I'm bored.

"I'm serious, man," Lenny insisted before Sal could answer.

"That's what scares me. What if I tell the police about all this?"

"Go ahead. But I know you won't."

Picturing Gallagher and more stress doing so, Sal sighed.

"I'll tell 'em what a bum English teacher you were."

Sal grinned. "They'd never believe you, because I wasn't."

"You passed me, didn't you?"

"I had no other choice. Pass you or get you back. So, what happens? I get you back here."

Lenny laughed subdued. "I was the worst."

Sal erased a heading. "You still are. You just transferred your false sense of values into society like the others."

"I'd only deny it if you told 'em," Lenny scoffed quietly. "Got the tools stashed where nobody 'll ever look."

About to reword another heading, Sal looked up. "Probably in my car trunk."

Lenny grinned. "Better then puttin' 'em in mine."

"Lenny, you're slippery, know that? You complained about missing tools. And *you* were the thief all along." Hammering and sawing dwindled, ceased, and Sal glanced out the hall window. "You even accused Charlie of stealing. You're something else."

"Not really. Just slippery," he agreed with a grin.

A real winner, Sal concealed.

"But you should've seen that Sheryl. Even you would've gone for her. Oo-ee."

Sal became annoyed. "I doubt it."

"Come on. You wouldn't go for her if ya had the chance?"

Sal looked up. "Not really because I'm happily married and love my wife. That would be deceitful, dishonest, and wrong, something you wouldn't understand."

"What's being married got to do with anythin'?" he inquired with that same callous indifference that always disturbed Sal.

Here we go again, Sal thought during Lenny's muffled laughter.

"You're weird, man."

"*I'm* weird? Don't judge all men by what you feel between your legs." He glanced at the carpenters sitting on the ground before Wally apparently holding another meeting. "*You're* weird. And these are immoral times, trust me. The real world is based on truth and honesty, not falsehood and deception."

"Oh, man, here it comes," Lenny breathed.

Tolerance, Sal warned. Try to change his thinking, if possible, rather than get annoyed, he urged, how he handled similar attitudes with his worse students. "Lenny, I didn't ask you to come in here."

"I thought you didn't go to church," Lenny pursued.

"I don't."

"Don't you believe in God?"

Oh, man, *not* again. Sal lowered his pencil to the desk. Clasping his hands behind his neck, he leaned back and the chair squeaked. "Sure I do. Can't I believe in God without going to church? Besides, what's that got to do with being honest and faithful to your spouse?"

Lenny stared briefly at Sal's reflective face, stretched, and rose. "Ah, this is gettin' too deep for me."

Sal shrugged. "Suit yourself."

Lenny left and Sal picked up his pencil.

Quincy entered next, placed sheet of paper on Sal's desk, and sat in the same metal chair. "How do you spell *resignation*?"

Assuming he was referring to him because of his fight with Happy, Sal almost dropped the pencil. Spelling the word slowly while staring down at the short, upside down paragraph, Sal had trouble reading Quincy's poor penmanship.

Quincy swung the paper right side up.

I need a vacation while I'm supposedly on vacation, Sal reminded himself, realizing that Quincy was referring to himself. "You're quitting?"

"That's right."

"How come?"

Quincy rose. "It's a long story." He shrugged, smirked, and left.

Pam appeared in the passageway. "What's going on?"

Act IV, maybe, he answered and told her about Quincy's resignation. "Too bad. Just when he was developing some nice forms."

Eying Sal staring out the window at the noisy carpenters, Pam giggled. "Figured it was something like that. I just saw him whisper something in Doris' ear. I think Quincy, Happy, Doris, and Roy are all friends," she revealed accurately, staring out Sal's window. "They're all outside in Roy's car, talking."

Sal joined her at the window and both eyed the blue Chevy. Sal studied Roy, Doris, and Happy in front, and Quincy leaning forward with his arms resting on the back of Roy's seat. No wonder Happy defended Doris, he suddenly understood and scolded himself for overlooking what seemed so obvious now. But is this it? Is HUD really firing them or are they quitting? he evaluated, cautiously optimistic about either possibility. Surely Lisa must have told hubby about them but maybe not about the loafers who were still loafing despite Marcel's presence, he realized incredulously. But so what if the foursome were replaced? he analyzed, aware how much their inefficiency had hurt the flood victims. It's too late to turn things around even if we could replace them with better people. Had HUD installed the right leaders from the start, trailers would've been set up long ago. It's the same blundering comedy of errors that often occurs, despite our supposed genius. Because we're imperfect and other reasons, his other self philosophized.

"Well, that's the end of 'em," a voice announced.

Both turned to Skip. Grinning, he jerked his hair in place and slumped down in the metal chair.

"They're fired?" Pam queried, still staring at them out the same window.

"Yeah. All of 'em, Roy, Doris, Quincy, and Happy."

Pam folded her large, freckled arms and pressed them under her breasts. "Really?"

"Just heard it from a reliable source."

Returning to his seat, Sal dropped Quincy's form into the waste can with a grin and sat. "You mean Christ has finally risen?"

Pam giggled. "Who told you?"

Skip yawned. "Marcel."

"Who's replacing them?" Pam asked.

"Nobody. They're irreplaceable," Sal deposited impudently and smiled again.

"Not sure," Skip confessed. "But I think that tall dude with the crew cut, Barney Layton, is replacin' Roy."

"Hear the latest?" Norm inquired while entering.

Sal studied his gray coveralls briefly, clasped the back of his neck and slouched comfortably.

"Yeah," Skip replied. "HUD just put Dinger in charge of operations."

Pam broke up.

"Wouldn't surprise me none," Sal commented, and the group regarded the sound of approaching footsteps in the hall.

Passing by, Roy glanced at Sal and the others and Marcel followed him entering his office. I guess this is *really* curtain time, Sal announced. "Isn't that just nice," he muttered and a relaxed smile engulfed his often troubled face. Now what? he asked, hearing more oncoming footsteps.

Smoking a cigar and wearing a sporty, navy-blue summer shirt over a pot belly, Barney Layton glanced inside while walking past also. He closed Roy's door behind him and it reopened fifteen minutes later. The trio processioned past Sal's office. Each took turns eyeing them and they left out the side door.

Time to check out how the other women are reacting, Sal decided and rose. Reaching the urn, he ventured another cup. Sipping, he noted Carmela quietly separating blues from recent inspection sheets. Another older, unidentified man was sitting alongside Rota, talking quietly to her.

Sal noticed Rota's distraught expression.

They're going to fire her? She practically lives here. The woman's invaluable, relatively speaking. Are they insane?

The front door swung open dramatically and in stumbled Doris sporting a sneer. Angling around her desk, she opened the middle drawer, and began hurriedly stuffing pencils, letters, and paraphernalia into her pocketbook. She emptied the other drawers similarly, slammed each shut, and left.

Sal poured his remaining coffee down the drain and discarded his paper cup and several others. He walked to a cabinet, pulled out a drawer and pretended to be checking a file folder.

"Oh, ah'm sure you're pretty enough to handle everything," he overheard the man tell Rota, and the man squeezed her hand affectionately.

I guess she's safe, he concluded, almost guffawing upon sensing that the man was making a pass at her, and he returned to his desk.

Marcel entered, made what Sal considered was an unnecessary, stupid correction of the new log's heading and left.

Chapter 34

Xeroxing the new form in the radio room, Tuesday morning, Sal inhaled cigar smoke and Barney and Happy entered his office.

"If you think you've got enough pull to fire me, you're full a shit," Happy resonated angrily, and Pam looked up from reading a paperback novel.

"Don't cuss at me," Barney drawled back.

Looking through the passageway, Sal observed Barney's crew cut, his slightly-hunched back, and Happy.

"Ah've got friends that'll take care of me. Don't you never fo-get it," Happy declared. "In the White House," he fumed.

Sal glanced at Pam who shrugged.

"Oh, ah got friends, there, too. We all have friends somewhere," Barney snorted back.

"Now there's a truth," Sal muttered for Pam's benefit, and she obliged again.

"So you better just cool it," Happy completed. "Or ah'll cool you, buster."

"You ain't coolin' nobody," Barney warned, "but yo-self."

"Sounds like a cooling period," Sal whispered.

Pam covered another outburst with her book.

"We'll see about that," Happy snapped and stormed out of Sal's office.

The cigar smoke intensified, and Sal pictured Barney standing before the passageway evaluating him watching copies fluttering into the bottom tray. I'll wait till he cools down, Sal decided, picturing introducing himself, and Barney left.

The next morning Sal looked up from his desk. He eyed Quincy glancing at his own short-sleeved shirt and matching beach shorts while entering. God, is this a stage or what?

"Just bought this. Whaddaya think?"

"Very nice. You and Rota make a nice pair." A pair of what? "Get yourself a racket, and you'll be all set," he added and grinned over both puns.

Quincy sat alongside. "A racket?" he inquired, frowning as if he had been offended. "What do you mean?"

Talk about paranoia, Sal thought. "A tennis racket." Slow down, fella. You're suffering from formitis.

Quincy regrouped his tuff into a point. "We're goin' on vacation," he revealed unconvincingly.

You've been on one, son, Sal concealed. "Thought you resigned." God, can't HUD even fire people properly?

"Nah. Changed my mind."

"Really?" The others changed their minds too? "Where 're yo' all goin'?" he drawled, "to the Bahamas?"

Quincy registered annoyance.

Footsteps sounded and both caught Doris peering inside with folded arms as she passed and entered the radio room.

"Haven't decided yet," Quincy answered uncomfortably. "Well, guess I better be packin'," he added and left.

"So, how 're yo' all been managin' without little ol' me?" Sal overheard Doris ask Pam.

It's shore been a mite quieter, Sal drawled to himself.

"Oh, I think Rota's still having troubles," Pam tried to soften. "But I think we're getting help."

"Think yo' all can handle everythin' while we're on vacation?" Doris deliberately specified which sounded equally unconvincing.

Sal walked to the passageway. Pocketing his hands, he leaned against the jamb. "So? You're *really* going on vacation?"

Doris yawned awkwardly. "Yeah," she answered. "The place was really startin' ta get onto ma nerves."

"Where are you heading? To the next disaster?"

Holding the opened novel before her, Pam struggled to keep a straight face.

Doris looked away to avoid Sal's eyes, left, and he returned to his swivel chair.

Pam appeared at the passageway. "Thought she was fired with the rest of them."

Sal shrugged. "Who knows about government jobs. Maybe you get a vacation with pay before they fire you. Of course they've been on vacation."

Pam's radio blared and she hurried back to her desk.

"Just Molly and me," Sal started singing happily.

Giggling sounded, then stumbling, as though Pam missed her chair this time and Sal sniffed into laughter.

The kitchen eventually became the oracle for airing speculation and rumor about the episode. Some men insisted that the four hadn't really been fired, disturbing Sal. Others claimed that Civil Service workers needed a hearing first.

"Of course, yo' all gotta work before you can call yo' self a Civil Service worker," Norm drawled.

"That leaves you out," Skip teased with a laugh.

Fingering his black beard, Phil declared that the foursome were going on sick leave because they were mentally sick.

A familiar voice, belonging to a face containing two large, grotesque lenses, wanted to know who ate all the doughnuts.

"The flies," Norm answered.

Dinger opened the empty refrigerator for the third time and scratched his head for the second time. Checking inside the freezer compartment, he carried Rota's half-devoured ice stick to a corner like a delighted chimp.

Rota entered. According to Millie, Roy had influential HUD friends who were arranging for the foursome to be transferred to the Wilkes-Barre, Pennsylvania disaster area.

Lyman shook his head. "All of 'em should be strung up. How they can screw up and not get canned, beats the shit out of me. You realize what's going to happen once they get there, if that's true?"

Skip snapped his hair in place. "Yeah. It's like adding a disaster to a disaster."

Drinking coffee, that is, pouring it into what resembled a black abyss, Phil laughed with the others. "Can't anybody stop them?"

"Yeah, God," Skip retorted. "But he's too busy working on the next disaster. Did you catch Happy yesterday morning? Somebody told him about an earthquake in Alaska, and he got so excited, he started tremblin' hisself."

Norm laughed with the others.

Skip shoved his hair in place. "Once he gets his back pay for loafin', he'll have enough bucks ta trade in the Barracuda for a Mercedes."

Vinny pulled his red hunting cap down, despite the heat. "Yeah, he's buying the one that Elm Chevrolet pulled out of the Chemung."

Phil lowered his cup. "One way to tell if they've really been transferred. See if Quincy's clothes are still in his bedroom."

"Checked this morning," Norm obliged. "They's still there."

"What's the matter? They didn't fit?" Lyman asked, and laughter followed again.

"That don't mean nothin' if they're there," Skip defended. "If I owned his threads, I'd a left 'em behind too."

"Did Roy empty *his* drawers?" Phil asked. "That's where you should check."

"No sense, man," Skip responded. "He's been wearin' the same ones for weeks. It matches his cowboy uniform."

Hammering started outside, slowed, then stopped, as if the operator was tired.

"I saw Doris empty out her drawers," Sal admitted innocently.

"And you watched?" Skip stabbed.

"What did Roy ever see in her?" Mike asked.

"Her loud mouth kept him from keeling over dead, man," Skip provided.

Phil lifted his cup and sipped. "That's funny, I thought he was all aong."

The banter continued similarly until the group sauntered up front, and mingled with the usual loungers.

"Not sure if I should sit here or behind Doris' desk, now that she's gone," Rota told a nearby group. "I'm so confused. Mr. Cardenas says she's been fired. She claims she's on vacation, and Mr. Layton isn't sure."

"Sound pretty normal to me, Ro," Skip chirped. "Like Roy always said–" Breaking off, he frowned and turned to Sal. "What were his famous words?"

Sal shrugged. "He was always lost for them."

Norm demanded a moment of silence to commemorate the foursome's departure. "It's the same thing Roy always gave us."

"Hang in there, Rota," Skip shouted, standing near the urn. "It ain't the desk. It's the woman behind the desk that counts."

"Rota should stay put," Norm told the others nearby beyond her hearing. "She can screw up from there as good as anywhere."

"Right," Skip agreed. "The difference between the two broads is that Doris' voice carried to Chicago. Rota's only a foot because of the windbags blasting away before they bounced here."

That night, all left except Rota who was determined to figure out what Doris had been doing for six weeks.

The ultimate absurdity occurred the following morning. Sal was checking several inspection sheets in the cabinets up front. Pam was writing HUD numbers in the new log in the radio room when the front door opened and the foursome entered–possibly in order to check what they might have left behind, Sal assumed, but they soon mingled with the others and even joked with them near the percolator.

Marcel and Barney entered next, and out stumbled the loungers pretending that they were heading for the different sites.

I wonder if our new leaders will ever find out what they *really* do all day? Sal questioned.

Marcel whispered something to Barney who nodded and glared at the foursome.

I better get back to my desk before I puke, Sal sneered, and hurried down the hallway.

"I think they're really leaving now," Pam announced.

Both looked out of Sal's window at Quincy fitting a suitcase into the humming Chevy.

Sal regarded Roy at the wheel, Doris sitting alongside, and Happy in back. "How come the band isn't playing?" he muttered and Pam giggled. "They screw up and even get to have that car?"

Pam giggled again. "Yes. That's their reward."

"Not sure about the others, but I think Lyman's right about Roy. *He'll* be heading for Wilkes-Barre or the next disaster."

Pam stopped giggling. "Why do you think so?"

"They didn't take away the car," he reasoned accurately, and the Chevy drove away.

Chapter 35

The courier arrived sometime later, and the men emerged from their hovels because it was payday. Swarming inside, they noticed Marcel and Barney. Slowing, they even converged almost orderly before Rota who distributed their paychecks with Marcel and Barney's help.

Since checks were missing or contained wrong amounts again, Sal appreciated receiving his but was disappointed about no raise. Marcel and Barney offered to look into matter, left, and so did the group immediately afterwards.

The courier brought a box of numbers for Sal to give to Homer. Since neither Marcel nor Barney knew how much Sal had accomplished, Sal saw little chance of gaining respect or receiving enough authority to make important decisions. Even if possible, speed and efficiency had long since been lost, he regretted and entered his car. But steps piled high so close to the narrow macadam road, prevented him from reaching the trailers quickly. Nor was Homer among the loungers playing poker in several different trailers or elsewhere. Returning to the office, he noticed the four teachers who had returned from blocking a trailer. Having received their checks, they were standing near the urn complaining to Marcel about not receiving raises, and Sal joined them amid the usual sound of screeching saws and hammering outside.

Though they argued that Roy had written "Give this man a raise" and signed it on the slips of paper that each was holding, Marcel claimed that Roy would have had to sign an official pay-increase voucher for their raises.

Lacking anything in writing, Sal sensed that his chance of receiving one was slimmer than theirs.

But I have nothing to lose to give it a shot, he decided.

Collecting their slips almost reluctantly, Marcel admitted that he was unfamiliar about such matters and agreed to call Millie.

Carmela had gone to the bathroom, Rota was checking the files, and the five hopefuls followed him to Carmela's desk. Sliding on top of it, Marcel picked up her phone.

How did *she* get a phone before me, the one who needed it so badly? Sal protested as Marcel dialed.

Millie claimed ignorance about such raises or vouchers, adding that scribbled requests were worthless.

"Anybody could have written them," Marcel relayed to the men.

Did you really expect anything else? Sal asked himself.

Marcel hung up, slid off the desk, and Phil demanded to know why their requests were worthless when so many meaningless HUD papers weren't.

Appreciating Phil's outspokenness, Sal watched Marcel frown effectively at the carpet, as if he were deeply sorry.

"Handwritten copies of anything are always worthless," Marcel scoffed indifferently.

Where did you dig up that stupid half-truth? In fact, the opposite is probably true in a court of law, Sal surmised. Well, what do you know? Say hello to another jackass.

Phil burst out laughing and all contemplated his face behind his huge, black beard. "A signature's a signature, whether it's written in pencil or horseshit. Where've you been?" he asked, surprising and pleasing Sal about his audacity .

Vinny repositioned his red cap unnecessarily. "Roy signed it," he also insisted, and Marcel seemed to appreciate the chance of turning to a less intimidating face. "Which makes it valid."

Marcel accidentally turned to Phil looming like an angry bull ready to charge. "Okay," he seemed to concede. "Write your names on separate slips of paper and I'll see what I can do."

Sure you will. Why would you? There's no recognition or money in it for you, Sal mocked cynically.

"Retroactive to July 21, the day Roy gave 'em to us," Phil ordered angrily.

God, could I use the extra money, Sal knew, tuning in to the hammering and wailing saws, and Marcel insisted that a one-step raise would hardly amount to much. More bullshit, he thought. "Maybe not for you, but it does to us," he contributed and Marcel eyed him. Precisely why we still have unions, he reminded himself. To protect us from unjust assholes like you. Were I Marcel, I'd fight to get raises for deserving employees like us. Too bad he didn't do his homework and find out how hard all of us worked.

All turned to Phil removing another slip of paper from his shirt pocket ceremoniously. "I grossed $817 for 198 hours as a G-4. I could make $940 as a G-5, a difference of $123 bucks. Want to check?"

It's nice when others do their homework besides me, Sal responded.

Marcel eyed the slip, shook his head, and Phil grimaced angrily at him.

"Why should I lose all that money?" Phil snarled and the rest agreed.

"I'll look into it," Marcel promised again, and he glanced at several men arguing with Rota about their paychecks. "Retroactive to July 21," he

334

consented unconvincingly, regarding each of the four teachers staring at him.

A pause followed, seemingly filled with the other's sarcastic doubt.

"I can only make recommendations," Marcel maintained. "Others approve or disapprove them. I appreciate your situation and sympathize with you," he began in a new tone. "Roy Nichols wasn't the kind to worry about bigger problems, much less–" he began and broke off, as if he refused to reveal more. "Fair enough?" His bushy eyebrows rose and fell and the teachers eyed him disbelievingly. Marcel slid off the desk. He was about to leave when the phone rang and he answered it.

Unsure where to spot trailers, a contractor demanded to know Roy's whereabouts. Marcel offered to send someone there with a map, hung up and Sal volunteered.

"Can you get there fast?"

Are flies buzzing the sink? "Yes." He was about to dash off, when Marcel asked him if Roy had a map of Kensington Park, a site that had just opened.

"It doesn't matter. I Xeroxed every available map, including Kensington. I'm the Xerox man, remember?" he announced and Marcel almost smiled.

Chapter 36

The next morning Barney Layton called a meeting outside, and the men grouped close to the office amid a thick fog. Barney emerged from the doorway smoking a cigar. Pausing on the top landing above the steps, he surveyed the men. Out stepped Marcel and a boyishly-faced man flanking him to his left. Removing his cigar, Barney announced that the foursome were gone, and he absorbed reserved applause and curious mumbling, as if the men sensed a threat to their loafing. He introduced himself as the new Director of Field Operations. Marcel Cardenas was in charge of expediting trailers and solving related problems, and Tom Littrel, Millie's assistant.

Great titles, Sal inserted sarcastically, standing near Skip, Norm, and the teachers. What about Grannis? he was almost tempted to ask him. Mr. Abomination in person, he announced.

"Our job's getting flood victims into trailers quicker than we've been doing," Barney declared.

There's an understatement, Sal thought.

"September 1 is gonna be our deadline for that. We gotta get 'em all out of here immediately," he stressed with a Southern drawl, and waved at them shrouded in mist. "Put 'em in available site, whether there's a pad, water, or what. Even before water and gas is hooked up."

Exactly what I told Craig to do weeks ago, Sal reviewed. Had Roy used the loungers for that, he would've been successful, despite Doris' behavior. In fact, screwed-up files would've have been immaterial along with the stealing, the incompetence, and so much more.

"There's no sense—" Barney said, interrupting Sal's thoughts, but a saw had started up, interrupting him.

All turned around in order to search for the culprit.

"Somebody tell whoever that is, to knock it off," Barney ordered gruffly.

Breaking away, Skip trotted past a pile of steps barely visible because of the dense fog, and Barney reinserted his cigar like an old Navy commander waiting for a sailor to tie down a noisy flap. The saw appeared to cut another piece hurriedly before halting and Skip returned. Removing his cigar, Barney explained that the victims were better off managing without electricity or even water, than remaining cooped up in churches, schools, and the Armory. "For the time being ah want you all to continue what you been doin' till ah get squared away with operations."

Oh, great, Sal inserted. You just gave them permission to continue loafing and disappearing.

"From what ah hear, we need tighten' up internally. We could use some foreman. One for the inspectors and one for the maintenance men. Any volunteers for foreman of inspectors?" he enunciated, surveying the men, which they started doing amongst themselves.

Volunteers? Sal protested with disbelief. What the hell kind of stupid way is that to find the right men? Another idiot, he labeled.

Barney stuffed the cigar back into his paunchy face, and Marcel and Tom began craning about, searching for raised hands.

Sal stared with amazement at Barney's bristled face and his narrowing eyes because of his own smoke. What the hell's going on? Sal continued raging. How could all of them be jackasses?

"Foreman of Inspectors," Barney repeated. "Volunteers?"

Considering Lyman, Skip, Norm, and the four teachers who worked hard blocking trailers, Sal settled on Lyman and was about to raise his hand.

"Dinger," someone suggested, interrupting him, and cackling laughter filled the damp surroundings.

Having apparently expected another name, Barney resumed examining the group. "How about you, Scott? We met and talked yesterday. Don't be bashful," he added, and heads began turning every which way. "Where's Scott Washington?" he blurted.

Oh, for God's sake. Where the hell is your brain? Another idiot that doesn't know anything about basic parliamentary procedure, Sal groaned in disbelief, unaware that Barney had ignored Lyman and Norman who had raised their hands in order to nominate him.

A young black, standing with several other young blacks off to the side, raised his hand almost reluctantly.

"Oh, there you are," Barney responded.

"But I don't know anything about–"

"Don't worry about it," Marcel interrupted him.

Yeah, sure, Sal suppressed. Guess who's going to spend God knows how long breaking him in?

"Now I need a maintenance foreman," Barney piped up and started reevaluated the faces.

Pulling himself together, Sal regarded Lyman again and particularly Skip who was fast, accurate, and knowledgeable about electrical and plumbing problems. Skip can even hook up gas stoves and repair gas burners, he knew. "Skip Reynolds or Lyman Bludiamond," he shouted.

Heads turned to regard the teacher with the gold-rimmed glasses and wavy hair strewn with gray and Barney ignored him.

"Where's that Justin fella? Met him yesterday also."

Who the hell's he? Met him yesterday? How's that for great

qualifications? Sal questioned. What if he had met Dinger, Miles, or a horse?

"Don't be modest," Barney thundered, disturbing Sal for sounding close-mindedly military. "Modesty don't help get trailers set up."

Neither does stupidity, Commander, Sal stormed.

"Where's Justin Sheepsma? Oh, there you are," he said, noticing him raise his hand as reluctantly as Scott had.

I bet both of them 'll fade into the fog, Sal predicted accurately. You don't need foreman. It's stupid, he added, picturing them getting raises. Except for Dinger and Miles, our group worked perfectly together without one.

"I just started two days ago," Justin seemed to protest with humble embarrassment.

Sal looked away in disgust.

"Hell, ah just started today," Barney bellowed, drawing laughter, aggravating Sal further. "Okay, you're in charge of the maintenance men."

Unbelievable. Almost as bad as how we sometimes choose candidates for public office.

"Well, I don't know," Justin answered, smiling self-consciously.

"Don't worry about it," Marcel insisted.

Sure, why should you? That'll mean more work and responsibility for me.

"Okay, that's it. I'll see both of you guys in Roy's old office," Barney declared and checked his watch as if the counterattack was minutes away. He opened the door and all followed him noisily inside.

What about my nominations, asshole? Sal objected, entered, and hammers and saws resumed with frenzied enthusiasm. No way am I going to tolerate his bullshit. Fuming, he excused his way ahead of several men, strode down the hall, and entered Roy's office.

Barney was already rearranging papers, pencils, and other items on the desk.

Sal regarded the diamond in a black onyx ring on Barney's fourth finger squeezing his cigar against his middle finger.

"Oh, Sal. Just the man ah wanna see," he boomed and repositioned the electric pencil sharpener near several different stacks of Quincy's forms. "You seem ta be the only one that knows what the hell's going on around here. Bastards in town are overcharging us, and you know about what that one block company tried ta pull with them defective block. Couple of contractors told me you had connections outta town where you live."

Sal placed his hands on his waist. "Well, I can't guarantee anything," he admitted modestly. "Send 'em to me, and I'll do my best to get the best price for *cured* block, he emphasized. But I want to talk to you about–"

"How about this Bob Updike?" Barney interrupted, squinting because of his swirling smoke. "Is he as good as he claims? He's trying to get HUD to sign another contract for him ta block a hundred more trailers."

Sal recommended him highly and Barney nodded.

Sal answered other concerns and eventually criticized Quincy's forms. At least we agree on something, he smiled, eyeing them landing in the waste can. "I'd like to give you some background on some of the men," he proposed like a college professor and mentioned Lyman. "He's an excellent maintenance man, and–"

"Ah know about Lyman," Barney quickly interrupted him irritably, upsetting Sal who heard someone enter his office.

Probably Scott or Justin, he sensed. "But you chose Scott as the inspection foreman," he objected quietly and emphasized that Lyman was a hard worker.

"Oh, he's a good man," Barney conceded quickly, as if fearing that Sal would consider him prejudiced against blacks, despite having chosen Scott.

Sensing that Barney knew nothing about Lyman and most likely hadn't even met him, Sal became so upset that he couldn't think clearly momentarily. He even forgot to mention that Lyman had been the only one to work voluntarily and independently at Edgewood. "I think Lyman should be the inspection foreman," he finally blurted amid heightened sinuses that prevented him from sounding convincing.

Barney frowned. "What the hell's the difference?"

Barney reminded Sal about his own narrow-minded, domineering father. It's the difference between what I know about a man's performance and your stupid selection of someone that neither of us know about, Sal fumed and managed to pull himself together. "The guy's intelligent, hardworking, and very capable," he finally verbalized. "He's also mature and knowledgeable about everything connected with trailers and inspecting them. And he's not afraid to get involved, even with tough, maintenance work. He's got the right attitude, knows what has to be done, and works hard at everything," he delivered, as if lecturing in class. "And then there's Skip Reynolds–" he attempted but noting Barney's head starting to shake negatively, Sal cut himself off.

"Scott 'll do the job," he simply declared gruffly and began puffing away erratically at his cigar.

Where did HUD dig up this clown? Sal rebuked. Geezus Krist, man, why Scott? You're related to him? he stormed with a laugh, picturing a Southern white man related to a black, then struggled to control himself again. "I don't get it," Sal popped out. Footsteps distracted Barney, and Sal noticed Scott entering his office What? You can't even focus on me? he directed at Barney. "Lyman should be chief inspector because of what I just said." For God's sake, get a grip, man. I'm not stupid. "All you guys are the same," he suddenly scolded the man, astonishing himself. "You think you're back in the military."

Having dealt with all kinds of men in the Service, Barney simply continued puffing away, dispensing him.

"And Skip should be maintenance foreman," Sal also insisted, but although appreciating his own assertion before someone in authority, he had mistakenly whined. He was about to list Skip's qualifications, but Barney was already checking the hall.

"Never heard of 'im."

Sal dug his fingers into his waist nervously. "How could you for God's sake? You just got here." Shit, he scolded, sensing that sinus prevented him from sounding more convincing again.

"Don't worry about all that. I'll take care of it."

Sal recalled promising Norm he would ask Barney about his raise. "You might not know Norman Meriwether, but he also does a good job and is cooperative. He surely deserves to be a G-5."

Barney tore out his cigar angrily. "If ah hear another word about that man's raise, I'll blow ma stack," he stormed.

Sal's mouth opened in dismay. You just did, Commander.

"The man's gonna be fired,"

Staggered, Sal stared at the man's face containing lines of age. What the hell?

"That's right," he told the lean face with high cheekbones. "He's been pesterin' me about it ever since I got here. If he'd work more and worry less about a raise, maybe he'd get one."

"I worked alongside of him. He's a good worker."

Barney reentered his cigar and ignored him.

Why is it that the first thing the new employers do–supposed leaders– is to fire good folks indiscriminately? Loose cannons cutting down quality employees, he labeled Barney. Asshole, Sal repeated. Bend, goddamn it. Give, he cried, unaware that he was picturing the Board refusing to give teachers a raise, and he looked away in further disgust.

Barney noticed his expression. "Ah can't worry about him or anybody else right now," he moderated.

Oh, good. Let's not worry about others. Fine statement from our new leader. Shit.

"We got a job to do, and we're gonna do it without worrying about raises," Barney insisted. He questioned Sal about various operations and received almost begrudging answers from the devastated, shadowy face suggesting that he needed another shave.

Sal answered a final question and Scott appeared before the doorway. Barney introduced him to Sal who shook Scott's hand, exchanged a few words, and excused himself past, in order to nurse his outrage, and walked up front. Noting Marcel helping Rota, he waited for an opportune moment and asked him if anyone had added his name to the list for raises.

Marcel didn't know and suggested that Sal ask Tom Littrel sipping coffee near the urn. Sal approached him, introduced himself, and questioned him.

Tom glanced at the list stuffed in his pocket and slid it back. "I don't know anything about *your* name," he emphasized, as Sal had anticipated. "Roy writing names on slips of paper is the wrong procedure anyway."

No kidding, Sal revived, annoyed about finding himself forced to grovel about money again. "What if I wrote my name on a file index card now? Maybe you could give it to the right HUD person."

Tom agreed with a shrug as if some imaginary ledger had to be balanced for him to do anything or as if nothing could be given away unless something was received in return. Disinterested, Tom explained that HUD · needed to know how many trailers contractors blocked daily, and he handed Sal a sheet to fill out and give to the courier. "Inspectors should be able to tell us that."

Another form? You're kidding, Sal disagreed. Realizing that Tom had no interest about the raises, Sal decided not to hold back. "How the hell can that ever be determined accurately?" he barked at the youthful face. "Inspectors don't hand in their sheets till late at night or the next day. Some of them even forget to do so until days later. It's stupid. A waste of time. What are you going to do with that information anyway?"

"Do it anyway," Tom urged like Marcel in that same stubborn, narrow-minded manner that Sal despised. Accepting the sheet, he left in despair.

Chapter 37

Norm appeared in Sal's office the next morning and revealed that HUD had fired him.

How come it's so easy to fire a good man? Sal stormed inwardly, sitting behind his desk, and shook his head sympathetically. "They should've given you a raise, not fired you. I'm sorry," he apologized sincerely. "Some men are just idiots."

Wearing another clean pair of coveralls, Norm shrugged good-naturedly. "Bad enough not being appreciated. But–" he attempted and broke off in a choked voice that moved Sal, and he regarded Norm with embarrassment and compassion.

"Gettin' too old for stuff like this," Norm added, extended his hand, and Sal rose.

Eying the man's pleasant face, Sal frowned. He felt large, rough fingers shake his hand. He walked around his desk, gave the man a hug, and Norm left. Sal swallowed down a lump. Damn. The way some supposed leaders behave never ceases to amaze me, he raged again. Realizing the courier had arrived, he pulled himself together again and walked up front.

The courier had just handed Rota the daily bulletin and some papers which she began perusing immediately. "Oh, my," she announced, "Pam's been promoted to a G-4, and Wally's gonna be a G-7."

You've *got* to be kidding, Sal repeated, one of his favorite phrases.

The four teachers laughed along with others, and the usual saws and hammering started up during their indignation.

"Geezus Krist what an outfit," Miles fumed.

"What about *our* raises, considering how hard *we* worked as HUD's blocking team?" Phil demanded nearby.

"That's it," Rota insisted. "They're the only ones."

"Let's see that thing," Mike demanded.

"Hey Dingle. You *didn't* get a raise," Skip shouted above the outside noise.

Dinger approached, sweeping back his hair. "I didn't even expect one."

"Why not, Ding? You're a quality loafer," Skip insisted.

The indignation subsided, and the foursome and Sal reasoned that competent or not, Wally qualified because he supervised eight men.

"Seven," Vinny disagreed. "The eighth got wounded after taking Wally's course on safety."

Mike insisted that HUD rewarded Wally for teaching Andre how to saw off his leg.

Skip disagreed, claiming he got a raise for building the largest kite ever.

Phil said it was for inventing the lopsided step.

Sal viewed the raises as the epitome of stupidity. Listening for a spell, he returned to his office and resumed working on the new log. Whoever authorized those raises is either blind, insane, or works somewhere else, he fumed. Nevertheless, he veered into the radio room, congratulated the surprised and elated Pam sincerely, and returned to his desk. Aware that his classic head still had a few shakes left, he used one up.

Minutes later, a man entered and introduced himself as "Stewart Garcia who was wearing a flashy tie bulging out between the lapels of a loud sport jacket.

Sal evaluated the man's well-tanned face suspiciously. This guy's been sunbathing at Lisa's pool? Rising, he shook his hand and accepted his card.

"I'm one of HUD's special field representatives," Stewart announced.

Won't hold it against you. Nice card, he thought, reading it, and he sat. Character 4,376? he entertained, bracing himself. "What can I do for you?"

"Mr. Layton sent me here," he began and flashed a smile. "Have you been having trouble getting block and supplies from manufacturers?"

Not in the mood for any more stupidity, Sal looked away briefly. "You might say that," he understated and described the Keely-Justin fiasco and the Mathews and Loomis episode.

"I can solve your problems. It's simple. You need to start dealing with out-of-state companies," he ordered rather than offering a suggestion, Sal noticed, and then Stewart seemed to pause as if awaiting Sal's congratulations for having come up with a great idea.

Giggling sounded from the adjacent room again, as if the owner were picturing Sal's smirking face.

Stewart glanced at the passageway briefly. "Prices would be cheaper and–"

"Excuse me," Sal interrupted and the giggling increased. Tolerance, he warned himself still again. "First of all, arranging with out-of-town companies could take oh, about eighty days with luck,"

The giggling intensified.

What did you do, take a course on salesmanship or read *The Power of Positive Thinking*? "It would probably take weeks before we got the first delivery. After the eighty days," he enunciated. "Didn't Mr. Layton tell you? We're trying to close shop by September 1."

"Yeah, but let me finish," Stewart insisted indignantly, weakening Sal's tolerance. "Now, I thought of setting something up for the contractors. It should include the contractor's name, how many blocks they need, when they're needed them, where they have to be delivered and–"

"Wait a minute. Hold on." Is it possible? he stormed, beyond despair. "Are you referring to putting together some kind of form?"

Stewart pocketed his hands under his colorful jacket contentedly, as if he had just banked a large lottery check. "Well, yeah. Of course," he sing-songed suggesting that Sal were stupid. "How else can you keep track of things? Mr. Layton told me to check with you."

Sal glared. About what? he was almost tempted to ask sarcastically, feigning stupidity.

Pam broke up and Stewart glanced back at the empty passageway.

Where does such driftwood drift in from? "All we do is make forms," he sing-songed.

Stewart's eyebrows raised and lowered offendedly.

"You really want to help right now? Forget the damn forms. Start making phone calls to anybody you think might sell block here in Elmira or the surrounding towns, not a thousand miles away. Oh, it's a royal pain in you-know-where, and it's boring. You might telephone for an hour and get nowhere, or hit somebody with a half a cube once a day. Whatever, it's nothing exciting. You want that? Go for it," he threw at the face. "And make sure *you* devise your own forms, not me."

"Well, pardon me, if that's the way you feel about it. That's why I suggested–"

"Yes, that's the way I feel about it," Sal interrupted, stimulating a burst of giggling from Pam. "All you guys want to do is make more red tape. You want to make connections with out-of-state companies? You want to make forms? Go ahead. Be my guest," he stormed. "Just leave me out of it."

"Okay, okay," he cried, raising hands up and waving them while heading for the door. "Forget it."

"Yeah, forget it," Sal sneered at the empty doorway. "Soon as it gets tough, the tough get going–out the door," he muttered and resumed working on the new log.

"Is it safe?" a deep voice resonated shortly afterwards.

Sal looked back up and regarded a familiar face. "Why not?" This is just a stage anyway.

Daryl grinned, introduced himself again, and entered.

What now, brown cow? Sal concealed half-rising to shake his hand. Hasn't this stage had enough? Sitting, he listened to Daryl continue his story.

Temporarily single and homeless, Daryl was working odd jobs to earn money. He lived wherever possible, mostly in his "rattletrap van," as he put it, and slept in a pup tent at night, "weather permitting."

Having completed three years of college, he hoped to finish the fourth at Elmira College and planned to marry a girl from Elmira afterwards.

Sal suppressed a sigh. Where do they dig up these guys? Much less hire them as contractors? he first analyzed.

"Keep this under your hat but I snowed Barney. Tried to make him think I had a crew, but I've been working like a dog knocking trailers off myself. Made him believe I was gonna stay on afterwards. Guess he fell for it. That's why he's letting me block a couple a more trailers. He thinks I have a crew.

Oh, God, Sal moaned internally. Just what I wanted to hear. "You're a con artist," he responded, sighed, and familiar giggling followed. "Know something?" he began, as if pausing to evaluate himself aloud. "Maybe it's the face. But people are always telling *me* their stories."

Daryl smiled. "You've *got* a kind face."

"Oh, that's it?" Sal answered and finally laughed. "How do you know I won't tell Barney?"

Daryl regarded the empty passageway curiously during renewed giggling and looked back. "Ah, I checked you out."

"Oh?"

"With the guys before. They said you were cool, the kind of guy to check out."

I'm already checked out. I'm trying to check in. Aware of his knowledge about operations, particularly inspection sheets, Sal almost felt proud. Is this guy just another HUD dud? he questioned next, smiling over the rhyme this time as Daryl rambled on about himself. Or does he *really* have any feeling for the flood victims? Surely a guy living in a van can't be all that bad, he reasoned, recalling his own youth. "So, what do you want me to do for you?"

"Nothing right now, thanks. I'll talk to you later. I've gotta get back to work," he added, shook Sal's hands and left.

Curious about whether or not Quincy turned in hand tools, power equipment, and office supplies exposed to possible thievery, Sal hurriedly left to check his trailer. Stepping inside the side door, he heard voices and strode down the hallway. Pausing before the kitchen, he peered inside. Seated haphazardly around the table were two muscular men wearing t-shirts containing the words *The New England Six.*

Eyeing him, they started explaining (or perhaps justifying, Sal sensed), that they had recently driven down from Boston "to help the flood victims," one of them said, which Sal's creative mind translated into "so you can make some quick bucks at the victim's expense."

Barney gave them permission to move in? Sal questioned, nodded, and eventually broke away in order to check the tool room still lacking the padlock. What else is new? he addressed also, realizing that the hand tools were gone. Entering Quincy's office, he noticed only a rusty hammer, a bent screwdriver, and a box of paper cups near several piles of blank inspection sheets on the table. Hearing more voices, he backtracked to the living room.

The encounter between young, robust men and Sal was predictable. Regarding his tag suspiciously and curiously, they feared that he would evict them. Evaluating such a group that resembled the New England Patriot's defense, Sal introduced himself casually like a modest professor about to start the new course. Disregarding empty beer cans and bottles scattered on a dirty, smeared floor sporting a small Pennz Oil drum almost overflowing with soiled paper plates, Sal casually asked them if they had seen any equipment "*lying* around," as he deliberately put it. How come everybody is so in love with *laying,* when they should practically always use *lying*? The dog *lies* down, he emphasized inwardly.

Drinking beer, several grunted that they hadn't.

Wonder where everything went? Sal considered throwing in, plus a sarcastic "Comfy?" but wasn't sure how they would take it and changed his mind. "How're you doing?" popped out instead. Looks like you found a spacious garbage can, he concealed, surveying the messy floor.

Appreciating that such a sedate-looking man didn't evict them especially since he surely appeared to be an official, two of them lowered their cans to the small table before the sofa. Noticing his concern, they even volunteered to clean everything up, surprising him.

I should try ordering this muscular bunch out and have them throw *me* out? he entertained with a laugh. No way. Watching them scurry sheepishly about picking up empty cans and soiled paper plates like mousy housekeepers, he even smiled. What missing tools? he teased. "You guys are living here now?" he nevertheless inquired, forever curious about everything.

"Yeah," a crew-cut man with bulging biceps seemed to confess, heading for the oil drum with paper plates that loomed odd in such a powerful grip. "Couldn't afford renting a motel or shit like that. Not with the prices in town," he justified and lowered the plates into the drum carefully in order to impress Sal about their pretended concern about tardiness.

"No problem." How can such big men be so pleasant and respectful? Muscles don't need verbal reinforcement. They speak for themselves, he answered.

Another man claimed to have "shacked up" in the bedroom with a young female he "picked up" near Southside.

Picturing a former student, Sal refused to ask for her name. "Just don't forget to change the sheets."

Their husky blast of laughter encouraged him to leave and he checked the bathroom. Ugh, he inserted, blaming them rather than Quinsy for the dirty towels on the floor and those draped over what was a slimy sink. Ah, the housekeeper 'll clean it up, he confided sarcastically to himself, squelching another laugh. Ought to charge them rent and pocket the money. To make up for no raise, flashed a thought, and he left.

Inhaling a foul odor outside, he observed the saturated ground and suspected an overflowing septic tank. He noted it on his pad, and reentered his office.

Barney appeared and removed his cigar. "Hey Sal, we need locks on the trailer's doors next door. Everybody and his brother's been using the john there. Some guys are even living there."

No kidding, Sal responded and almost smiled. But sensing that Barney was trying to "pass the buck" in order to avoid a confrontation with so much muscle, he nodded and revealed the possible septic tank problem.

"So I noticed. What's causing that?"

It's called defecation, man, Sal mused. "The septic tank is probably overflowing."

"Thought you told me it was just emptied."

"It was," Sal agreed and both left to check the surrounding ground.

"It don't seem like the office bathroom gets that much use," Barney offered.

Nobody stays here long enough to use it, man. They probably have been using Quincy's bathroom to keep out of sight, he concealed, aware that in addition to using the toilet, hundreds of men including the *New England Six* were also washing, and showering daily, including Wally's crew and contractors. "Grand Central Station's men's room probably gets less use, Chief," he explained with a smile.

Barney bent down to study a sudden trickle.

This man isn't too swift either, Sal concluded. "Somebody just flushed."

"Telephone call, Mr. Layton," Pam shouted from the office's side window.

"I'll call the septic people," Sal told Barney's back.

"Yeah, do that," Barney responded without turning.

When am *I* going to get a phone? Sal questioned again, using Carmela's to call their number that he found in the *Yellow Pages*.

The truck arrived the next morning. Hopping out, the driver to inspect the saturation along with Rota, Barney, and Sal, Rota having insisted that she needed a break.

Sal shook his head. A break to check a stink? Whatever turns you on.

The driver recognized the problem immediately. "Ya need a new overflow system."

"I don't think so," Sal disagreed and ordered himself still. Let the Chief handle it.

Puffing away, Barney withdrew his cigar as all continued studying the saturated ground, Rota insisting that the oozing water was a spring.

"How much would that cost?" Barney asked.

Glancing at the noisy carpenters while calculating carefully, the man appeared to find the amount on Rota's breasts. "Two hundred and fifty bucks."

Great, Sal mocked sarcastically. A hair below Rip-Off City for something we don't need.

The man explained everything in detail and turned to the tall, stooping Barney who had worked every conceivable HUD project and development after retiring from the Navy twenty years ago, Sal had learned.

Barney removed his unlit cigar. "What if we just have it emptied?"

All *right*! Nice going, man. Sometimes intelligence does seep in, much like certain nasty fluids seep out, Sal dramatized with a laugh.

"How often would we have to empty it?" Barney inquired.

Depends how many showers and flushes folks take, Admiral, Sal left unsaid.

The driver's face had a field day. He frowned, squinted, and maneuvered his lips. Shrugging, he scratched his ear.

"We just emptied her two days ago and she's full up?" Barney questioned.

A feminine pronoun again, this time to describe something as repulsive as a septic tank? Sal criticized and gave his tired head another shake. If women only knew the depths of men's abuse.

Rota headed for the office, and the septic man devoured her legs as if he were a sailor on leave after spending two months at sea.

Barney turned to Sal watching the carpenters banging away with frightening enthusiasm. "If we can get away with emptying her, say, only twice more by September 1, at forty-five bucks a shot, that's ninety bucks altogether. We'll save $160."

Is this guy for real? Worrying about a few measly bucks? "True," Sal nevertheless agreed, almost laughing at the paltry sum compared to what had been lost, broken, stolen, and wasted on useless manpower. Yet, watching Barney make the necessary arrangements, Sal appreciated his concern to save the government money. If more people were like him, the country wouldn't be in such debt, he assumed innocently.

"Put up a sign on all bathroom doors," Barney told Sal. "And mention something about cutting down on showering because the septic tank keeps overflowing," he barked without removing his stogie.

Why not just tell the men to shower at home? "I'll take care of it," he responded with a nod and spent a half hour devising signs that he posted inside both trailers' the bathrooms.

Late the next day, Barney stepped into Sal's office. "Something's got to be done about the trailer next door. Just came from it. It's a pigpen."

I guess the *New England Six* stopped housecleaning, Sal realized.

"I want you to tell them to move out. We just can't have this."

Thanks, Sal returned underground.

"What if Hugh Brennig comes over and sees it?"

Who's he? Sal ridiculed with a laugh. He's more invisible than the loungers and just as worthless. Sal nodded and entered the trailer.

Stepping inside the noisy living room, he greeted the same sprawled group drinking and joking again. No way am I going to try to evict them, he decided and reminded them to clean up the mess again. "It's a health hazard," he threw in as if he were a Public Health Department inspector.

"Tiny," so nicknamed because he weighed over three hundred pounds and possessed huge pectorals bulging against his dirty t-shirt, lowered his beer can and collapsed it in his hand in order to impress or frighten Sal, he sensed.

Nice try, Sal withheld, but a ten year old can do that.

"How about if we clean up like last time?"

Sal eyed the overflowing Pennz Oil can. What last time? he suppressed, sensing that they had stopped doing so the moment he left. "Surely that can be arranged," he assured facetiously, and almost broke up. "I'm just relaying orders. You might want to confirm that with Barney," he added cheerfully. Where the buck *really* stops.

"Catch 'im later," Tiny flung.

Sure you will. I should I worry about something that doesn't involve helping the victims? he entreated, shrugged, and departed.

Chapter 38

Resuming working on the new log, Sal encountered such major inaccuracies as omitted serial numbers, manufacturers' names, and more. Doris had even mistakenly dispatched six trailers to Corning he also learned. I'm going to have to check some sites personally in order to correct such problems, he realized. Driving to Skycrest, he was stunned to find an empty trailer parked near the entrance. Probably abandoned because the toter couldn't find where to drop it off and nobody was here to help him.

I guess he didn't want to waste time and bucks hauling it back here, he surmised accurately. He jotted down the serial number and other pertinent information on his pad and found another trailer parked on a nearby side street. Checking its serial number, he discovered that it should have been delivered to a victim's personal property. How do I indicate such discrepancies in the log? What do I write? he questioned. Forget it, he answered, realizing that he couldn't, nor could anyone else. He drove back, mentioned the two trailers to Barney (who frowned) and eventually finished the new log.

Sal soon learned that Marcel had left to straighten out Corning's records which were suffering similar problems. In fact, whoever was in charge, hadn't filed inspection sheets, much less had anyone given them to the contractors whose vehement complaints had filtered back to the Holding Point office.

Sal became Barney's troubleshooter and assistant in the succeeding days though Barney never acknowledged it to him. Sent to new parks, Sal often radioed back the usual problems concerning gas, electricity, and much more. He also found himself requesting more trailers, personally directing them inside sites, and dramatically radioing Pam about the site's grand opening afterwards. Though the insane hiring had stopped, loungers continued signing in and out like before.

Major problems soon arose. Because bulldozers had to remove a curb and fill in a ditch near one new park's entrance, Sal radioed Barney, using Pam's radio.

Although he explained to him that he had to delay the grand opening until late afternoon, Barney dispatched a dozen trailers before twelve anyway, stunning Sal. Consequently, trailers ended up in a clogged line before the entrance, and Sal stood alone on the busy street struggling to direct traffic while answering the radio and appeasing an angry site engineer and his men.

Timing the completion of work at another park where Daryl was blocking a trailer, Sal couldn't find the site inspector to make the final approval. To save time, he radioed Barney to send the ten trailers anyway, and with Daryl's help, positioned them upon their arrival. Though HUD didn't require contractors to inspect trailers, Daryl even helped Sal do so, surprising him. Finishing without finding any problems hours later, Sal radioed Barney that the site was ready for contractors and their blocking crews.

Shortly afterwards a HUD vehicle pulled up along the nearby dirt road and a man wearing sunglasses exited. "Who released this park?" he asked Sal gruffly and removed his glasses.

Approaching with Daryl and two other contractors, Sal watched him slip the glasses into his short-sleeved shirt pocket. "I did."

"By whose authority? Who are you?"

"Sal D'Angelo." An intelligent earthling who still gives a damn about the victims and will till the end, he commented proudly, unaware how stressed out he was. "I authorized myself," he added flippantly.

Daryl and the contractors broke up.

"You weren't around and the pads were ready. We just finished checking out ten trailers that are all ready," he flung cheerfully. "That's the name of the game. Getting in and inspecting as many trailers as possible in the fastest time."

"You had no business releasing this park. That's not your job."

Nobody has even defined my job, he grumbled inwardly. "How do *you* know what my job is? Sorry, I've got no patience or the time for this. It's too stupid. Why knock success?"

Frowning, the man looked away indignantly.

"What's the problem? Where the hell have *you* been?"

"None of your damn business. That's not the point."

The male ego again. Asshole number 342. "In fact, it is. Had you been here, I wouldn't have had to do *your* job. The point is I *did* your job, and I did it well," he asserted. *My way*, he repeated still again. If I get fired, I'll be teaching soon anyway, thank God, he repeated again.

"Who the hell are you, talking to me like that?"

Sal didn't care if the man was Hugh Brennig. "I introduced myself before. Weren't you listening?"

The others laughed again.

"You guys are all the same. Somebody finally does *your* job, and you're upset because it bothers your ego. What the hell's the difference who does what or how, as long as trailers get set up as fast as possible?"

"We'll see what difference it makes," he retorted, strode angrily to his car, and sped away.

Sal turned to Daryl. "I can tolerate mistakes, because we're only human. But pettiness, narrow-mindedness and incompetence? Plus loafing while others are suffering and desperate? No way."

Daryl nodded.

If we could've only had the right leaders from the beginning, Sal repeated still again with a touch of remorse, and he returned to the office.

Having learned about the incident, Barney scolded him, although mildly, Sal appreciated. "You really didn't have the authority," he maintained several times, and Sal waited until he reinserted a small, smoking stud in his mouth.

"Four extra families are going to be getting into trailers a day earlier because of me and that contractor, Daryl. I defy anybody with even half a brain to argue about that," Sal deposited coolly.

Barney eyed him curiously.

Hoping to shift Barney's attention elsewhere, Sal deliberately complained so vehemently about Roy, Doris, Happy, and the general complacency, incompetence, and apathy, that Barney's cigar moved left, right, back, and even up and down like a semaphore flag.

"They sure were some bunch," he agreed through his soaked cigar, and Sal returned to his office.

Waiting for him, Scott handed him a batch of inspections sheets and both corrected some omissions. Sometime after Scott left, Daryl entered and asked Sal if anybody would mind if he moved into one of the trailers in the field. "It beats getting stuck in my van or pup tent, especially when it rains."

Sal looked up from checking an inspection sheet. "Thanks for all your help," he sidetracked momentarily.

"No problem."

Sal shrugged. "I don't see why not. Everybody else has slept in them on an off. Just keep the place spotless, and don't tell Barney I gave you permission. And stay a jump ahead of the toters. They're starting to move trailers out by the dozen."

"No problem. Thanks." He shook Sal's hand, and left.

Signing out that night, Sal stepped outside into the semidarkness and paused. What the– Where's my car? Adjusting to the city glow, he found it almost hidden between separate piles of steps. He also noted steps stacked throughout the parking area, against the fence enclosing the trailers in the field, and beside Wally's makeshift workshop, all of which several mornings of dense fog had hidden. Surveying the area beyond the office, he even observed a plantation of them lining the far fence. "The guy's gone insane," he muttered, pushing a pile aside that was blocking his door. How're people supposed to get in and out of the parking area? he demanded, removing several from the front of his car. Driving away, he had trouble maneuvering around stacks along the gravel road. For God's sake, man, turn off the faucet, he stormed. Reaching the macadam road, he sped out the front gate and headed home.

Chapter 39

Barney entered Sal's office Thursday morning and announced that two veteran HUD inspectors were arriving from New York City and Houston respectively in order to assist with inspecting.

You *can't* be serious, Admiral, Sal protested disbelievingly. "What for? We've got tons of inspectors."

"These guys got experience."

You mean that they're professional loafers? "We've got some good inspectors," he enunciated. "I told you about Lyman who also does maintenance work. Then there's Skip, the four teachers, and–"

"They're gonna be lodging with open expense accounts at the Holiday Inn," Barney interrupted.

He's so wrapped up in himself, he doesn't even hear me.

"In case ya need 'em for anything."

Yeah, I need them to stay out of my office and *not* bend me out of shape. I give up, Sal announced inwardly. "Uh huh," he responded, realizing that he had no other choice. You mean they're going to be on vacation at government expense, Sal redefined. Are they bringing their wives? Need them? he protested, barely hearing Barney rambling on about them. They'll be needing *me* to explain operations! I'm invaluable, and they're going to waste my time. "Okay. Thanks for letting me know."

Pulling up inside a government vehicle later, the men had trouble finding a parking space between the piles of steps. Entering Sal's office, they introduced themselves, shook hands, and apologized for not knowing anything about inspecting or anything else.

Nice, Sal thought, having learned that they were salaried as G-11's. Couldn't you have at least lied about your ignorance? he objected with a laugh. "No problem," his other self agreed. God, what a phony I've become. Oh, I think I'm goin' out of my mind–over dopes like you, he hummed, following the Beatles' tune inwardly, as the two men spoke enthusiastically about their availability and eagerness to help. Why wasn't HUD dumb enough to send badly-needed *maintenance* men? he enunciated, and eventually briefed them about the disaster generally. Dinger's even worth more than these free-loaders, he reflected and delayed his own work for almost an hour in order to explain how to inspect a trailer, fill out an inspection sheet, and much more.

Thanking him, they repeated their vow to offer him expert help.

Oh, really? Why? *You're* going to look for some experts? he objected, eying them heading out the door.

Several hours later both men returned and admitted botching up their inspection sheets. Could Sal spare some new sheets and help fill them out properly?

Thanks. Had they been experts, they could have inspected five trailers by now, Sal suppressed, complied, and they promised to be more careful and thorough next time.

You mean about screwing up?

That night, Daryl slept in a trailer. A heavy sleeper, he woke in the morning. Thinking the trailer was moving, he assumed he was dreaming and fell back asleep. A car horn soon woke him up completely minutes later and he rose with a yawn. Peering sleepy-eyed out the window, he noticed the county-side seemingly floating past. Realizing that the trailer was being towed south on Route17, he shouted repeatedly for the driver to stop, but the loud-sounding diesel kept obliterating his voice, and he gave up.

The toter finally pulled inside Shady Hollow, a newly opened trailer park, stopped, and turned off the motor.

"I can't come out," Daryl bellowed again.

Surprised, the toter climbed out, shut the door, and scrutinized the trailer perplexedly.

"I'm naked, man," Daryl insisted frantically and the toter walked to the bedroom window. "My clothes are in my van parked near where you picked up this trailer."

The toter scratched his head, frowned, and caught sight of a triangular-shaped head poking out of the opened window. "What the hell 're you doing in there? Who the hell 're you? You got a woman in there?"

Daryl removed the screen. "No. I'm alone. I'm a contractor. I work for HUD. I slept in the trailer. I just woke up. I got nothing to wear. I left my clothes in my van. Maybe you got something for me to wear? Anything, man?"

The toter grinned. "I don't know. I'll check." He did and returned with an odd piece of oily burlap.

"That's it?" Daryl remarked, accepting it.

"Yeah. My clothes is at the cleaners."

"Oh, man."

"What can I say?"

"Are you heading back to the office? Where you picked up this trailer?" he specified.

"Yeah. Soon as I dump it. I gotta check in with your secretary. But ya ain't supposed ta be in this kind a trailer while I tow it. It's against the law. Come on up front."

"Shit," Daryl uttered with a frown and wrapped the piece around his waist. But stepping out gingerly, he had trouble walking to the cab in his bare feet and finally made it.

The driver parked the trailer between designated stakes and returned to the Holding Point. Mountains of steps forced him to park near the office, some distance from Daryl's van, and out stepped Daryl clinging to his sarong.

Seldom missing much, Skip happened to be standing before the window above the couch during the usual sound of sawing and hammering. "I'll be damned. Tarzan just arrived."

Puzzlement rearranged expressions.

"I'm serious. Take a look."

Several men, including Sal, gathered before the window, and regarded Daryl struggling to make his way toward his van. Mistakenly glancing at the carpenters and the office window seemed to hurry Daryl into floundering. The burlap started slipping off. Unable to pull it up, Daryl gave up. The burlap dropped and catcalls and whistling followed. Barely discerning his van because of the steps, Daryl struggled to zigzag between them.

"What the hell?" Phil cried with a laugh.

Hammering and sawing stopped.

"A streaker," Phil said.

Whistles disturbed the pleasant warm morning, plus cheers and several toots from a lounger's parked car.

"Oh, my," Rota chirped.

"I do believe I've experienced it all," Sal confessed.

Chapter 40

Most of the trailers were dropped off at the various sites by Friday afternoon, September 1, and that part of the enormous task was finally completed except for the blocking, electricity, gas, and so much more. In other words, that was just the beginning of unbelievable problems that were destined to follow which HUD should have handled immediately after the disaster, Sal knew. Sitting behind his desk, he sympathized with hundreds of flood victims still living in cramped quarters. Looking back, he realized that he should have acted more decisively, possibly even complained to Brennig or higher-ups about Roy. His fear that Roy would fire him for doing so had been mostly rationalization, he now recognized.

He also sensed that his inability to speak up like Phil (until much later), was somehow related to his psychological makeup, genes, and accumulated stress from teaching, plus his overbearing father who constantly suppressed him during his early youth whenever he disagreed with him. And how come you didn't communicate with Barney, reveal all the problems that ensued since he arrived, especially about the loungers, tons of probably unnecessary steps that Wally is still turning over, even Marcel's unnecessary new log? he scolded. I was too stressed out and I'm not an informer.

Sal stared out the hall window at the carpenters moving about lazily. Hoping to encounter similar situations, so that he could act more resolutely and prove to himself that he had learned and grown, he forgot that everyone approached each experience with whatever was their ability at the moment.

Though vaguely satisfied about having devised an accurate, comprehensive, well-organized file index system containing considerable information that eliminated four logs, he knew that quick, intelligent action was needed during a disaster, not meaningless paperwork.

But he was mostly annoyed that he felt forced to create another log just to satisfy a man's ego. Had Marcel been a woman, maybe she wouldn't have been so headstrong, he evaluated innocently.

Though he appreciated his endeavors at Skycrest, he also felt satisfied and proud that he and Skip had released all the trailers at McArthur Park almost singlehandedly. At least I got away with bopping Happy.

He had been amazed at how callous, complacent, and indifferent others could be during a disaster, particularly the loungers who complained angrily about the pay foul-ups, even though all of them had hardly worked.

About to grumble internally that the world contained few good people, he pictured Skip, Lyman, Norm, and others, including the four teachers and even Rota who always gave her best, changed his mind and even smiled.

Sal also recognized again that faulty leadership was responsible for so much loafing, not the loungers. After all, wasn't it human nature *not* to rush into working if you could get away with getting paid for doing nothing? he reasoned, forgetting that possibly bored, some might have even appreciated doing something meaningful rather than loafing.

He tuned into Barney accepting congratulations from Rota, the contractors, and even the loungers up front.

Leaning back, squeaking his chair, Sal clasped his neck. Barney's like a general who just won the war, he scoffed, visualizing the tall, stooping, crew-cut man receiving handshakes from everyone. Little do they realize what *really* went on, he knew, refusing to join in. All he did was reach a decision that a kindergartner could have made weeks ago.

Besides, bypassing men like Lyman, Skip, and Norm was too unconscionable, like a publisher passing up a great novel for fear of profiting less. Of course, saving Uncle Sam a few bucks on septic work was truly brilliant, Sal reviewed sarcastically. But neither Barney, Brennig, nor anyone is thinking about easing the flow of trailers that are now arriving in droves, he protested. It's like massive reinforcements and supplies pouring in unnecessarily after the battle is won.

Heading for Roy's office, Barney passed Sal's doorway.

"Unit fifteen" sounded over Pam's radio, and because she was Xeroxing inspection sheets, the new Chief veered inside to answer it.

"Barney Layton here, over," Sal discerned.

"We need some numbers 'cause a fleet of trailers is waiting to come in, over," Homer honked from his nose.

"What the hell's he talking about?" Barney complained, breaking Sal up.

Returning to her desk, Pam struggling to suppress her giggling. "I'll take care of it, Mr. Layton," she offered, did, and Barney drifted into Sal's office.

"I think we ought to slow down the influx of trailers," Sal suggested hurriedly in order to prevent Barney from sidetracking him.

Barney removed his cigar. "What? What do you mean? Why?"

Sal explained, adding that excess trailers would have to be toted back at unnecessary government expense.

"Ah, that's no problem. It's better to have too many trailers than not enough," he scoffed and left.

Oh God, Sal thought, aware that gloating prevented Barney from thinking clearly.

The courier arrived with the checks later. Fuming about no raise, the four teachers converged in Sal's office in order to hand in their inspection sheets and they complained. Settling down, they decided to protest to Wayne Jankowski, rather than Barney who seemed to lack the power to help or the inclination during such a momentous day, they agreed. They left shortly afterwards, and Sal resumed working on the blocked trailer count for Tom which he had procrastinated completing because of its redundancy.

The following morning, the men signed in and most whistled out to their favorite slots for the day, except for a few diehard coffee-drinkers. They're taking advantage of Barney now and he doesn't even know it, Sal recognized. Barney still doesn't know anything about inspections or the blues and doesn't seem to care either, Sal also sensed. I'll brief him. But not until he calms down, he added and walked up front to check a folder in a cabinet.

"This job's really getting out of hand," whispered a lounger holding a cup of coffee nearby.

Verifying a serial number on an inspection sheet, the slender English teacher with hairy arms poking out of a short-sleeved shirt regarded him curiously.

"Can't afford to play so many holes, man," he confessed.

"I'll bet," Sal quipped and slipped the folder back between two folders. Realizing he had nothing to lose, he decided to see Wayne about his possible raise also, despite realizing that his chance of getting it was less than slim. It might even be fun. Reaching the Rand after lunch, he met Floyd leaving Wayne's glass-enclosed office. They exchanged greetings and Floyd complained about wasting all morning trying to get paid for setting up over three hundred trailers.

"They owe me over a hundred thousand."

Sal almost sympathized with him until the figure registered. And I'm worried about a measly two hundred bucks? Nevertheless, Sal thanked him for doing a great job. They shook hands, parted, and Sal approached Wayne sitting behind his desk talking on the phone.

Twentyish and hardly resembling his father, Wayne interrupted his conversation and offered Sal a seat alongside him.

Studying the young man who resumed speaking on the phone, Sal would have preferred that he sported long hair or wore outlandish clothes which might have suggested opposition to the present hard-nosed establishment. But wearing a white shirt and drab tie lacking the sportier Windsor knot, he looked too clean-cut and patriotic to be open-minded, Sal reasoned.

Probably resembles his mom, Sal concluded. Looking through a glass partition into the large office room containing many desks ahead of him, he observed Tony Grannis. Holding a cup of coffee, he was talking and laughing with several men. Must be nice getting paid for being on a perpetual coffee break.

Wayne hung up, apologized for keeping Sal waiting, and they exchanged the usual formalities. Sal described Roy's promised raise and asked why he hadn't received it yet.

Wayne rested his white-sleeved arms on the desk, suggesting he welcomed a change from a boring morning. "Because we never received anything in writing from Roy," he answered, fluttering his blue eyes superciliously. "Or a pay-increase voucher. The other guys were here this morning. They're in the same boat."

Here we go again. "Why not accept those slips of paper that they gave you, the ones with Roy's handwritten approval? Those guys worked hard." Unlike the loungers, he suppressed. "Considering so much government waste, they deserve raises," he insisted, aware that despite his own weak argument, he would have to make a case for them before he could for himself.

"How do we know that was even Roy's handwriting?" Wayne countered.

"Oh, come on. Four teachers conspired to pull off a forgery?" he scoffed in annoyance. "Including me? I don't think so. But you're missing my point."

"We follow rules and regulations."

Here we go with the rules and regulations shit, like they come from God, Sal sneered. Whenever you sense your own inhumanity or close-mindedness, blame it on rules and regulations or God.

"Since we didn't get the proper pay-increase vouchers, we could hardly send those handwritten sheets to Washington."

"Why not? Truth should always supersede ignorance, especially rules and regulations. You know those guys didn't forge Roy's handwriting. He wanted to give them raises and had the authority to do that. Therefore, you should draw up the necessary vouchers so that they get raises, including me, since I'm not lying about them or me. Why he didn't take care of the pay-increase vouchers or whatever the hell that is, I don't know." Except that he was an asshole, he concealed. "You still have the chance to do the right thing and draw up the necessary vouchers."

"Not really."

"Bullshit," Sal growled.

Wayne looked away momentarily. "There aren't many things humans do that they can't undo. Especially in this case."

"What I think is immaterial. The question is one of proper

procedure," he uttered stiffly. "Besides, Roy's no longer with us."

"You mean that getting fired or transferred from a job cancels out everything or anything somebody said or did beforehand? Come on. What if a judge pronounces someone guilty and gets fired or dies an hour later or the next day. Does that nullify his verdict?"

Wayne shrugged indifferently, looked down, and Sal stared at him regarding a letter on his desk.

You're already old, man, because you're unmovable and unloving. What's going to happen when you're forty? He'll be worse than his father, unless he changes, Sal answered.

Wayne turned to laughter emanating from the men surrounding a nearby desk.

"Didn't Roy have the authority to give raises?"

"Yes," Wayne conceded somewhat reluctantly.

"Okay, so there you are. You should honor that. Don't you see my point? It's so simple."

"That depends on *your* viewpoint. Not mine. You might not realize it, but if it wasn't for proper procedures, we'd have chaos."

"Sometimes we have chaos *because* of *supposedly* proper procedure, like right now?" Hello.

Wayne shrugged again.

"Why follow so-called proper procedure when it hurts five good men? Don't you get it? Give all of us raises and you'll feel good about having done something positive and just. We're all quitting to start teaching soon. What about all the stupid raises you gave out?"

Already shaking his head, Wayne stopped. "Which ones? What do you mean?"

Sal paused to reflect. Not too anxious to fault others for his own benefit, he mentioned Wally and Quincy. "Plus those G-11 brass you sent here. And all those lame ducks who are still overpaid for slurping coffee and loafing around doing nothing," he finally chose to reveal.

Wayne shrugged again. "I don't know anything about all that," he dispensed, as Sal had secretly predicted. "There's just nothing we can do about you guys now, even if we wanted to."

"We both know that the right people with the right authority could give us raises. Even make us G-11's if they wanted to. This all boils down to finding the right people and getting them to do that, follow?"

"Yes," Wayne conceded, surprising Sal. "But I don't have the authority, and I don't know the right people."

"So, find 'em, damn it. For the sake of justice. Do the right thing, man." Where's your conscience? he suppressed.

"Even if I did, I probably couldn't influence them."

"How do you know if you don't try? The problem is you're indifferent, like so many others. You're one of those couldn't-care-less degenerates. You don't want to bother or get involved. There's no money in it for you," he unloaded. He glared at Wayne who looked away as if he were bored, annoying Sal still again. It's the same problem since the beginning of civilization, he concluded, namely the lack of compassion for others, folks not really wanting to help folks."

Wayne looked back. "How come none of you guys submitted a voucher?"

"We didn't even know what that was or that we should have submitted one. We're just teachers, he almost cornered himself into popping out. Besides, we trusted Roy. He promised us raises, and we assumed we would get them." In other words, he wasn't a man of his word among a ton of other inadequacies, Sal withheld.

Wayne frowned. "Maybe Marcel forgot to submit proper authorization to us," he seemed to vacillate. "I'll check," he added, surprising Sal and left. Minutes later, he returned with Sal's pay folder and sat. Rummaging through his papers, including Sal's celebrated four-dollar voucher, he shook his head. "Nothing here except this, an authorization to change your job classification from maintenance man to inspector."

Sal laughed. "They *hired* me as an inspector. That's what I've been ever since I started."

"Not according to this."

"What was I before?"

"It doesn't say."

"Whatever," Sal dispensed impatiently, irritated by what he viewed was more stupidity. "What about a raise for these last two weeks?" he specified. You're begging, he scolded. I don't even give a shit about the money. It's for my wife and family, he justified, eyeing Wayne. I could practically live in the woods if I had to. There's something wrong with your head, man, he considered uttering. It keeps swinging back and forth, not up and down.

"Sorry, there's nothing we can do about it."

What, about your head? "What about giving us a raise for the next two weeks?" he asked, realizing that he had reached the bare minimum.

"That depends on whether or not we receive proper authorization and how long that would take before it's approved."

"What can you do to speed it up?"

"Nothing."

Congratulations, Sal condemned. God are *you* worthless.

"See Millie. Maybe she can help."

"Okay. Can I see her now?" The problem is, I've never seen a woman's now, he teased, recalling an old joke, and he almost laughed at his own absurdity.

Wayne offered to check, surprising Sal again, and left. He returned shortly afterwards. "Yes."

You're kidding, Sal thought and Wayne directed him to her office. Pausing before her desk, Sal reintroduced himself and reminded her that she had hired him in June. Seems like years ago, he thought, sitting in the chair that she offered him.

"Oh, yes, I remember," she said with a nod. She sniffled throughout his explanation about the raises, and responded similarly. "Marcel must not have submitted authorization. It got lost or maybe it's just delayed."

Sure, Sal thought.

She promised to check with Tom Littrel about a raise to cover the final two weeks. "If Marcel tells you that ya'all will get a raise, I'm sure ya'll will get it," she offered encouragingly.

"Tom's got my file index card with my name on it," Sal ventured despite picturing the remote possibility of its value.

Millie blew her nose, apologized because she had to leave and pick up a prescription for her sinus condition, and Sal left.

Driving home that night, Sal accurately concluded that his final two-week check wouldn't contain a raise. At least it was fun chopping Tom apart, something he deserved for being hardnosed and immovable, Sal labeled and broke into a grin.

Chapter 41

The following day, September 4, word spread that all temporary HUD employees were going to receive a special check covering all back pay, plus the pay period Sal had discussed with Wayne and Millie.

Consequently, the office trailer was overloaded with heavy loitering and serious coffee-clutching throughout the day.

Accepting his check with curiosity after the courier arrived, Sal wasn't surprised about not receiving a raise. At least they're consistently incompetent, he scorned.

None of the other teachers did either and they complained anew. Phil and the three others suggested seeing Wayne again. They bid Sal goodbye for good and left. Sal telephoned Tom from Barney's empty office, and Tom not only conveyed ignorance concerning Sal's situation, but claimed that he didn't remember the file index card Sal had given him, as Sal had anticipated.

You're lying or just another bright, incompetent bastard, Sal labeled. "Didn't Millie talk to you about our raises?" What the hell kind of people are these? The same as certain others that live throughout the world, he answered. Don't they realize that life isn't really about money or one's job but how you treat one another and yourself?

"From what I gathered from her, if you're getting a raise, it will go into effect as of August 31 and will cover however long you work beyond that. I believe I remember signing it," Tom said.

"August 31? I'm quitting today. That only covers four days," he complained, unaware that his final check wouldn't arrive until a month later and wouldn't include those days either.

"That's the best I can tell you," Tom replied disinterestedly.

Not really. You're supposed to admit that you're another asshole. "Why didn't you do something when I gave you the card?"

"I haven't had a chance to look into it."

Ah, what's the use? Sal grumbled, hung up in disgust, and returned to his office.

Daryl entered towards evening, sat alongside, and asked if Sal wouldn't mind staying after everybody left, in order to help him load spare wood into his van and truck

Sal contemplated the man's odd, triangular face and pointed chin. What spare wood?

Daryl elaborated and Sal laughed. "Why not? You're a good soul. You deserve it. Yes, why not?"

"Thanks, man," he responded and left.

That evening, Sal shook hands with Lyman, Dinger, and even Miles who were quitting that day. They signed out for good, as did Kevin, Terrance, and others. Sal also said goodbye to Barney, Skip, Wally, and Craig and the women who planned to stay on as long as possible. Lacking the usual loungers who also signed out, the office fell quiet, save for Rota still at her desk.

The front door opened and in stepped a young man wearing a leather belt supporting an assortment of tools around his waist. "Telephone man," he chirped, pausing before Carmela sitting behind Doris' desk reading some papers. "I'm here to an install a phone."

Heading for the door in order to meet Daryl, Sal paused. "You're kidding. At this hour? Who's it for?"

The man checked his order. "Got me. It looks like you're just getting an extra jack for one of your rooms."

Probably for me, Sal sensed. But you're about two months too late, he almost laugh and avoided shaking his head. Exiting, he met Daryl as planned, having learned that he intended to build a shed on five acres that he recently bought outside the city. Sal helped him load some 2 x 4's, and miscellaneous wood into Sal's car and Daryl's truck, and Sal followed him to his barren land. They unloaded both vehicles in the dark, returned for more and dropped them off also. They shook hands afterwards, wished each other luck, and parted.

Having signed out, Sal headed back to the office in order to clear out his desk. Weaving between the piles of steps on both sides of the curved road, he arrived and parked. Exiting, he lingered long enough to survey the overwhelming piles, but refused to shake his head. Stepping inside, he was surprised, not because Rota was still at her desk, but because a policeman had perched himself on it beside another officer standing nearby.

"Sal D'Angelo?" the officer inquired, slid off Rota's desk and approached him.

Say no, Sal warned. "Yes," he responded, accepted what appeared like a small folder and opened it amid a pounding heart. You're under arrest for stealing wood, he precluded. You fool, he scolded.

"That's a warrant for your arrest ordered by Judge Julius Goodman. Mr. Bernard Hills is charging you with third-degree assault. I'm afraid you'll have to come along with us. Read 'im his rights, Joe."

Shit, Sal thought. He looked up and contemplated the officer's seemingly sympathetic face. Bernard Hills? Who's he? Happy! he cried. Barely hearing Joe verbalizing his rights, he forgot to ask if he could call his wife or a lawyer, much less if he were going to jail. "That happened long ago," he protested, as if length of time were a factor. "How come I'm just getting this now?"

The officer placed hands on hips, laughed, and glanced at Joe. "We hardly have time for stuff like this. Too many officers tied up with the flood. I'm surprised you got it so soon."

"Can ya hold it down a little, fellas?" a quiet, inconspicuous voice inquired.

Accepting the cuffs, Sal regarded Rota and almost burst out laughing.